MW00791731

DEAD IN THE FRAME

Also by Stephen Spotswood

DEAD
IN THE
FRAME

A PENTECOST AND PARKER MYSTERY

STEPHEN SPOTSWOOD

DOUBLEDAY *New York*

Copyright © 2025 by Stephen Spotswood LLC

Penguin Random House values and supports copyright. Copyright fuels
creativity, encourages diverse voices, promotes free speech, and creates a
vibrant culture. Thank you for buying an authorized edition of this book
and for complying with copyright laws by not reproducing, scanning, or
distributing any part of it in any form without permission. You are supporting
writers and allowing Penguin Random House to continue to publish books for
every reader. Please note that no part of this book may be used or reproduced
in any manner for the purpose of training artificial intelligence technologies
or systems.

All rights reserved. Published in the United States by Doubleday, a division
of Penguin Random House LLC, New York, and distributed in Canada by
Penguin Random House Canada Limited, Toronto.

www.doubleday.com

DOUBLEDAY and the portrayal of an anchor with a dolphin are registered
trademarks of Penguin Random House LLC.

Jacket images: (prison bars) Pict Rider / iStock / Getty Images;
(woman) Simona Dumitru / Moment / Getty Images
Jacket design by Michael J. Windsor and Emily Mahon

Library of Congress Cataloging-in-Publication Data
Names: Spotswood, Stephen, author.
Title: Dead in the frame / Stephen Spotswood.
Description: First edition. | New York : Doubleday, 2025. | Series: Pentecost
and Parker mystery ; 5 | Identifiers: LCCN 2024005719 (print) |
LCCN 2024005720 (ebook) | ISBN 9780385550468 (hardcover) |
ISBN 9780385550475 (e-book)
Subjects: LCGFT: Detective and mystery fiction. | Novels.
Classification: LCC PS3619.P68 D43 2025 (print) | LCC PS3619.P68 (ebook) |
DDC 813/.6—dc23/eng/20240212
LC record available at https://lccn.loc.gov/2024005719
LC ebook record available at https://lccn.loc.gov/2024005720

MANUFACTURED IN THE UNITED STATES OF AMERICA
10 9 8 7 6 5 4 3 2 1
First Edition

To Lillian and Will—You changed my life.
To everyone who fell in love with them—You did, too.

Judge me by the enemies I have made.

—FRANKLIN D. ROOSEVELT

CAST OF CHARACTERS

WILLOWJEAN "WILL" PARKER: The right hand of brilliant detective–turned–murder suspect Lillian Pentecost. When she gets hold of whoever's built a frame around her boss, there's bound to be blood.

LILLIAN PENTECOST: The most famous resident of the Women's House of Detention. Can she survive long enough to discover who put her there?

JESSUP QUINCANNON: A millionaire philanthropist who devoted his life to the study of murder. Until someone decided to turn him into an exhibit in his own Black Museum.

ALATHEA: Quincannon's fashion-plate bodyguard. Mistake her for stupid, and you're a fool. Mistake her for soft, and you're dead.

SILAS CULLIVER: Wide-shouldered, smooth-talking lawyer in charge of stocking Quincannon's museum with its bloody exhibits. Is there a reason he's avoiding Will Parker like the plague?

DR. RYAN BACKSTROM: A brain surgeon who thinks a lobotomy can fix all your ills. Did he do some quick and dirty surgery on Quincannon?

JUDGE MARTIN MATHERS: An old friend of Quincannon's father. If this bitter letch has any secrets, he's clutching them tight.

VICTORIA PELHAM: An elegant slice of the upper crust with a dark past. Rumor has it she killed one lover. Did she go for a matched set?

MAX ROBERTS: Veteran reporter working the crime beat for *The New York Times*. He's willing to sacrifice an old friendship for a juicy headline.

TIMOTHY AND ELAINE NOVARRO: A charismatic preacher to the working class and his devoted wife. Why did they score an invitation to Quincannon's murder, and did one of them play a starring role?

BILLY MUFFIN: Former hitman who was on the scene for the killing and has now gone to ground. Can Will dig him up in time to pin a murder on him?

WALTER BECK: Police photographer and recent widower who is willing to do anything to get to the bottom of his wife's death.

DETECTIVE DONALD STAPLES: NYPD golden boy and no friend to our duo. Getting to snap the cuffs on Lillian Pentecost is a dream come true.

LIEUTENANT NATHAN LAZENBY: Still the best homicide cop on the NYPD payroll, he's been told that meddling in this case will cost him his badge.

FOREST WHITSUN AND PEARL JENNINGS: New York's preeminent defense attorney and his long-suffering co-counsel, who have been tasked with proving that Lillian Pentecost didn't pull the trigger. But can they succeed when their own client is keeping the truth from them?

HOLLY QUICK: Pulp crime writer and Will's better half. She has decidedly intimate experience with detectives and is ready to go sleuthing herself.

ELEANOR CAMPBELL: Devoted housekeeper, baker of scones, keeper of secrets, and a woman you don't want to see on the other end of a double-barreled Winchester.

DR. OLIVIA WATERHOUSE: A criminal mastermind who's made a habit of stomping on the richest worms in the Big Apple and beyond. She has an offer Lillian Pentecost might not be able to refuse.

DEAD IN THE FRAME

CHAPTER 1

Grimm knew something was wrong even before he turned on the light. It was the smell. Burnt powder and wet copper and that particular rot you get only with something that used to be a human being. He'd smelled it plenty in the war. In the moment before he flicked the switch, he said a silent prayer.

Please don't let it be one of my friends this time.

The bare bulb in the office ceiling ignited and Grimm closed his eyes. Too late. That split second had already been burned into his mind, so he opened them again.

Another prayer unanswered.

"Aw, Briggsey."

His partner was slumped over his desk, right arm dangling at his side, gun hanging from his fingers. The blood sprayed across the threadbare carpet, almost to the door.

No, Grimm thought. All the way to the door. There were flecks of red speckling the pebbled glass. One thick spot dotted the second *i* in INVESTIGATIONS.

"That's a keeper," Briggs would have said.

Something inside Grimm lurched, and he couldn't tell if it was his stomach or his heart. He didn't have time for either to settle. With insides squirming, he stepped forward to examine his dead partner.

He reached toward Briggs's head but stopped. What about fingerprints?

Hell, he thought. *It's my office. My prints are everywhere.* Besides, he wanted to see Briggs's face.

He gently tilted that cinder-block head to the side.

If not for the entry hole above his right ear, it could have been any other Friday night at the bar. Briggs after one whisky too many, laying his cheek against the liquor-stained wood and telling the bartender, "Don't worry, I ain't sleeping. Just cooling this side of my face."

It could have been the night that Grimm had sat down next to him and started talking about what to do now that their respective careers as police officers were done—Grimm because of his tongue, Briggs because of his fists. At some point, Grimm brought up, so casually and spontaneously, how there were a lot of private operators working the city.

"You think we should be private dicks?" Briggs asked. "Those guys are assholes, Danny."

"Yeah, but they get paid good money to be assholes."

Now he was dead, and one way or another it was Grimm's fault.

He tilted his friend's head back. Gently, like he didn't want to wake him. As he did, he noticed there was a sheet of paper in the typewriter. He leaned in and read.

Danny,
    I'm tired of the scramble. Tired of working to
make things right. There ain't no getting back to even
in this world and I'm done trying.
    Goodbye. I'm sorry.
    Briggs

Briggs had said something like that to him just last week. The lunk could get real maudlin when the drink got on top of him.

A car horn sounded somewhere on the street outside, and Grimm snapped to. How long had he been standing in here, leaning over a dead man?

He should call the cops. They'd come, all right. Probably in record time. Suicide note or not, they wouldn't pass up a chance to get Daniel Grimm in a box.

No, he had things to do.

He opened the battered filing cabinet and retrieved the file on Zachary Boon. Inside were the notice of receipt for Lydia Boon's check, the photo, and the blackmail note.

The cops would get a real kick out of the photo. Probably pass it around the station house. Grimm figured Lydia Boon had had enough heartache.

He rolled up the file and slipped it inside his jacket before retrieving the .45 he'd taped behind the filing cabinet. Briggs had said it was a clean piece, and Grimm had no reason to doubt him.

With what he figured was his last look at his partner, Grimm left the office, closing the door softly behind him, then moved to the back stairs. He knew a bar about twelve blocks south where he could find a quiet corner to think.

Think about who might have murdered his partner.

Holly paused her narration, then added, "That's the end of the chapter. What do you think?"

"I think the same thing I thought the first time I read it," I told her. "It's a knockout. I don't know what you're worried about."

I tried to see what her face was doing, but that was tough to do while driving. We were on a particularly curvy stretch of highway, and while the Packard handled smoothly—it was a '47 model and barely off the assembly line—I could only account for my own steering. It was mid-October and the leaves had changed, so a lot of drivers had their eyes on the trees instead of the blacktop.

We'd spent the last three weeks sharing a Catskills cabin. Holly to finish her novel, me to keep her occupied between chapters. No phone, no newspapers, no nosy neighbors wondering who those two women were from New York City. Sisters? Cousins? Do cousins kiss like that in New York?

A lot of occupying got done.

Now we were on our way back, my first-ever vacation complete, and Holly's first novel in the books, so to speak. The finished product sat in her lap—a stack of 247 typewritten pages held together with a binder clip. She'd typed "The End" only two nights before and had proclaimed it "not bad." Which is the highest praise she ever heaped on herself.

"I'm worried it's too easy," she said. "When you get to the end of that chapter and Dan Grimm tells you it's a murder, how surprised are you?"

"At this point, not at all."

"Will, be serious. How surprised were you the first time?"

"I don't know if I'm the best gauge to use," I said. "I do this for a living, after all. I have an eye for clues."

"The people who read this will have read a hundred mysteries like it," she reminded me. "They'll have an eye, too."

"Why don't you save all the copyediting questions for Marlo and Brent? They know this stuff better than I do. The fictional variety, I mean."

Marlo and Brent Chase were the owners of Strange Crime Press and Holly's novel was their third book out of the gate, the first two being collections of short stories from their now-defunct *Strange Crime* magazine. Holly also shared their bed on some nights when she wasn't sharing mine.

If you're wondering how that kind of setup works, the answer is an orderly calendar and an open mind.

"I want to know your opinion precisely because you have real-world experience," Holly explained. "Also, Marlo and Brent have been editing my work for so long, I worry they've gotten a little blind to my tricks."

"You have tricks? I know about that one where you take my necktie and—"

"Stop stalling. I promise I won't be upset, whatever you say."

That was a promise no one could keep. There was a direct line from those 247 typed pages straight to her heart, and I didn't want to say anything that might leave a bruise.

"Okay," I started. "Let's break it down. Did I know it was a murder? Sure. But I was already leaning that way because it's a crime novel. Then there's the blood. His desk faces the door, right? I remember the layout from Chapter One. Anyway, there's blood splatter in a straight line to the door, but the entry was on the right side of his skull and he was facedown. The mechanics don't work."

I kept one eye on the road and one on Holly's fingers, which were plucking at the hem of her gabardine slacks, telling me that her nerves were about a six out of ten.

"You were real subtle about it," I assured her. "It's a coin flip whether the casual reader sees it. Now, they'll probably pick up on the fact that the suicide note is typed and Briggs can't type. I mean, who's two-finger-pecking out a suicide note when a pencil is right there? But none of these are the questions you should ask."

The plucking paused.

"They're not?"

"Nope," I said. "You want to know if, using these clues, I could figure out who did it, and I could not. I wasn't lying when I said the ending was a shocker."

"Really?"

"Really truly. The whole time I'm thinking it's someone close to Grimm and Briggs, because they got his voice in the note. Later, when there was the thing with the dead dog, I started thinking it was what's-his-face. Berthol. It never crossed my mind how Grimm joked to Vickie that Briggs was his secretary. What was the line?"

" 'I pound the pavement, he keeps the office in order,' "

Holly said, quoting it from memory. "'I tried to put him in heels, but he said it made his toes hurt.'"

"Right! She knows the heels are a joke, but she doesn't know all of it is, so she assumes Briggs knows how to type. And slipping it in as postcoital pillow talk? Perfect. Nobody remembers pillow talk, fact or fiction."

"Is that so?"

Her hands had stilled and she was looking at me rather intently.

"Hey, I'm not saying I don't want to listen. But in real life, I'm still trying to get my legs to stop shaking. In your book, they're going to be bailing out of the chatter to flip back to page eighty-nine."

"You remember the page number?"

"Page eighty-nine, second paragraph down, begins with the line 'The zipper caught halfway and Vickie snarled, "Just tear the damn thing off, Dan."' Speaking of which, why don't you read that bit? I think there might be a typo in there somewhere."

"Let the typo stay," Holly said. "I don't want you driving into a tree."

She was smiling now and her voice had lost that edge.

A few minutes later she asked, "Do you think Lillian would know who did it?" referring to my employer, who is frequently cited in the papers as "the most accomplished female private investigator in New York City." They could cut the "female" and still be sticking to the truth.

"She's Lillian Pentecost," I said. "She'd probably know who did it just by looking at the cover."

Holly had follow-up questions, but only a few. Then she put the typed manuscript back into her handbag and placed her hand on my knee. It stayed there all the way back to the city.

It was midafternoon when I deposited her and her manuscript at her apartment in Morrisania. After which I continued on to Brooklyn, my destination the brownstone that had served as my home and office for more than five years.

That's how long I had served as Ms. Pentecost's leg-woman, office manager, sounding board, and occasional prodder. That doesn't fit nicely on a business card, though, so all mine said was:

WILLOWJEAN PARKER
Associate Investigator
Pentecost Investigations

Three weeks gone with no phone, no papers, and no mail had been a slice of heaven, but I was looking forward to diving into whatever had piled up while I was away. Ms. P had said she'd put business on hold, but I doubted she could go that long without picking up a new client. She'd probably been running all over the five boroughs, multiple sclerosis be damned.

Hopefully she hadn't gotten into too much trouble while I was gone.

That was what I was thinking when I turned the corner and saw the police cars centered around our front steps.

My mind went to some bad places. I didn't even bother parking the car. Just left it in the middle of the street and started toward our door.

"You stop that! You stop that right now!"

Our housekeeper, Mrs. Campbell, yelling from somewhere inside. Angrier than I've ever heard her.

A beat cop stepped in front of me, said something about how I couldn't come any closer. I didn't get a chance to ask him why, because that's when I saw a pair of figures step out of the open doorway and onto the top of the stoop.

Lillian Pentecost, followed by a cop in a sergeant's cap.

"Boss!" I yelled.

She looked up, blinking in surprise or at the sun.

"Will?"

She looked like she'd been yanked out of bed. Mismatched in an off-white blouse and a pair of winter-weight gray plaid slacks, her braid half done, that streak of silver hanging over her face in an unkempt hank. No jacket, no tie, and, I realized very quickly, no cane. She wouldn't have been able to use it anyway, because her hands were cuffed behind her back.

"Call Mr. Whitsun," she said, as the sergeant directed her down the steps and into the back of an unmarked sedan. "Tell him I am in need of his services."

Whitsun was a lawyer, but not our usual one. He was a top-notch criminal-defense attorney.

The sergeant slammed the door shut. I pushed past the beat cop and ran up to the car, pressing my forehead against the window.

"What's going on?" I shouted. "What's the charge?"

The sergeant slapped the roof of the car, but Ms. Pentecost managed to shout the answer before it sped away.

"Murder," she cried out. "The charge is murder!"

CHAPTER 2

I ran up the steps and into the brownstone, and if that sergeant had tried to stop me, I'd have been under arrest, too.

I turned to go into the office, but another cop blocked my way. Over his shoulder, I saw one going through my desk, one kneeling in front of the safe and pulling out its contents, a fourth holding a camera and snapping a picture of something on Ms. Pentecost's giant oak desk, and a fifth actually sitting on the desk, legs dangling, while he flipped through my boss's calendar.

I didn't have a gun on me, and so all five men still have their kneecaps. In lieu of lead, I was about to hurl some invectives when I heard a bellow in a Scottish brogue.

"One more step, and you're gonna get it!"

I went around the corner to the dining room, where I found another half-dozen officers, all huddling around the entrance to the stairs, with Eleanor Campbell barring their way. Even cops are hesitant to bull-rush a woman who, in her gray curls and apron, could pass as their grandmother.

She was testing them, though. One hand was on the door-frame, the other secured around a rolling pin that she had raised above the head of the man directly in front of her. He was in a suit, not a uniform, though he'd still gone for police-blue.

His face was turned away, but I knew the haircut. On the

other side I'd find fair hair and kind eyes and an open, friendly face that would look good on a poster for a Western about a young sheriff come to rid the town of its no-good varmints.

I wouldn't have seen that movie, but only because I'd met Detective Donald Staples before. I was rooting for the rolling pin.

Mrs. Campbell spotted me above the crowd and her face lit up in relief.

"Will! Will—you tell them they're not allowed up there."

All eyes turned to me as I shouldered to the front of the line. A few kept their snickers to themselves. A few didn't bother.

Staples didn't laugh. But he did say, "Miss Parker. When your boss said you were on vacation, I guess she wasn't lying."

I was still dressed for cabin-lounging in a blue flannel shirt and a pair of denim dungarees rolled up to the knee. Both had numerous stains and not a few scorch marks caused by errant sparks from the cabin's fireplace. My red curls, hidden under a white kerchief, were tangled and filthy. Half of the specks on my face were freckles, the other half dirt.

It had grown too cold the last few days to bathe properly at the nearby spring, and heating up well water for sponge baths had become too much of a hassle. If I'd known I would have had to address a crowd, I'd have at least spritzed on some perfume.

"Tell your maid this warrant covers all property of Lillian Pentecost, living quarters included," Staples continued. "If she doesn't stand aside, I'll have her arrested for interference."

I took the document out of his hand. I'd seen enough warrants over the years that it took me only a few seconds to pick out the important bits: "Lillian Pentecost," "all property owned by," "suspected murder," and the judge's signature, which I knew Staples was too straight to forge.

"Suspected murder of who," I asked.

Staples looked at me like I'd grown a third arm.

"Are you serious?"

"This isn't an early Halloween costume. I've been up in the Catskills, no phone, no papers. I get home and I find my boss being led out in cuffs. So, yeah, Donald. I am serious."

He looked at me with something like sympathy.

"Jessup Quincannon."

"That bum? What did he say she did?"

Staples shook his head.

"He's the victim, Parker. Quincannon's the one your boss murdered."

If you've been reading along with these glorified case reports, you know the name Jessup Quincannon. For the uninitiated, Quincannon is—make that was—a wealthy philanthropist who was regularly referred to in the papers as "a connoisseur of crime and murder."

He loved the topic so much he kept a private showroom of objects de awfulness—murder weapons, blood-splattered clothes, bits and bobs found in the pockets of famous killers and victims. Every so often he invited a few other lucky freaks to come look and listen to him hold court. Those get-togethers were known in the press as the Black Museum Club.

The last time I'd seen Quincannon was only a handful of weeks before. When Ms. Pentecost had threatened to kill him.

All of this flashed through my mind, but not quick enough for Staples.

"Pick up a newspaper, Parker," Staples said, snatching the warrant out of my hand. "Or ask your maid. She can fill you in. Right now, we are going to execute this legally authorized warrant to search the premises. That's the entire premises, all three stories and the carriage house out back. Anyone standing in the way gets brought up on charges. Those charges may not stick. I know you and your boss have friends in high places. But I'll tell you one thing. The pull you have isn't enough to get her out of this. Not with the evidence we have."

Whatever traces of sympathy that I might have glimpsed on his features had vanished. I looked to Mrs. Campbell. She still had the rolling pin raised and was waiting for me to give her the nod in one direction or the other. As much as I wanted to see Staples get cracked, I didn't want to see her led out in cuffs, either.

"All right. You had your little speech. Now here's mine," I told the self-righteous detective. "First, you will refer to that woman behind you as 'Mrs. Eleanor Campbell.' She is a hell of a lot more than a maid, and you better memorize her name. Next, my room is one floor up, second door on the right. The .45 in the nightstand and the Browning in the holster hanging on the closet door are registered; the knives at the bottom of the unmentionables drawer are not required to be. Please refold everything when you're done rummaging. And third, your warrant specifies all property owned by Lillian Pentecost. That carriage house is deeded to one Eleanor Campbell—told you to memorize the name—so if you want to step foot in there, you'd better come back with another warrant or I'm going to tell her to take the safety off that rolling pin. If that doesn't frighten you, look up what happened that time she caught a burglar. I think you'll be impressed. I know the medical examiner was."

I had a fourth item lined up. Something about how Staples wouldn't know solid evidence if it bit him on the ass, but we were interrupted by an officer poking his head around the corner. It was the beat cop who'd been guarding the street outside.

"Detective, we've got a backup on the street. Some damn woman left her car parked in the middle of the road. You want I should call a tow truck?"

Now that I listened, I could hear a chorus of car horns.

"The damn woman will move the car herself," I told him. Then I looked at Mrs. Campbell and nodded. Reluctantly, she lowered her blunt instrument and stepped aside. Staples waved his men up the stairs.

"For what it's worth, Parker, I know this isn't easy."

"You're right," I said. "That's not worth shit."

I went outside to move the car.

CHAPTER 3

It took longer than expected. The vultures of the Fourth Estate had arrived. Carrion-eaters are a necessary part of any landscape, but that's hard to appreciate when yours is the corpse they're picking.

"Parker! Is it true? Is she arrested?"

"Has she confessed?"

"Why'd she kill him? What did he have on her?"

All my replies were three words or less and unprintable, unless their editors wanted to get fined.

I caught the eye of Max Roberts from the *Times*. He didn't shout any stupid questions because, at least in his professional life, he wasn't a stupid man. He gave me a look and mouthed the words "We need to talk."

My boss and I had traded favors with him on occasion. By my count, we were up by at least two. That might come in handy, but first I needed to get the lay of the land.

I was opening the door to the Packard when a flash went off. I dived inside, but it was too late. Some rag had my country-cousin ensemble immortalized in celluloid.

As I backed away, one of the reporters ran to a nearby car, jumped in, and started following, desperate for some sort of scoop. I didn't want to lead him right to Mrs. Campbell's door-step, so I took him on a scenic tour of Brooklyn's narrower streets. Eventually I caught lucky and swerved around a delivery truck just as it was pulling out of an alley. It blocked the road long enough for me to make my escape.

Fifteen minutes after I left, I arrived one street over from where I had started. The back door of the brownstone let out onto a little courtyard, on the opposite side of which was the carriage house that Mrs. Campbell was the deeded owner of. Its front door opened onto the adjacent street.

It was a tiny, two-story affair—all red brick and slate tile. I honked twice and the front door was opened by the woman herself. I jumped out of the Packard, made sure there were no cameras in sight, and hurried inside.

"Sorry for the delay," I said. "I had to shoo off a buzzard. Do you want to tell me how the world fell apart in three weeks?"

"It all started when—" was all she managed to get out before I cut her off.

"Hold on. I've got to make a call."

She directed me through the sitting room to the little kitchen and the phone nook recessed into one wall. Through a window I could look across the courtyard and see the silhouettes of police officers moving through the brownstone.

I dialed Forest Whitsun's number.

I don't make a habit of memorizing the phone numbers of defense attorneys, not even the one the papers call "the real-life Perry Mason." It's just that for much of September, Whitsun had been our client. Now, it seemed, Ms. Pentecost was going to be his.

A woman's voice came on the line.

"Forest Whitsun's office, Pearl speaking. How may I help you?"

Pearl Jennings was Whitsun's associate and, though we'd met only briefly, she impressed me then as one of the sharper tools in the drawer.

"Pearl, it's Will Parker. I need to speak to Whitsun."

"Did they arrest her?" she asked.

"Son of a . . . Yes, they did. About twenty minutes ago."

"You should have called right away," she said.

"I'm sorry, I was—"

"Let me get Forest."

There was the sound of footsteps, then silence, then more footsteps but with softer heels, then a man's voice.

"They arrested her?"

Even with three words, Whitsun could still squeeze that folksy twang in there.

"Yes, they arrested her," I snapped. "Now Staples and his merry band of assholes are taking our home apart top to bottom."

"I assume you saw the warrant."

"I did and it's legit."

"All right, I'll get a copy of it later," he said. "First, I've got to find out where they've taken her."

"I can be at your office in thirty minutes."

"No!" he barked. "Stay where you are. Where are you, by the way?"

"I'm at Mrs. Campbell's."

"Good, stay there."

"Whitsun—"

"There is nothing you can do, Parker," he said. "Let Staples do his job. And let me do mine. I'm damn good at it."

"Look here, counselor. For you to do your job, you have to be officially hired and I haven't signed a contract or cut a check."

"No, but Pentecost did," he said. "She put me on retainer."

"What? When?"

"Three days ago." I heard Pearl say something urgent in the background, but I couldn't catch it. "I've got to go. Remember what I said. Don't do anything."

Click.

I hung up, then sat down at the little table under the kitchen window. The one where Mrs. Campbell took her morning tea. There were dark, teacup-size rings in the wood—the reason she was always shoving doilies in my direction. The cobbler's children go barefoot, and all that.

"Is he going to help her?"

I turned to the housekeeper hovering in the doorway, eyes heavy with worry.

"Yeah, he's off to save the day, I guess," I said. "You want to tell me what exactly he's saving her from?"

She cocked her head toward the sitting room.

"Come on. I laid everything out while I was waiting for you."

Her sitting room was a big, open affair with a scattering of overlapping, multihued rugs covering a stone floor. There was a sewing machine in one corner and a wood-burning stove in another. A trio of comfortable, overstuffed armchairs, a similarly comfy sofa, a few end tables, and enough lamps to make up for the lack of windows filled the room. The walls were covered with a collection of small oil paintings, depicting hills and seascapes and moors.

Fifty years ago, I was told, the room had contained a quartet of cow stalls. Fifteen years ago, it had held a Model T. Now it housed my favorite Scotswoman.

There was a folding rosewood table set up in front of one of the chairs. The few times I'd been in her house it had held jigsaw puzzles or sewing projects. Now it held a stack of newspapers and what looked like a piece of mail addressed to our boss.

"Did you yank all this out from under Staples's nose?" I asked, as I took a seat in the chair.

"The letter was right on her desk," she said. "Wasn't nothing to put it in my apron pocket. The newspapers I already had. I figure the best way is for you to read the stories and ask me questions as you go. I can't tell a story start to finish like you can."

Sometimes it was easy to forget that Lillian Pentecost didn't hold the copyright on cunning.

"I'll get the percolator on. Figure you'll be wanting some coffee."

She lit the woodstove, then disappeared into the kitchen and left me to my homework.

I started with the letter. No postmark on the envelope. Inside was a familiar card printed on a thick, creamy paper—an invitation to one of Quincannon's Black Museum Club salons. Ms. P received at least two a year and, unless coerced, always declined.

MR. JESSUP QUINCANNON CORDIALLY INVITES YOU TO HIS HOME ON TUESDAY, OCTOBER 7, TO DISCUSS AND VIEW MATERIAL RELATED TO THE MURDER OF MR. PATRICK EBBERS AND THE SUBSEQUENT DEATH OF MRS. ANNA PENTECOST, MOTHER OF FAMED DETECTIVE LILLIAN PENTECOST.

Refreshments will be served beginning at 7 p.m. with the presentation to begin promptly at 8 p.m.

That bastard.

During a case last winter, we had discovered that Quincannon had sheltered a murderer from discovery. That murderer had gone on to kill at least one more person and put a gun to the head of the woman who'd recently been caressing my knee.

In response, Ms. Pentecost began throwing monkey wrenches into Quincannon's pastime. Keeping his collection stocked with murderous souvenirs required the complicity of customs officials and the bribery of police. Hard to do when those officials are threatened with discovery or flat-out fired.

Quincannon retaliated in turn.

Not long before I left for the Catskills, my boss learned that Quincannon had gotten his hands on a family keepsake— a painter's box filled with long-dried tubes of oil colors. During an impromptu visit with Ms. P to his Black Museum, I learned that the box had something to do with her mother's murder.

When Ms. P had demanded the box of paints back, Quincannon had refused, threatening to make it the center of one of his salons. A threat he'd apparently decided to make good on.

Mrs. Campbell came in and put a kettle down on the flat top of the stove. I held up the invitation.

"When did this arrive?" I asked.

"A little before seven-thirty last Tuesday. Right when I was clearing her dinner plate," she said. "Messenger service brought it."

Hand-delivered and at the very last minute.

"I was there when she opened it," Mrs. Campbell continued. "She read it, then dropped it like it had grown teeth."

"Did she say anything?" I asked.

Instead of answering, Mrs. Campbell busied herself straightening a perfectly straight painting.

"This is where I remind you that I need to know everything, swear words included," I told her.

She turned to me, her expression about as somber as I've seen outside of church.

"She said, 'I'm going to kill that man.' "

"Okay. Maybe develop amnesia on that one."

She snorted. "I can keep a secret well as you, lass. Keep reading. I'd start with the *Times* if I were you. I'll be in the kitchen while the water boils, keeping an eye on those bastard bobbies."

I turned to the newspapers, starting with the *Times,* as instructed. The first thing my eyes landed on was a photo of

Quincannon from the shoulders up. If you looked at it, you'd see a ruddy seventy-one-year-old with a head of white wavy hair and a long mustache to match, its ends waxed to a needle point. A man with strong features and the kind of wise, patrician bearing that political campaigns are built on.

What the photo didn't convey was how his eyes gleamed when he landed on the topic of murder, how his voice quivered with pleasure as he ran his fingers over a cut-throat razor that had been used to leave a woman bleeding out in a gutter.

Philanthropist and Murder-Expert Shot Dead; Detective Lillian Pentecost Key Witness
BY MAXWELL ROBERTS

Last night, local philanthropist, financier and crime aficionado Jessup Quincannon was shot dead in his Washington Heights home during a meeting of the infamous Black Museum Club. The investigation is ongoing and police officials will not comment on their progress. However, wanted for questioning is famed detective Lillian Pentecost, who made headlines last month by handing those very same officials the solution to three outstanding murder cases.

A collection of his friends, associates and other guests—including this reporter—were gathered Tuesday evening at the invitation of Mr. Quincannon, who had promised to deliver a bombshell revelation. That revelation, he told his guests, was regarding the untimely, perhaps scandalous, death of Miss Pentecost's mother, Anna.

Little is known of the background of the famed detective prior to her arrival in New York City some years ago and her subsequent rise to fame as a keen investigative mind.

At 8:15 p.m. the guests were congregated in the first-floor conservatory of Mr. Quincannon's uptown mansion as the host lingered over his third-floor collection of crime memorabilia, commonly called his Black Museum, after the famed Scotland Yard exhibit. At that time, Lillian Pentecost was seen arriving and taking the elevator up to the third floor.

Moments later, two shots echoed down the mansion's spiral staircase. Several guests ran up to investigate the sound, including this reporter. Mr. Quincannon was found lying dead on the floor, a bullet wound in his head. Lillian Pentecost was absent, having fled the scene.

Damn.

If Max's goal was to make readers think, "Lillian Pentecost is a murderer," without coming right out and typing it, he'd done his job.

I read the rest, but it didn't get better. It didn't help that Ms. P was the only guest actually named. The rest were "a respected lawyer," "a retired judge," a "charismatic minister," and "assorted others."

Was that the *Times* playing it safe, or Max pulling his punches? He never did like to pick a fight with people in power.

What was even more curious was the sidebar I found on the jump page.

The Last Words Of Jessup Quincannon
BY MAXWELL ROBERTS

Less than an hour prior to his death, Mr. Quincannon invited this reporter to join him in his private office for an exclusive interview. His office, located on the second floor of his stately Washington Heights home, is modest for a man who has made millions for himself and others from his cunning investments. It's also unassuming for someone who has made a study of murder and the men and women who commit it.

Mr. Quincannon argued that he and those few he invited to his salons were part of a greater majority.

"You need only look at your own newspaper," he declared. "What are those first pages devoted to but the bloodiest, the most sensational stories? My fascination is the world's fascination. We are drawn to the taboo, the forbidden. And what is more taboo than the taking of another human life?"

Asked why he thought some people might be drawn to real-life stories of grotesque acts, Mr. Quincannon said that it was part of human nature and should be studied as such.

"There are those who would have you believe that acts like these are committed by only the basest sort of man, but we see again and again that this is false," he said. "Even the wealthiest, most educated among us are capable of succumbing to our darkest impulses. We talk about these things in the town square. I am merely elevating it to the discourse of the salon."

When asked about the subject of that night's salon—an obscure murder involving the family of famed detective Lillian Pentecost—Mr. Quincannon remained circumspect other than to say, "I can't abide a hypocrite."

That was it. Only seven column inches. I wondered what had been left on the editing-room floor.

And how did Max score an invitation in the first place? Quincannon was notoriously private, his club even more so.

I dived deeper into the stack.

The rags made hay out of the murder for a couple of days, before more fuel was added to the fire. On Friday, police "arrived at the home and office of Lillian Pentecost, where they served a warrant to collect evidence."

Three days ago. The same day she'd put Whitsun on retainer.

By now coffee and tea had been served, and Mrs. Campbell was planted in the chair opposite me.

"This evidence they collected on Friday? You know what it was?"

"Her gun," she said. "The derringer."

"Just the derringer?"

She nodded.

That was odd. We had several firearms in the house. Most were on file, and the ones that weren't were hidden so well I wasn't too concerned about the police discovering them.

But they only wanted the two-shot derringer. The one I'd requested Ms. P purchase years ago as a "just in case."

Something queasy occurred to me.

"Did she take the derringer when she left for Quincannon's?" I asked.

It wasn't unusual for Ms. Pentecost to go armed. In fact, shortly before I'd left for vacation, she'd mentioned that she would have to rely on firearms more in the future, her multiple sclerosis making swordplay a challenge.

Mrs. Campbell peered into her cup, like she could find the answer in the tea leaves.

"I don't know," she admitted.

Double damn.

There wasn't much else in the papers. Nothing useful, anyway.

Tomorrow's editions were sure to bring fresh horrors: the police storming the brownstone, the arrest, new digging into Ms. Pentecost's past and her feud with Quincannon. They might even find out what had happened when she confronted Quincannon about the painter's box.

Alathea, Quincannon's bodyguard, had been there. She could tell reporters how Quincannon had made my boss practically beg him to give the box back, and how even after she had begged, he'd refused. She could tell them what Ms. P had said right before we walked out.

I don't need to look back at my notes. I remember the words exactly.

"*If you ever . . . Ever! Come near my family or my friends again, I will put you in a grave myself.*"

I wasn't sure if Alathea had seen Quincannon's face when my boss said those words, but I had. He'd believed it.

So had I.

CHAPTER 4

I was no Lillian Pentecost, but I could fill in the blanks. Staples and company had arrived three days earlier with a warrant for a single gun—the derringer. Today they had come and taken Ms. P away in cuffs.

The bullet was a match. No way Staples would make this play with anything less.

I went into the kitchen and called Whitsun again. Through the window I saw the NYPD continue to mill in and out of and through the brownstone. The warrant covered all three floors, which meant they were in the third-floor archives.

If they were planning to go through every file in the joint, they could be there until spring. There were hundreds of boxes, tens of thousands of newspaper clippings, case notes, typed and otherwise.

When I'd first started working for her, Ms. P had cautioned me against committing anything to our notes that might cause trouble if they were to ever become public knowledge. That was why many of our reports had some very conspicuous holes in the narrative. We also used a handful of codes and ciphers that nobody was cracking anytime soon.

At the time, she'd explained away the prohibition as protection against burglars. Now I was wondering if she'd also been planning for just this kind of eventuality.

There was no answer at Whitsun's office. I hoped that

meant that he and Pearl had found Ms. Pentecost and were in the process of prying her loose.

My next call was to Max Roberts at the *Times*.

"What the hell, Max," I said as soon as he picked up.

"Will?"

"Got it in one."

"Look, I'm scrambling here," he said. "Can I get a quote on the arrest?"

"A quote?"

"I'm on deadline."

I took a deep breath because I'd been told that's a good way to keep from screaming obscenities.

"I'm still catching up," I told him. "I need to know what really happened that night."

"If you read my story, you know what happened," Max said.

"Lillian Pentecost 'fled the scene'?" I said, soaking his words in as much contempt as I could muster. "Did you see her running away? How fast was she sprinting with her cane?"

"Hey—you want to argue semantics, there's a job opening in editorial," he snapped. "She went upstairs. There were gunshots. By the time we got up there, she was gone. If that isn't fleeing, get her to explain it, because she wouldn't take my calls."

"Can't imagine why."

"It's a tough business all around," he said. "Now, how about that quote?"

I gave him a quote. It wasn't fit to print. Then I hung up.

Telling Max off felt good, but what next? Whitsun had said to stay put and keep my hands to myself.

"To hell with that."

"What did you say?" Mrs. Campbell called from the other room.

"I said I'm going out!" I called back.

Not dressed as I was. I ran outside, retrieved my suitcases

from the Packard, and dragged them in. I rummaged for something moderately unsoiled and came up with a pair of dark denim pants and a thin black turtleneck.

I hadn't brought a pistol with me on vacation. There was one secreted away in the trunk of the company Cadillac, but that was parked around the block in full view of cops and reporters.

I did have a wicked little switchblade that I'd picked up at a country store in the Catskills. I tucked that into my pocket, splashed some water on my face, did what I could with my hair, and went back downstairs.

"Lock the door when I'm gone," I told Mrs. Campbell. "Nobody gets in without a warrant."

"Where are you off to?" she asked.

We were a two-woman ship now, and lying didn't feel right, so I told her. I'd say that she thought my idea was both safe and smart, but I don't want to lie to you, either.

I went outside, hopped in the Packard, and drove north.

By the time I got to Washington Heights, the sun was within spitting distance of the horizon and Quincannon's mansion was haloed in orange light and ugly shadows. A three-story Victorian sitting in the middle of an acre of shrubbery and trees, all of it surrounded by an eight-foot-high wrought-iron fence that wrapped around the block.

Edgar Allan would have loved it.

I parked the car right outside the front gate, got out, and pushed the buzzer. I waited half a minute, pushed it again, then put my thumb on it and kept it there.

Not a peep from the speaker.

I looked up the cobblestone front walk. The sun was disappearing behind the house, and its shadow was starting to crawl slowly, inexorably, toward me. There was one dim light in a basement window, but that was all.

Not one to give up easily, I took a walk around the block. In front, the cobblestones cut through a tended lawn, but around the edges of the property, it was all thick trees and dense brush, and as I turned the corner of the block, I lost sight of the house itself.

Halfway down that block, the branch of an elm hung over the top of the fence. It was still several feet too high for me to jump up and grab. But invention is the mother of necessity, and risky ideas are the grandbabies.

I pulled the Packard around and eased it as close to the curb as it would go. I waited for the sun to do its disappearing trick, then got out and looked around. There were lights on in nearby buildings, but no faces visible in the windows.

Fingers crossed that Quincannon had neighbors who kept themselves to themselves, I hopped on the hood of the Packard, then climbed up onto the limb. It creaked perilously but held. I'd spent five years with a traveling circus learning from any and every performer who'd let me, so heel-toeing it across the limb and down the trunk on the other side of the fence was child's play.

Once on the ground, I made my way through the trees toward the house. I didn't know any entrance but the front door, so I moved in that direction.

I emerged onto the lawn and was about to step onto the walk when I heard a twig snap. That was all the warning I had before a shadow tore itself away from the darkness and tackled me to the ground.

I landed hard, half on grass, half on cobblestones, fully stunned. I was on my back, my assailant straddling my chest. They had an arm pressed against my throat. Something dark and feathery hung over my eyes.

I grabbed hold of whatever it was and yanked. My attacker yelped in pain and toppled off me. I scrambled backward on the ground and, as soon as my legs were free, threw a kick at my opponent's face.

Instead of a satisfying crunch, all I got was air. Suddenly, there was an arm wrapped around my ankle and a pair of long legs clamped around my thigh. I was forcibly rolled onto my side.

I grabbed the switchblade out of my back pocket and was fumbling to hit the button when my attacker spoke.

"Please stop that, Miss Parker. A little more pressure and you won't be walking out of here."

I looked down the barrel of my leg at my attacker. In her black sweater and matching slacks, Alathea could have been my twin. If you ignored her extra six inches, long black hair, flawless porcelain skin, and fashion model figure.

She wasn't the type to bluff. Another inch and my knee would be shredded. I forced myself to relax.

"All right," I said. "I'm done fighting if you are."

After a couple of seconds to make sure I was on the level, she let me loose. Slowly we got to our feet, neither of us taking eyes off the other.

"What are you doing here?" she asked.

"I rang the bell, but nobody answered. Thought I'd better investigate."

"I disconnected it. Too many reporters."

"Still—better safe than sorry. Good thing we're both in black. Hides the grass stains."

She smiled, but there was no feeling behind it. She slowly swiveled her head, taking in the full 360 of our surroundings. We were standing in the middle of the long front walk. Twilight was sucking the light out of the world. Other than the rustling of the trees and the sound of a car horn a few blocks over, it was eerily quiet.

"You're an intruder, Miss Parker. I believe I would be within my rights to shoot you dead."

A chill started at my tailbone and went straight up to my ears. I didn't know much about Alathea. Not even a last name. We had a file on her in the archives, but it was little more than rumors.

From all the people Quincannon had to choose from, he

had hired her as his bodyguard. That told me everything I needed to know.

"You could do that," I said. "But you'd need to go all the way back and get a gun, and I don't want to put you through all that trouble."

She gave me a disappointed look, then pulled up the bottom of her sweater. The grip of a snub-nosed revolver curved out of the waistband of her slacks.

"I'll ask again," she said. "What are you doing here?"

I played it straight.

"I've been out of town the last three weeks," I explained. "I get back, I find your boss is dead and mine is getting hauled away. I'm told to stay out of things, but I've never mastered that trick, so I figured I could come here and . . . I don't know. See if I can get a bead on what really happened."

"What happened is your employer killed mine."

"Bullshit."

She plucked a scrap of dead leaf out of her hair and dropped it on the ground.

"I'm afraid it's true," she said, searching her tresses for more detritus. "I was there."

"In the room when she shot him?" I asked. "The papers didn't mention that."

"In the room less than a minute later."

"That's sixty seconds, Alathea. Think about what you could do with sixty seconds."

She actually thought about it as she combed through her hair with her fingers. Or at least that's what I assumed she was doing behind those dark eyes.

"Mr. Quincannon was alone in his museum," she said. "There are no windows on the third floor. Nobody used the elevator except your employer, and nobody could use the stairs because there was a crowd of people at the bottom, all looking up because they'd heard the gunshots."

She shook out her mane, satisfied it was free of foliage.

"The only person we know was present was Lillian Pentecost."

"No offense to your powers of perception, but I do this for a living," I said. "Let me have a look around."

I took a step in the direction of the house, but she put herself in my way.

"I'm afraid I can't do that."

"One little peek. I won't touch anything. I promise."

I tried to go around her, but she moved again, putting a hand firmly on my shoulder. There was a lot of muscle connected to those manicured nails.

"There are rules, Miss Parker."

"You care about rules?" I couldn't imagine that anyone who'd been employed by Jessup Quincannon was on hand-holding terms with ethics.

"I care since I'm the executor of Mr. Quincannon's estate."

My eyebrows did a thing.

"You're the executor? What about Silas Culliver?" I asked, referring to Quincannon's personal attorney and bagman.

"I suppose he didn't trust Silas with that responsibility."

"But he trusted you?"

She gave the smallest of shrugs.

"He knew that deceit wasn't in my nature," she said. "What you see is what you get."

A gun-toting ice queen who was built like a Rockette and could tackle like Joe Stydahar.

"A judge's order will grant you access to the house," she said. "In the meantime you have my word that the crime scene will be preserved."

I didn't know how far her word went. But she had me out-armed and out-argued, so I gave in. She walked me to the gate.

"I don't suppose you've had any conversations with the press about the last time Ms. Pentecost and I were here together," I said, thinking about Ms. P's last words to Quincannon.

"I have not," she said. "But I have told the police."

"Thanks for that."

"I try not to lie to the authorities except when absolutely necessary."

As Alathea unlocked the gate, she said, "Can I tell you two things you probably don't want to hear, Miss Parker?"

"Sure," I said. "You didn't break my knee or shoot me, so why not?"

"I don't know exactly what Mr. Quincannon had on your employer," she said. "But I do know he planned to reveal Lillian Pentecost's secrets to a room full of people."

"What are you saying?"

"I'm saying that having your secrets splayed out for the world to see is more than enough reason to commit murder. Even for someone as forthright as Lillian Pentecost."

She was right: I didn't like hearing that. I stepped through the gate and onto the sidewalk.

"You said there were two things," I reminded her, as she closed the gate behind me. "What was the second?"

Without cracking a smile she said, "You stink."

CHAPTER 5

I retrieved the Packard and drove until I found a phone booth. It was getting late, but I spent a nickel calling Whitsun's office again.

Pearl answered.

"Where have you been?" she asked after I told her who was calling. "Mrs. Campbell said you were out. Out doing what?"

There was an edge to her voice, like she thought I might have been doing something unwise and possibly criminal.

"Nothing you need to worry about," I lied. "What's going on with Ms. Pentecost? Did you get her loose?"

"She's under arrest," Pearl said patiently. "That means a bail hearing. There's one scheduled for Wednesday."

"Wednesday! Why not tomorrow?"

"Wednesday is a miracle. They tried scheduling it for next week, but Forest went to town on them. You can thank him when you see him."

"How about I do it now?" I suggested. "Put him on the phone."

"He's busy writing half a hundred motions. I'm busy writing the other half. You can talk to him Wednesday at the courthouse."

I asked a question I already knew the answer to.

"What about her gun? Was it a match?"

Pearl's voice dropped an octave.

"Yes," she said. "It was."

Damn it.

"Did you . . . did you ask her about it?"

"She says she didn't have it on her. It was in her desk the whole time, but . . ."

But it was her word against the bullet they pried out of Quincannon.

"All right. I'll be at court Wednesday with checkbook in hand. I don't want her behind bars a minute longer than necessary," I said. "Speaking of which, where do they have her?"

I knew the answer to that one, too. If you were a woman in New York City and the cops pinched you, there was only one answer. But I wanted to hear Pearl say it and she did.

"The House of D."

The Women's House of Detention squatted at the intersection of Greenwich and Sixth Avenues—a concrete gargoyle that cast a shadow across the whole of New York City.

I parked the car across the street, got out, and stared at its ugly face. There were lights scattered in the eleven floors' worth of windows, but even if one of them belonged to Ms. Pentecost, I had no way of knowing which.

It was late, but there were still people on the street. Some of them gave me curious looks, but none lingered. They probably thought I was some inmate's sister or girlfriend.

I knew the area well. A few years back, I'd dated a Macy's stockgirl who had a fifth-floor apartment on Christopher Street. She had a sideline pinching dresses and brassieres and selling them to the women, and some of the men, in the neighborhood.

Sweet kid. I wondered if she was still there, or if she'd gotten caught.

If she had, she might be somewhere in the guts of that

concrete meat grinder. I really hoped not. I knew a lot of hard women who'd come out of there broken.

In some ways Lillian Pentecost was harder than any of them. But her multiple sclerosis symptoms could appear out of nowhere. Or out of somewhere, like not enough sleep, not enough food, too much stress.

That all worried me, but not as much as what Alathea had said.

Was Lillian Pentecost capable of murder?

Sure, she was. But so am I. So are you. It just takes the right circumstances.

There were things in my life, past and present, that, if you poked hard enough, might make me lash out without thinking. If I had a knife or a gun at hand, I might use it.

Was my boss guilty?

Her gun was a match. She'd gone to Quincannon's angry and, to give Max his due, "fled the scene" was probably the right way to describe her quick getaway.

It didn't look good.

The alternative was: She was being set up. There were plenty of people who might want to build a frame around my boss. People she'd help put away; their friends and family; quite a few politicians; half a hundred police officers she'd shown up over the years.

Not to mention the enigma we knew as Olivia Waterhouse. A criminal mastermind who focused her efforts on digging up dirt on the rich and powerful, and who had been responsible for more than one visitor to the morgue.

We hadn't heard from her in months. Maybe she'd been busy planning this.

Then I remembered a phrase my boss liked to remind me of. That thing about the guy with the razor. The simplest explanation was most often the truth, and the simplest explanation was that my boss had shot and killed Jessup Quincannon.

Triple damn.

I got back in the car and drove away. As I crossed over the Brooklyn Bridge and the lights of that borough spread out before me, I tried to get my face in order for when I saw Mrs. Campbell. But all I could think about were bullets and razor blades and how easy it would be to push someone to use either.

CHAPTER 6

From the journals of Lillian Pentecost

I am in my cell.

I have been allowed some paper and a nub of pencil. Mr. Whitsun also asked that I be provided with a cane, but that request was denied. Prisoners are not allowed weapons.

A pencil, a notebook, and the clothes I was wearing when I was arrested. That is all I have.

I was able to speak with Mr. Whitsun briefly at the station house before being transferred here. His instructions were: "Write down every detail about how they treat you. The worse, the better."

I imagine he will use it to bolster a request for bail. So I write.

Upon admission to the Women's House of Detention, I was made to strip and shower in freezing water. I was then given a medical exam by a man who identified himself as the clinic doctor. This included a cavity search. It was invasive and inhumane. I'm afraid I did not comport myself well. I can't imagine any rational woman could, under such circumstances.

I was left bleeding.

I told the guard this as I was escorted to my cell.

"Just wad something up in there," she suggested.

Which is why my shirt is missing a cuff.

Mr. Whitsun, if you are indeed reading this, do not feel the need to tread lightly or couch this testimony in euphemisms. The shame here is not mine, nor am I the only one to suffer in this manner.

The House of D—as it is called by the women who are imprisoned here—is a shame to the entire city. Meant to hold 450, at the time of this writing it contains many more. I know this because the cell I am in was built for one, but now holds two. Many of the other cells I passed had three or even four prisoners.

My roommate's name is Valeria Lincoln. She arrived the day before I did and is awaiting trial for assault.

"She went after a dozen guys," the guard who escorted me to my cell said. "Bit one's ear clean off. You should watch yourself with her."

Valeria was asleep when I arrived and has remained so.

I apologize for my handwriting. My hand is shaking and holding the pencil has become difficult, though I think it is less from my multiple sclerosis and more from hunger. I arrived too late for dinner and have not eaten since yesterday.

Do not tell Eleanor this. I would not put it past her to come pounding on the door of the prison in protest. I've been hungry before. I have been in more dire straits.

Though I was a younger woman then.

I am rambling. I should sleep.

That is no easy feat here. Hundreds of women whispering, snoring, coughing, yelling, and breathing creates a dull roar, a muted cacophony that is always present, even in the dead of night.

So though I am exhausted, I remain awake.

I cannot help pondering who has put me in here. I was not lying when I said that I did not murder Jessup Quincannon. I did not bring my pistol with me that evening. It was, to my knowledge, in the middle drawer of my desk.

Someone has framed me. And I have made it appallingly simple for them.

I was surprised when I received the invitation to Quincannon's salon. I had thought he would hold the painter's case he had stolen from my father's house as leverage against me. A sword of Damocles forever dangling.

Perhaps our last confrontation convinced him that I would not bend to extortion. At any rate, I was thrown off-balance. No, let me be honest in these pages. I was enraged.

The invitation arrived so late I had little time for thought. I decided to go to his salon and convince him. Threaten him, if need be.

It was after eight p.m. when the taxi dropped me off at Quincannon's. After I pushed the buzzer and announced myself, Quincannon's bodyguard, Alathea, walked down to the gate and let me in.

She told me she had informed her employer of my arrival and I was to be sent up immediately.

As we entered the front door, I passed a woman in a gold lamé evening gown smoking a cigarette. I recognized her but could not put a name to the face. Once inside, Alathea walked me to the elevator. I expected her to accompany me, but she did not.

As the doors shut, I noticed someone in the hallway behind her—Max Roberts from the *Times*.

So that was Jessup's plan, I thought. To splash the story of my family's scandal across the front page.

The elevator doors closed and proceeded upward. It's a slow machine. It seemed to take an eternity, though it was likely only a handful of seconds. Under times of stress, I've found that time can become elastic.

As the car approached the third floor, I heard two sharp, muffled raps. A mechanical problem, perhaps. I briefly entertained the terrible thought that I would become trapped in there. Locked in a cage while my secrets were paraded in public.

When the doors opened onto Quincannon's third-floor museum, I noticed the smell first. It smelled like death, if death has a smell. Quincannon was lying on his back on the floor in the center of the room. Gunpowder still hung in the air; blood was beginning to seep from the wound in his temple.

As I approached the body, I took in the room. There were some new additions—a battered Victorian writing desk sat against the wall; a scorched teddy bear slumped on a pedestal in one corner. Otherwise, little had changed from when I was there a few weeks prior: glass cases filled with memento mori (blades, bullets, photos, scraps of bloodstained clothing); the wall mounted with larger artifacts, like the bullet-riddled car door that Will said must have belonged to Bonnie and Clyde, though I question its authenticity.

I saw no one else, but I cannot testify that I was alone. There were dark corners where someone could have hid. I should have conducted a thorough search, but I was distracted.

Inside the glass case closest to the body sat the painter's box, just as it had been a month prior. Its top open to reveal a cache of ancient, long-dried tubes of paint, the inside of the lid used as an easel. The smears of ochre. That particularly vibrant blue. The very paints that had been used to create the painting that hangs behind my desk.

My eye was drawn to a small leatherbound notebook lying beside the body. I picked it up and examined it. From the first line, I recognized it as a detailed—and lurid—description of a chapter of my personal history I wished to keep private.

What I did next was foolish, I admit. I could hear alarmed voices echoing up the stairs from the first floor. Very soon, someone would come up to investigate. The police would be called. Everything in the room would be logged as evidence.

I thought about hiding the notebook on my person, but quickly realized that I would almost certainly be searched. So

I put the notebook in my pocket, took the elevator back down, and retraced my path out of the house. I walked several blocks before hailing a cab, and returned home. I burned the notebook in a metal bucket in our courtyard.

All foolish, I know. As I said, I was not thinking clearly.

Someone has gone to a great deal of effort to frame me. The timing was immaculate. From the moment I entered the elevator to go up to the time I exited the building was perhaps two minutes in total. A very tight timetable to accomplish a murder.

How they managed to do so with my gun, I do not yet know. I saw the weapon several days before and then not again until the police arrived for it.

My invitation to the salon came at the last minute. Likely at Jessup's instruction, so I would not have time to disrupt his plans.

I wonder when the other guests received theirs. With enough time to plan a murder, perhaps?

Another question: Was it an enemy of Quincannon's, and I am merely a scapegoat; an enemy of mine; or one who despised us both?

Two birds with one bullet, as Will might say.

Private property does not exist in a prison cell, and so I have written some of this in cipher, as you can see. Ask Will for the key. Tell her it's the brisket recipe. She'll understand.

My hand is sore from gripping this nub of a pencil. I believe this is all I know that might be helpful. At least all that I am willing to discuss at this time.

Now I think I will sleep. Or try.

CHAPTER 7

Knock, knock, knock.

"G'way," I muttered.

More knocking. I rolled over, remembering too late that I wasn't in my bed but on Mrs. Campbell's sofa. I hit the floor with a thud.

"You all right?" Mrs. Campbell called from the kitchen.

"I'm fine!"

I looked at my watch. It was a little after seven a.m. Another tap-tap-tap at Mrs. Campbell's front door. Quiet, like the person was afraid of bruising their knuckles.

I peeked through the curtain to see a question mark standing on the mat. I call him a question mark because I didn't know the man, and because that was the general shape of him. He was one of those tall sorts who've developed a permanent slouch in his spine.

The rest of him was slouched, too: the lapels of his brown suit, the cuffs of his trousers, his too-long salt-and-pepper hair, his face, which was mostly chin but not in a pleasant way. Even his eyebrows were slouching.

Actually, those eyebrows looked familiar, but I couldn't place them. Then I noticed that he had a satchel hanging off his shoulder and a notebook and pencil poking out of his breast pocket. He turned toward the window and I spied a camera hanging from the strap slung over his shoulder. I jerked the curtain closed.

"Ah, crap."

Mrs. Campbell came in from the kitchen. She was dressed for the day in a purple and white paisley number, her steel-gray curls carefully pinned.

"Who is it?" she asked.

"Reporter," I said. That's where I must have recognized him from—the scrum from the day before.

Another knock. More insistent.

"Miss Parker!" he called through the door. "I need to speak with you!"

I had to bite my tongue to keep from telling him what I needed him to do. If I did, that would confirm that I was indeed in the carriage house, and reporters were much like rats—if you saw one, you knew there were a hundred more waiting in the wings.

Luckily, Mrs. Campbell knew what to do with vermin. She pressed her nose against the door and shouted, "Get out of here, you dobber! Right this minute or I'll sic the coppers on you. There's about fifty right out front and I'm sure they'd love to take their nightsticks and—"

"He's gone," I said.

The man was loping away, peering back over his shoulder as he ran, probably afraid a horde of New York's finest were about to be hot on his heels.

"What were they going to do with their nightsticks?" I asked our housekeeper.

"Mind your business."

With that bit of slapstick behind us, I did my best to do as Whitsun and Pearl and Alathea had suggested—keep my hands to myself.

I started with a few personal errands, like making use of Mrs. Campbell's claw-foot tub and her collection of lotions and tinctures, including a lemon-scented syrup that turned the water yellow and bubbly. An hour later, I let the last of the Catskills swirl down the drain.

Smelling civilized again, I went about finding a long-term garage to store the Packard. The air had an autumn snap to it, and a convertible top wasn't going to come in handy anytime soon. On the drive there I dropped my three weeks of cabin-wear off at a laundry. And on the walk back, I stopped at a newsstand and picked up every daily they had on the rack.

Errands accomplished, I installed myself at Mrs. Campbell's kitchen table with a cup of coffee and a fresh scone, and began picking through the papers.

It was as bad as predicted. Worse, even, because of the photo. I use the singular because it was practically the same shot in every paper, all taken from slightly different angles as Ms. Pentecost was led down the brownstone's steps.

As I read, my eyes kept being drawn to it, to her face. Some wit had once commented that she had a very masculine profile, almost like John Barrymore. As if Barrymore weren't the prettiest thing in tights.

The photo did something to her face, though. Her nose, always on the verge of hawkish, looked bent out of true; those sharp cheekbones were blunted; the blue-gray eyes, only one of which was original, seemed confused and dimmed.

I started putting my coffee cup over the picture each time I opened a new paper.

The bylines changed and the adjectives got shuffled, but the tone across the board was: She probably did it. It was almost as bad as the arrest itself. Arrests could be undone. But once a story is read, you can't yank it back out of readers' heads.

The only rag that had something truly new was the *Free City Press,* which had somehow managed to get a list of Quincannon's guests and, unlike Roberts, wasn't squeamish about printing it.

The story put names to the retired judge, the minister, the doctor, and so forth. No one who rang a bell. Then I got to the last name on the list.

"Billy Muffin?"

Mrs. Campbell, who was standing at the sink tending to some dirty dishes, turned her head.

"Never heard of them. That a recipe in there?"

"Billy's a man," I explained. "And definitely not a treat."

"Oh?"

"He's a killer."

Specifically, a killer for hire. I'd never met him, but his name had cropped up in more than one of the files in our archives. Back in the day, Muffin had been one of the men the mob turned to when they wanted somebody snuffed but didn't want to get their hands dirtier than they already were.

Quincannon liked to pepper his parties with the occasional monster, and Muffin definitely qualified. I didn't know the count, but the bodies to his name were rumored to be in the double digits.

A gunman at a party where someone was shot? Why the hell was my boss getting stitched up for it instead of him?

It was time to make some calls.

The first was to Whitsun's office, where I was told by a temp that neither he nor Pearl was available.

Next, I rang the House of D to inquire about getting in to see my boss. I knew from past experience that prisoners were allowed only one visitor a week, aside from their lawyer. I was informed by a secretary whose politeness was paper-thin that Ms. P was off-limits to everyone and that I should check back after her arraignment.

"After her arraignment she'll be out on bail," I said.

"Then you can talk to her then, can't you?"

I hung up before she did.

Next on the list was Lazenby. Lieutenant Nathan Lazenby was our man at the NYPD, and while we didn't always see eye to eye, we regularly scratched each other's back.

I couldn't even get past the desk sergeant.

"He's out."

"When will he be in?"

"Don't know."

"Will he be back today?"

"Don't know."

And so forth.

Finally, wanting to hear a friendly voice, I called Holly. She hadn't seen the papers yet, so I had the displeasure of relating to her the unfortunate events that had transpired while we were incommunicado.

"Do you want me to come over?" she asked, when I was finished.

"Thanks for the offer, but there's nothing to do but wait. I can probably manage that on my own."

By midafternoon, I was wondering if I shouldn't have taken her up on the offer. At least we would have had enough players for a game of hearts.

Miraculously, no more reporters had come knocking, though a neighbor from across the street stopped by to hand-deliver a flyer for a Halloween jamboree that could just as easily been slipped under the door. We sent the snoop on her way unsatisfied.

I was considering a walk to the library—all Mrs. Campbell had on hand were worn paperbacks about horny duchesses—when there was a knock on the kitchen door. Staples's smeared face peered at me through the thick glazing of the window.

I opened it but kept the chain on.

"If you don't have a warrant, you don't come in," I told him.

"I'm only here to inform you we're finished with the house," he said. "You can go in. Though the warrant still stands, so we might be back."

My anger wouldn't fit through the crack, so I unlatched the door and opened it wide.

"You're really loving this, aren't you?"

Staples didn't flinch. He was a cop, so he was used to people getting in his face.

"I go where the evidence takes me."

"The evidence, huh? Which led you to our doorstep and not to the mob button man who happened to be on the scene when a body hit the floor. What about Billy Muffin?"

"Don't worry. I have plenty of questions for Mr. Muffin when I see him."

"What do you mean when you see him? You haven't grilled him yet?"

Now he flinched, his eyes flicking down to touch the ground then back up again.

"He was not on the premises when we arrived."

It took me a second to make sense of what he'd said.

"Hang on. You mean Muffin *fled the scene*? I use that phrase because I'm told it's the right one for when somebody skedaddles before the cops show up. Instead of chasing the bona fide murderer, you—"

"Billy Muffin has never been convicted of murder," Staples said.

"I'm sorry," I said, with as much sarcasm as two words would hold. "I mean the man suspected of a couple dozen killings. Instead of chasing him, you go after my boss?"

Staples had buttons as big as dinner plates, and it was usually child's play to push them. This time he wasn't taking the bait.

"Your boss also ran," Staples reminded me, in an infuriatingly calm voice. "She clearly had a grudge against the victim. She was alone with him when he was killed, and she was in possession of the gun that killed him."

"A .41 rimfire thrown out of that derringer and through a human skull? And it's clean enough that you got a warrant off it?"

He shook his head. "The first shot went into a book mounted on the wall. Nicely preserved and a perfect match."

I didn't respond. I didn't know how.

"You can hate me all you like, Parker. But if you're looking for who to blame, talk to Lillian Pentecost."

He turned and walked back across the courtyard. I recovered in time to yell, "I want a list of everything you took out of that house!"

"You'll get it!" he called back, not even bothering to look over his shoulder. Then he was through the back door of the brownstone. A minute later, I heard a car start up and drive off.

"I don't care about any bullets," Mrs. Campbell said from behind me. "She didn't do it."

"Of course she didn't," I said.

I wish I could have said it with more confidence.

When we re-entered the brownstone, Mrs. Campbell went straight for the kitchen while I made a beeline for the office. The room had a gently ransacked quality. Papers were scattered across both of our desks; drawers were open, as was the floor safe. My stash of 5th Avenue candy bars was missing.

The large oil painting on the wall above Ms. P's desk was still there. The woman in the blue dress lying in the shadow of a tree. I'd half expected it to be taken as evidence. That it wasn't suggested the cops didn't know about the connection between it and the painter's box that Quincannon had gotten his hands on.

Not that I knew the connection, either. I was only speculating. The colors in the box were the same as in the painting. Did Ms. Pentecost's mother paint it? Did this Ebbers guy?

Another question to throw on the pile.

After I gave the office a once-over, I went upstairs. I checked Ms. P's bedroom first, finding it mildly ruffled but mostly intact. Then I went to mine.

My drawers had been turned out, as had my closet. Everything was in a heap on the bed: clothes, knives, the Colt, and the Browning. My tiny bookshelf had been emptied and the books left in a pile on the floor along with my collection of playbills.

They'd gone digging under my bed and pulled out my stack of pulp magazines. Those were carpeting the floor.

In contrast, the copy of *Vice Versa* a friend had mailed me from L.A. in flagrant violation of the Comstock Act had been placed carefully on top of my dresser. It had been opened to a poem about two lovers holding hands while walking down the street. No one had scribbled "Dyke" across the page, but the message was clear enough: We know what you like, Parker. And we can put our hands all over it.

I took my time putting everything back, even going to the trouble of taking an iron to my rumpled blouses.

I was procrastinating.

Eventually, all my own possessions were back where they belonged, and I couldn't put it off any longer. I went up to the third floor.

The third floor of the brownstone was one open, high-ceilinged space dedicated to rows and rows of tall shelves, packed tight with the boxes we used to store case notes and photographs, the occasional scrap of evidence, and other bits and bobs Ms. P had picked up during her career.

In the center was an Egyptian rug, a spacious armchair, and a standing lamp that provided light when the skylights would not. Ms. P spent many a long night sitting in that chair, or sprawled out on the rug, poring over cases, old and new, looking for connections, tugging at threads.

The chair and lamp had been moved to a corner to get them out of the way. In their place were file boxes. Dozens of them, some stacked, some lying on their side. Folders were everywhere. There were gaps in the shelves where the boxes had been.

What had they taken? Our files on Quincannon, certainly. Those had grown considerably over the last few months and included detailed descriptions of how Ms. P had interfered with his hobby.

Viewed in a certain light, it wouldn't look good. There was

no paying client setting us on Quincannon. You didn't have to tilt your head far to interpret it as obsession, or a vendetta.

But there were plenty of other files that might be of interest to the police. Like evidence of particular officers who were inept, corrupt, or both. If the cops had helped themselves to individual files, we might never find out.

I made space in the middle of the rug and pulled the chair back to its usual spot and then the lamp. When I did, I noticed an ugly crack running the length of its Tiffany shade. Someone must have knocked it over.

That was when the tears came. I'd been fighting them all day. At least I'd kept the waterworks turned off when yelling at Staples.

How dare they? Lillian Pentecost was worth any ten of them put together. She had laid more criminals in their lap than I could count, and this is how they treated her?

The crying jag didn't last long. Once it was over, I started sorting through the mess.

Eventually Mrs. Campbell came up to help. Putting everything back where it belonged would have been a fool's errand, so we settled for making some general piles.

"The boss can tackle the finer details when she gets home tomorrow," I told her, as we sorted.

It was early days then, and I had hope.

CHAPTER 8

The lobby of the New York City Criminal Courts building was a beehive. Everyone in it was buzzing, and a lot of them had stingers. It was always like this—cops brushing against lawyers against crooks against press against however many clerks and secretaries and paper pushers it took to keep the wheels of justice grinding fine.

That morning felt different. Every third face was turned toward the front door, waiting for the paddy wagon carrying prisoners from the House of D.

I checked my watch. It was running late. The two-mile trek from Greenwich Village to the courthouse at 100 Centre Street in Lower Manhattan, which should have taken ten minutes, was pushing half an hour.

At the twenty-eight-minute mark, the door swung open and Whitsun and Pearl walked in, Whitsun in a hickory-brown suit and Pearl in a blue-gray two-piece with a pencil skirt that whispered at the knee.

Flashbulbs went off. Pearl blinked and turned away, while Whitsun smiled and gave them his good side. I don't know why he bothered. With the baby blues of Jimmy Stewart and the bone structure of Gary Cooper, all his sides were good. Though I'd seen what happened when you got on his bad one.

The reporters swarmed.

"Forest, Forest—did she do it?"

"What about the gun, Forest?"

"The DA says he's going for life. Will you talk plea?"

Whitsun, who had a couple inches on most of them, raised his hand like a schoolmaster asking for silence. Eventually the little tykes quieted.

"Gentlemen, there will be time for questions after the arraignment," he said. "But I will say now that this arrest is the result of a long-standing grudge the police in this city have against Lillian Pentecost. She's showed them up I don't know how many times. You can go back in your archives and count the headlines. No, gentlemen, I think you'll find this so-called iron-clad evidence is little more than papier-mâché. Now, please excuse me. My client should be here shortly."

It was a good, quotable speech, but the journalists weren't satisfied, and as soon as he was finished, they started lobbing questions. Pearl was left unmolested at the edge of the mob. Probably because the reporters assumed she was a secretary rather than a lawyer herself. There weren't many female legal eagles, and even fewer Negro ones.

She casually scanned the crowd. We'd met a few times, so she knew my face, but her eyes skipped right over me. I forgave her. With the long blond wig, thick glasses, and makeup that did away with my freckles, I looked more like Lauren Bacall's dowdy, nearsighted cousin than Will Parker. My black victory suit, its skirt not even hinting at knee, made me indistinguishable from every other secretary or stenographer in the joint.

The disguise was to protect both me and the reporters. If one of them tried to get a quote from Lillian Pentecost's girl Friday, I was in the mood to bite their nose off. Maiming a reporter was probably a crime even in New York City.

Although every bone in my body wanted to stay rooted in the lobby so I could get eyes on my boss, I pried myself away and hurried to the stairs. I followed them up to Judge Hugo Creed's fifth-floor courtroom and reclaimed my seat in the back row, which was being held for me by a very handsome stringer for the London *Times*.

"I absolutely adore New York accents," he'd confided before placing his hand on what I would say was the small of my back, except backs must extend lower across the pond.

I put up with it. It got me a spot in what had quickly become a standing-room-only courtroom.

I was starting to be concerned that my disguise wouldn't hold up. I was surrounded by reporters, many of whom knew me on sight, and some of whom weren't exactly dull. Max Roberts was one row up and across the aisle, and he knew me better than any of them, though he was busy brushing off questions himself.

I needn't have worried. No one's eyes were on me. They were all moving from the side door where defendants were traditionally led in to their watches and back again. After ten minutes of this, our collective impatience was interrupted by the sound of footsteps, popping flashbulbs, and a burst of shouted questions from the reporters in the hall who hadn't managed to nab a seat.

Everyone craned their neck around in surprise. Were they coming in through the visitors' entrance? A moment later, Whitsun and Pearl walked through the big double doors, Ms. Pentecost sandwiched between them. No cuffs, but no cane, either, wearing the same now-rumpled clothes she'd been arrested in. Except the sleeves of her blouse were rolled up.

Was that a torn cuff? What the hell had they done to her in there?

I realized why they had her come in that way. To parade her in front of the reporters. To make sure every paper got art for tomorrow's front page. The great detective brought low.

As they walked up the center aisle, Ms. P scanned the gawking faces. Her eyes passed over me without pause. No recognition, but certainly fatigue. Her good eye was bloodshot, and the lids of her glass one looked red and raw.

There were no shouted questions from the reporters in the courtroom. They knew better. Judge Creed was at that moment taking his seat.

Creed didn't look like a bruiser. He was thin and graying, with a face that was all bifocals and no chin, and spindly arms that looked hard-pressed to pick up a gavel. Books and covers, though. He'd had so many people tossed out of his court, it was said that his bailiffs liked to compete for distance.

Ms. Pentecost took a seat at the defense table along with her lawyers. A moment later Creed took gavel in hand and gave a hard rap.

We were off.

I won't give you the blow-by-blow. If you've ever had the displeasure of sitting through a court hearing, you know how boring it can be. Like a tennis match played by snails.

Besides, this was an arraignment. There were only two questions to answer: Was the defendant pleading guilty or not guilty, and how much was bail?

The answer to the first came quick enough. Ms. Pentecost got to her feet to say the two magic words in a voice that carried nicely to the back of the room. Then Whitsun served the ball.

"Your Honor, we would like to petition the court for bail at this time."

"What say the prosecution to the matter of bail?" Creed asked, directing the question to the prosecution table.

Keith Bigelow was one of the only people in the DA's office we'd never had dealings with, which is probably why he'd been chosen for this gig. Approaching sixty, he was a little short and a little round, and he had a snowy beard and hair in the same shade. He could have played Santa, or maybe one of his elves.

He took his time standing. Then he put his hands in his pockets and sighed, like he really had to ponder the answer.

"Well, Your Honor," he began. "Murder in the first degree is a serious charge. There's a lot of very compelling evidence. I'm not sure bail is proper."

Ball to Whitsun.

"Only last month, the district attorney's office granted bail in a first-degree murder case—the Salvatore case. I believe that was also in front of you, Your Honor. Maybe Mr. Bigelow is unfamiliar."

A lob to Bigelow, who frowned and looked back at the other suits sharing the prosecution table with him. One of them whispered something and Bigelow nodded.

"Yes, yes. Salvatore. I see your point. Except Mr. Salvatore—and correct me if I'm mistaken—is the owner of a rather modest laundry service. Now, Miss Pentecost, on the other hand, is a woman of considerable means. She has contacts around the globe, or so I'm told."

Back to Whitsun.

"Mr. Bigelow's insinuation that my client will not stay to face these spurious charges—face them and prove them false—is insulting," he declared. "Lillian Pentecost has assisted the police and the DA's office on any number of occasions and—"

"Which will hold no water in this court, Mr. Whitsun," Creed cut in. "There will be no favoritism in this or any other New York City court of law."

That was bullshit, but everyone should have goals.

"I'm sorry, Your Honor," Whitsun said, managing to sound contrite. "I would also like to remind the court and Mr. Bigelow that Ms. Pentecost is a very ill woman. This short time in a prison cell has already severely impacted her health. You cannot in good conscience have her spend another night there."

To Bigelow.

"I believe there are physicians at the prison, are there not?"

To Whitsun.

"Your Honor, these physicians are hardly qualified to treat something as serious as multiple sclerosis," he said. "With your permission, I'd like to read an account of my client's first night in jail, which includes her experience with the prison doctor."

The judge reluctantly gave permission, and Whitsun picked up a sheet of paper, both sides covered in script.

You've already heard what she had to report, but this was my first time. Three sentences in and I was ready to take a crowbar to somebody. Beside me, the Brit reporter squirmed in his seat.

Creed cut Whitsun short.

"That's enough, Mr. Whitsun," he said. "There's no jury here to sway, sir. And I won't have that kind of incendiary language in my court, do you understand?"

"Yes, sir, I'm sorry," Whitsun said. "Believe me, I'm not comfortable using it. But I think it goes to illustrate the point that—"

"One moment, Mr. Whitsun," the judge said, turning to Bigelow. The prosecutor had his hand raised.

"Mr. Bigelow," the judge said, "do you have an objection?"

"No, sir. Not an objection, per se. I was only thinking that if Mr. Whitsun is concerned about the quality of care at the Women's House of Detention, then the state would gladly agree for Ms. Pentecost to be attended to by her personal physician. If that's all right with Your Honor?"

Creed nodded and smiled. "That's a fine idea. It certainly sounds like it addresses your concerns, Mr. Whitsun."

It took a second for Whitsun to get his feet back under him.

"Your Honor, it's not solely the matter of my client's health," he said. "In the interest of judicial fairness, I think that bail, even if it's a high amount, should—"

Creed cut him off again. "Mr. Whitsun, it is a common occurrence for bail to be denied in the case of murder, especially in the first degree."

"Your Honor—"

"Bail is denied."

There was more. Something about scheduling motions and getting things on the calendar, but I wasn't listening.

Ms. Pentecost wasn't coming home. Not that day. She was going back to the House of D.

When Creed gave his gavel one final rap, I jumped.

The judge stood and so did every reporter in the place. Half ran for the door to go call in the story, while the other half began shouting questions at Whitsun and Ms. P and Bigelow.

I remained slumped on the bench, head swimming, stomach sinking.

The Brit stepped on my foot trying to get to the aisle, and that snapped me out of it in time to see Ms. Pentecost being led away by a pair of bailiffs.

When she neared my row, she stumbled forward, reaching out and catching the back of the bench in front of me. As one of the bailiffs helped her steady herself, she said in a whisper that I could barely hear over the thrum of the reporters, "I did not do this."

Then she was gone.

CHAPTER 9

"What the hell was that in there, Whitsun? Where was the real-life Perry Mason the papers are always gushing about? Where was he? I want to meet that guy, because his substitute stood there and let *Miracle on 34th Street* hand him his ass."

I was shouting, but I didn't care. We were upstairs in a private room at Zanotti's, a second-generation Italian joint two blocks from the courthouse. It was frequented by a lot of lawyers, judges, the occasional NYPD brass. Rank-and-file cops preferred Flannagan's around the corner.

If either Whitsun or Pearl was bothered by my tirade, it didn't show.

"We knew going in that bail was going to be a long shot," Whitsun said.

"Nobody told me."

"It's the publicity around the case," Pearl explained. "The evidence. Ms. Pentecost being who she is. They were bound to make an example."

"I thought we had a shot with the health angle, but Bigelow was waiting for it, and, yes, you're right, he sucker-punched me," Whitsun admitted. "I'm gonna have to study up on him before we go in there again."

It's hard to keep yelling when your target agrees with you.

"Did Ms. Pentecost know?" I asked. "That it was a long shot?"

Whitsun nodded.

"We told her. But she already had an inkling," he said. "Now, do you want to calm down and take a seat so we can talk about what comes next?"

No, I didn't want to do that. But pacing a groove in the carpet wasn't going to help my boss. I sat.

Pearl pointed to the side of my face. "You've got a little pancake around your hairline."

I was still in the victory suit, but I'd ditched the wig and glasses and washed the makeup off—or most of it off—in the restaurant bathroom. I dipped a napkin in a glass of water and scrubbed.

"What's the plan?" I asked. "Whatever it is, it needs to include whatever paperwork it takes to get inside Quincannon's house. Alathea says she's leaving the crime scene untouched, but I don't know how far I'd take her word."

Whitsun and Pearl exchanged a look.

"She says that, huh?" Whitsun said.

"I might have dropped by and asked," I said. "It's her call, since Quincannon made her executor of his estate."

Whitsun leaned back in his chair.

"Huh. I didn't know that. Wonder why he didn't leave it to his lawyer."

I stopped scrubbing. If there was any makeup left, it would have to stay.

"His lawyer's a shark. More so than average, I mean," I said. "Anyway, I want to visit the scene. Find out who was standing where when. Then there's Ms. Pentecost's gun. Somebody would have needed to steal it, use it, then return it. There was fingerprint dust all over the drawer it was kept in, so I guess Staples did his job. I'd like to know what prints they pulled."

Pearl nudged Whitsun and nodded.

"Yeah, all right," he said.

"Yeah, all right what?" I asked.

"You're hired."

"What do you mean, I'm hired?"

"I mean, I've got other investigators that I like to use," Whitsun said. "But if I told you to lay off and let them do their job, would you listen?"

"Hell no, I wouldn't," I said, starting to stand again.

Whitsun waved me back down. "Don't go getting riled up. Like I said—you're hired. If you're going to be doing the work, we might as well use you. But we've got to talk about what the work is."

There was a knock at the door and a pair of waiters delivered a bottle of Chianti and three plates of various pastas with all the trimmings. One of them was obviously new on the job and his lip curled in disgust when he slid Pearl's plate in front of her. He didn't know Pearl and Whitsun had helped the owner out of a jam and in return she didn't get turned away at the door. If she noticed the sneer, she pretended not to.

"What did you mean about what the work is?" I asked when they left. "The work is to find out who killed Quincannon and framed my boss."

Whitsun tried to talk around a mouthful of mezzelune.

"Whf, yesh tha—"

"Obviously, that would be the best outcome," Pearl said for him. "But you've got to start thinking like an investigator for the defense. You're not finding out who did it, but anyone who could have done it, who wanted to do it. Every motive, means, and even the barest chance of opportunity. That's what we'll need at trial. You understand?"

I must have nodded, because Pearl nodded back and tucked into her meal. My stomach was still somewhere south of my knees, so while my pasta went cold, I did the math.

A murder trial took months to put together. Sometimes we handed the DA a killer and it was a full year before we were called to testify.

A year Ms. Pentecost would spend in the House of D.

No, I thought. We were going to find the real killer and we were going to be quick about it.

The real killer. Because she didn't do it. She'd whispered as much.

A voice in the back of my head—one that only slightly resembled my father's—asked the question I didn't want an answer to.

If she did it, would she tell you?

Yeah, I thought. Yeah, she would. Because I'm her friend and we trust each other.

To which that voice responded with another question.

Why'd she feel she needed to tell you she didn't do it at all? Wouldn't she expect a good, trusting friend to know she was innocent?

I didn't have an answer to that one.

Luckily, Whitsun distracted me by handing over the notes Ms. P had scribbled in her jail cell.

"Some of this is gibberish," he said. "She says you can decode it. Something about a brisket recipe?"

"Then it's going to have to wait," I told him. "I need a Bible to translate it."

Whitsun put down his fork, opened his briefcase, and pulled out a well-worn King James.

"Are you kidding me?" I asked as he handed it over.

"Comes in handy," he said around a mouthful of pasta. "Always nice when you can quote gospel to a jury."

Ms. Pentecost didn't know the whole book by heart, but she had a few choice bits memorized. I, on the other hand, needed to cheat. For the "brisket recipe" I turned to Daniel, found the bit about the three guys in the furnace, and started deciphering, writing the translation into my own notebook.

I paid the most attention to her account of the night of the murder. The timeline was tight but not impossible. One of the guests could have been waiting up there, or even have sprinted up the steps when they saw Ms. P get in the elevator.

That included Alathea. She would have been armed, after all. Also, she'd always played chaperone in the past. Why not this time?

I mentioned this to Whitsun, and he nodded.

"She's certainly someone to look at," he said. "But my favorite is still this Muffin character."

Finally, something we agreed on.

We also agreed we should keep to ourselves the bit about Ms. P stealing Quincannon's notes and burning them. No use giving the authorities any more ammunition than they already had.

We talked for a while longer. Whitsun handed me a laundry list of chores—who to talk to, what questions to ask. I kept my mouth shut and let him think he was being useful.

"I'll file a motion to get you access to Quincannon's house," Whitsun said. "But I can't make people talk to you, you understand?"

"For that, I'll use wit and charm."

Pearl laughed. Whitsun looked skeptical.

"Oh, I've got both, counselor," I said, standing. "I just don't waste them on you."

CHAPTER 10

I was passing through the main dining room of Zanotti's on my way to the exit when I caught a familiar pair of eyes. There was some subtle semaphore, then the body connected to those eyes got up and walked past me down the hall and into the men's lavatory. A quick look around to make sure no one was watching, then I followed and locked the door behind me.

The bathroom was a single-seater, and at six feet and change and broad as a bricklayer, Lieutenant Nathan Lazenby took up most of it. He was dressed in his best black wool and his dark beard, liberally sprinkled with silver, had been trimmed to something more patron saint than mad monk.

"You've been avoiding my calls," I hissed.

"I'm sorry, Will. I couldn't chance it," he said. "I've been told in no uncertain terms not to go anywhere near this case."

We were almost chest to chest, so I had to tilt my chin up to berate him. It probably blunted some of the impact, but I didn't care.

"You could have at least warned her it was coming."

"I told her Staples had her in his sights."

"You should have come and fetched me."

"I offered and she said no, absolutely do not go get you."

That took some of the wind out of my sails.

"Why would she do that?" I asked.

"She wanted to make sure they knew you were up in the mountains the whole time. You're the one with the history of shooting people, remember."

"Person. One person. In self-defense."

There were some close calls, though.

A few years back, Lazenby himself had locked me in an interrogation room and grilled me on the shooting of a huckster spiritualist. At the time, he'd really believed I'd done it.

I didn't blame him. I'd pointed a gun at the woman and would have put a bullet between her eyes if Ms. Pentecost hadn't been there to stop me. It was only when every gun in the brownstone was fired and their bullets examined under a microscope that I was cleared.

The point is, Ms. P was right. If the cops thought there was the barest possibility I'd been in the city when Quincannon was shot, I'd have been in the frame, too.

I hopped up on the sink, heard the porcelain give a creak, and hopped back down. I settled for wedging myself into a corner by the door and crossing my arms.

"You should have come and gotten me anyway," I huffed.

He gave a "maybe I should have" shrug.

"Look, the brass is keeping an eye on me," he said. "But if there's anything—"

He was interrupted by a tap at the door.

"Occupied!" he bellowed.

We listened as a pair of patent leathers went scurrying away. By the time the footsteps faded I had my next words ready.

"Assuming you were about to offer your assistance, short of being seen in public with me, then I've got an errand for you," I told him. "Billy Muffin. I understand he was present at the murder, but is currently unaccounted for."

"Staples is looking," Lazenby said.

"Could you look, as well? Without stepping on his toes?"

"Probably," he said. "Rumor has it Muffin's out of the murder business and into armed robberies. He's been holding up illegal poker games. The victims aren't talking, and nobody's been killed yet, so it hasn't been a high priority. I could probably make it one."

"Thanks," I said. "I'd really like to have a chat with the man. Also, if you could get me the medical examiner's report on Quincannon, I'd greatly appreciate it."

"The DA's office has all the evidence from this case in a vise. How am I supposed to do that?"

"I have faith in you, Lieutenant."

"Fine," he said. "But if you have to call me again, use an alias. Use . . ." He looked around the room and came up with a name.

"Seriously? You expect me to do that?"

"You will if you need to talk to me. This case is a bear trap. We both need to step carefully."

Lazenby sighed and looked at the door.

"I should go," he said. "Tell Lillian to be careful in there."

He left, but I didn't follow. Instead, I latched the door again, then sat down on the toilet and rested my chin in my hands. Some people do their best thinking on the can. I'm not usually one of them, but I wasn't looking for a brainstorm, merely the beginnings of a to-do list.

As much as I didn't want to admit it, Lillian Pentecost was out of commission for an unknown amount of time. Papers needed signing, people needed calling. Ms. P's physician, Doc Hubbard, for one. He needed to be told to prepare for a field trip to the House of D.

What else?

Lazenby was on Muffin, but there were the other guests to track down. For most of them, I had nothing but their names.

Also, I needed to give a quote to the press. Too much silence would make it look like I was hiding, which would look like I thought Ms. P was guilty.

Actually, there might be a way to kill two birds with one—
The door to the bathroom rattled.

"Occupied!"

Frustrated footsteps hurrying away.

It was getting so a girl couldn't ponder in peace.

CHAPTER **11**

I met Max Roberts at a little hole-in-the-wall on Forty-third Street, a couple of blocks from the Times Building. The place was known for good burgers, strong martinis, and deep booths that offered the luxury of privacy. I'd managed to walk out of Zanotti's without eating anything, so I was halfway through a burger with all the fixings when Roberts appeared next to my booth.

"Hey, Max."

"Will," he said, tossing his leather satchel onto the seat across from me, then following it in. "Long time since we've met up in here."

"Pretty long."

It occurs to me that I haven't done much to describe Max Roberts, a handsome sort if you've got a thing for assistant principals. He was a hair past his fiftieth birthday, and the years were starting to catch up with him, but he was still winning the race. The gray sidewalls above his ears had encroached in the five years we'd known each other, but not unpleasantly. The paunch he'd been nursing had grown, but the bifocals seemed to be the same prescription.

He was also still wearing the same brown two-breaster with matching tie. No surprise there. He had four of the things hanging in his closet.

He gave a sniff.

"I thought you stopped getting extra onions on your burgers."

"I started again about five minutes after we broke up."

Did I mention Max and I were a couple once upon a time? And by "couple," I mean we coupled for about three months five years previous. Max was the reason I now had the "no dating reporters" rule. Also "no dating anyone old enough to have sired me."

"If you're gonna yell at me again, I'd rather skip it," he told me. "I've got a deadline."

"No yelling," I assured him. "You said you wanted a quote. I'll give you a quote."

His face lit up, then quickly darkened.

"What's the catch?"

"Tit for tat. You tell me about the night of the murder and the people there. I give you an exclusive quote from Lillian Pentecost's right-hand girl."

He considered it.

"You don't talk to anyone else?"

"You and you alone."

He considered some more.

"All right," he said finally. "What's the quote?"

I shook my head.

"Uh-uh. Tit first, tat later," I said. "How'd you get invited to Quincannon's party? Don't skimp. I don't have time to play footsie."

Max waved down the waiter and ordered a double martini, hold the olives. He hadn't changed his favorite drink. Then he leaned back into the soft vinyl of the booth and began.

"I got a call from Quincannon that morning," he said. "I'd been poking him for years to let me into one of his Black Museum salons. Never a bite. Now he says I can come over and write a story on it and get an exclusive interview to boot. The only catch is his guests are off-limits. I can't use any of their names. Except one."

"Lillian Pentecost," I guessed.

"That's right. He sent over a contract. Three pages of legal mumbo-jumbo that basically said if I name any other guest, the *Times* can get sued down to the thumbtacks. I didn't care. I wanted in, so I signed. My editor signed. I went."

That was why the *Times* played it coy with the names. Quincannon was dead, but that piece of paper wasn't.

His martini arrived and Max took a long sip. Then another.

"I get there right at seven. Nobody else is there yet. His assistant—have you seen his assistant? Jesus. She takes me up to his office, where Quincannon is waiting to have our interview. I had a whole—"

I interrupted. "I want to know everything he said. Not just the paragraphs that made it into print."

He peered at me over his bifocals like I was a schoolgirl looking for a scolding.

"I was about to say that I had a whole notebook full of questions, and I got to ask exactly one, with two follow-ups," he said. "He made it pretty clear, pretty quick, that it wasn't an interview. Just a chance for him to stand on his soapbox. It lasted exactly three and a half minutes. Every word he said, minus the hellos and thank-yous, is in that article."

"Then what?" I asked.

"Then he had his girl escort me downstairs. I asked if I could get a tour of the Black Museum. She said no. I asked if she'd mind answering a few questions, and she said hell no and to have a glass of wine. So I had a glass of wine."

"And then?"

"If you've read my story, you know."

"Come on," I said. "You were there an hour before Ms. Pentecost showed up. What was going on between the lines?"

"Between the lines? It was a weird group," he said. "And not weird like I expected."

"What do you mean?"

"I thought it'd be a bunch of well-to-do with a taste for tragedy. It was more hodgepodge."

"Who was there?" I asked.

"Didn't you see? *Free City* already printed the guest list."

"They're just names to me. I want your impressions. Feel free to talk fast. I know shorthand."

He talked, I dashed and dotted.

- Dr. Ryan Backstrom (mid-forties; blond hair, blue eyes; pleasantly statuesque). A wunderkind brain surgeon with a fascination for abnormal psychology.

- Reverend Timothy Novarro (mid-forties; dark hair, eyes, and complexion; the sharpest pencil-thin mustache you've ever seen). Novarro operated out of a storefront church and was rumored to be a closet Commie.

- Elaine Novarro (early forties; blond; a little severe). The "seen and not heard" type of wife.

- Victoria Pelham (mid-fifties; long brown hair, dark eyes; a pinup figure paired with upper-crust poise). When she was eighteen, Pelham married a railroad baron. He had a massive heart attack not long after, and Pelham has been working her way through the money ever since. People whisper, "Black widow," when she walks by, but never quite loud enough for her to hear.

- Judge Martin "Hang-'Em-High" Mathers (somewhere south of Methuselah; no hair; mostly cataracts). An old friend of Quincannon's father. He'd been on the bench in Louisiana and moved to New York City in his dotage.

- Silas Culliver (forties; bald as a newborn; built like a
  Notre Dame linebacker). Quincannon's pet lawyer
  and the man tasked with helping him procure
  exhibits for his macabre collection. An asshole with
  the diction of a duke.

- Alathea (late twenties; Snow White if she was
  raised by seven assassins). In Max's words: "When
  she gave me a look, I wanted to run, but I didn't
  know in what direction."

- Billy Muffin (late thirties; redhead; kind of
  squirrely). Back in the day, if you wanted someone
  gone and you didn't need to be quiet about it,
  you called Muffin. He worked for any and all
  of the families, as well as the occasional private
  individual. Rumor has it that he took a slug in the
  leg, which caused him to lose a step.

There was also a cook and a waiter hired for the event, but
Max didn't get their names. Add Ms. Pentecost into the mix and
that made twelve people on hand for the murder besides the
deceased himself.

I took Max's descriptions with a grain of salt. He had his
blind spots. A nice pair of legs, for one. Also, he was slow to
criticize anyone in authority. He thought, despite all evidence
to the contrary, that if someone had a seat at the high table, it
was because they had earned it.

"All right, so you show up to the party. What happens
next?"

He glanced at his watch.

"Come on, Max. Spill."

"There's not much to spill," he said. "Everyone knows I'm
a reporter, so nobody wanted to chat, except for Novarro, who

wanted to talk about the city's social policies. And Mathers, who asked if I'm a Jew. He's a joy. You'll love him.

"A little before eight, Quincannon comes down. Does a round of the room. Ignores me completely. Says he's making some last-minute adjustments to his presentation and disappears back upstairs. Shortly after that, I go looking for the bathroom. It's occupied because the preacher's wife spilled a drink on herself. Guess she couldn't handle her liquor. That's where I am when I see Alathea walk your boss inside and put her in the elevator. Right after that, we hear the gunshots. There's some confusion, because people think it might be part of the show. An atmosphere thing. Then Alathea comes running in from somewhere. She bolts upstairs. The doctor, Culliver, and I follow."

"What about Muffin? Did he go up?"

"I didn't see him."

"Where was he when the shots were fired?"

"I don't know, Will," he said. "I was waiting outside the bathroom, remember?"

His voice had taken on that tone that I recognized from the final days of our ill-fated fling—a grating whine that was both apologetic and aggrieved.

"All right. You ran upstairs—then what?"

"Alathea goes in first. She's got a gun. Pulls it out of one of those thigh holsters you enjoy. She checks the body. Then the doctor, Backstrom, confirms it. After that it was the cops' show."

He looked at his watch again. This time with emphasis.

"I understand you're in a bind," he said, "but I've got a story to write. I shouldn't even be here. There are still people in editorial who remember that you and I were an item."

"Is that what we were?"

"You know what I mean. If they think I'm playing soft they'll yank this and give it to one of the young Turks trying to knock me off the crime beat, and there are plenty of them."

There was the whine again. That "the whole world is out to get me" bellyaching that I'd lain in bed and listened to on so many of our stolen afternoons.

He reached into his satchel and pulled out a fresh notebook and a worn-down pencil.

"Enough tit for now. What's the official statement from the offices of Pentecost Investigations?"

My first instinct was to tell him to shove it. But Max had played it straight and I might need him again, so I gave him what he wanted.

"Lillian Pentecost is innocent of these charges. Not only will we prove that, we'll hand the police and the district attorney the real killer. As Lillian Pentecost has done countless times in the past."

He finished scribbling and looked up.

"Nice jab."

I shrugged. "I can do subtle when I need to."

I could tell he wanted more, but he was smart enough not to push. He slipped his notebook back into his bag, then put his elbows on the table and leaned forward, looking at me over his bifocals again, less the disciplinarian and more the father figure.

"I'm sorry it has to be this way," he said. "This can't be easy."

"Don't sell yourself short, Max. Chatting with you isn't the worst thing in the world."

"You know what I mean. You spend all this time catching killers, and then your boss goes and . . ." He shook his head, leaned back, and downed the rest of his drink.

Then it hit me.

"You think she did it."

He wiped away some gin that had dribbled down his chin.

"Come on, Will. Look at the evidence."

"Exactly," I snapped. "Look at the evidence. In what world is Lillian Pentecost—who is smarter than you and me put together—going to walk into a party, shoot a guy, then go home and put the gun back in her desk for the cops to collect at their leisure?"

My voice had risen enough for patrons at other booths to peek over to see who was shouting. I didn't care.

"Believe me, Max," I said, "if Lillian Pentecost ever wanted somebody dead, you'd be lucky to find a body, much less any evidence."

Max had been the target of worse tirades, and he didn't flinch. He looked at me mournfully and said, "Yeah, sure, Will. But smart people do dumb things, and a lot of them are locked up for murder. You should know. You helped put some of them there."

CHAPTER 12

After Max left, I sat in the booth for a while, stewing over his last words. He probably thought he was doing me a favor. Preparing me for the worst.

That was one of the reasons we hadn't worked out. That and the postcoital griping. I was young and new in town, and he thought he needed to educate me about the big, bad city and the evil in the hearts of men.

Didn't believe me when I told him I knew plenty about big and bad and had seen my fair share of the inside of men's hearts.

What had he said?

Oh, right. "You're a twenty-year-old girl. What could you know?"

Like I said: The guy's got blind spots.

I decided I needed to see Ms. P. I needed to talk to her about that night, and I needed to do it now.

I paid the check and asked the waiter if I could use their phone. He said sure and I dialed the House of D. I got the same charming secretary as before and asked politely to schedule a visit with Lillian Pentecost.

"Are you her lawyer or a family member?" she asked.

"No, I'm her—"

"Visits are limited to lawyers and family members," she droned. "The latter will be required to provide proof of blood relation."

"I've visited prisoners before. Those aren't the rules."

"Visitation rules for prisoners awaiting trial are under the discretion of the warden," she said. "For Mrs. Pentecost, that's lawyers and immediate family members."

"What about speaking to her on the phone?"

"Phone calls are limited to lawyers and—"

"Let me talk to the warden," I demanded.

"I'm afraid she's not available. Would you like to leave a message?"

I left one. I didn't think she'd pass it on.

I drove back to Brooklyn in a rage. I was angry at the secretary, at the warden, at the district attorney's office, who'd probably asked for visits to be limited so they could sweat Ms. P.

I was angry at Max for planting that seed of doubt.

Who was I kidding—the seed was already there. Max had simply watered it. But damn him for thinking he was doing me a favor.

Back at the office, I gave Mrs. Campbell a firsthand account of the bail hearing—she'd caught the basics over the radio news—then I installed myself at my desk and tried to type up the notes from my conversation with Max. I say "tried" because I kept fumbling the keys.

"Couldn't handle her liquor" became "coydnt hamdlr her liqur."

"Alathea goes in first" turned into "Althea goess inn fiirtt."

Eventually I stopped abusing my Remington and sat and thought. Or tried not to think.

I was failing at both when Mrs. Campbell knocked on the door and poked her head in.

"That reporter's back. He's knocking on my front door asking for you."

Something in my smile made the housekeeper flinch.

"Delightful," I said, walking around her and through the back door and across the courtyard to the carriage house.

I couldn't beat the crap out of Bigelow or the warden or

Staples. I couldn't drag the entire justice system into the street and kick its teeth in.

But I could punch a reporter.

I barreled through Mrs. Campbell's kitchen and sitting room, then flung open her front door, revealing the same slouch of a man who had come knocking two days earlier. He was wearing a different wrinkled suit, still with the camera and satchel over his shoulder.

He stumbled back in surprise, tripped over his heels, and landed on his rear on the asphalt. It's not as satisfying to punch somebody who's down, so I settled for yelling.

"Listen, buddy. I don't care what rag you're working for, you don't get a quote. Not now, not ever. Now get on your sticks and scram!"

I was winding up to slam the door when he yelled, "I'm not a reporter!"

I paused.

"Please," he said. "I'm not a reporter. My name is Walter Beck. I work with the police crime lab. I need to speak with you."

"Do you have a warrant?" I asked. "We have a rule. No warrant, no cops."

"I'm not here on police business," he said in a hushed voice. "It's a personal matter."

He looked up and down the street. He had the air of a man waiting in line at a brothel.

"I don't know what your game is," I said, "but we're not taking cases at the moment."

He unhunched his shoulders long enough to say, "I think you'll take mine."

"What makes you say that?"

"Because I'm the one who framed Lillian Pentecost for murder."

CHAPTER 13

I dragged Walter Beck inside and tossed him into the least comfortable of the sitting room's chairs. Then I stood over him and did my best to loom. While I did that, Mrs. Campbell locked and bolted the door.

"Say what you said again," I told him. "Slower this time."

"I framed Lillian Pentecost for the murder of Jessup Quincannon," he said, setting his camera and satchel on the floor.

"You killed Quincannon?"

"No, no, no. Of course not." He made it sound like I'd insulted him. "I didn't kill him. But I did frame her."

Mrs. Campbell stepped up and asked, "How exactly did you do that?"

That was my line, but I let her have it.

"It was really very simple," he said, switching his gaze between the two of us. "I worked the case. I had access to the evidence. It was relatively easy to replace the bullet taken from the crime scene—the intact bullet that did not enter the body—with one of the samples we had from Lillian Pentecost's derringer."

"What samples?" I asked.

"From the Belestrad murder. We still have all those bullets on file."

You know how I mentioned that time Lazenby suspected

me of putting a bullet in a woman and tested every gun in the house to make sure I didn't? This was that time.

Beck's story was plausible. His delivery was off, though. No pride, no passion. Like he was reading the instructions on a box of Rinso because he really wanted to get those stains out.

Mrs. Campbell broke away from Beck and went across the room and started doing something in one of the tall cabinets in the corner. I looked at him with fresh eyes. Monster? Madman? He didn't look like either, but they rarely do.

"So you decided to frame Lillian Pentecost? For what? Kicks?"

"I did it because I want her to investigate—"

Whatever he was about to say was cut off by the angry Scotswoman walking up and pointing a Winchester pump-action at his head.

"All right, laddie," Mrs. Campbell growled. "We're going to give that smug detective a call and you're going to tell him exactly what you just told us."

Beck swallowed the lump in his throat and shook his head. "No, ma'am, I will not."

She pressed the barrel against his forehead.

"Son, you very much will. Or I will open your skull to the air."

Incredibly, he didn't soil himself.

"Then I'll be dead and you'll never be able to prove anything," he said, his voice wavering only a little. "I was very careful. No one knows what I did and there's no evidence. But . . . but if Lillian Pentecost takes my case. Really takes it and investigates. Then I'll confess to everything."

I didn't like the way Mrs. Campbell's finger was curled around the trigger. I reached out and gently shifted the barrel to the side. Now if she got a twitch, he'd lose his hearing and not his life.

"There are easier ways of hiring us," I noted. "Ones that don't involve a felony or putting my boss in prison."

For the first time, he showed some emotion.

"I tried," he said. "I called. I wrote. Three times I wrote. And three times all I got was 'I'm sorry but I don't believe I am best suited to help you. I would be happy to recommend other investigators.' I've tried other investigators. I said that in my last letter. I need Lillian Pentecost."

He hadn't quoted Ms. Pentecost's refusal letter verbatim but he came close. I could do it word for word because I'd typed two thousand of them. That was a lowball on how many people Ms. P had turned down over my years with her.

Three times he said he'd written. Walter Beck . . .

"Your wife," I said. "Your wife committed suicide."

"She did not commit suicide!" he shouted.

Even though she was the one with the shotgun, Mrs. Campbell retreated a step.

Beck took a deep breath and repeated more calmly, "She didn't commit suicide. She was murdered. I want Lillian Pentecost to prove it."

"How do you expect her to do that when you've put her in prison?" I asked. "I don't know if you've heard, but they denied bail."

He shook his head.

"I know how you work," he said. "You're the one who goes out and gathers facts and clues and you bring it back to her. You can still do that."

The fact that he had us pegged so neatly only stoked my anger. No, it wasn't only that he thought he knew us. It was the matter-of-factness. The lack of smugness.

He should be cackling maniacally. He should be twirling a mustache. How dare he be so ordinary?

"Will you accept my proposal?" he asked.

His proposal! Like he was selling a used car. I had the impulse to snatch the shotgun out of Mrs. Campbell's hands and see how far I could shove the barrel down his throat.

I managed to quash it. I had a better idea.

"All right," I said. "You've got us up against a wall. I'm not promising anything, but I'll hear you out. Let's head over to the office and you can tell me about your wife."

He smiled, but not in triumph.

"I don't think so, Miss Parker. I heard Detective Lazenby talking about that machine you have set up in there to record people in secret. No, no, no, I don't think so."

He wagged a finger at me and that I didn't snap it off is a miracle of restraint. Now what?

During my years with the circus, I'd regularly played substitute to this or that lovely assistant, most frequently for Mysterio. When the show went off-script, like, say, Mysterio shoving his hand into the top of my corset and pulling out a string of handkerchiefs, instead of immediately elbowing him in the teeth, I'd ask myself, What would Lulu do? Lulu being the usual owner of the corset.

Lulu would peek down her cleavage and say, "I wonder what else is down there?"

Which is what I did, setting the magician up to say, "Not much, but give it a few years."

The audience laughed and Mysterio kept all his teeth and I kept my job, if not my dignity.

So when I felt my elbow twitching, instead of acting on my first impulse, I asked myself: What would Lillian Pentecost do if presented with Walter Beck?

The answer came quick and clear and was about as palatable as letting Mysterio have a free grope. I took one of the other chairs, then turned to Mrs. Campbell.

"Eleanor, can you find me a notebook and pencil?"

Mrs. Campbell is about as sharp as they come, so she pivoted with balletic grace.

"I've got one in a drawer here. Just sharpened the pencil, too," she said. "I'll put some coffee on."

However, instead of putting the shotgun back wherever she found it, she propped it in a corner, where it would be close at hand. Because she was also nobody's fool.

With the kettle on the stove, Beck and I settled into our respective chairs. Mrs. Campbell stationed herself in the kitchen, out of sight but certainly within earshot.

Will Parker: Tell me about your wife, Mr. Beck.

    Walter Beck: She was beautiful. And very sweet. Cheerful and kind. And unprepossessing. You understand?

WP: I know what unprepossessing means, yes. Why don't we start with some biography? Like her name.

    WB: Susan. But she liked to be called Susie. Susie Elizabeth Beck. Formerly Grigg. We were high school sweethearts back in Portsmouth. That's in Virginia.

    Married in 1942, right before I shipped off. She lived with her mother during that time. I took a round in my stomach and spent three months in England. Then got sent home in September '43. Spent a year recovering. Susie never left my side.

    While I was bedridden, I enrolled in correspondence courses. Photography and law enforcement. When I saw the job at the crime lab advertised in a magazine, Susie and I agreed it was a great fit. We moved into the city in April '44.

    It was a dirty little cupboard of a place. Eventually I got a raise and we moved to where we are now in Jackson Heights. Or where I am now. She's . . .

WP: All right, Walter. Take a minute if you need to.

    WB: Not necessary. I've told this story enough.

    We were happy. She was happy. Not as much in the first apartment. There was barely enough room to breathe. But she helped find our place in Jackson Heights and after that, things were better.

WP: Did she work?

    WB: She had a secretarial job at a travel agency a few blocks away, in Elmhurst. She didn't have to. I made enough. But she'd done volunteer work while I was overseas and gotten into the habit of working. It would have been temporary. We were going to have a family, you see?

She started there not long after we moved apartments. That job really seemed to perk her up. Made her smile.

WP: *She wasn't smiling before?*

WB: That first place—we barely had windows and what we had were facing another building. Not a bit of sunlight. She used to joke, "Walter, you could use our living room as a darkroom without changing a thing."

But she was much happier when we moved. We had a party. Invited friends, co-workers. We were talking about children again. Now that we had the room.

It doesn't make sense. She wouldn't have done it. I tell you, she wouldn't.

WP: *Tell me about what she wouldn't do.*

WB: On July nineteenth, 1946, I came home from work. I'd been gone since dawn. A burglary at Fordham University. Detective Staples had wanted all the photographs printed right away.

I had told Susie not to stay up. I was surprised when I found all the lights on in the house. Every single one, it seemed. We never did that. I went into the bedroom first, but the bed was still made from that morning. Then I went into the bathroom, and that's where I found her.

The tub was full.

She was . . . she . . . um . . . There were lateral incisions stretching from the crook of her elbow down to her wrist.

The water was . . . black.

My straight razor was lying on the floor.

I didn't touch her. I've seen enough crime scenes made a mess of by family members. I called the police straightaway.

WP: *Who worked it?*

WB: Lieutenant Lazenby.

WP: *Lazenby is good.*

WB: The best when it comes to homicides. That's why I was so disappointed when he eventually closed the case as a suicide. There were no prints. But there wouldn't be if he used gloves.

And the light switches, remember? We never had on all the

lights. Living room, bedroom, kitchen, the lamp by the bed. All at once.

Then there was the wine.

WP: What wine?

WB: They found red wine in her stomach. The medical examiner did. Quite a lot of wine. Susie didn't drink to excess. She was raised Quaker.

The lieutenant said . . . He said sometimes people fortify themselves. But where was the bottle? There was no bottle of wine in the house.

Before you ask, there were seven places that served red wine within ten blocks of our apartment. The police checked. Susie hadn't been seen at any of them.

There were an additional twenty-three within a half-a-mile radius. The detective I hired checked them as well. Nothing.

The lieutenant was very kind. Or he thought he was being kind.

He said these things were unexplainable. But that's our job, isn't it? That's my job. His job, your job, Lillian Pentecost's job. To explain things.

WP: If you know my job so well, I imagine you know the questions I'm about to ask. Did your wife have any enemies that you know of?

WB: Not a soul. Everyone loved her.

WP: What about at the travel agency? Maybe she rubbed a customer the wrong way?

WB: She was a secretary. She typed up itineraries or sometimes called to arrange flights or trains. She didn't work with the customers. At least that's what her employer said. The detective looked into it and didn't find anything. I have his report in my bag.

But I've always wondered if there was something that was missed. A customer who took a dislike to her or . . . or something else. And this person kept it secret until . . . I mean, nobody would know, would they?

WP: How about you? Anyone with a grudge?

WB: I work for the police, Miss Parker. I imagine I have a lot of enemies. But I doubt any of them know my name. You didn't, and I've been in the same room with you many times. You didn't even recognize me.

WP: Ever testified in court?

WB: No. My photographs get used, but I'm not the one presenting them. I'm . . . I've been told I don't make the best witness.

WP: Who was this other detective you hired?

WB: Darryl Klinghorn. I believe you're familiar with him.

WP: I am. I was. Klinghorn was very thorough.

WB: Yes. His report was quite extensive. All dead ends.

That's why I need Lillian Pentecost. Because I know she can succeed where others have failed.

You tell her that if she finds my wife's killer, I'll confess everything. I'll tell the press, the police, whoever will listen. I'll tell them how I did it and why.

WP: You know you'll go to jail, right?

WB: I don't care. As long as I get answers. As long as my Susie gets justice.

WP: If we do this and find that it's a suicide? What then?

WB: Miss Parker, I swear to you on my life and on the memory of my wife, she did not kill herself. Somebody did this to her. That person is still out there.

It was a good line. Over-rehearsed, but as Beck reminded me, he had practice telling this story.

He opened his satchel and pulled out a thick leather document holder so packed with paper the stitches were starting to pop. A few of the pages had been typed by the police and the rest—half a novel's worth—by Darryl Klinghorn.

I gave it a quick flip-through, asked a few more questions, then cut Beck loose, giving him the admonition that I wasn't going to do squat without Ms. P's say-so.

"I understand," he said before walking away. "Thank you, Miss Parker. Thank you for helping me."

As if he were any other client.

Once he was gone, Mrs. Campbell went over to the corner cabinet and replaced the Winchester.

"What are we going to do about that one?" she asked.

What, indeed?

It seemed to me there were three options. The first was to investigate the death of his wife, and hope Beck made good on his promise. Option two would be going hard on Beck. He sold himself as a man with nothing to lose. But people can always lose more.

Then there was option three—ignore Beck and keep working the Quincannon case. If Beck was on the level, both about faking the evidence and not being the killer himself, that made our murder a lot simpler.

Nobody broke into the brownstone and stole Ms. Pentecost's derringer and then broke back in and replaced it. There was no criminal mastermind. Someone showed up with their own gun and killed Quincannon and then won the lottery when Beck decided to tamper with the scene.

Three paths diverge in a wood. Each of them had pitfalls, but I wasn't the one chancing the plunge. The woman whose life was on the line was stuck in the House of D and I was forbidden from seeing her.

I could send a message through Whitsun, but then I'd have to let him in on Walter Beck. Once I did that, the decision was out of our hands and in his. Even if I did it in code, he'd still know something was up.

Three paths.

I needed to talk to my boss. But how?

My eyes landed on the flyer advertising the Halloween jamboree.

"Huh."

"What?" Mrs. Campbell asked.

"How are you with a needle and thread?"

CHAPTER 14

From the journals of Lillian Pentecost

After three days of silence, my cellmate spoke to me.

We had passed a handful of words. Good mornings and good evenings; helpful but curt directions on what to bring to the showers; where to store my few possessions.

Otherwise, Val remained silent.

It was the day after my arraignment and I was writing in this journal, which Mr. Whitsun was able to procure for me in order to keep a record of my incarceration, as well as my thoughts on the case.

Val had been lying silently in his bunk since lunch when he abruptly stood up. Pressing his hands against the ceiling, he twisted from side to side, eliciting a series of cracks from his back.

Then he went to the door of our cell and shouted out the barred window.

"Hey, Judy! Judy! You got any of that liniment you've been using on your leg? My ribs are killing me."

I did not hear Judy's response, but it must have been in the negative, because Val groaned and turned away.

I should take a moment to describe Val. I would find out later that he much prefers this over Valeria and, whenever possible, lives his life as a man.

I will refer to him as such in these pages.

He is around thirty years of age, large, not quite six feet but approaching it, and broad, though little is fat. He is dark-complected, with a naturally stern face, but an affable demeanor when he wishes. His close-cropped, curly black hair is slicked back using a pungent brand of pomade that he bought from another prisoner.

When I arrived, he had been wearing what he had been arrested in. In this case, a men's shirt and trousers that had been rudimentarily tailored. We had both since been ordered to change into prison uniforms—shapeless blue smocks tied around the waist. The linen is so rough I'm convinced Eleanor could use it to polish silver.

Still standing, Val untied his smock and pulled it high enough to reveal a collection of brutal-looking bruises leading from below his right breast down to his navel. He gingerly pressed a finger to one of the bruises and hissed. He looked to me.

"I've seen you limping around. They give you anything?"

"I'm afraid there's no liniment for my condition."

"Just my luck," he said. "Or, I guess, just your luck, but you know what I mean."

He went back to examining the bruises.

"Were those incurred before your arrest or after?" I asked.

"Before," he said. "Cops didn't do this. Not this time."

"I was told when they first admitted me that you had been arrested for biting someone's ear off."

"Not completely off," he said. "Took a chunk, though. In my defense, the guy and his buddies were looking to rape me."

"That does seem like an excellent reason."

"Tell it to the cops. These guys are saying I started it, and there's more of them than there are of me, you know what I mean?"

I told him I did. Then he went back to his bunk and the silence resumed. Twenty minutes or so later, he spoke again.

"Whatcha scribbling?"

"Notes on my case. As well as anything of interest about my treatment while incarcerated."

"Like what?"

I saw no harm, so I turned to a previous page and read aloud.

"'Yesterday evening in the mess hall, I dined alone. Or as alone as one can be in this place. No one spared more than a handful of words for me. By now they know the crime for which I'm charged, and my profession when I'm outside these walls. Perhaps a private detective is too akin to an officer of the law for their comfort.

"'When I stood up from my table to bus my tray, one of the guards bumped into me, causing me to stumble and my cup and plate to fall to the floor. It was clearly deliberate, and he stood over me while I picked them up.

"'Most of the guards here are women, and the few men seem little more than ornamental intimidation. This one's name tag read ANDREWS. I wonder if I have done something to draw his ire. I do not recognize him, but the faces of officious men all blend together after a while.'"

Val laughed.

"I like that," he said. "*Officious.* That's a good word."

"Thank you."

"Andrews is the weaselly-looking one, right? Big teeth, can't grow a mustache? He wasn't here my last go-round. But I know from one of the girls that he was a cop before this."

That was telling. The step down from police officer to prison guard is rarely taken willingly.

"You're wrong about why everyone's keeping their distance," Val added. "I mean, shoot, we all know the difference between a flatfoot and a shamus."

"Then why?"

"We don't know where you fit, do we?" Val said. "We know you're a big shot. We know you're in for murder. Usually women your age it's husbands, but it wasn't your husband, right?"

"It certainly was not."

"You a lesbian?" he asked. "I ain't flirting. Only asking because of the clothes you came in with."

I shook my head.

"Not as such, no," I told him. "To be blunt, there has been little space in my life for sexual relations with men or women, and I have no interest in making room."

"Smart," he said. "Women are trouble. Men, too. Though I like a little trouble sometimes, you know what I mean? Or maybe you don't."

"I assure you, I am not a virgin."

"Yeah, those are pretty scarce around here," he said, chuckling. "Anyway, people will warm up to you. Then you'll have to figure out why they're cozying. It'll probably be money. Buy me a brush from the commissary. Buy me some tobacco. Things like that. Then again, you got a nice face. Somebody might make a pass."

"Why are you cozying up to me?" I asked.

"I could use some tobacco."

He held his expression for a moment, then burst out laughing.

"I'm kidding," he said. "I'm just friendly. I'd have done it sooner, but I figured you'd get bail, and who wants to go to the trouble of making friends with someone you're never gonna see again, you know?"

"You've been in the House of Detention before."

"Yep. Six weeks in '38 for vagrancy. Two months in '42 for the same, but that got dropped. It was still two months, though. Then nine months in '44 for prostitution. Same in '46. First was bullshit. Second wasn't. Gotta eat, you know? This time it's a bunch of stuff, but mostly assault."

After some coercing, Val eventually told me about his most recent arrest.

"Last Saturday I tied one on at home," he explained. "Then I got bored. Drunk and bored is a bad mix. I head over to this Irish joint I know. Usually, I stick to the Italian places, because I can pass, but there was this girl I was looking for who I knew hung out there. Sometimes I like trouble, remember? Anyway, I take a seat at the bar and manage to get two drinks ordered and downed before some creep grabs me and says, 'Hey, buddy, whites only in here.' There's some disagreement. They start dragging me out by the collar and then someone goes, 'Hey, this guy's got tits.' That's when things got rough."

He did not need to elaborate on what "rough" meant. I'd seen the bruises, after all. I tried to begin a conversation about how he might be able to prove he acted in self-defense, but Val showed little interest, seemingly resigned to his fate.

Eventually he pulled a copy of *Holiday* out from under his mattress and lost himself in descriptions of foreign travel. I let him be and continued writing.

The next morning, a guard arrived—not Andrews—and I was told my personal physician was here to conduct an exam.

It seems Mr. Bigelow's suggestion was not merely strategic.

I was taken to the clinic, which brought back unpleasant memories of my first day.

I was tired and still achy from sleeping on the cell's thin mattress. I did not know if I had the patience for Dr. Hubbard's usual round of tests. But at least his would be a friendly face.

A curtain had been set up around one of the beds, and Dr. Hubbard was standing next to it, in intense conversation with the clinic doctor, the one who had conducted my initial "examination."

"I don't care how things are done here," Dr. Hubbard was saying to him. "In my world—the sane, civilized world—we do not conduct physical examinations in full view of whoever happens to walk by. Oh, hello, Lillian. Get behind the curtain and on the bed. I'll be with you in a minute. What was I saying? Right. The civilized world. Are you familiar with it?"

I went through the curtain and was surprised to find a nurse waiting for me. She was leaning over the bed, flipping through what I assumed was my very robust medical file.

I was struck by her hair—wavy and blond and not tucked under a cap—and her uniform, which strained against her exceptional cleavage and ended just above the knee, showing off calves made taut by two-inch heels.

What nurse, I wondered, would wear heels?

Then she looked up and said, "Have a seat, boss. Do you want the full report or the back of the book?"

CHAPTER **15**

I consider anytime I can surprise Lillian Pentecost a victory.

"Admit it. I got you."

She almost sort of smiled.

"That uniform isn't exactly . . . regulation," she noted.

"That's what I told her," Hubbard said, slipping through the curtain. "They'll think I'm some sort of letch."

"That's kind of the point, Doc."

Nurses get overlooked all the time when they're standing next to a doctor. The problem was that my face was known to more than a few of the guards, as well as a bunch of the prisoners. Thus the abbreviated hemline and the padded bra to go along with the wig and makeup.

I wanted to keep their attention on my tits and not my face. And if Nurse Palmer didn't really seem to do all that much, they'd figure Hubbard kept her around to polish his stethoscope.

"I suppose it won't be the worst thing that's ever been said about me," he grumbled as he opened up his medical bag. "By the way, you should keep your voices low. The curtain is thin and even stupid people get curious."

You've never met Hubbard before, so let me do the honors. He's in his sixties, with white hair, a perpetually stubbled but kind face, and the beginnings of jowls. An affable hound dog. He's another tall one, but rather than loom or slouch, he's always sliding over a chair and putting himself on a level with his patients.

As for why he was willing to go along with this little ploy, it was simple. Lillian Pentecost had a tendency to foster loyalty in her nearest and dearest. Not all of them would kill for her, but many would help her bury the body.

"Back to the original question," I said. "The long or the short?"

"The topic?"

"The identity of the person who framed you."

"How much time do we have?" she asked.

Hubbard, who was laying out various instruments on the bed, answered for me.

"I've informed that so-called doctor that this initial exam—which I will actually be performing, so be prepared—will take at least half an hour, though we can probably extend it to forty-five minutes without suspicion. Subsequent visits, every week I am told, will be limited to fifteen minutes. Which, to be honest, is quite a bit more than you usually permit me when left to your own devices."

Ms. P gave him a look that I thought was reserved only for me.

"Pout all you want, Lillian—I'm going to make the most of this," he said. "I don't care who killed who. I only care how this hellhole is aggravating your disease. Now, I want to start with a reflex test, so take off your shoes and we'll work from the ankles up."

She did as instructed, then turned back to me and addressed my initial question.

"Use your best judgment," she said. "Tell me everything you think I need to know."

I did.

It was good that we had business to conduct. It took my mind off how she looked.

All her features were skewed out of true by fatigue, eyes red-rimmed, hair held together with the bare minimum of bobby pins. I didn't have a measuring tape, but I was sure that streak of silver running through the auburn was an eighth of an inch wider. Also, they had her in prison attire. The kind of thing you'd shove a toddler into because they couldn't be trusted with buttons.

I did my best to ignore it all and described Beck's visit, along with his claims and demands. Eventually I presented the three choices as I saw them: go along, attack, or ignore.

Throughout this, Hubbard was working her over, having her stand, sit, squat, bend, knocking on this and listening to that. At that moment, he had her arm lifted and was palpating her lymph nodes so I wondered if she'd been too distracted to hear my three options. I was about to repeat them when she asked, "How are you sleeping?"

The question took me by surprise.

"How am I sleeping? You're the one with steel wool sheets and a few hundred roommates. Don't worry about me—I'm sleeping fine."

"Your eyes are bloodshot," she said.

"It's the makeup. I'm allergic."

"Your face is thin. There's a hollowness."

Hubbard looked up from his pawing.

"You do look a little worn down. I didn't want to say anything before."

"You don't have to say anything now," I snapped, which is not an easy thing to do while whispering.

Hubbard blushed and went back to his prodding.

"Fine," I told Ms. P. "To be honest, I haven't slept in my room since I got back. I've been sleeping on the sofa in the office."

"Why?" she asked.

It was embarrassing. I didn't want to talk about it. I don't even want to type about it, but she'd asked, and I owed her an answer.

"I tried sleeping in my bed that first night and I kept waking up, sure I was hearing someone break into the office. I go down, and of course there's no one there, so I go back up and try to sleep. Then I hear something, or think I do, and startle awake, and get up and go down again and so forth. Eventually I got tired of it, so I decided to bunk in the office."

"Are you sleeping better there?" she asked.

"Sure," I lied. "I mean, it's not the Ritz, but I'm getting enough winks."

Ms. P made one of those noises of hers, but it might have been Hubbard pushing against her gut. I took advantage of the pause.

"I repeat the question: How are we handling this? Kid gloves, an iron fist, or . . . I don't know what the third analogy would be."

"All three," she said.

"I'm not following."

"We continue the investigation into Jessup Quincannon's murder," Ms. P explained. "We also look into the death of Susie Beck. While at the same time not ignoring Walter Beck. He is at best an extortionist and at worst a murderer. Possibly twice over."

"Twice? You think his concern about his wife might be a case of the fellow protests too much?"

"There is precedent."

Hubbard held up a finger.

"While it's fascinating to watch the pair of you work—I'm really quite lost, by the way—we are nearing the forty-minute mark."

I did my whispering double-time.

"Investigating Quincannon and both Becks is a tall order," I said. "I've got nearly a dozen other guests and assorteds to interview, and that's if you're only including everyone in the house that night. Speaking of the house, Whitsun called this morning. Says the judge gave the green light for me to get into Quincannon's tomorrow. Who knows what leads that will turn up. That's all before I start digging into a cold suicide. This could take . . ."

I couldn't bring myself to say "weeks" and settled for "a while."

"I understand," she said.

"We need to get you out of here. You can't stay in this joint. You'll . . . You just can't."

She turned to Hubbard.

"Robert, what is your prognosis?"

Hubbard flipped open the notebook where he'd been jotting numbers.

"Heart's good, breathing's good, reflexes could be better, but they could always be better. Balance is certainly worse, but not egregiously so," he said. "Are you in pain?"

She shook her head.

"No, no pain."

"Then all in all, you're in adequate health, considering the circumstances. Although your socket is irritated. You've been sleeping with your eye in again, haven't you?"

She nodded.

"Don't do that. If you do, don't wear it the next day."

"Other than that, is there anything concerning?" she asked.

Hubbard sighed.

"If you're asking me if you're healthy enough to stay here, I don't think anyone is healthy enough to stay here. But you haven't deteriorated much since your last checkup. That's all I'll say. I'm going to go talk with this clinic butcher and buy you a few more minutes."

Hubbard slipped through the curtain, and Ms. P turned back to me.

"You see? It's not so terrible."

"It's the goddamn House of D."

"I've had worse accommodations," she said. "One of these paths will prove fruitful. We'll find a murderer or satisfy Walter Beck, or both."

She reached out and patted my hand, like an auntie comforting a frightened child. Was she saying all that to make me feel better? I didn't know. I never could tell when Lillian Pentecost was lying.

I chose to believe her. What good was the alternative?

"I do have one request, if you don't mind," she said.

"Fire away."

"You'll be seeing Dolly Klinghorn, I imagine."

That was Darryl Klinghorn's widow, who had kept the agency running after he was killed.

"I will. I figure she might know something about Susie or Walter Beck that didn't make it into the file."

"Then tell her I have another case I'd like her to look into. An assault at a bar in the East Village. One involving a Valeria Lincoln, who is currently incarcerated here."

She gave me the details and I promised to pass them on.

"Any suggestions on how to tackle things? Quincannon, Beck, or otherwise?" I asked.

She had a few and spent a minute relaying them. Then Hubbard returned.

"I'm afraid we're done here," he said. "I didn't want to argue too stridently—otherwise they might decide not to allow me back next week."

"Thank you, Robert," Ms. P said. "Will, if you don't mind, I'd like to speak with Dr. Hubbard in private for a moment."

"Right," I said, a little flustered. "I'll . . . um . . . I'll be right out here."

I made sure my wig was on straight and slipped through the curtain. The clinic doc gave my outfit a judgmental once-over. I made Nurse Palmer return his frown with a smile.

What were Ms. P and Hubbard talking about?

Had she been lying? Had she concealed how bad her symptoms were?

Whatever it was didn't take long, because half a minute later, Hubbard was coming out, hat in one hand, bag in the other.

"Come, Nurse Palmer. We have other patients to see."

Then we were walking away. Down the hall to the elevator. I hadn't even said goodbye.

Will Parker wanted to run back and hug Ms. P and tell her it was going to be all right. But Nurse Palmer would keep her eyes fixed straight ahead, so that's what I did.

I never said a bad word about Lot's wife again.

CHAPTER 16

Hubbard and I said our goodbyes a few blocks away. When I asked what the private confab had been about, he said it was a personal matter and nothing to concern me.

I told him I was concerned regardless and he said that was unfortunate and maybe I should take an aspirin.

Despite the smartassery, I let him drive off unmolested, then went to a nearby pharmacy that had a phone booth where I could make a couple of calls.

I had three roads to go down and there was no use waiting.

"This is Mrs. Crapper calling for Lieutenant Lazenby."

This time the desk sergeant put me right through.

"Lazenby here."

"First, I can't believe I have to use that name," I said. "Second, any luck on ferreting out Muffin?"

"We got a report that a private poker game was hit last night. No one's talking, but sounds like Muffin, so we know he's still in the city. We just don't know where," he said. "Also, I'm getting the medical examiner's report on Quincannon, but I'll have to get it to you roundabout."

"Roundabout is fine, as long as it arrives eventually," I said. "While you're picking up groceries, can I add something to the list?"

I translated the growl that came over the line as "I'd love to do you another favor—please let me know what."

"You handled the death of Susan Beck, right? What do you remember about that case? And what can you tell me about Walter Beck as a specimen?"

There was a long silence on the line.

"You there, Lieutenant?"

Finally, he said, "Your boss is in jail on a murder charge and you want to know about an old suicide? What gives?"

"Walter came to us about his wife's death," I said truthfully. "He thinks foul play."

"I know," Lazenby said. "He's told me. He's told anyone who will listen. I'll ask again, why are you wasting breath on this?"

It was a good question, but I had a good answer.

"I feel the same way," I told him. "But you know how Ms. Pentecost is. Just because she's locked up, doesn't mean she won't take cases."

"All right, but why do you want information about Wally?"

Wally? Walter Beck was a Wally?

"Because when a wife dies—suicide, murder, or choking on a walnut—I always look at the husband first. I don't care if he's the one writing the check."

There were maybe five people in the city with a better nose for bullshit than Nathan Lazenby and one of them was my boss. But I'd had years of practice pulling fibs on both of them, so in the end he bought it.

"Wally's a good guy," he said. "A hard worker. Not the brightest bulb, but you don't need to be a genius to take pictures. His wife's death nearly broke him, though. Sweet girl."

"You knew her?" I asked.

"I met her once," he said. "A few years ago at a housewarming party. Wally invited a bunch of people from the force. Wally's not exactly a charmer, so I was surprised when I met his wife."

"Surprised why?"

"She seemed a little out of his league—young, pretty, full of energy. Wally kind of . . ."

"Slouches?"

"Yeah, that's it," Lazenby said. "But I don't question love. Although . . ."

"Yeah?"

"There was something melancholy about her."

"How exactly?" I asked.

Another silence, but not quite as long this time.

"Something in her face when she thought no one was looking," he said. "I can't explain it better than that."

Lazenby had the touch when it came to understanding people. If he said Susie Beck was melancholy, I believed him.

"When she killed herself a year later, it wasn't the biggest shock," he added. "Not to me, anyway."

I asked a few more questions, but none that went anywhere. Then I asked if he could include the Beck crime scene photos along with Quincannon's.

He said he would.

"But like I said. It'll have to be roundabout."

"Mrs. Crapper thanks you."

I hung up and took one of those calming breaths. Hearing Lazenby talk nice about Walter Beck and not being able to tell him that the man was an evidence-tampering piece of shit hadn't been easy.

I dropped another nickel and gave the operator a number.

A voice that still held a hint of its midwestern accent answered.

"Klinghorn Investigations, Dolores Klinghorn speaking."

"Hey, Dolly," I said. "Will Parker. Got time for some girl talk? Preferably in person?"

"For you, Will, anytime. You know where my door is."

I did, and since her basement apartment was only a few

blocks away, I was knocking on it five minutes after hanging up. When Dolly let me in, she didn't bat an eye at my nurse getup. She was a woman in the same game. She'd probably worn a costume or two herself.

The last time I'd spent any significant time at Dolly's, I had been investigating the death of her husband, which had occurred while he'd been helping Ms. P and me track a killer. Coincidentally, Darryl Klinghorn had died at least partly because Jessup Quincannon had kept that killer's identity a secret.

The place hadn't changed much, at least not the little dining nook off the kitchen. There was already a cup of coffee and a slice of pumpkin pie waiting.

Dolly hadn't changed much, either. She was still a fiftyish blonde going elegantly gray who preferred to stitch her dresses herself. Today's was a blue-and-white-check number with puffy half-sleeves and white bows in strategic places.

She looked like she'd stepped out of the Sears and Roebuck catalog. Nothing about her suggested she was the third-sharpest female private eye in the city.

"This Quincannon business is ridiculous," she said, once we were working on our coffee and pie. "They think that Lillian Pentecost is going to shoot somebody with her own gun? Then take it home with her? Who do they think they're talking about?"

See what I mean about sharp? She didn't say Ms. P wouldn't shoot somebody. Only that she wouldn't be dumb about it.

"What can I do to help?" she asked. "You name it, it's yours."

I don't know what she was expecting, but it wasn't Susie Beck. I gave her the same line as I did Lazenby. That Walter had come to us, and Ms. P wasn't letting something as inconsequential as being in jail keep her from investigating.

"If you have a copy of Darryl's report, I don't know what else I can tell you," she said.

"What about Beck himself?" I asked. "You get a read on him?"

"I only met him twice, but he seemed . . . well, kind of pathetic. Desperate, too," she said, taking a sip of milky coffee. "He came to us in . . . I think November last year. He paid the retainer and Darryl started working background on the wife. See if he could get a whiff of someone with a grudge, or a reason she'd want to kill herself. One or the other. Worked it for a couple of months, put a report together, along with a bill. That was the beginning of January. The retainer was long gone by then, but Beck couldn't pay the balance, so we held on to the report. That was my rule. We'd gotten stiffed too many times. Darryl suggested he write your boss, since she was known to take cases pro bono. Walter said he already had, but he'd try again."

That would have been Beck's third and final letter to Ms. Pentecost.

"It wasn't until this past August that he was able to get the money together. I handed him the report then," Dolly added. "Not that he was happy with it. He insisted Darryl must have missed something. But, my God, you know what Darryl was like."

I did. If there was a stone, Darryl Klinghorn would look under it and then write three paragraphs about the experience.

I picked up my fork to take a bite of pie and was surprised to find it had vanished.

"You want another piece?" she asked.

I was about to say no, but my stomach answered loudly in the affirmative. I had been too nervous about my visit to the House of D to eat breakfast. For that matter, I had no memory of eating dinner the night before.

Dolly was carving out a second piece when she went, "Huh."

"Huh what?" I asked.

"Something Darryl said about the Beck case," she said, sliding the pie onto my plate. "Not sure it means anything."

"Meaning is relative," I said, already taking a bite. "What was it?"

"That maybe I should have been the one to take the travel agency," she said. "The place where his wife worked."

"Why did he think that?"

She shook her head. "I'm not sure. We were staking out this no-tell motel in Jersey City. This was right after Beck had come to us saying his pockets were empty. Not long before Darryl— well, before he died. Anyway, we were in the car and he said something about the travel agency and how maybe I should have taken it because I have a lighter touch. But right after, we spied the mark going into a room with her brother-in-law and we had to get busy. He never brought it up again and I never asked."

What about Susie Beck's place of employment made Kling-horn think his wife would have had a better chance than he did? Did that mean he missed something, or thought he did?

Food for thought.

Dolly and I spent a few minutes exchanging professional gossip—who was new in town, who was going out of business, who got his fingers broken because he'd used them to tickle the spine of a mob boss's girlfriend. Long enough for me to finish my second slice of pie and down my coffee.

I also asked her if she had time in her schedule to do a job for us.

"Honey, I always have time for you."

If that sounds like flirting, it's not. She's just that nice. I gave her details about the Valeria Lincoln assault.

"Sounds like fun," Dolly said. "I'll get started first thing tomorrow. And I'll give you the family discount."

"Thanks," I said, getting up and retrieving my coat. "I won't turn down the cut rate. Lawyers are expensive."

At the door, Dolly said, "You know, if you're ever looking for extra work, I could always use somebody. It's mostly cheating spouse stuff, but it's steady."

"I appreciate the offer," I said. "But being Lillian Pentecost's right hand is steady enough."

"Well, the offer's always open."

As she closed the door behind me, I thought about the message hiding underneath her midwestern politeness. The one that said: Things change. And murder raps are hard to beat.

CHAPTER 17

As I pulled up to the brownstone I was surprised to see a figure in an olive-green overcoat and matching cloche stepping out of a cab. This figure had about three inches and forty pounds on me, the latter distributed to the most pleasant of locations. I knew this because I'd just spent three weeks in the Catskills meticulously mapping them.

"What are you doing here?" I asked Holly as the driver manhandled a suitcase out of the trunk.

"I got a phone call from a Dr. Hubbard. It seems Lillian told him to call me," she said, trading the cabbie a handful of bills for the case. "She thought you might need company."

"Weren't you going to hole up with Brent and Marlo and edit your novel?" I asked, grabbing her suitcase and following her up the steps.

"That doesn't really require us to be in the same room," she said. "Though there are benefits. All I need is a copy of my manuscript, which I have. And a telephone, which you have. Also, you are to give me—and this is a thirdhand quote from Lillian—'the lot.' Which sounds very provocative, but probably means—"

I had my key out to unlock the front door when it swung open, revealing Mrs. Campbell.

"Hello, dear. Let me get that."

She snatched the suitcase out of my hand and disappeared into the house.

"Hang on a minute," I said, hurrying to catch up.

The housekeeper stopped and swiveled, and I almost ran into her.

"Doc Hubbard called," she announced. "He said to make sure you didn't skip meals, and that Miss Quick would be coming over to visit. Maybe now you'll keep to your room at night."

She directed her gaze to the open office doorway. I followed it to see the pile of blankets on the sofa.

"That was . . . I couldn't sleep, you understand?"

Her expression softened.

"I do, dear," she said. "I know exactly. Being alone in a house takes some getting used to. With Holly here, you won't have to."

I was outnumbered and surrounded. But at least I knew what Ms. P had been chatting with Dr. Hubbard about. Not her problems, but mine.

"I'm going to take Miss Quick's things up to the guest room," Mrs. Campbell said before adding to Holly, "You can sleep where you like, dear. But you'll need space for your clothes, and this one's closet is chockablock."

The housekeeper disappeared up the stairs and Holly deposited coat and hat on the hooks inside the front door, revealing a green-and-white candy-striped dress that showed off half her legs and most of her arms. It was the sort of thing that, should I go out in public wearing it, would make people look for the St. Patrick's Day parade.

Holly, with her summer-browned skin and thick black waves of hair that had been growing out since spring, made it look good. Better than good. We'd been apart only a few days, but it already felt like too long.

She caught me staring.

"Don't worry," she said, wiping some condensation off her glasses. "I know you're busy. I won't get in the way. Also, why are you dressed like you're posing for the cover of *Spicy Detective*?"

I explained about the ploy to get me in to see Ms. Pentecost.

"I'm not worried about you getting in the way," I told her. "But we just spent three weeks together. Aren't you tired of me?"

She walked over, wrapped her arms around my neck, and kissed me.

When she finished, she ran her tongue over her lips. "Not yet," she said.

I did not drag Holly upstairs immediately, for which I deserved a merit badge. Besides, Mrs. Campbell was in the guest room unpacking Holly's things, and while our housekeeper apparently knew me down to my bones, there were some things I didn't want her overhearing.

Instead, I took Holly into the office, shoved my blankets to one side of the sofa, and we sat while I brought her up to date on events, including the extortion scheme. Holly had long ago proven she could keep a secret.

"My God," she said when I was finished. "That's rather genius. The scheme of replacing the bullet. Or maybe not genius. That's an overused word. Very cunning, though. And brazen. Seeing the possibility for tampering and acting that quickly."

"Do you mind not heaping praise on our extortionist?"

"I suppose a photographer would have an eye for detail," she continued. "For shape and composition. There's some interesting psychology there."

"Holly."

"I know, I know," she said. "Interesting but irrelevant, as my editors like to say."

We moved on to more relevant material, such as the other characters at Quincannon's that evening and Max's assessment of them.

"Quincannon was such a son of a bitch that I wouldn't put it past any of them to murder him, including the caterers," I told her, after running through the list. "My personal favorite is still Billy Muffin. It seems to be Max's, too. Second to Ms. Pentecost, of course, but he doesn't know about Beck and the swapped bullet."

"This is the same Max Roberts you told me about when we were listing our respective exes?" she asked.

"It is. But don't hold that against him. He usually has much better sense."

Holly pursed her lips in the way she does when she's dicing up a sentence.

"Spit it out," I prompted.

"It's just that when you were listing the suspects, you didn't mention him," she noted.

She wasn't wrong. I hadn't been thinking of Max as a suspect.

"What would his motive be?" I asked.

She shrugged. "What are anyone else's motives? I'm not asking because you and he were lovers. Or maybe I am. I don't think I get jealous, but who's to say? All I know is, you shouldn't overlook a writer. We can be very devious."

I was mentally adding Max to my tally of suspects when the phone rang. It was Pearl confirming my visit to Quincannon's house the following morning.

"Forest wants me to remind you to bring a camera," she said.

"Certainly."

"And to take lots of pictures."

"That's what a camera is for."

"He also has a list of questions he'd like you to ask," Pearl added. "Would you like me to read them off or can we pretend you know how to do your job?"

"Let's pretend and save time."

After I hung up, Mrs. Campbell poked her head in long enough to ask if there was anything in particular we might like for dinner, as she was going shopping. There wasn't, and she left.

I must have had on a face because Holly asked, "What's wrong?"

"Our decision not to tell Whitsun and Pearl about the swapped bullet," I said. "I understand the reasoning. If they move on Beck and he doesn't flip, that's a bridge we can't get back. But lying to your lawyer is usually a bad play. I'm worried is all."

She pursed her lips again.

"I might have a solution," she said. "Not to the problem, but to the worrying. Temporarily, at least."

"What's that?" I asked.

"I was thinking that before Eleanor comes back, we could go upstairs and you could take my temperature."

We spent some time checking each other's vitals, but once the stethoscope was tucked away and my body started to resolidify, the worry returned.

"Here's my biggest problem. Or one of the biggest, anyway," I said, staring up at my bedroom ceiling. "How the hell am I going to work the Quincannon murder and dig into Susie Beck at the same time? Every minute I waste is one more Ms. Pentecost spends eating jail food."

Holly slid off the bed and began rummaging through her discarded clothes.

"You could hire Dolly Klinghorn to investigate Susie Beck," she suggested, pulling out a pack of Chesterfields and a lighter. "She's very keen. And she already knows the case."

"Yeah, Dolly's a sharp one. But when I'm working Susie Beck's maybe-murder, I need to keep an eye out for dirt on her husband. He might still be our killer, after all. Which means I'd have to tell Dolly about the extortion, and if I'm not telling Whitsun and I'm not telling Lazenby . . ."

"I see," Holly said, lighting her smoke, then sliding back into bed next to me.

She inhaled, exhaled, and we watched the smoke trail up to spread softly against my bedroom ceiling before melting away.

"If this were one of my stories, the detective would tie Walter Beck up and threaten to pry off his fingernails," Holly said.

I glanced over at her.

"I'm not saying you should do that," she clarified. "Simply pointing out that it's an option."

"Believe me, I've thought about it," I admitted. "But the man had an angry Scotswoman hold a shotgun to his head and he didn't blink. I think he'd lose all ten fingernails before he cried uncle."

Another column of smoke and then, "I could do it."

"Pry off someone's fingernails?"

"Investigate Susie Beck," she said, reaching over and ashing her cigarette into an empty can of Folgers I kept on my nightstand for that purpose.

I turned on my side so I could look at her straight.

"You're not a detective," I said. "You're a writer."

"Really? Is that what I am?"

"I'm being serious."

"So am I," she said. "I've spent my entire adult life writing about detectives. Before you say that it's different, of course it's different. I know that. But it seems that a lot of the Beck case is phone calls. At least to start. Speaking with her co-workers and so forth. I'm assuming Mr. Klinghorn provided a list."

Holly had seen one of Klinghorn's reports before and knew how thorough they could be.

"He did."

"There you go," she said, blowing out another plume. "I'm very good on the phone. Or at least I'm less—well, you know. You can write up some questions for me and everything."

"What if Susie Beck was really murdered?" I asked. "One of these people could be the killer. Have you thought of that?"

Holly gave me a look that I'm pretty sure Ms. P taught her.

"They can hardly kill me over the phone, can they?"

I didn't like it, but I couldn't think of a good reason to say no. It wasn't like Holly was the sheltered type. The divot above her breastbone—a bullet wound eleven years younger than she was—attested to that.

"All right," I said. "Phone calls only. Anything needs to happen in person, you pass me the ball. Deal?"

"Deal."

We shook hands. Then we leaned shoulder to shoulder against the headboard and she smoked her cigarette with one hand and played connect-the-dots with the freckles on my stomach with the other.

After a minute, I asked, "When did you first think of this? You helping out with Beck?"

"Downstairs when you were explaining his demands," she said, smoke curling out around the edges of her mouth. "I waited to bring it up because I thought you needed . . . well . . ."

"To be loosened up?"

"I didn't say that."

"You didn't need to."

I rested my head on her shoulder and thought about the dangers of surrounding myself with smart women.

CHAPTER **18**

The next morning found me again pressing the buzzer outside Quincannon's iron gate. In my oversize handbag I had: my Kodak, twenty rolls of film, enough flashbulbs to last, three notebooks, half a dozen pencils and accompanying sharpener, and assorted detritus.

For once, I left the gun at home. Alathea would only confiscate it, and if she wanted to kill me, she'd already had several perfectly good opportunities.

The woman in question emerged from the front door and made her way down the walk. She was wearing a pair of voluminous black slacks and a wide-collared white satin number unbuttoned far enough to flash collarbone. An oval of polished jade hung from a silver chain around her neck.

I was holding my own in a thundercloud-gray suit over a lavender blouse—a combination that Holly assured me "cut a dramatic silhouette."

"Thank you for coming on a Saturday morning, Miss Parker," Alathea said, as she escorted me inside. "Mr. Quincannon's house is yours. At least for the next two hours. I will also be available to answer whatever questions you have, within reason."

I was tempted to haggle over the definition of *reason,* but two hours wasn't much time.

"All right," I said, taking out my camera. "Let's get to work."

Over the next 120 minutes, I filled three notebooks, shot seventeen of twenty rolls, wore two pencils down to nubs, and burned through every single one of those flashbulbs. If I were to include every interesting detail and every answer to every question, I'd be nosing into *War and Peace* territory.

Even with hindsight in my favor, it's still a crapshoot on what I should include and what I should chuck, but I'll give it a go.

First, the house.

Quincannon's mansion looked haunted on the outside, but was pleasantly plain on the inside, at least if you stayed below the top floor. The first floor consisted of an airy entryway and sitting room; a high-ceilinged conservatory decorated in a clean, modern style; a long kitchen that gleamed with new appliances; as well as the obligatory bathroom located in a nook halfway between the front door and the conservatory.

There was a narrow set of stairs off the kitchen, and if you took them down, you'd find an impressive wine cellar and a small suite of rooms given over to Alathea—bedroom, den, bathroom. Lots of bookshelves, plenty of art on the walls.

Go up to the second floor and you'd find Quincannon's office, which was not too far removed from the one in our own brownstone, as well as the master bedroom with bath, and a seemingly little-used guest bedroom.

Then there was the third floor and Quincannon's collection.

There were two ways to get there—a wide, curving staircase that did one revolution per floor, and a freshly installed elevator.

I timed both during my visit. The stairs could be taken two at a time and traversed in less than seven seconds. The elevator, so new it still smelled of oil and paint, took exactly fifteen seconds from doors closing to doors opening. About the slowest elevator I'd ever ridden, but it still made things tight for our murderer.

Next, the Black Museum.

I could have gone the rest of my life without visiting it again. An open space devoid of a single window. Instead, illumination was provided by rows of hanging bulbs hooded in green glass. Their light reflected off the dark-wood wall and floors, and off the rows of waist-high, glass-topped cabinets displaying blood-soaked bits and baubles.

Broken blades, hunks of bone, gleaming razors, scribbled notes, spent bullets—each one commemorating a murder. The larger exhibits were mounted on the wall. There were framed sketches, a map whose streets had been pockmarked by red *X*'s, a bullet-ridden door supposedly splattered with Bonnie Parker's blood.

There was a writing desk I hadn't seen last time—one of those glorified schoolboy things that people pay a mint for. I opened the lid. The bottom was lined in green velvet. Pinned to it was a letter.

Dear Boss,
I couldn't help myself. She was . . .

The sentence cut off in an inkblot. Like the writer's hand had been yanked away.

"Bullshit," I muttered. "Has to be a fake."

"Mr. Quincannon was always very discerning as to authenticity."

Alathea's voice came from right behind me, but I managed to stay inside my skin. How did she move so quietly on hardwood in heels?

"Anyone can get taken," I said, turning away from the desk and moving a handful of steps to the one glass case that was open. The one that was conspicuously empty. The painter's box had been taken as evidence, of course.

I took a picture.

"Here's where the first bullet went in," Alathea said, walking across the room.

She pointed at a small, empty shelf on the wood-paneled wall. Right above the small table holding the telephone. Both the shelf and the phone were smeared with fingerprint dust.

"It went into some kind of book, right?"

"A textbook on phrenology signed by Edward Rulloff," she said. "Mr. Quincannon explained who that was to me once, but to be honest I didn't pay close attention."

"Did he tell you about all the exhibits?" I asked, trying for nonchalance and failing.

"If you're asking if he told me about the painter's box, I only know that it was important to Lillian Pentecost and played a key role in a murder that would mortify her to the soul. His words."

Mortify her to the soul. What a gem.

"Where did you find the body?" I asked.

Alathea directed me to a spot on the floor halfway between the open glass case and the wall where the bullet hit. There was the smallest spot of dried blood on the wood.

I took a picture.

"How was he positioned?"

I expected Alathea to describe what she'd seen. Instead, she lay down on the floor and carefully arranged her limbs, making smaller and smaller adjustments until she was satisfied.

"Like this," she said.

I took a picture.

"Was there much blood?"

"Not really," she said, still playing dead. "There rarely is with such a small caliber. No exit wound, you see?"

I didn't ask how she knew that bit of trivia.

"You don't have to take my word for it," she added. "The police took more than enough photographs of the body."

I grunted. I didn't trust any photos where Beck's finger had been on the shutter button.

"Stay there a moment, if you wouldn't mind," I said.

"My pleasure."

I walked back to the open case and stood over it as if examining what had once sat in the now-empty space. I drew an imaginary gun and turned.

Quincannon/Alathea was six feet away, feet pointed toward me. I squeezed an imaginary trigger and an imaginary bullet went into the imaginary book propped on its shelf on the wall. I took three steps, which brought me to Alathea's feet. My imaginary barrel pressed against Quincannon's head.

The second imaginary shot did the trick.

The prosecution's story would be simple: Ms. P gets off the elevator, walks to the glass case to retrieve the painter's box, Quincannon tries to stop her, she draws and fires, misses, advances, fires again, hits, then flees.

It was hard to miss with that first shot at such close range, even with a derringer, but perfectly understandable if you're suffering from multiple sclerosis. It did suggest that whoever murdered Quincannon wasn't an expert shot. That pointed away from Billy Muffin. Alathea, as well.

Unless that was the goal. Either could have shot Quincannon in the head and then fired the second shot into the wall to make the cops suspect an amateur.

Both could also have legitimately missed with their first shots. Thing went wrong even for experienced killers.

I glanced down and saw Alathea looking up at me with an unreadable expression.

"All right," I said. "You can Lazarus yourself."

She stood, brushing off the back of her midnight-black trousers while I went around the room, taking snaps of every exhibit in the joint.

"Where's all this junk going to go?" I asked, picking a jar off a lacquered shelf and shaking it. The dozens of teeth inside rattled like popcorn in a pan.

"Most of it will be sold off to private collectors," Alathea explained. "Some pieces have been specified in the will to be given as gifts. I believe Victoria Pelham will receive Sendak's lighter. The writing desk goes to Backstrom. Silas is handling all of that, as well as going through the books and tallying Mr. Quincannon's holdings in preparation for a final audit before the will is executed."

"Speaking of the will, Whitsun would like a copy," I said. "So would I, for that matter."

"I'll ask Silas to send you one."

Culliver wasn't our biggest fan, so I wasn't going to hold my breath.

"Enough sightseeing," I announced. "Let's get down to business."

Which brought us to the night of the murder.

Again, I won't give you everything. If I did that, there'd be whole paragraphs describing the maid service that showed up that morning to dust and scrub; Alathea's afternoon run to the dry cleaner's to pick up Quincannon's favorite suit; that the caterers had to toss nine pounds of oysters because they found out one of the guests (Victoria Pelham) was allergic.

Just because I sat through it, doesn't mean you have to. Here are the essentials, all given while sitting on beautifully sculpted, exceptionally uncomfortable chairs in Quincannon's first-floor conservatory.

5:00 p.m.: The caterers (Mrs. Sara Johnson and her son, William) arrive and begin cooking and setting up.

6:45 p.m.: Quincannon retires to the third floor to jot down some notes for that evening's presentation. Usually he did these presentations on the fly but he "wanted to get his words just right," according to Alathea.

7:00 p.m.: Max Roberts arrives and is escorted up for his so-called interview. Less than ten minutes later, Alathea escorts him down to the conservatory. Her story jibed with the veteran reporter's.

"He did not seem well pleased," she said. "He made threats."

"Threats?"

"To print the guests' names," Alathea explained. "He said that because the interview was so brief, it went against the spirit of the contract signed by him and his editors and should be considered void."

"What did you say?"

"That I was not a lawyer, and that he should have some wine or leave, but if he disrupted the proceedings, the choice would be taken out of his hands. He chose to have a glass of wine."

7:15 p.m.: Reverend Timothy Novarro and his wife, Elaine, arrive. Each arrival follows the same pattern. Guest hits the buzzer at the front gate; Alathea walks out to escort them in; coats are dispensed with in a hall closet, which gives Alathea a chance to look for suspicious bulges.

The Novarros were first-timers to a Black Museum Club soiree. They'd come by the previous winter trawling for donations. Quincannon spent an hour talking theology but sent them away empty-pocketed. Alathea suspected he invited them because he generally enjoyed poking fun at God-botherers.

7:25 p.m.: Dr. Ryan Backstrom and Victoria Pelham arrive back-to-back. The doctor had been part of Quincannon's orbit for a while. Pelham had been a member of the club since its founding. She and Quincannon were "very close."

"How close is very?" I asked.

"They were lovers on and off for years."

The thought of Quincannon putting his hands on another human in an intimate fashion made me shiver.

"Were they on or off when he died?"

"I'm not sure," Alathea said. "She used to come over every Saturday evening during those weeks when she was in the city, which she was for most of this past spring. Mr. Quincannon requested I be out of the house on those nights. He discontinued the request in May. But then reinstated it in July. She travels frequently, so I assumed she had left town and returned. I've since reconsidered."

"Why is that?"

"The evening of the salon was the first time I'd seen them together for some months," she explained. "The way they moved around each other suggested distance. The way he held his head. How she angled her pelvis away from him. It was clear that they were not currently in a sexual relationship."

The pelvic-angle bit sounded a little weak to me. Then again, they'd laughed at fingerprints at first.

It was interesting, though. Lovers on the rocks. Always a good motive.

7:30 p.m.: Billy Muffin arrives. He was "Quincannon's latest plaything," Alathea explained. Quincannon had invited him over earlier in the summer to chat about Muffin's career as a contract killer. He always liked to have a "live specimen" at his parties.

A specimen suggested something that could be kept safely under glass. I've known plenty of killers, and they're more like tigers. You can cage them, and they might play tame for a while. But stick an arm in and you'll be batting lefty the rest of your life.

7:35 p.m.: Silas Culliver arrives with Judge Mathers, propelling the retired judge in a wheelchair. Mathers, like Pelham, had been a member of the club since its inception. Though Alathea had the impression it was more out of obligation to an old friend of Quincannon's father than true friendship.

7:45 p.m.: Max and Silas get into an argument about the finer points of contract law. There's no shouting, but enough loud hissing that Alathea has to come over and remind Max that his continued presence is at her discretion. Max goes for another glass of wine, while Silas heads upstairs to palaver with Quincannon.

"What about?" I asked.

"I imagine his decision to invite a reporter to the salon."

"Why was that, by the way? In the past, he wouldn't even admit that the Black Museum Club was an actual club."

"I think you know," Alathea said.

"He wanted to smear Ms. Pentecost in the press."

She nodded.

"Your boss was a real asshole."

"He was . . . complicated."

7:55 p.m.: The complicated asshole in question comes downstairs, with Silas at his heels, and makes a brief appearance. There are about five minutes of what Alathea called "holding court," where he passes a few words with his guests, pelvises tilting to and fro.

Eventually Quincannon pulls Alathea aside and tells her he's going back upstairs to finish his notes. He asks that she phone him when Lillian Pentecost arrives.

8:10 p.m.: People start to get restless. Dr. Backstrom asks when Quincannon plans to begin and says he has an early surgery in the morning.

Elaine Novarro has had one too many and sloshes wine on her dress. Alathea gets her some soda water and directs her to the bathroom across the hall from the elevator.

8:15 p.m.: The front gate buzzer sounds one last time. Ms. Pentecost has arrived.

Alathea uses the house phone to call Quincannon on the third floor and tell him that Lillian Pentecost has arrived and sounds ready to storm the gate. Quincannon responded giddily—Alathea's words.

"I can't imagine Quincannon giddy," I said.

"Maybe that's not the right word. Excited to the point of breathlessness."

"That's so much worse."

Quincannon tells her to let the lady in, then to go down to the wine cellar and bring up the bottle of Chateau Haut-Brion Burgundy 1922, which he's been saving for just this sort of occasion.

8:17 p.m.: Alathea collects my boss and puts her in the elevator, then descends to the wine cellar to play fetch. The Haut-Brion had been misfiled in 1932, and so she doesn't hear it when . . .

8:18 p.m.: Two gunshots are heard echoing down the stairs. The crowd responds accordingly. Mrs. Johnson, the cook, yells down the basement steps to Alathea to tell her something has happened.

Alathea runs back up to the conservatory. Culliver, who is standing at the foot of the stairs looking up, tells her what he heard.

She draws her pistol and runs up the two flights to find the Black Museum empty, save for her boss, whose head has been freshly aerated. She makes a circuit of the room to make sure no one is hiding behind any of the cases. After that, Backstrom confirms the new hole in Quincannon's head is fatal.

8:20 p.m.: Alathea uses the phone underneath the punctured book to invite the police to the party.

Last came answers to assorted questions, of which I had many.

"Why call the cops? The woman uses a cane. You could have caught her."

"I thought about chasing her down, but ultimately decided not to," Alathea told me.

"Why is that? Avoiding grass stains?"

"Avoiding bullets, Miss Parker. As far as I believed, she'd shot and killed my employer. I don't know about you, but I eschew gunfights whenever I can. So many terrible things can go wrong."

Ask a biting question, get a biting answer.

"Speaking of bullets, according to the cops, Billy Muffin wasn't there when they arrived. Did you happen to see him leave?"

She shook her head. "I did not."

"Was he there when you ran upstairs from the wine cellar?"

"I don't know."

"Was anyone not there who should have been?" I asked.

She closed her eyes as if trying to picture the layout of the conservatory.

"Silas was there," she said. "He told me about the shots. So were Backstrom and Novarro. The judge, of course, was still in his chair. The waiter was there, as well. Elaine Novarro was in the bathroom, I believe. Victoria was outside having a cigarette. I'm not sure where the reporter was, though I saw him upstairs shortly after, so he might have been in the conservatory and I simply missed him."

So the two women and Max were unaccounted for, but any of them—excluding the judge, unless he was faking—could have run up the stairs and back down again. How they'd do it without being seen by everyone else, I didn't know.

"Anyone in that room have bad blood with Quincannon?"

She leaned back in her chair and stretched her long legs out in front of her, digging the heels of her pumps into the conservatory's Persian carpet.

"That's a very knotty question."

"How so?"

"Mr. Quincannon never really seemed to care if he was liked or not," she said. "He preferred to be admired. Respected. I think that's why Lillian Pentecost infuriated him so much. Because she refused to bend to that desire."

"My boss isn't the bending type," I said. "The question still stands about bad blood."

"Some minor grudges," she admitted. "Culliver and he were always bickering. Usually about the logistics of obtaining this or that item for the collection. He and Judge Mathers sniped some. And, of course, there was always a certain amount of tension with Victoria Pelham."

It's hard to make the word *tension* sound lascivious, but she managed.

"It's an odd group of people," I said, remembering Max Roberts's comment about the guest list. "Small, too. Was Quincannon's popularity waning?"

"Usually, these things are planned out weeks in advance," Alathea said. "This party was rather last-minute. Barely a week's notice."

"Why was that?" I asked.

"I think he had been vacillating on exactly how and when to unveil this latest . . . find," she said, referring to the painter's box. "I know Silas cautioned him against such a public display. I suppose he'd finally made a decision and didn't want to wait."

"Speaking of last-minute," I said, "it wasn't an accident that Ms. Pentecost's invitation arrived less than an hour before the big reveal, was it?"

Alathea shook her head.

"He wanted the invitation delivered early enough that she could attend, but too late for her to interfere."

If Quincannon was there, I'd have shot him again for good measure.

"Ms. Pentecost says you didn't frisk her. That go for all your guests?"

"Mr. Quincannon's rule was that his salon guests were not to be interfered with," she explained. "I did frisk Mr. Muffin, however. I'm loyal, but not to the point of foolishness."

"And?"

"He did not carry a gun into the house."

That hardly ruled him out. A gun could have been planted earlier, or he could have snuck back outside and retrieved it.

Which reminded me of something.

"When we're done here, I'd like to take a circuit around the outside," I said. "Take a few pictures."

Her hand traveled to her sternum and she tapped the jade pendant with a manicured fingernail.

"I'm afraid you won't find it," she said.

"Find what?"

"A way inside."

Tap, tap.

"You're sure?" I asked.

"There was an incident some years back. A journalist tried to gain entrance and take photographs of Mr. Quincannon's collection. He managed to climb a trellis to the second floor and was prying open the window before he was discovered. Mr. Quincannon hired me shortly after. I insisted on making adjustments."

"What sort of adjustments?"

Tap, tap, tap.

"I hired a retired cat burglar to examine the house and make recommendations on how to improve security," she said. "Mr. Quincannon implemented all of them. No scalable surfaces; sturdy windows; reliable locks. No one entered this house without my knowledge, Miss Parker."

I thought that was bullshit. Alathea was out of the room hunting a bottle of Burgundy. She couldn't guarantee anything.

However, the retired cat burglar sounded like Jules—a friend of mine who knew his business. I made a note to give him a call.

"You're very thorough," I said.

"It's my job."

Tap, tap, tap, tap.

That was when I realized that the tapping was a tic. Alathea was pissed. She'd been paid to do one thing—keep Jessup Quincannon's soul, assuming he had one, holding hands with his body. She had failed.

The ice queen had a crack. I stuck a wedge in and pushed.

"That *was* your job," I noted. "But, hey, at least you get the consolation prize of being his executor. You get to sign papers and help figure out who gets his collection of teeth."

If looks could kill, I'd have been dead twice over.

"Is there a question, Miss Parker?"

"How did you two get along?" I asked.

"We got on well," she said, without hesitating.

"Want to elaborate?"

She thought about it for a moment.

"We had a very simple relationship," she said. "He paid me and housed me and trusted me to keep him safe. He trusted me not to ask questions, and he never asked them of me. Now, would you mind answering a question for me, Miss Parker?"

"Shoot," I said, immediately regretting my phrasing.

Alathea crossed her legs in that way that some women can do, that's both a promise and a threat, and that I have absolutely never practiced until my knees hurt.

"Something's changed," she declared. "Something about you and your understanding of this case. When you scaled the fence the other evening, you were . . . desperate. Not only because your employer was in jail, but because you didn't know if she was guilty or not. Now you're sure, aren't you? You have that swagger back."

"You think I have a swagger? How sweet of you."

She kept going, not letting me play it off.

"All those questions about the evening of the murder, but none about the days leading up to it. If Ms. Pentecost were indeed framed, someone would have had to break into her home, steal her gun, use it to murder Mr. Quincannon, then replace it. That suggests considerable cunning and long-term planning. But you haven't touched on that aspect at all. No questions about who might be capable of such a scheme. Or people's whereabouts in the days before the murder. For example, Silas was in London the three days prior to the murder.

Not that he couldn't pay someone to procure Ms. Pentecost's gun. It's what he specializes in, after all. But still . . . it's interesting that you have so thoroughly neglected that aspect of the crime."

Alathea wasn't just a walking, slinking threat of violence. She had a brain on her, too.

"Don't worry," I said. "I'll get around to those questions when I interview the guests."

She leaned forward over her crossed knees, putting her face within a few feet of mine. I did my best not to inch back.

"Impressive."

"What is?" I asked.

"You're a very good liar."

Shortly thereafter, Alathea escorted me down the front walk. As she was unlocking the iron gate, she said casually, "The funeral is tomorrow."

"The funeral? Quincannon's funeral?"

She nodded. "It was a concession made by Mr. Whitsun. He rescinded his motion to hold the body at the morgue in exchange for granting you swift access to the crime scene."

That's why this got arranged so quickly, and on a Saturday morning to boot. A funeral would be interesting, though. I wondered how many of Quincannon's party guests would be in attendance.

"Where's it being held?" I asked.

She told me the name of a Bronx church, then held the gate open for me to step through. "It's a private service. Invited guests only."

That meant hanging outside the cemetery gates, maybe with binoculars, and ambushing people when they came out. Not a way to make friends, but nothing I hadn't done before.

"Would you like to be mine?" Alathea asked.

"Your what?"

"My guest," she said, shutting the gate. I heard the thick lock snap into place.

"I'd love to," I said. "But why the offer?"

She stood there for a long moment examining me, her perfect porcelain face bisected by the iron bars.

"Someone killed my employer, Miss Parker," she said at last. "If it wasn't Lillian Pentecost, as you so clearly now believe, I'd like to assist you in discovering who. If you get the chance to introduce me to them, I'd be ever so grateful."

With that last bit of promised violence, she turned and slunk back up the walk.

CHAPTER 19

From the journals of Lillian Pentecost

As Val predicted, the other inmates have decided that I am worth approaching. Though there have been no sexual overtures as yet, there have been requests for money, advice, and other assistance.

The money I will arrange on a case-by-case basis through Mr. Whitsun and only for essentials from the prison commissary. The advice and assistance—usually regarding legal matters—I give freely, as much as I am able.

Although I had one woman ask if I would mind calling the judge and request she be set free. This caused quite a bit of amusement among the others at the lunch table.

"You think if she could do that, she'd be in here gabbing with us?" one said. "Get a clue, Ethyl."

I did have one notable interaction. A girl approached me—her name was Beth. She could not have been more than seventeen. I had helped her sister, she said, some years back, at one of our Saturday open houses.

"She was a nursemaid for some rich bitch up around Central Park," Beth told me. "They'd stitched her up for stealing this diamond. But really it was the bitch's eldest who'd done it. Pawned it and put the money right up her nose. Sarah—she said you figured it out in ten minutes. Ten minutes! Without even leaving your house. Anyway, I wanted to say thank you."

I told her it had been my pleasure and asked after her sister.

"She's doing swell. She got married. I'm gonna be an aunt—can you imagine? I'm hoping they let me out before the baby's born."

I thought all this might have been a prelude to asking me to assist with her own troubles, so I asked what she was incarcerated for.

"Wrong place, wrong time," she said, then walked away.

Not all of my interactions have been so pleasant. The guard Andrews will go out of his way to bump into me and, during one instance in a crowded hallway, shouldered me forcefully into the wall and held me there for several seconds.

I have also taken to carefully examining my meals before eating, after discovering a prophylactic submerged in my stew.

I still do not know what I have done to warrant this treatment.

Val and I continue to grow more familiar. I learned about his upbringing in Harlem, and the circumstances that led him to being kicked out of his home. It is a familiar story—one I've encountered many times in my career, and more frequently since Will came into my life.

I told him of my request to Dolly Klinghorn. He was appreciative, but skeptical that it would lead to anything.

"When it comes to people like me, the law is just looking for an excuse."

Val also peppers me with questions about my life and career, as well as about my disease.

"Did the sclerosis do that?" he asked one day when I was cleaning my prosthetic eye.

I shook my head. "No. My eye was taken."

"What do you mean, 'taken'?"

"I mean a man removed it by force."

He cringed, his hands moving as if to protect his own eyes.

"Jesus, Lil. That's brutal," he said. "I hope you got him back for it."

"I did."

I might have smiled when I said it.

"This thing is going to kill you?" he asked later. "This disease?"

"It could," I said. "Eventually."

"If I had that hanging over my head, I'd roll the dice like you do, too."

The comment startled me. But not because it wasn't true.

Mr. Whitsun has requested that I write down what I know about Jessup Quincannon. When I said that he should ask Will to consult our third-floor archives, he said that those had been "ransacked and rummaged" by the police.

Will did not mention this when we met. Probably because she thinks it would upset me.

It does.

I started formalizing the archives—putting things in some semblance of order—shortly after being diagnosed with multiple sclerosis. Someday this disease will begin pecking away at my memory. It already fatigues me to the point of fogginess on some days.

Thus, the archives: organized in a way that suits me personally.

Now undone.

I am determined not to dwell on this, and so I will do as Mr. Whitsun asks. I will write about Jessup Quincannon.

Will can speak to our more recent interactions, and much

of Jessup's life has been publicly documented, but I will relate one anecdote about the first time I met him.

I was young. Not far removed from Will's age. I had worked several cases, some of which had garnered attention, but I was still an unknown. It was a surprise to me when, on one of my first visits to New York, I should find myself recognized.

I was attending a party at the home of a wealthy dowager—the reason is complex and irrelevant to this story. The guest list included some of the most influential men and women in Manhattan. I had very little experience navigating such settings and was feeling more than a little overwhelmed, so had retreated to a table in the courtyard from which I could watch the partygoers through the open French doors. Soon a man came out and sat across from me.

"You're Lillian Pentecost, aren't you?" he said.

As you may have already guessed, this was Jessup. He was in his physical prime, hale and hearty, hair just starting to turn silver. Perhaps it is hindsight, but I remember noticing a certain intensity. Like he was taking in every detail of the world around him and peering at it through some internal microscope.

I confirmed my identity and he introduced himself.

"My father's people," he said, nodding to the group inside. "The crème de la crème of New York."

He said it with such scorn it intrigued me.

"You think otherwise?" I inquired.

"I think the milk has gone sour," he proclaimed. "Don't let the beauty fool you. Beneath this excess, the sparkle and sheen, you will find all the usual rot of the human condition. The standard vices. The casual horrors. You of all people must be familiar with that. That business in New Orleans. Truly horrible stuff."

He went on to describe details of a case that had brought me some measure of fame—details the papers had failed to print. I was surprised that he knew so much.

"One hears things," was all he said by way of explanation. "Are the stories true, though? People exaggerate."

I told him that what he knew of the incident was, in its broadest details, correct.

"So young, and a woman. Yet you've lived more than many ever will."

"I lived, but others died," I said. "Some most horribly."

He waved that off.

"Yes, yes. But you've felt something. Something primal."

"Terrified, Mr. Quincannon. I felt terrified."

He leaned forward, eyes bright with genuine curiosity.

"Would you do it again, knowing what you know now? Risk your life for others. Strangers, even?"

I did not reply without hesitation, but in the end I said that I would.

He sat back, his expression one I had grown quite familiar with—a man's amusement at my perceived naïveté.

"Well, you are young," he said.

Our attention was drawn then to a loud burst of laughter that came wafting through the French doors.

"My father is in there somewhere," Quincannon said. "Making money. That's what he does. He puts money in places. Investments that make more money, and then he'll take that money and put it somewhere new, and if something does not make him money, if it displeases him, he will throw it away without a second thought. Like an apple he has found a worm in."

The way he said it, I wondered if he was not speaking of himself. But I stayed silent. I recognized that he was not addressing me, but the glittering world on the other side of that doorway.

Eventually Jessup turned back to me.

"No, Lillian," he said, his expression one of barely concealed anger. "I do not think the world past those doors or anyone in it is worth saving."

Events at the party quickly drew me away, and I forgot about Jessup Quincannon until some years later, when I learned of his fledgling Black Museum Club.

I remember thinking that his obsession around murder and murderers was a way of verifying the contempt he already felt. He viewed himself as an outsider, and he invited other men and women to sit with him, apart from the throng, and to look in and remark on the rot beneath the diamond sheen.

I might have been one of those sitting with him if not for a fundamental disconnection between how he viewed the world and how I did—one that would become clearer the more we interacted. That there is hidden decay beneath the skin of the world is something that we could agree on. But he turned his eye to killers, I to the victims. He believed that if you are the person being acted upon against your will, then you are weak. If you are weak, then you are not worth consideration. That, I think, was the corruption at the heart of Jessup Quincannon.

I wonder what in his life led him to that conclusion. And why so many others seem to believe the same.

———————————

I find myself unable to sleep again. I have been thinking about the girl Beth, and her sister, Sarah. It eats at me.

I recall the case. I remember how clear it was that the diamond was stolen by someone in the family, and how it took only a few phone calls to confirm my suspicions.

I remember all of that, but for the life of me I cannot remember the girl herself. I do not remember her face or her voice or what she was wearing or any word that she said.

I would discount this as an isolated incident, but I have spent the last hours thinking about the women, and the occasional man, who have taken advantage of our open house to bring their troubles to me.

I have discovered many instances where, again, I remember the problem but not the individual. Nothing at all of them.

Is this the common vagaries of human memory? Or is it the multiple sclerosis beginning to peck away?

Or worse?

Have I, over the years, come to value the puzzle more than the people? Am I more akin to Jessup than I would like to believe?

I do not care for that thought at all.

The evidence of what happens when you start thinking of people as problems that need to be solved is all around me, packed two or three to a cell, and they spend their nights crying.

As sometimes I do, as well.

CHAPTER 20

Sunday, but not a day of rest. Quincannon's funeral was scheduled for noon, but before I went to withhold my respect, I had to make a detour.

When I'd gotten back to the brownstone after my two hours with Alathea, I'd found that Lazenby had left a message for me.

"He said the package was waiting at the butcher's on Fifty-first Street," Mrs. Campbell told me. "I assume you know what that means."

It wasn't the toughest code to crack. Which is why I was on the train at ten a.m. on a Sunday, heading to Borough Park.

I'd left Holly asleep in bed. While I had been peppering Alathea with questions, she'd spent much of the day tracking down Susie Beck's old co-workers.

We were focusing on the women in the office because of Klinghorn's comment about needing a softer touch.

However, when she found them—if she found them—they were either unavailable or could provide nothing that wasn't in the file. One girl had moved to Cleveland and barely remembered Susie. Another was on her honeymoon in St. Louis and her mother didn't know what hotel they were staying at.

The owner of the travel agency had sold the business in January, retired to North Carolina, and promptly died. None of the old staff was still there, and the new owner hadn't bothered to keep records.

All we had to go on was Klinghorn's report. But I was starting to wonder if his casual mention to Dolly of the travel agency being an untapped lead wasn't wishful thinking.

At 10:20 I emerged onto Fifty-fifth Street, rounded a corner, and started walking north. Driving would have been quicker, but I was just paranoid enough to worry that Staples might have a man on me, and I didn't want to tip anyone off to where I was headed next.

Unlike with Nurse Palmer's décolletage, I was costumed not to draw eyes. My black A-line landed a good two inches below my knees. It was paired with a gray cardigan, some scuffed Mary Janes, and an oversize handbag that even my great aunt Fifi would dub dowdy.

I felt like I stood out anyway. It's not that Borough Park was entirely Jewish, but there were as many yarmulkes as fedoras, and even some peyes mixed in.

I turned onto Fifty-first Street, and halfway up the block stopped at a narrow rowhouse whose canary-yellow paint had faded almost white. I climbed the steps, lifted the knocker, and rapped. Footsteps approached. The door opened and—

"Miss Parker! Come on in."

"Sam Lee?"

The young roustabout–turned–morgue orderly was dressed for a funeral, too—black suit, white shirt, black tie.

"Looking sharp," I said.

"Thank you, miss. Come on in. Mr. Levy is in the back."

I followed him down a narrow hall, dodging scattered baseball gloves and windup toys, and past the kitchen, which still smelled of fried eggs and fresh bread, to a small bedroom in the back of the house.

Last time I'd been in that room it had housed Hiram's mother-in-law. Now it was stripped of all but the bed frame and mattress, which held a scattering of typed pages, two piles of photos, and the man of the house.

Hiram had bought his suit at the same sale as Sam Lee, his in a thirty-four short instead of a forty-two long, though he had ditched the jacket and tie. As he was sitting directly under the room's ceiling light, I could see the glint of silver hiding in the black of his hair and trim beard.

He looked up from the photo he was examining.

"Will," he said. "It's good to see you."

"You, too. Where're the kids and the missus?"

"My wife took the children to the zoo. They've been wanting to go, and the weather is pleasant."

Hiram wasn't the sort to lie to my face, so the kids probably had been hankering for the zoo. But I knew the real reason his wife had chosen that morning to absent herself.

The last time I'd been to his house, she had cornered me and dressed me down for getting her husband tied up in our cases. A lot of people shunned him for taking apart bodies for a living, but he kept at it because he was talented and he believed it was the best way he could serve the community that ostracized him.

The work meant a lot to him and helping us put his job in jeopardy.

She had said all this very quietly and very calmly, and it had felt exactly how she meant it to—like a knife slid in slow and deep.

"Sorry for the cloak-and-dagger," I told him. "Lazenby can't be seen on our step, and I probably shouldn't be seen on yours. At least your office step. Pretty sure I wasn't followed here."

"You weren't," he said with more surety than I had. "Isaac phoned from the delicatessen on the corner. I asked him to watch for you. No one was following. No men on foot and no cars."

I must have looked impressed, because he shrugged and said, "I am not so much a pariah that I can't ask a favor or two."

I turned to Sam Lee.

"What about you?" I asked. "What are you doing spending your Sunday with your boss?"

For a year now, Sam Lee had been acting as Hiram's chief assistant and unofficial student. Hiram had notions he could get him into the medical program at Howard University down in Washington, D.C.

"Mr. Levy has me over for Sunday breakfast," he explained. "If I'm around the boardinghouse on Sundays, my landlady Mrs. Henry drags me to church with her. I don't know what she's more interested in, finding me Jesus or finding me a wife. I'm not much interested in either.

"Besides," he added, "I want to know what I can do to help Ms. Pentecost."

"Look," I told him. "You can't do anything. Neither can Hiram. Even me coming here is taking a chance, Isaac on the corner or not. They know Hiram helps us. By 'they,' I mean the cops and the DA, both of whom can make things rough."

I felt foolish schooling Sam Lee, a Negro who had grown up south of the Mason-Dixon Line, on how hard the long arm of the law could hit, but I wanted to drive the point home.

"This is true," Hiram chimed in. "It could mean losing your job or, worse, it could ruin your chances to get into Howard. We keep our heads down. Understand?"

Sam Lee nodded. "Yes, sir. I do."

With that bit of awkwardness out of the way, I took a seat next to Hiram on the bed and looked at the snapshot in his hand. A woman lying in a tub, slashed wrist thrown over the side, her naked body obscured by blood-blackened water.

Susie Beck.

"Ugly," I said.

"Sad is what it is," Sam Lee answered.

"Yeah, that, too."

Hiram put that picture in one of the piles and picked up another, a close-up of her wrist. He examined it for a few seconds, then sighed and put that picture on the pile with the rest.

"What do you think?" I asked.

"I think it's both sad and ugly," he said. "But nothing to suggest it isn't a suicide, if that's what you're wondering."

"I don't see any hesitation marks," I said, leaning over to peer at the second photo.

"They don't always have them," Sam Lee said. He looked to Hiram, who gave him the nod to keep going.

"I've seen a couple of suicides since I've been here," he continued. "A lot of times they've got to work up to it. But sometimes they don't have to. They have it in their head what they're going to do and get on with doing it."

It had been too much to ask that Hiram would see something that the other examiner had missed. But hope springs eternal.

"Thanks for taking a look," I said. "Is that other pile of photos what I think it is?"

He handed them over.

"A selection of photos from the Quincannon killing," he said.

I flipped through. Quincannon's body on the floor—looking smaller and frailer than Alathea. A close-up of his face, eyes open but not in shock. Like he'd seen it coming and wasn't surprised in the least.

An even closer shot of the bullet wound. Half an inch over his right eye. The photographer had even managed to capture the flecks of gunpowder tattooed around the wound.

The photographer.

It occurred to me that Beck had almost certainly taken this picture. And here it was, sitting on the same mattress as photos of his dead wife.

Hiram broke me out of my revelry by reading from a typed document with the medical examiner's seal on the top.

"One bullet, small caliber at very close range, entering the head just above the right orbit at a slightly upward angle. It fragmented almost immediately, the pieces traveling through the frontal and parietal lobes, some retaining enough momentum to strike the back of the skull."

"Any chance these fragments could be jigsawed together to compare against the bullet they pulled out of that book?"

Hiram shook his head.

"I'm afraid it was quite decimated," he said. "Why do you ask? Do you think it might have come from a different weapon?"

I was getting tired of lying to my friends, but again it had to be done.

"Just one of many theories the boss is playing with," I said, keeping my eyes on the photos and off Hiram.

Lazenby had included a picture of the mounted book that the first bullet had gone into. A two-inch-thick tome, now with a ragged hole between the words STUDY and OF.

Six inches to either side and the bullet would have hit the wall, flattened, and been in no shape for a comparison. Ms. Pentecost might have still been arrested, but Beck wouldn't have been able to tamper the way he had, and she might have at least made bail.

I scooped up both sets of photos and slid them into my handbag.

"Thanks for playing go-between," I said. "I'd stay and chat, but I've got a funeral to get to."

I said my goodbyes and left. I was passing Hessel's Delicatessen (FRESH MEATS! WE MAKE OUR OWN PICKLES!) and was about to cross Thirteenth Avenue when Sam Lee caught up with me.

"Hey, Miss Parker," he said, huffing only a little. "Can I steal a word?"

"Sure," I said. "Take two. We're having a sale."

We crossed the street together, then paused on the corner. North up Thirteenth, a man was taking a rake to the lawn of the yeshiva that Hiram's children attended. Farther south, people were moving in and out of the bakery, the drugstore, the tailor's. An elderly gentleman in a wide-brimmed black fedora was directing a pair of beefy men loading a sofa onto a truck.

Nobody paying attention to the goyim on the corner.

"What's the deal?" I asked.

He shoved his hands into his pockets and scuffed the toe of one of his size-thirteen oxfords into the sidewalk. He looked like a little kid getting ready to ask for permission to go to the ballgame.

"You know I appreciate all you've done for me, right?" he said. "Setting me up with Mr. Levy. Helping me find a place to live."

"Sure," I said. "Anytime. Don't mention it."

I might have blushed. I've never gotten comfortable with being thanked, even when I might have deserved it.

"I don't want you to think I'm ungrateful."

"Never crossed my mind."

"It's just that Mr. Levy is always on me about going to medical school. Almost as bad as Mrs. Henry is about Jesus and a wife. And maybe I will go to Howard. I don't know."

He looked over my shoulder like he was trying to catch a glimpse of his future somewhere up Thirteenth Avenue. If he saw it, he didn't wave. He looked back to me.

"You keep telling me to keep my head down and not help out—"

"Now, Sam—"

He held up a hand.

"Let me finish, all right?"

That kind of assertiveness was out of character for him. He'd also pried his hands out of his pockets and gotten his toes under control.

"Go ahead," I said.

"You don't have to tell me things are tricky right now. I was nine the first time a police officer shot at me. I know what's what," he said. "You and Ms. Pentecost are my friends. If I want to help, you let me help. I'm not a child, Miss Parker. I can take my own chances. You understand?"

Now it was my turn to scuff my toe.

"Yeah, I hear you," I said. "If I treat you like a kid, I'm sorry. I always wanted a little brother, but it's not fair to cast you in the role. If I ever try to teach you how to suck eggs again, I give you permission to kick me, all right?"

He finally cracked a smile.

"All right," he said. "You need any help, don't count me out ahead of time. Deal?"

"Deal."

We shook on it, then he said so long and ran back to Hiram's. I watched him go, idly wondering who he reminded me of. Myself at his age or myself at my age?

I glanced across the street and caught the eye of a rotund man with Coke-bottle glasses and a beard down to his belly sitting on a chair outside the deli. The all-seeing Isaac.

I nodded. He didn't nod back.

Fair enough.

I headed for the subway.

CHAPTER 21

I've always thought funerals were a rotten way to spend a Sunday. Even the funeral of someone you're glad to see gone.

You've got a whole, fresh week right in front of you. You're thinking about everything you need to do, want to do. Planning out your life. But to get there, you've got to slog through a reminder that said life is finite and all your plans don't mean bupkes.

This particular reminder of my mortality was being held at a churchyard in an obscure corner of the Bronx whose surrounding homes looked fit for a funeral themselves.

Was it still a funeral if the guest of honor was getting cooked in his casket?

Alathea informed me as much when she met me at the top of the subway steps. Quincannon was being cremated.

"What are you doing with the ashes?" I asked.

"He's requested that I scatter them throughout the city," she said. "Concentrating specifically on the Upper West Side, where he grew up."

"Don't tell anyone," I warned her. "Property values will plummet."

The churchyard held a small stone chapel and about four city blocks' worth of gravestones, all encircled by a head-high stone wall. Next to the church was another building—a squat stone affair with a tall chimney that I assumed was the crematorium.

I followed Alathea through the side entrance of the chapel. We were using the side because the front was swarming with journalists. Some of Staples's boys had been recruited to keep the Fourth Estate in line, but that didn't stop the reporters from shouting their questions when they saw me.

"Parker! Parker! Did she do it?"

"The DA says he wants life. Will Whitsun deal for a lower sentence?"

"Would you say Pentecost is languishing in prison?"

The door closed behind us, cutting off the sound of the free-for-all outside. As I paused inside the door to let my eyes adjust to the dimness of the chapel, I allowed myself a moment to regret not changing clothes between errands.

Sure, my black dress was funeral-appropriate. But I felt frumpy next to Alathea, who was decked out in a tweed suit that must have been custom-dyed to match her jade necklace.

Custom-tailored, too. Unless skirts came off the rack with hidden holsters sewn into the back panel.

What kind of woman comes packing to a funeral? Other than me, I mean.

The chapel was as cold and stony inside as it was outside, and barely big enough to fit the seventy or so people in attendance. At the front was a raised space that accommodated a podium, some waist-high vases filled with flowers, and an open coffin.

While Alathea conferred with an older man who was either a minister or getting his Halloween costume together early, I approached the guest of honor.

Quincannon appeared much as he had in life, that full head of silver hair lacquered for the last time. His skin, always tight to his skull, was a smidge tighter, his suit a little big. Of course, it had been originally tailored for someone who was breathing.

The mortician had done an excellent job covering up the bullet hole in his forehead. I could barely make out the outline under the makeup.

I have to give you some context for what I did next. You see, I had a friend back at the circus, and one of his jobs was to create exhibits for the House of Oddities. That included some startlingly realistic human bodies, or at least body parts.

I glanced around to make sure no one was looking, then reached my hand into the coffin and touched its occupant's hand. Dry, cold. Kind of waxy.

I moved my hand up to the face and did the same. I pinched the cheek.

Yep. That was a corpse, all right. My hope was dashed that this was all some elaborate plot by Quincannon and that he was hidden away somewhere cackling to himself while Ms. P got charged for a fake murder.

I let go of Quincannon's cheek, remembering too late that skin loses its elasticity after death. The flesh remained raised, the imprint of my fingers still clearly visible.

"What are you doing?" a voice whispered behind me.

I recognized the impeccable English tones, so I wasn't surprised when I turned to find Silas Culliver looming over me. Looming, because he was built more like a linebacker than a lawyer.

For those of you who haven't met the man tasked with helping grease the wheels to stock the Black Museum, here's what I saw: a bald head balanced on a set of wide shoulders, and a torso that could have been three anvils stacked one atop the other, all supported by a pair of legs a lumberjack would have spent five swings on. This construction was draped in what I assumed was the finest black English wool.

"A pleasure to see you again, Silas."

"How did you get in here?" he asked, looking around as if searching for a mouse hole I might have crawled out of.

"I invited her."

He turned to find Alathea standing behind him. Even in two-inch heels, she had to look up to meet his eyes, but her gaze did the looming for her.

"She works for the defense, Alathea."

His condescension bordered on contempt, and I half expected violence to break out, but instead of slapping him, she merely smiled.

Which was, in retrospect, much more terrifying.

"I understand that, Silas," she purred. "But what harm can it do? What was it you said? That they have the haughty bitch dead to rights?"

It was like watching a pair of spatting siblings face off over the last candy apple. Silas blinked first.

"She's your responsibility then," he snapped, before barreling back to the pews.

"Such a charmer," I whispered. Alathea's response was to get a firm grip on my elbow and lead me to an open spot in the far-left corner of the front pew. Once we were seated, I glanced over my shoulder.

"Bigger turnout than I expected," I said in a hushed voice.

"Mr. Quincannon had many people he could call friends," Alathea hushed back.

I looked closer. Some of them actually had tears in their eyes. It made me wonder what side of him they had seen. Not the side I had. The one that got a hard-on for death. That cozied up to murderers, threatened my boss, and got the woman I love almost killed.

My eyes wandered front to back through the crowd.

"I suppose the fossil in the wheelchair is Judge Mathers," I said to Alathea. "I'm supposing that because Culliver is sitting next to him. I'm guessing he played chauffeur again. And don't mistake this for me being chatty. Talking to you gives me a good reason to keep my head turned in this direction and get a view of the crowd. Speaking of which, I think that's Reverend Novarro coming in. Unless there's another Latin lover type among Quincannon's crowd. Looks like he left his wife at home. I'd feel self-conscious staring, but every other woman in the room and a couple of the men are doing the same. I wonder if that's Victoria Pelham all the way in the back. The veil makes it hard to tell. Is the guy in the far corner Backstrom?"

Alathea turned around in the pew to look.

"I don't think Dr. Backstrom is here," she said after a moment. "He was invited, though."

I was going to ask Alathea to point out any other celebrities in the audience, but the minister chose that moment to step up to the podium and begin the service.

Funeral services are rarely rip-roaring affairs, and this one was no different. The minister droned through some aphorisms, a couple of proverbs, and the usual dust-to-dust talk.

Despite the appearance of a couple Bible verses, the sermon was mostly stripped of religion. A pair of hooks jutted out of the wall behind the minister, and I wondered if they had held a crucifix. Taken down, I assumed, as part of Quincannon's wishes.

The ten minutes of oration was capped with, "Does anyone wish to come up and speak before we escort Mr. Quincannon to the crematorium?"

Usually nobody takes the bait, but not this time. Timothy Novarro was out of his seat and advancing to the podium before the minister could finish the question.

The older clergyman was so surprised it took him an awkward few seconds to cede the stage. Novarro slid into the spot behind the altar like it had been hand-carved with him in mind. He grabbed hold of the sides like a captain steering a ship, and began.

"A philanthropist. A millionaire. An obsessive. Infamous. Lonely. A man is never one thing," Novarro told the crowd. "This should not surprise us, but it always does. We are made in God's image, and God is never one thing."

His eyes were like a cool breeze, brushing across everyone in the room, a touch of contact and then gone.

"If you think about darkness, about evil, then that is what your eye is drawn to," he continued. "You see it everywhere. When you look in the mirror, all you see is the darkness in yourself. And so that is what you become. It is a self-fulfilling prophecy."

If his eyes were a cool breeze, his voice was like taking a dip in a warm bath. It was that thought—*this guy's voice is better than a hot soak*—that brought to mind the picture of Susie Beck.

Warm bath, cold blade, darkness.

That snapped me out of it enough that I had the presence to turn my eyes to the crowd and see how they were taking things.

Silas looked squirmy, Judge Mathers amused. Victoria Pelham was an enigma behind black lace.

I was taking in the rest of the mourners when the doors at the back burst open and a man ran in holding a camera. He fired off a series of shots, the flashes bouncing off the gray stone like lightning strikes.

Alathea was out of her seat while the afterimage was still fading from my corneas. If you're wondering if someone can run at speed while wearing two-inch leather pumps, the answer is yes.

The photographer fled out the door, Alathea about ten steps behind. Did photographers carry camera insurance? This one was going to need it.

The interruption barely disturbed Novarro, who continued as if nothing had happened. I missed most of what he said, keeping an eye on the door, but perked back up for the ending.

"I pray for the day when we will all see ourselves as clearly as God sees us. When we break free of the chains that we place upon ourselves. The day when we will all be free."

From your lips to God's ears, preacher.

CHAPTER **22**

"I need to witness Mr. Quincannon's remains being put into the crematorium. I assume you can make your own way out."

Alathea walked away before I could respond, leaving me standing alone at the pew. I forgave her abruptness. She was in a mood, having failed to catch the photographer, who had scrambled over the stone wall—a maneuver she couldn't quite match in her tailored tweed.

That was fine. I had suspects to meet.

Novarro was glad-handing it with a few people and in no danger of disappearing. But Culliver was pushing Judge Mathers toward the side entrance like he was training for a Soap Box Derby.

I very casually stepped into his path. If there hadn't been witnesses, I'm pretty sure I'd have been run over.

"Do you mind, Miss Parker?" he said. "Judge Mathers is infirm and I need to get him home."

I was preparing a snarky response, but the skeleton in the chair stepped on my line.

"Shush, Cueball," he croaked. "I ain't gonna get any more infirm in the next five minutes. Now, who is this pretty little thing?"

Mathers had probably been called rangy once upon a time, but all the meat had been picked off and gravity had done a job on his skeleton. His head was more liver spots than hair, and it looked like his features—nose, mouth, lips—were in the process of being reclaimed by his skull.

"This," Silas told the elderly man, "is Miss Parker. She's a detective. She's trying to prove that someone else killed Mr. Quincannon."

"Speaking of Quincannon," I said, "if you don't mind, I have a few questions for you about—"

Silas held up a meaty hand.

"Ah, ah, ah," the lawyer said. "Let me save you the trouble. I have no intention of speaking with you. Nor with Mr. Whitsun. Nor anyone else from Lillian Pentecost's defense team."

As he spoke, his fingers—sausage-thick with big, swollen knuckles—moved over his suit with surprising grace. Smoothing a crease, adjusting a cufflink, straightening the knot in his tie.

"Subpoena me, if you must," he continued, "but until I am on the witness stand, you will have nothing from me."

I tried to re-create Alathea's smile, but I must have missed, because he didn't flinch.

"What are you so afraid of?" I asked. "If you've got nothing to hide."

It was his turn to grin.

"Miss Parker, we all have something to hide."

"I don't!" That was from the skeleton in the chair. "I ain't got a thing to hide."

Silas leaned over and said into his ear, "We are not required to speak with her."

Mathers snorted.

"Don't tell me my business. I was a sitting judge for more than half a century. I know what I'm required to do and not do." He cranked his head up to look at me. "Come by whenever you'd like. We can chatter about anything and everything."

Cueball got in position to start pushing again, and this time I made way.

"When you do come, though, wear something short," Mathers said as he passed. "My knife might be too dull to cut steak these days, but I do like to see what's on the menu."

"Jesus Christ," Culliver muttered, as he wheeled the old pervert out the door.

Success. Of a sort.

I looked around at the swiftly departing crowd, most of whom were funneling out the front door. It was a slow-moving line and Victoria Pelham was second from the front, held up by an elderly woman in a dusty mink who seemed to have given up walking in favor of letting the breeze totter her in whichever direction it was blowing.

I hurried over.

"Excuse me—Mrs. Pelham?" She turned and looked at me, face a pale blur behind the veil. "If you go out that way, you're going to get mobbed by reporters. If you follow me out the side door, I can escort you across the cemetery and out the far gate."

She looked back at the door, where she saw the sporadic bursts of flashbulbs and heard the questions thrown by reporters at the departing mourners. She nodded, deciding that I was the better deal.

I led her the long way to the side door, passing by Novarro, who had gathered a few more into his orbit and was saying something about "the lifeblood of human kindness."

I stuck my head in as I passed and handed him a card.

"Reverend? Will Parker. When would be a good time to speak with you about your relationship with Jessup Quincannon?"

He paused his miniature sermon long enough to smile and take the card, fingers brushing against mine in the same way his voice had earlier.

"We have services every Sunday at noon and Wednesday evenings at seven o'clock," he told me. "Stop by whenever you like. I'd be happy to talk."

Two for three! Now to go for four.

I proceeded with Victoria Pelham to the side door, where I paused, poking my head outside. The reporters were busy swarming an ancient-looking Rolls-Royce that Culliver had made the mistake of parking out front.

While they were distracted, I led Pelham in the opposite direction, putting the chapel between us and the reporters, and cutting a path through the cemetery.

A very slow, meandering path.

I reached into my purse and pulled out a packet of cigarettes. "Would you like one?" I asked.

I wasn't a smoker, but I knew Pelham was, and I like to be prepared.

"Yes, thank you."

I tapped out two sticks, handed one to the former railroad baroness, and lit both.

During this exchange, she tossed the veil up onto the flat of her hat, and I almost fumbled the lighter. The woman was beautiful, and not the garden variety, either.

Large dark eyes animated a soft face that had collected its fair share of wrinkles, its owner being past fifty. But each crease looked carefully thought-out. If Ingrid Bergman looked like this in a couple of decades, she should consider herself lucky.

The only jarring detail was a nasty burn scar running across the left side of her neck. It was old, the scar tissue long since grown thick and gnarled.

If I happened to stare, Pelham was gracious enough to ignore it. We walked and puffed. Or she puffed and I faked it convincingly.

"My name is Will Parker, and I—"

"I know who you are," she said, but not in a snappish way.

"I'm glad we have this opportunity to talk," I said. "I went hunting for your address and couldn't find it. No phone number, either."

"I don't have a fixed address, Miss Parker," she said. "One of the concessions I demanded when selling my late husband's

business interests was the use of a private car on all of his former rail lines."

"You live on a train car? Doesn't that get cramped?" I asked.

"It's a very nice train car," she assured me. "And I can get off
in any city I wish and stay for as long as I like. Currently I'm at
The Carlyle. I enjoy hotels almost as much as I do trains. They
simplify things."

I didn't know about simple. Most of the hotels I frequented
were the sort where the furniture had been rearranged to hide
the bloodstains.

"You spend a lot of time in New York?" I asked.

"I do."

"Because of Jessup Quincannon?"

"I know a lot of people in the city."

"But you were good friends with Quincannon."

She paused at a particularly hefty monument to someone
named Grimké—a granite obelisk that ended well above our
heads. She leaned against it, crossing one leg over another,
graceful as a chorus girl sneaking a smoke in the alley between
numbers.

"I don't know if I'd say that," she said. "It's difficult for two
people who have spent so many nights pleasuring each other to
be mere friends."

I must have done something with my face because she
laughed.

"You did know we were lovers, didn't you?" she said, taking
a long pull on her cigarette.

"I did," I admitted. "I just didn't expect you to be so direct
about it."

"My God, your generation. Such prudes."

She tilted her chin up and blew a column of smoke straight
up, where it wrapped its filmy tendrils around the obelisk.
Holly would have called it clumsy symbolism, but I didn't
think Victoria Pelham did anything clumsily.

"Jessup and I hadn't known each other more than a handful

of hours before we fell into bed," she said. "There was a party. Some good conversation. Then some good sex. Then some more good conversation. We would rekindle it over the years. Whenever I spent any extended amount of time in New York, we would make time for each other."

"Saturday evenings?"

She smiled, allowing the smoke to curl out from between her lips and contour those well-crafted lines of her face. "You've been doing your homework."

"I am a detective."

"That was Jessup," she said. "So . . . regimented. You know, he wouldn't allow Alathea in the house when I was there. I think it was because he let himself be vulnerable when he was with me. He didn't want to chance anyone else being privy to that."

Quincannon vulnerable? A human being with friends and lovers and soft spots?

I didn't like it.

"Were you still spending time together when he died?" I asked.

She shook her head.

"No. The last time we were . . . together was in May."

Around the time Quincannon told Alathea she was free to spend her Saturdays at home.

"Was this hiatus because you hopped a train out of town, or because one of you called it off?"

"The latter," she said. "Jessup ended it. Abruptly and without explanation."

Pelham took one last drag and then dropped the cigarette into the weeds growing up around the edge of the monument. I dropped mine, as well, grinding both out with the heel of a Mary Jane. She started moving toward the gate again. I followed, keeping to her elbow as best I could without stumbling over headstones.

"He didn't tell you why?" I asked.

"He did not," she said. "I wondered if he wasn't courting someone new."

That was interesting. It would hold to the timeline. A two-month break and then back to telling Alathea to give him the house on Saturday nights.

"Any idea who?" I asked.

She stopped and looked back toward the chapel, where the throng of reporters was starting to disperse.

"It could have been anyone," she said. "He had eclectic tastes, as you know."

I didn't know and was going to ask for clarification, but she started moving again, quicker this time.

"It was his prerogative, of course. We were hardly exclusive, and I was more than happy to hop back on my train. I spent June in San Francisco. Lovely city, despite the weather."

I had never been and would have said so, but we were getting close to the side gate and there were more questions that needed posing.

"Flipping the calendar to the night of the murder, where were you when you heard the shots?"

If she was thrown by the segue, she didn't show it.

"Outside having a cigarette. I didn't know they were gunshots. Not until later."

"Did you come to many of the Black Museum Club's salons?"

"I had an open invitation. Though I rarely attended."

"Why come to this one?" I asked.

"Oh, I don't know," she said. "A whim."

Then we were at the gate. Since I'd offered to escort her to it, it would have been rude to bar her way. I held it open and we stepped out onto the sidewalk. I was hoping it would take a while to get a cab, but one was turning the corner and her hand was already in the air, flagging it down.

"I have a few more questions," I said. "Maybe I could ride with you back to The Carlyle."

"I don't think so," Pelham said. "Perhaps another time."

She dropped the veil back over her face, then slid into the cab and closed the door. If the cabbie was intrigued by a shrouded passenger, he didn't show it. He set the meter running and pulled away.

I turned back toward the cemetery. From the crematorium's chimney billowed a stream of black smoke that thinned as it rose, tracing a line up, up into the sky before disappearing from view.

I stood there, staring at that line, thinking about ashes and dust.

Unlike Quincannon, I wasn't the morbid sort, so I didn't think about it long.

I walked off to find a cab of my own.

CHAPTER 23

Finally, it was starting to look like I was investigating an actual goddamn murder case.

I had a collection of suspects, some invitations to chat, a few people I still needed to lay eyes on, and at least one "I'd rather eat boiled liver than spend a minute answering your questions." And only twelve days after the killing and six since Ms. P was thrown in the clink.

Splendid.

Meanwhile, Holly was tracking down the rest of Susie Beck's co-workers. The one who was honeymooning in St. Louis had finally called back. She remembered Susie as "quiet and pretty and mostly kept to herself," which was about as useful as a sack of lint.

"My God, I hope when I'm gone, people remember more than my hair color and that I wore glasses," Holly said when she gave me her report.

I hugged her close.

"Don't worry, sweetheart. You are supremely memorable."

She didn't know how to take that, which was fine by me.

I wasn't too concerned that Holly was coming up empty. The more I thought about it, the more certain I became about how the Susie Beck investigation would end.

The police said suicide. Klinghorn said suicide. Hiram and Sam Lee said suicide.

It was almost certainly suicide.

Would Walter Beck accept that if we put it in front of him? Something told me no. He'd dig in his heels and tell us to go back to the drawing board.

Which meant Ms. P's freedom came down to finding the real killer.

Which is why, when Monday dawned, I made it my priority to have a face-to-face with the remaining guests who'd been at Quincannon's the night of the murder. First on my list was Billy Muffin.

Mrs. Crapper rang up Lazenby again and asked how he was doing on locating our missing button man.

"Wherever he is, he's dug himself in deep," the lieutenant said. "He'll have to come up for air again eventually, though. If for no other reason than to make some money. My sources are telling me that the poker game he knocked over barely got him three bills. He's not the sort people would hide for free."

With Muffin on the back burner, I moved on to the low-hanging fruit.

Sara Johnson ran a tidy operation out of the kitchen of a basement apartment down the street from the Harlem branch of the YMCA. She cooked up a few hundred breakfasts and lunches a day that she and her family would run out to folks who preferred a fried fish sandwich over peanut butter and jelly.

The food was so good some of the mostly all-white construction crews working in the area got their lunch from her. She also had an upscale sideline providing canapés and fancy sandwiches for hoity-toits like Quincannon.

All of this I discovered secondhand from neighbors, which is as close as I got to the cook in question.

My knock on her door was answered by a young man in his twenties—her son, William, I presumed. I had to presume because when I introduced myself, instead of responding in kind, he said, "I know who you are. They said not to talk to you."

"Who said?" I asked.

"They did."

He shut the door gently, but the result was the same as a slam. I found a pay phone, called Whitsun, and did some yelling.

"I don't know if it was Staples or Bigelow, but one of them is sticking a foot out to trip me up."

"That's probably true," Whitsun said in an infuriatingly calm voice.

"Can't you do something about it? Make a motion. Write a . . . a whatever to the judge?"

"I do that and they'll say Mrs. Johnson and her son misunderstood them and they never said anything of the kind."

I uttered a rude word.

"This thing happens all the time," Whitsun informed me. "It's how the game is played."

"This isn't a game. Ms. Pentecost's life is on the line."

"You don't have to tell me that."

I cursed some more but eventually my nickel started running low.

"Listen, Parker," Whitsun said, "this can't be the first time somebody's built a wall in front of you. Hike up your skirt and start climbing."

I climbed. Not that wall, but another one. I was suddenly feeling very unwell and thought I should go see a doctor.

Ryan Backstrom's office was on the twelfth floor in a block of new office buildings near Mount Sinai Hospital and looked appropriately impressive for a man with a lot of letters after his name.

A bank of glass windows showed a waiting area with a handful of people and a secretary who had definitely not been hired for her cheery smile. Not the sort you could talk your way around, so I didn't even try.

"Excuse me," I said, poking my head in the door. "I was just on the elevator, and there's a man riding it up and down. He says he's looking for Dr. Backstrom and he seems very out of sorts."

Apparently that sort of thing had happened before, because the secretary didn't look surprised.

"Thank you," she said, getting up. "I'll go see to him."

Once she was on her way to the elevator, I crossed the waiting room, opened the only other door, and went through. If you're somewhere you don't belong, walk confidently and with purpose and half your job is done.

On the other side of that door were three more, labeled EXAM ONE; EXAM TWO; and PRIVATE OFFICE. I heard the murmur of voices behind the first, soft rustling behind the second, and silence behind the third.

I chose silence.

Backstrom might be a medical big shot, but space in Manhattan still comes at a premium, so his private office wasn't much bigger than my bedroom, and at least my bedroom had a window. His only contained a modest desk, a chair for him and one for a visitor, a bookshelf of medical tomes, a coatrack in the corner, complete with hat and coat, and a couple of diplomas and a pair of paintings hanging on the wall.

I sat in the visitor's chair and checked my watch. Hopefully, Backstrom liked to take a breather between patients. If not, I could be there a while.

On top of the desk was one of those ceramic heads that looked like it had been drawn on by a drunk cartographer. I had the urge to get up and try his desk drawers, but I checked myself. What did I think I was going to find? A calendar that said "Oct. 7, buy milk, kill Quincannon"?

I kicked out my feet, sighed, and busied myself going over what I knew about the man.

Before coming over, I'd rung up the one psychiatrist in our address book—Dr. Lydia Grayson. Both Holly and Ms. Pentecost were patients of hers, and while I'd never asked, I assumed the woman knew more than a few details about yours truly.

This was the first time we'd spoken, and I was surprised when the voice that came over the line sounded less like Freud, more like Franky from the fish market.

"No, I don't mind answering a question, Miss Parker. As long as it doesn't mess with the confidentiality of any of my patients."

Except she didn't say "mess."

Turns out she'd never met Backstrom but was familiar with his work. She was not one of his admirers.

"The man thinks that he can cut away mania or depression with a scalpel. Now, I don't subscribe to that masculine/feminine energy dichotomy, but you have to admit hacking at a problem with a sword is a pretty manly way to mess things up."

Lobotomies, she told me, have a surprisingly low mortality rate, considering you're poking a hole in someone's skull. But while very few things are worse than death, some come close.

"I've had a few people come into my office—brought by family, usually—who are trying to cope with life after a lobotomy," Grayson said. "Yes, Johnny isn't gnashing his teeth anymore, but he's not answering to his name, either."

Interesting. A man who liked putting skylights into people's skulls. I wonder if he decided to swap his scalpel for a pistol.

While waiting, my eyes went to the two framed paintings hung side by side on the wall. Both were of a man sitting in a chair smoking a cigarette. The one on the right showed everything as is: man in a chair, red cardigan, brown pants, eyes, nose, mouth, and cigarette. Not exactly a masterpiece, but otherwise a standard portrait of a dull-looking fellow.

The one on the left was painted in shades of gray with a hint of red to show the color of the man's cardigan. The body and chair were both disjointed, like one of those Cubist pieces that lets you peep at all a nude's parts simultaneously. The man's face was an ugly smear.

I was out of my chair getting a closer look at that second painting when the door opened and Backstrom walked in, startling both of us.

"I'm sorry. I didn't know Mrs. Pervis had sent someone in," he said, moving behind his desk. "Let me put these notes away and I'll be right with you."

"That's all right," I said, delaying the inevitable argument. "I was just taking a look at these paintings."

"Those were done by a former patient," he explained, opening his top drawer and exchanging one notebook for another. "It's a before and after."

"Before and after?"

"Before treatment and after," he explained. "The patient was an artist, but she was suffering from—well, a variety of maladies. As you can see, it severely impacted her ability to perceive the world as it really is."

"Yeah," I said. "That can be hard sometimes."

"Are you Mrs. Amaro?" Backstrom asked. "Denise Amaro? I'm sorry. Mrs. Pervis is usually good about keeping me on track."

I sat back down.

"No demerit required for Mrs. Pervis. And, no, I'm not Mrs. Amaro. My name's Will Parker and I'm an investigator, currently working for Forest Whitsun. The defense attorney? You might have heard of him. I'd like to ask you some questions about Jessup Quincannon."

It took a few seconds for Backstrom to catch up to all that, which gave me the opportunity to examine the man. He was an aging Nordic type, with a thick, heavy brow that provided shade for a set of narrow blue eyes that peered out at me like I was a Russian soldier who had wandered into his gunsight.

He spoke with a slight accent. Something from one of those countries that's mostly snow. Despite the brow, his mouth dominated his face and he probably lit up a room when he smiled, though I'd never know it.

"I'm sorry Miss—Parker, was it?" he said. "I'm afraid I'm going to have to ask you to leave."

He stood up to emphasize his point. I leaned back in my chair, crossed my legs, and laced my fingers across my knee to emphasize mine.

"Let me be frank, Dr. Backstrom," I said. "I'm not going to leave until I've asked my questions. Which you are free to not answer, by the way. It says so in America's fine print. But I am going to ask them."

"I'll have the police called," he said.

"You could," I conceded. "But I promise you I will make a scene. I have absolutely no qualms about flailing and kicking and screaming things like 'That man cut open my brain and I can't see, I can't see.' After which you can explain the misunderstanding to your patients, if any are left. And to the other doctors on this floor, though word probably won't get around. Doctors don't gossip, do they?"

It was a bluff, of course. I didn't have the time to get arrested. But Backstrom didn't know that. He was looking at me like a patient he couldn't diagnose. Eventually he connected the dots I'd laid out for him and sat back down.

"Ask your questions," he said. "I can't promise I'll answer them."

I slipped a notebook and pencil out of my purse and fired the first shot.

"How did you get involved with the Black Museum Club?"

He thought for a moment and must have decided it was a safe enough question to answer.

"Jessup came to see a lecture I gave. This was several years back. He approached me after and asked some very astute questions. He invited me to one of his salons. There was a speaker. I can't remember the gentleman's name, but he had killed his parents when he was young and had spent much of his life in institutions. It was quite informative. To hear things from that perspective."

"So you kept coming back for more perspectives?"

I must have failed to keep the skepticism out of my voice because Backstrom snorted and shook his head.

"The police were like this, too," he said. "You Americans and your stubborn refusal to look clearly and directly at the darkness in the world. This is why you entered the war so late, you know. It took a slap in the face like Pearl Harbor to break you from your stupor."

I could give my own lecture on the different shades of gruesome the world can come in, but my goal was to get answers, not to give them.

"My apologies, Doctor," I said. "I was simply trying to understand what drew you to Jessup Quincannon."

"I am a man of science," he declared in that way men of science do. "Jessup's gatherings were a unique opportunity."

"Did you go often?" I asked.

"I attended sporadically. My schedule is very full, you understand." He stressed that last bit to remind me I was sabotaging that schedule.

"You attended the October seventh salon."

"I did."

"Any particular reason?"

He shook his head. "It was a day when I was free."

"But you knew it had something to do with Lillian Pentecost."

"I knew only what was on the invitation."

I could feel Backstrom closing his shutters. I pitched a curveball.

"What did you think of Quincannon's philosophy?" I asked. "The idea that the act of murder can change a person."

Backstrom was shaking his head before I'd hit the period.

"No, no," he said. "That's where Jessup and I disagreed. I have no doubt that the commission of a violent act can fundamentally alter a man, psychologically speaking. But there is no physical change. It's quite the reverse. Abnormalities in the brain—particularly in the frontal lobe—result in people acting irrationally."

He leaned across his desk, seeming to forget he was here under duress.

"You say you work for Lillian Pentecost's lawyer," he said. "You should tell him to pursue this. As I understand, she suffers from multiple sclerosis, which I'm sure has resulted in fundamental changes to her brain. She might not have been able to appreciate that what she was doing was wrong. You understand?"

I did understand, but calling an interview subject a dirty bum was a good way to get yourself thrown out, threat of a scene or not.

"Did you get a chance to continue this argument with Quincannon that evening?"

He blinked, startled back into the nuts and bolts of a murder interview.

"Oh, well . . . no. I didn't really get a chance to speak with him."

"Not when he came down and made the rounds?"

He shook his head. "No, I don't think he did. Speak to me, I mean. I was in conversation with another gentleman. I don't remember his name—strikingly red hair."

That would have been Billy Muffin. Which saved me the trouble of a segue.

"This redhead—how long were you talking to him after Quincannon went back upstairs?"

"I really don't remember."

"Were you still talking with him when you heard the shots?"

He leaned back in his chair and tugged at his ear.

"Um . . . no. No, I think I had moved on."

Interesting. Not his answer, but the pause, the little ear-tug. Was he taking the time to remember, or was he conjuring something fictional from whole cloth?

"Did you see where Muffin went? The redhead? Did you see where he was when you heard the shots?"

"I'm afraid not. I was looking up the stairs. Not at the other people in the room."

From outside in the hall, I heard a door creak open, footsteps, a back-and-forth of muffled voices. I jumped ahead.

"You were the first to examine the body, weren't you?"

He nodded. "I was. It was clear there was nothing to be done."

"Did you notice anything out of the ordinary? Anything notable?"

"There was a bullet hole in his head," Backstrom said. "I found that notable."

"What about everyone else in the room? What were their reactions?"

"They were in the presence of a murdered man. What do you—"

There was a perfunctory knock and the door opened. Mrs. Pervis stepped in.

"Dr. Backstrom, Mrs. Amaro is waiting in . . . Oh." Contained in those ellipses was surprise that the room housed two instead of one, recognition of me as the woman who'd told the fib about the man on the elevator, and a dawning realization that she'd been bamboozled.

Backstrom might be the sort to avoid a scene, but Mrs. Pervis looked like she wouldn't mind one at all.

I pulled the rip cord.

"Thank you for your time, Doctor," I said, standing. "I'm sure we'll be speaking again soon."

I slipped past the secretary, down the little hall, through the waiting room and the hallway outside, and straight down the stairs, because waiting for an elevator ruins a good exit.

As I trudged down the twelve flights, something gnawed

at me. I wasn't as good a lie detector as the machine with that name, but I could generally tell when someone was weaving around the truth.

Backstrom had just lied to me. But hell if I knew exactly how or why.

CHAPTER **24**

Tuesday was a wash.

The morning was spent typing notes, answering correspondence, and paying bills, which insist on arriving even in times of distress.

The afternoon was spent at Whitsun's office in the Bronx, watching as he and Pearl ate a late lunch and filling them in on everything I'd learned so far.

They were as frustrated as I was that Muffin was in the wind, but perked up when I told them about Victoria Pelham.

"Juries love sex," Whitsun said, chomping on a particularly pungent liver-and-onion sandwich. "As a motive, I mean. Especially if there really was another woman. Pelham's got one husband in the grave. Under somewhat suspicious circumstances, as I understand it. Wouldn't take much to get a jury thinking she might not take kindly to being spurned by a lover."

I must have made a face because Pearl jumped in.

"What he means is it creates reasonable doubt," she explained. "Anything that can do that will be gold when we get to court."

The meeting didn't last much longer. They had clients waiting in the lobby.

"Get me some more motives, Parker," Whitsun called out as I left.

"Get yourself a breath mint, counselor," I cried back.

.   .   .

Some motives.

When we get to court.

They were working with a battle plan that extended months into the future. Ms. Pentecost needed out yesterday.

With that in mind, I got up bright and early Wednesday morning and drove to the Lower East Side and the address I had for Judge Mathers. No phone number, so I couldn't call ahead, but the man had said to stop by anytime.

He'd also asked for something leggy, but it was getting too cold for skirts, and besides I didn't take requests. He'd have to settle for a pair of wide-legged gray-check slacks, a white blouse, and a gray jacket that hid my shoulder holster and the Browning Hi-Power nestled inside.

When I pulled up to the dilapidated three-story on the eastern edge of the Bowery, I thought I'd made a mistake. I was under the impression Mathers had money. If anyone on this block had more than two bucks to their name, they were hiding their light under a bushel.

Don't get me wrong—the Bowery isn't all knife fights and boozers dying in the streets. There are bright souls living full lives in every nook and corner of this city, Skid Row included.

I've spent more than a few nights over at Sammy's just off Houston, where the down-and-out enjoy nightly cabarets in the shadow of the el and Sammy pays for the funerals of his regulars so they don't end up in potter's field.

Sure, his booze help put some of them in the grave, but who's counting?

The guy I stepped over to knock on Mathers's front door wasn't dead, just dead drunk, cradling a half-empty bottle of rotgut like a newborn. I knocked quietly so I didn't wake him.

I guess it was loud enough, because I was shortly greeted by a white-haired houseman in full coat and tails. The tuxedo was threadbare and faded to the point where it was a couple of shades lighter than the man's skin.

"May I help you?" he asked.

If he was ignoring how out of place he looked in this neighborhood, I would, too. I gave him my card and he went back inside. A few minutes later, he reappeared and I was escorted up to the second floor, passing by rooms that were dark and empty, until we got to a back bedroom that had been turned into a sitting room of sorts. If two ratty armchairs and a stained rug a sitting room made.

Mathers was in his wheelchair, positioned by the window, peering out using a pair of binoculars strung around his neck. If he noticed my arrival, he didn't show it. His mouth hung open and he was licking his lips, like a cat imagining pigeon pie.

Eventually, he lowered the binoculars and cursed.

"She drew the curtains," he said.

Not a bird lover, merely a pervert.

I must have made a sound because he continued, "I'm not a Peeping Tom. No, no. This woman across the alley. Her husband beats her, you see? He thinks she's whoring around."

He turned his chair to face me.

"He'll kill her eventually," he said. "Inevitable."

I looked over the top of his head out the window, but all I saw were drawn curtains.

"Have a seat. Take a load off those legs."

I did as he suggested, and the chair creaked ominously. I wondered if Mathers had dragged it out of an alley or had had his butler do it. He wheeled the chair closer, so his half-withered legs were almost, but not quite, touching my own. He was wearing a pair of striped pajamas that no amount of laundering would get white again. The air in the room was still, and it smelled like mildew and old wood and something worse underneath.

"So you're Lillian Pentecost's dogsbody. The one who can dig under old Cueball's skin."

"Will Parker, Ms. Pentecost's associate."

"What can I do for you, Miss Parker." The way he said my name, it was like a cold hand running up my thigh.

I had a whole bucket of questions waiting to throw on him, but my curiosity was piqued.

"Have you called the police?" I asked. "On the wife-beater across the way."

"Oh, Miss Parker," he said, sounding disappointed. "I think you and I both know they wouldn't do a damn thing. Slap on the wrist, if that."

He shook his finger like he was scolding a child. "'You stop beating your missus, or you'll get a stern talking-to.'"

Then he made a noise like laughter. There was a bird up in the Catskills that made that kind of squawk. Woke me up every morning at six. I'd wanted to throttle the thing.

"I have a few questions about the night of the salon," I said when he was finished. "When Jessup Quincannon was killed."

"Well, honey, you're shit out—"

He started coughing. It was an ugly, hacking cough and when he was finally done he had a stream of yellow spittle hanging out the gap between two of his few remaining teeth. It dribbled down his chin and onto his collar.

"Goddamn it. Jefferson!"

His body man appeared, towel in hand, wiping away the mess.

"This is what you have to look forward to, Miss Parker," he said, as his butler attended to him. "Your body makes too much of one thing—like spit and dandruff and liver spots. Or too little. Like hair and muscle and erections."

He flapped a bony hand at the butler.

"That's enough, Jefferson. Leave the towel and get out."

Jefferson did. The spit had left a new spot on Mathers's pajama shirt the same tobacco-stain yellow as his skin.

"What I was trying to say, Miss Parker, is that if you're

looking for the minutiae of who said what and all that, I can't help you."

"Can't, or won't?" I asked.

"Very much cannot. You see, my mind, like my body is rebelling. For example, I can remember the last words that Leroy Gross—he was a horse thief back in Louisiana in 1902—said before they led him off to the gallows. But ask me what I had for breakfast this morning, and it's a mystery. Though I assume it was mush. That's all Jefferson makes me for breakfast anymore. Calls it oatmeal, but it's mush."

He picked a scab off his dry lower lip, examined it, then flicked it to the floor.

"All I know about that evening is I arrived, there were people—some of whom I recognized, none of whom I liked. Cueball, of course. He drove me. That highfalutin piece of tail Jessup liked to diddle. A reporter, hang 'em all. Then someone told me that Lillian Pentecost had shot Jessup and he was dead."

"I imagine that came as a shock," I said.

He took a moment to think about it.

"Man like Jessup rubs a lot of folks the wrong way," he said. "Not that people need much of a reason to do a killing. I think I was more surprised that someone got around to murdering him before he could murder someone else."

He leaned forward in his chair and I caught a whiff of him—stale piss and rotting teeth.

"He always wanted to, you know. Murder someone. He held his little parties and talked all about philosophy and psychology, but he wanted it, you understand? Like some pimple-faced virgin. He wanted to know what it felt like."

I'd had a great-aunt like Mathers—so close to death she didn't care what anyone thought of her anymore. She passed her final days making anyone in her presence wish they were somewhere else. Mind you, she was senile and also kept running out into the fields at night, buck naked, so at least she had an excuse for her behavior.

Mathers was just a dirty old man, and I don't have much patience for those.

"Sure, I understand," I said. "The first time I met Quincannon I told him he got his rocks off on it."

Mathers reared back.

"Oooh! The tongue on you. Nasty little girl.

"But it's true," he said when he was done cackling. "Probably would have liked to have gotten his hands on your boss. That she did him in first—oh, he must be rolling over. Or swirling around, since he's only ashes now."

"What about you?" I asked. "Did you get your rocks off on it? Is that why you were part of his club?"

His grin vanished.

"Don't pretend you know me, girl. There wasn't nothing about killing Jessup could teach me that I ain't seen close up and in quantity."

He craned his neck around to look out the window, and for a few long breaths I thought the interview was over. Then he started talking again.

"I've known Jessup since he was a boy. I had money and his father put it to work to make more. Don't ask me how. Listening to Edgar explain it—Edgar was Jessup's daddy—it bored the hell out of me. Jessup, too. We bonded over that. Anyway, I came to his little parties because he invited me. I don't get many invitations anymore."

He looked back, and I think there were tears in his eyes. Tears for himself or for Jessup Quincannon, I didn't know.

"He called me. I remember that. He called to make sure I was going to come. That he'd send that bald bastard to drive me. He was so excited. Said he was going to flog Lillian Pentecost in the town square. I said, 'Fine, fine, Jessup, I'll come. But keep it short.'"

"Flog her?"

"That's what he said."

"How exactly was he going to do that?"

He waved a hand limply in the air.

"Who knows? Who cares? Nothing new under the sun."

No grins now. Whatever high-octane spite fueled him was running low.

"During the party, you were sitting in your chair near the foot of the steps," I said. "That gave you a pretty good view of the room."

"If you say."

"Was there anyone missing when the shots were fired?"

He didn't so much shrug as twitch his bony shoulders.

"Don't know," he said. "Told you, I don't remember specifics."

"Who did you see?"

Another twitch.

"Doctor, I think. Asked him about my gout. Man didn't know shit."

He looked over his shoulder again. The curtains in the window across the street had moved. They weren't wide open, but there was a gap.

"Don't you want to find out who killed your friend?" I asked.

Mathers looked back. The twinkle that had been in his eyes when I first arrived had vanished. He took a deep breath—his chest wheezing in and out like a threadbare bellows.

"Let me tell you something, young lady," he began, slowly kicking his chair toward the window until the back wheels bumped against the wall. "I put a thousand men in prison and sent another hundred or so to death by hanging. Not one of those rulings brought their victims back to life. No, honey, that's why Lady Justice has a blindfold on. She'll screw anyone, but she don't want to look at you while she's doing it. Those were Leroy Gross's last words. That Lady Justice is a blind whore."

He picked the binoculars up off his lap and twisted around in his chair, propping his bony arms on the sill.

"Eh, yep. That's a new bruise on her cheek. Bad one, too."

A hint of glee had returned to his voice. A spark of anticipation. Mathers wasn't watching out of concern. He was watching because he didn't want to miss it.

I'd thought Quincannon was rotten, but at least he bothered to cover it up. Mathers was reveling. Rolling around in it like a dog in his sick.

Still, even monsters are human.

"I think you're a liar," I told the liver spots on the back of his head. "I think you care plenty. I think your friend is dead—the one person who'd ever bother trying to pry you out of this shithole. I think you probably know everybody who might have a grudge against Quincannon, so why don't you tell me?"

He didn't turn around. Just kept the binoculars pressed to his face, hands shaking even with his elbows acting as a tripod.

"My memory is about as faithful as that whore across the street," he murmured. "Now, why don't you take that nasty tongue and get out."

I thought that was a fine idea.

CHAPTER 25

Back home in Brooklyn, Mrs. Campbell informed me that Holly had gone to see Marlo and Brent to discuss her manuscript. That was fine. I felt soiled by my time with Mathers and didn't want to chance contaminating her.

I had some lunch, spent a few hours in the basement getting started on developing those seventeen rolls of film from Quincannon's house, then came back up and typed out what useful things I'd learned from the old judge.

Not much.

Maybe his memory really was that bad. Still, he'd been able to pull the word *flog* out of the air without any trouble.

Was it worth taking another run at him?

Perhaps. But not right then. Right then I needed to get myself to church.

Timothy Novarro's Church of the Holy Redeemer was one of those storefront deals located on East 103rd Street in Spanish Harlem. The space was wide and shallow, with about a hundred wooden folding chairs set up in five long pews. A row down the center ended with what looked like a thirdhand pulpit.

The windows were covered over with newspaper and the tile floor belied the space's former life as a grocery. There was a wooden box on a table near the entrance with a narrow slit cut in the top where people dropped their tithes. More coins than bills, from the sound of the clinking.

Even on a rainy Wednesday night, four out of five of the chairs were taken, so I settled for one in the last row, draping my raincoat over the back, where it went to work creating a puddle underneath. The place smelled like wet wool and the ghosts of produce past.

I hadn't memorized the last census, but the people taking up the other seats looked like the population of New York City in miniature: white, Negro, Spanish—even a Chinese family. A few of the men had ties on, but not many. Children crawled around on the floor.

I'd seen a few tent revivals during my circus days, and this place had that feel. If anyone fell on the floor speaking in tongues, I was running for the exit.

A woman wearing a bright blue tea dress was flitting up and down the aisles. She wrangled the kids, showed people to their seats, smiled, laughed, said hello to every other person, each of whom greeted her like family.

Novarro's wife, I was guessing. She was about forty years old and a couple inches shorter than me, though her platinum-blond hair was done in bumper bangs that made up the difference. She was built like Holly—plump but in all the right places. She also shared Holly's skin tone—brown enough to throw her nationality into question.

She didn't strike me as severe, which is how Max had described her. She had the face of a bank teller—plain, cheerful, with a touch of lipstick.

At around seven p.m., Mrs. Novarro disappeared through a door in the back, and a moment later, the man himself emerged wearing a long black robe and black velvet stole across his shoulders.

He quickly took his place behind the pulpit and greeted the crowd as a whole.

"Good evening and may God bless us all."

The crowd, minus one, repeated, "God bless us all."

Novarro leaned forward, setting his elbows on the pulpit. Less like the captain of a ship and more like a housewife at a windowsill about to share some good gossip. If a housewife had smoldering eyes and a pencil mustache. When he spoke, it was in the same conversational tone he'd used at Quincannon's memorial.

"A man walks into your house wearing a fine suit, polished shoes, billfold bulging in his pocket. A good man. A godly man, even. Where do you put him? You seat him in your finest chair, of course. Serve him your best wine. You start cooking those T-bones you've been saving for a special occasion. This is a man of quality, after all."

A lot of the people in the crowd were nodding, but some savvy congregants refrained. They knew these parables always had a twist.

"There's another knock at the door. It's your neighbor from down the street. Torn pants, shoes with the heels falling off. The one who's always drinking cans of Blatz on the stoop at ten in the morning. You know him. He's smelled those steaks cooking and says he's awful hungry. Where do you sit him? You keep him in the hall, right? The man smells like beer. He curses. You've never seen him walk through the doors of a church in his life. But maybe you invite him in because you're a good Christian. You're charitable. He's not sitting in your living room next to that first guest, though. Oh, no. You're putting him at the kitchen table and he's getting served water."

You see where this is going. Eventually he got around to citing the official version of the story. James 2:1–5, if you're curious. Love thy neighbor, no matter the cut of their suit. Basic Sunday-school stuff, given new life by Novarro's rich vibrato.

I wasn't much for preaching, but it was a nice palate-cleanser to Mathers's bitterness. Brief, too. Thirty minutes after he started, he was wrapping up.

"We talk about God and judgment. God will judge this,

God will judge that. But what is God first? God is love. And what is He next? God is a mystery. So many churches are bent on solving that mystery. Looking for clues in the scripture. Pieces of a puzzle. But that doesn't interest me so much. The people in this room interest me. How we treat one another interests me. I believe it interests God, too. Thank you. God loves you. I love you. Be safe."

There was a healthy smattering of applause and Amens. Then the crowd stood as one and began to file out, though many stayed behind to chat with one another or to bend the preacher's ear.

I joined the line for Novarro and tried not to tap my foot too much as it inched forward. By the time I got to the preacher, most everyone else had left.

"Miss Parker," he said, smiling and shaking my hand. "I thought I spotted you in the back. I'm so happy you took my invitation. How did you find the service?"

"Surprisingly short."

If his laugh was fake, it was a good one.

"I don't have the patience for long-winded sermons," he said, lifting the velvet stole off his shoulders and draping it across the pulpit. "A lot of our parishioners, they work jobs that have them up before dawn."

"I found that last bit interesting," I admitted. "Judgment and mystery. I don't suppose that was for my benefit."

The question caught Novarro by surprise, and he actually seemed to consider it.

"I'm not sure," he admitted. "I don't write my Wednesday sermons ahead of time. I just say what the spirit moves me to say."

He unzipped his robe, revealing a pair of high-waisted brown corduroys and a simple white button-down. He slipped out of the robe and draped it on the pulpit with the stole.

Without it, he lost something of his mystique. Like catching Cary Grant scarfing down an egg salad sandwich at the Automat.

The door to the back room—probably a stockroom once upon a time—opened and the blond usher stepped out. In one hand she carried a metal case about the size of a portable typewriter and heavy enough that it made her lopsided.

"I got most of it down," she was saying as she came toward us. "The rain didn't help. We really need an intercom. I wonder if— Oh, hello."

There was a quick introduction. The blonde was indeed Elaine Novarro. When I was identified as "Miss Parker from Lillian Pentecost's office," there was a flash of something in her eyes.

Alarm?

"Thank you for coming all the way up here. I hope you enjoyed the service."

"I did. Is that a stenographer's case?" I asked.

She opened her mouth to respond, but her husband got there first.

"Elaine used to be a court stenographer. Now she sits in the back room and listens to me and types out my sermon. Then I turn it into something a little more polished for Sunday."

"We also mail the finished sermons out to people across the country," Elaine added. "Someday we hope to get it on the radio."

For me, radio was for baseball, the news, and the occasional episode of *The Shadow*, but I made the appropriate noises. Then I dived in.

"I'd like to ask you a few questions, Reverend."

"If you don't mind doing it while we clean up," Novarro said.

I told him I didn't, and he and his wife started folding up the wooden chairs and stacking them in a corner.

"What exactly was your relationship with Jessup Quincannon?"

I asked the question of her husband, but his wife answered.

"It was hardly a relationship," Elaine said. "We only met the man twice. We were courting him for donations. Along with every other philanthropist in the city."

"Personally, I don't even like asking for tithes," her husband added. "Going around begging for money takes time away from preparing sermons, or visiting parishioners, or my prison ministry. If it wasn't for Elaine pushing me to find donors, I'd be preaching from the gutter."

I knew a touchy subject when I heard one, and money almost always is.

"Timothy and I met with Mr. Quincannon in his home. This was last winter, shortly after we opened here," Elaine explained. Her stack of chairs had reached eye level, and she started work on another. "We talked to him about the ministry and our church and our plans."

"I'm guessing Quincannon wasn't too interested," I ventured.

"He was more interested in engaging me in a rather murky conversation about morality and the existence of the human soul," Novarro said. "He wasn't exactly rude, but he was certainly trying to test my boundaries. Still, I've heard far worse visiting prisoners in Rikers, though Elaine certainly hasn't. Some of his language was . . . vibrant."

"I was fine, dear," his wife assured him.

"How did you respond?" I asked, thinking about Whitsun's craving for motives.

"I did what I do with the prisoners," Novarro said. "I didn't take the bait. When he realized I wasn't going to play his game, he had us shown out."

Novarro and his wife had made short work of the chairs, which were now folded in nice, even stacks against the wall. Elaine retrieved a mop and bucket from the back and went to work on the wet tile, while the pastor walked over to the tithe box.

"If your meeting was a bust, why invite you to the salon?" I asked.

"I have no idea," Novarro said, pulling a set of keys from his pocket. "It came as a complete surprise, didn't it?"

"It did," Elaine said, furiously mopping.

"You hadn't spoken to him or seen him since last winter?"

"Not a word," Novarro said.

He used the tiniest key on the ring on the padlock holding the box closed and flipped open the lid. Inside was a scattering of bills and a pile of silver and copper. There was also a cloth bag, into which Novarro began scooping the money.

"To be honest, I wasn't going to go," he said. "But Elaine reminded me that the church coffers were getting low and beggars can't be choosers."

"Even if the tithe was coming out of the Devil's pocket?"

"I don't believe Jessup Quincannon was the Devil, Miss Parker," Novarro said. "Though I do think he was tormented by them."

"He certainly is now," I said.

Novarro tried to hide his smile.

"Miss Parker, that is very unchristian of you."

"Reverend, you have no idea."

Suddenly Elaine was between us, dripping mop in hand.

"Do you mind emptying the bucket, dear? It's a little heavy for me. And maybe get the heater going in the car?"

"Of course, sweetheart."

Novarro handed off the bag of cash to his wife, then retrieved the bucket and lugged it outside, leaving me and the missus alone. She managed to keep a smile simmering, but it was less bank teller and more bank manager: skeptical and ready to deny your loan application.

"Did you get the chance to ask Quincannon why he invited you?"

"We only spoke with him briefly," she said. "He thanked

us for coming and told Timothy he hoped he'd find the evening entertaining."

She walked over to the pulpit and began folding her husband's robe and stole.

"You stayed in the conservatory the entire time?"

"Yes. We spent most of the time telling anyone who would listen about the church."

"Until you had your accident."

"My what?"

"You spilled wine on yourself, didn't you? Then you went to the bathroom?"

Elaine fumbled a fold and had to start over.

"Yes. It was very clumsy of me."

"That's where you were when you heard the shots?"

"Yes. Though I didn't know what they were," she said. "I didn't know anything had happened until I stepped out and saw people running up the stairs."

"When you came out, did you happen to see Billy Muffin? He was one of the guests. Short guy, red hair."

"I don't think so," she said. "I remember him being present earlier. A civil servant of some kind? We tried to talk to him, but he didn't seem—"

The door swung open again and Novarro reappeared, drenched from head to toe.

"It's still raining a bit," he said, wiping water out of his eyes.

"My goodness," Elaine exclaimed. "We need to get you home or you'll catch your death."

She tucked the bundled robe under one arm and looped the other through the arm of her sopping husband.

"It's been very nice meeting you," Elaine said, making it sound almost sincere.

"Yes, you really must come back," her husband added.

I had more questions, but Elaine was already ushering her husband out the door. He paused long enough to hold it open for me and waited for me to step through. It was indeed still pouring outside, but a shallow awning left over from the building's grocery store days provided a few feet of relief.

A beat-up Buick was parked across the street, its engine running.

Novarro turned to his wife and said, "You go get in the car. I'll be right there."

Elaine was saying something about catching a chill, but Novarro cut her off.

"I'll only be a minute, Elaine."

Reluctantly, she ran across the street, pulling her raincoat over her head to keep her bangs from collapsing.

Novarro took a step toward me. Instinctively I glanced up and down the block. Not a lingering congregant in sight.

"I didn't want to say anything in front of Elaine," he said. "I don't take violating an oath lightly. But I feel moved by God."

Oh, good, he wasn't about to strangle me. This was a good-old-fashioned proposition.

"I've heard your name before," he continued.

"Really?" I said, prepared to bat down his pass. "Where was that?"

"From John Meredith."

I felt suddenly heavy and lightheaded at the same time. My hand rose to my face, fingers pressing against the inch-long scar cutting through the freckles on my left cheek.

"How did . . . He's out?"

"No, he still has some time left on his sentence. He's one of the prisoners that I've ministered to in Rikers," Novarro explained. "He's really a very changed man. He deeply regrets his actions. I think someday he'd like to tell you that in person."

He reached out and squeezed my shoulder and said something, but it was lost under the sound of the rain beating on the top of the awning.

"What?" I asked.

"I said do you need a ride anywhere?"

I shook my head.

"I hope to see you again, Miss Parker. Get home safe."

Then he was running across the street to the Buick, where his wife sat watching intently.

I'd had more questions. But my mind had gone blank. Rushing into that now-vacant space was the feel of a fist driving into my gut, the collision of boot on my ribs and my face, lying curled on the sidewalk, sure it would end with a bullet or a blade.

It took a few minutes, but eventually I got up the courage to walk to the car and drive home.

CHAPTER 26

From the journals of Lillian Pentecost

Yesterday Val and I were awoken in the predawn hours and then ushered down the hall while our cell was searched.

We were not singled out. Several other cells on our floor were also ransacked. According to Val, it's not an unheard-of practice when they find contraband circulating among prisoners.

Whatever they were searching for, they did not find it, and fifteen minutes later we were allowed back into our cell.

Our mattresses had been stripped. Our few clothes were in a pile on the floor, their pockets turned inside out. Our meager possessions had been rifled through. Val's copy of *Holiday* was lying in a corner, torn down the spine.

Beside it was my prosthetic eye, its fabricated iris a spider-web of cracks. I picked it up and it fell to pieces in my hand.

It is not a fragile object. Someone had placed it on the ground and very deliberately stepped on it.

Andrews had been one of the guards searching the room. I am quite sure that if I were to examine the bottom of his boot, I would find slivers of my eye embedded in the heel.

I still do not know the reason for this aggression.

It was not until later that I discovered that the journal I had been writing in was missing.

Fortunately, anything incriminating, such as my meeting with Will under her guise as Nurse Palmer, was written in a cipher. Usually an unnecessary precaution, but clearly not in this case.

I did not write everything in code, though. Such as the description of my first interaction with Jessup Quincannon, as well as ruminations about my disease and my memory. All of it is innocuous, but the thought of it being read by that man is humiliating.

In other circumstances I would confront Andrews. But these are not those.

I was distraught for a time, and Val helped calm me. He will arrange with another woman to store this new journal in her cell when I am not writing in it.

It will be tedious, but so much of prison life is.

———————————

Friday, October 24. Eleven days in the House of D. Can it be so few? Without stimuli, time can become extraordinarily elastic. Minutes stretch into hours stretch into days.

I feel like I've written that before.

This morning, I was taken to the clinic for my now-weekly appointment with Dr. Hubbard. When Will, again disguised as Nurse Palmer, asked how I am faring, I told her I am well and joked that the rest is probably good for me.

She asked about the eye patch, and I made up an easy lie.

"I'm afraid I've irritated the socket again," I said. "I think I can do without a prosthetic in here."

Dr. Hubbard examined the socket, which he did find mildly inflamed, because it always is. Will made a comment about pirates.

Then Robert asked me the question he always asks during our appointments.

"Are you in pain?" Not merely referring to my eye, but in general.

I never consider it a lie when I tell him no, though, in fact, I am always in pain. My fingers, my knees, the muscles of my back all constantly ache from the strain of living with this disease.

Pain has been my constant companion for some time. Almost as faithful as the uncertainty this disease carries with it.

But there is nothing to be done, and it is nothing that can't be borne.

"No, Robert. No pain."

"Are you sure?" Will asked. "No offense, but you look like you haven't slept in a couple days."

Eleven, I wanted to say. I had not slept the whole night through in eleven days.

Instead, I told her, "Communal showers and uniforms do tend to dull one's glow."

Perhaps she believed me. In the past I've been able to lie to her. But as she's grown keener, I find myself caught out more often.

I hope she believes this lie. I fear she blames herself for my predicament.

Our time was much briefer than last week. That was a "full workup," Hubbard explained, while this was merely "kicking the tires." Consequently, we were allowed only fifteen minutes.

I spent most of that time reading a summary Will had typed of her work since our last meeting. Her tour of the crime scene, Jessup Quincannon's funeral, her conversations with the various guests.

She was very concise, but it was still a difficult task to read it all in the time allotted, and to do so while Dr. Hubbard manipulated me like a rag doll. By the time I was finished, our time was nearly up and I was exhausted.

"Any thoughts on my next move?" Will asked. "I mean, I

know I've got to crack the caterers. And I've got to take a run at Culliver, but I need something to jimmy him open. I don't know what else I can do about Muffin. Lazenby's on it, or so he says. Then there's Beck. Holly's been helping on that front— I hope that's okay. Honestly, I've been contemplating making a runaround. He swapped bullets. That means he has the real one hidden somewhere, probably in his apartment. Yeah, a bullet is small. But the guy works long days, sometimes long nights. If I got in, I might have hours to hunt. Then again, he knows how we operate. He might have stashed it at work. I'm not up for a second-story job in the crime lab. Maybe I should leave Beck alone, focus on solving Quincannon. I get the sense Backstrom was holding something back. And what about Novarro? He just so happens to be playing father confessor to John Meredith, the guy who put me in the hospital during the Collins case. Was that a coincidence? Did he bring it up to throw me off my game? I can't tell. What do you think?"

All of this I am able to transcribe in retrospect. In the moment it was a blur. I could barely make sense of it. Will was standing there, an anxious look on her face, waiting for me to say something.

I finally told her, "I trust your judgment."

Clearly not the guidance she was seeking.

"Okay, but . . . I make the wrong move, it could burn a bridge, and you'll be the one standing on it when it goes up in flames."

Robert must have seen that I was in distress.

"I'm going to go talk to the clinic doctor about your diet," he said. "I'll try to buy a few more minutes."

He slipped through the curtain, leaving us alone.

In my mind, I tried to sort through Will's notes. What did I know of these individuals? Nothing about Backstrom or the Novarros. I knew of Billy Muffin, of course, but had not heard his name in years.

I remember reading about the scandal around the death of

Victoria Pelham's husband. Whispers that he was a cruel man. Judge Mathers is known to me, as well. We crossed paths years before. If man is possessed of a soul, Mathers's has long since been lost.

Was any of this useful to Will? I couldn't decide.

Also, I could not get that girl out of my head. The one whose sister I'd helped. The sister whose name I could not recall.

"Will. Would you do me a favor?"

"Anything, boss."

"I assume you've canceled our Saturday open houses until further notice."

"Naturally," she said. "I mean . . . it's not like you can run them from in here."

"When you return home, have Mrs. Campbell make the usual calls. Put out word that they will recommence tomorrow. You can counsel visitors in my absence."

Panic flared in her eyes.

"I can't do that," she said.

"You most certainly can."

"No, I mean I can't." She was clearly angry now, but Robert had left the curtain slightly open and he and the clinic doctor were visible through the gap. She had to say the following through a smile and clenched teeth.

"In case you haven't noticed, I have a lot on my plate," she hissed. "Which I usually wouldn't complain about. Except the stakes here are a little higher, as you are in jail, framed for murder, denied bail, and—"

I reached out and took her hand and she stopped. For a moment, I feared one or both of us would cry.

"Please, Will," I whispered. "It's important to me."

Before she could respond, the curtain was yanked open by a guard—not Andrews, thankfully. Robert was standing behind him.

"Lillian—they're telling me you have to go," he said. "But I'll ask about getting you some better food, all right?"

There was no chance to respond before the guard led me away. I could not catch Will's eyes, and as of writing this, I still do not know what she will do.

I feel like I've failed her.

When the elevator passed the floor to my cell and continued down, I have to admit I panicked. Any abnormality in prison can prove hazardous.

"Where are we going?" I asked the guard.

"You've got a visitor," she said.

"I didn't think I was allowed visitors."

"You are if they're family."

CHAPTER 27

I trust your judgment.

It wasn't the first time she'd told me that, or something similar. This time felt different. Like she was convincing herself as much as me.

Now she wanted me to pile our Saturday open house on top of everything else?

Standing across the street from the House of D, I felt lost at sea and in danger of drowning. I didn't need to put in a call to Dr. Grayson to understand why.

I didn't exactly grow up in the most stable of homes. When you have a father who would as easily kick you as kiss you, there's not much you can rely on. Except for the drink and the violence. I always had to keep on my toes.

That came in handy when I ran away and joined the circus. I found it easy to jump from act to act, to learn new tricks on the fly.

I did that by clinging to the things that never changed. Little things, like the balance of the throwing knives. The width of the tightrope. That each playing card was two and a half by three and a half inches and only the queen of hearts had a divot in the center.

Little islands of stability in a sea of swirling circus chaos.

For the last five years Lillian Pentecost had been my rock.

Unchanging. Always there. The very fact of her allowed me to go out and dance on the heads of pins or whatever the situation called for. As long as she was waiting at home.

Now she wasn't. She said she was okay, but I could tell she was soft-pedaling it for me. I'd had to repeat myself a couple of times, and there were moments when I was sure her mind wasn't in the room at all.

I trust your judgment.

That made one of us.

I didn't want to think about that, so instead I kept my eyes on the main entrance of the prison. As we left, Hubbard told me the guard said Ms. P was being taken down to the visitors' area.

To see who?

Not Whitsun. I'd called him the night before to give him an update. He told me he wasn't seeing Ms. P until Monday at the earliest.

Was Bigelow making a play? If he was the type to tell witnesses to stay quiet, he might be the sort to meet with defendants sans counsel.

I did half an hour of waiting and watching before I saw my mark exiting the front doors. There was no mistaking him. First, he was better-dressed than most of the crowd—a clean black suit and tie, all buttons properly done, and a matching fedora with the kind of brim that had gone out of style two decades before.

He was tall and lanky, with narrow shoulders and long limbs—a sort of Ichabod Crane silhouette. Or maybe Ichabod's father, since this man was somewhere north of seventy.

It was the nose that did it. That suggestion of a hook. The eyes she must have gotten from her mother. His, I would notice later, were brown.

I intercepted him as he crossed Greenwich Avenue.

"Mr. Pentecost?" I asked.

He blinked and stared at me, dazed. A lot of the people

coming out of the House of D looked like that. Surprised that there's a world where sunshine still exists.

"Yes?" he said finally.

"Please excuse the nurse's uniform. I'm Will Parker. We've spoken on the phone. I work for your daughter. What are you doing for lunch?"

Within an hour, Holly, Adam Pentecost, and I were sitting around the dining room table at the brownstone finishing lunch and chatting.

"It's not that I don't trust Pastor Pike to carry on the good work of the church. But there are some congregants—older ones, mostly—who are used to me. They confide in me where they might not with anyone else. Also, being retired, I have the time to travel to our more remote parishioners. Or spend more time with the sick ones, or the ones too old to really make it to regular services. Things Pastor Pike might not have time for. I try not to step on his toes, and he assures me that I don't. Though he is a bit of a glad-hander, so who knows. Eleanor, the pork gravy was delicious. And the biscuits! You have to send me the recipe for the biscuits."

"I did send it to you," Mrs. Campbell said from the dining room doorway. "You cocked it up."

His eyes widened as the memory struck home.

"Right, yes. Dill instead of chives. Essence of pickles. Not my best effort."

The Reverend Adam Pentecost was, in no particular order: a voracious eater, struggling cook, amateur bird-watcher, moderately good woodworker, lover of novels, semiretired man of the cloth, and president of the committee to replace the Devilbliss Bridge, which was nearing collapse thanks to a combination of time, vandalism, and termites. I knew all this after a fifteen-minute car ride followed by a thirty-minute lunch, because he was also, above all else, a talker.

The man was an open book, and he didn't mind turning the pages for you. Basically the flip side to his daughter, who shared little. At least with me.

Mrs. Campbell, it turned out, had known the good reverend for donkey's years and gave him a big Scottish bear hug when she saw him, then insisted on using some leftover hog bits to cook up a fresh batch of gravy, which she said quite proudly was his favorite.

While they were catching up, I'd taken the opportunity to hang up Nurse Palmer. A nurse, a minister, and a writer sitting down to lunch sounded too much like the setup to a bad joke.

"How did I get started on all that?" Reverend Pentecost muttered, nibbling at a rim of biscuit.

"You were saying you're retired," Holly reminded him.

"Oh, yes," he said. "Essentially, I am. But I still have a host of nonspecific and mostly voluntary duties. Which means I came down to the city only for the day. I'll take the train back up this afternoon. Though, of course, I'll find extended lodging for . . . well, for the trial."

That ushered an awkward silence into the room. Luckily Holly could always be counted on to put a silence out of its misery.

"That's silly," she said. "About finding lodging. There's a perfectly good guest room upstairs."

"I thought you were staying in there, dear."

"Only temporarily," Holly said, looking my way. "Probably only a few more days."

I nodded. Holly couldn't bunk with me forever. Eventually I'd have to get comfortable sleeping in an empty brownstone.

"No hotels next time you come," I told the retired minister. "Although hopefully there won't be a trial to come down for."

"Yes, of course," he said, sipping his water.

Holly stood. "I should really get back to work," she said. "My own work, not the . . . the other project. Marlo pointed out that if I insist on having the father gutted, I mean really eviscerated, then I must do something about the blood. The killer would have it all over her dress. Does she have a change of clothes there? And what does she do with the bloody garments?"

Adam Pentecost stood and shook her hand.

"I'm sure you'll figure it out. It was a pleasure meeting you, Holly."

"And you. It adds a lovely bit of context to Lillian. She's always going on about how context is important."

With that, Holly went upstairs to mop up some blood and Ms. P's father sat back down. With just the pair of us, I could ask the questions I'd been holding in for an hour.

"If you don't mind, and I'm not insisting—what did you and your daughter talk about during your visit?"

If he was put off by my directness, he didn't show it.

"Yes, well, a number of things," he said. "I caught her up on everything going on back home. My home, I mean. I recognize that she doesn't see it as her's anymore. Also, I told her about the phone calls."

"Phone calls?"

"From reporters. Most are rude enough that I don't feel guilty hanging up on them. But there was also a Mr. Bigelow," he explained, dabbing a bit of pork gravy off his chin with the corner of a linen napkin. "From the questions he asked—and Lily confirmed my suspicions—he was looking to nail down her motive. I think that's the right phrasing. 'Nail down'?"

"That works. He was asking about the theft of the painter's box?"

"That, and, well . . . about Lily's mother. My wife. The circumstances around her death. Whatever this Jessup Quincannon was planning to sermonize on the night of his death."

Reverend Pentecost laid his napkin out on the table and began folding it.

"I'd been expecting the call," he said, matching one corner to another. "I'd heard through the grapevine—small towns are really wonderful in that fashion; awful and wonderful—

that he, or people from his office, had been calling around to various town officials. I don't think he found much. It's all new people in those positions now. I say new, though some have been there for a decade or more. And last month there was a fire in the basement of the old schoolhouse. That's where they stored all the old court records. Sheriff's reports, that sort of thing. Everything was lost. Mr. Bigelow seemed very dissatisfied when he finally got around to calling me."

More folds, shaping a neck and a tail.

"Did you satisfy him?" I asked.

"No, I don't think I did," he said, adding more folds to the napkin. "I explained that I am quite an old man and he was asking about events decades in the past. The human brain has quite an amazing capacity to subsume events—whole years, even—especially when they are traumatic."

He finished folding, leaning forward to place the linen swan in the center of the table. I don't know if he was smiling because of his origami skills, or because he'd admitted to telling a fib.

"I learned how to do that on my honeymoon," he said, nodding at the swan. "From a waiter in Boston. I made him do it three times until I had it down."

"Although," he added, "my wife was the artist."

There was a long stretch of silence after that.

I was in the middle of puncturing it when Mrs. Campbell delivered coffee and suggested the two of us move the show into the office while she cleared the table, which we did. In the office, I took the sofa and he the stiffest of our guest chairs.

"It's my back," he said when I offered him something more comfortable. "Fifty years of standing at a pulpit have practically welded it straight. Now, what were you saying about the trial?"

"That Bigelow will find somebody who'll talk. If not him, then a reporter. Unless your town is devoid of gossips."

"I'm afraid not," he said. "We have our share."

"In that case you should brace yourself. One way or another, your wife's murder will get dredged up. It could get ugly."

Reverend Pentecost frowned, and I thought it was because he was imagining how ugly things could get. Then he said, "Lily's never told you, has she? About what happened to her mother."

I shook my head.

"She hasn't," I admitted. "In fact, until you called up last month, I didn't know you existed. I knew she had a father, mind you. Just not one who was alive and well and baking pickle biscuits."

Another frown. This one of the indecisive variety. He peered down into his coffee, like he could find his next words in the swirl of the milk.

"Lily has always divided her lives quite firmly," he said. "It started after her mother died, I think. Keeping things close. When she shared what was going on in her head, I always had the sense she was holding back. Perfectly understandable. Adolescent girl, preacher's daughter. But . . ."

He looked up and his eyes caught the painting above the desk, as if for the first time, and he let out a little "Oh."

"Look," I said, "if you don't want to talk about it, I understand. I'm only worried that—"

"Lily's mother wasn't murdered," he said, still looking at the painting. "She was accused of murder. The murder of a man she was in love with. With whom she was . . . Well, they were having an affair. He was killed. Brutally. She was arrested and put in jail. Before the trial, she committed suicide in her cell."

I probably should have said something along the lines of "I'm sorry. That's awful." Instead I blurted, "Jesus Christ!"

At least it made him smile.

"I've talked to him about it quite a bit," Reverend Pentecost said, finally moving his eyes from the woman in the painting to the one on the sofa. "Although I'm ashamed to say Lily and I didn't discuss it much, then or in the years since. Surprisingly easy to avoid, all things considered."

The undercurrents were dark there. Dark and deep, with

unspoken thoughts swimming below the surface, and I sensed that some of them had teeth.

I had questions. A thousand questions. I forced myself to ask only one.

"What else did you two talk about? Other than the phone calls?"

It was a life preserver, and Ms. Pentecost's father grabbed it gratefully.

"Not much," he said. "Half an hour is precious little time. I spent much of it apologizing."

"Apologizing for what?"

"For calling her in the first place," he said. "About the theft. I knew it would make her angry. I should have let it lie. If I hadn't, things would be so different."

"Look, Reverend—"

"Adam, please."

"You're my boss's father, so I don't think so. How about we settle for Mr. Pentecost?"

"That would be acceptable."

"Mr. Pentecost—it wasn't your fault," I said. "She was going to find out about it anyway. Quincannon sent her an engraved invitation. Somebody took advantage of the circumstances to kill him and—not to get too deep in the weeds—a second someone is taking the opportunity to frame your daughter for the murder. What I'm saying is the tally sheet of responsibility is a long one, and your name is so far down the list it hardly figures."

He sat there for a moment, looking like he was thinking of a rebuttal. Then he nodded.

"I suppose you're right," he said. "There was nothing I could do."

He took a sip of coffee and then added, "The same could be said of you."

I didn't understand what he meant and told him so.

"That you hold no responsibility for the predicament that Lily finds herself in," he explained.

"Who said anything about me?"

"My daughter during our visit. She seems to think that you might be running yourself ragged—that's how she put it—because you feel culpable. Being away when this happened. You might feel that if you were here you could have prevented it."

"Now, that's . . ."

I stood up from the sofa.

"What I mean is . . ."

No. Even on my feet the rebuttal wouldn't come.

Because it was true. If I'd been there, I could have talked her out of going. Or at least gone with her. Everything would be different. She certainly wouldn't be in jail accused of murder. But, no, I was on vacation. Five years, and the one time I leave, this happens.

I don't know how much of that was playing across my face, but it must have been quite a show. Mr. Pentecost reached up and took my hand.

"I made a thousand choices leading up to what happened with my wife," he said. "I know because I've had time to count them. Wondering what I could have done differently that would have resulted in her being alive today. Every bit of it was wasted energy. What will be will be, and all we can do is learn from it. We must contend with the world that is, not the one that was, or the one that could have been. Now, sit down, I'm getting a crick in my neck."

I sat back down.

There was another awkward silence, and this time we let it breathe for a while. Then something occurred to me.

"That whole spiel about you feeling guilty. Did you really talk about that with your daughter, or were you using that as a way to sneak in a personalized sermon?"

"We chatted about so much," he said, hiding his eyes back in his coffee cup. "An old man can't be expected to remember everything."

I sipped my own coffee and pondered apples and trees and the trajectory of falling fruit.

CHAPTER **28**

After Adam Pentecost left, promising that next time he was in the city we would be his first boardinghouse of call, I went upstairs to see how Holly was handling the viscera. I found her at the desk in the guest room, papers spread around her. But it wasn't her manuscript. It was the Susie Beck file. She perked up as soon as I entered.

"I think I might have found something," she said, stubbing out her Chesterfield in the Folgers can. "I was looking for names. I figured out what to do with all the blood, by the way. It was really quite simple. I'm embarrassed I didn't think of it sooner. Anyway, I was looking for names. That bartender in Chapter Seven—the one who tells Grimm about the blackmail letter? I need a better name than John Baxter. It's not really a bartender name, and he needs a good one since he comes back later."

She dug through the file until she found a particular page.

"One name caught my eye. Louis Ballard. I thought, well that's a nice name. He was one of Susie Beck's co-workers. Since we were focusing on the women, I had initially skipped over him. Anyway, by the time Mr. Klinghorn wrote about him, he had left the travel agency."

She handed the page to me.

"What am I looking for?" I asked.

She stood up and put her finger right over where Klinghorn

had written Ballard's job as of a year ago: a waiter at the White
Clover.

Nine out of ten detectives wouldn't have included that
detail, but Klinghorn was the obsessive sort, God rest his
greasy soul.

The White Clover was a cabaret joint that, until recently,
had catered mostly to gay men. A raid had shut its doors last
month, and word on the street was they were staying shut.
And, while you didn't have to be homosexual to work there, it
sure helped.

"In the report Ballard is quoted saying he knew Susie
Beck to say hello to," Holly said. "They passed the time with
small talk, but nothing serious. But what if he was lying and
Mr. Klinghorn picked up on that?"

We'd assumed when Klinghorn mentioned to his wife that
she should have taken the travel agency, it was because Dolly
would have a better touch with women. But Klinghorn had
been a professional. He'd interviewed thousands of women. A
gay man, on the other hand—I could see that throwing him.

We moved down to the office.

If Ballard had a phone, Klinghorn hadn't included the number, and there was no Louis Ballard in the phone book. Luckily,
I knew more than a few of the former staff of the White Clover.

I went through two bartenders, three waiters, and a drag
singer before finally finding a manager who told me he heard
Louis had gotten a job at a pet store in Greenwich Village.

That seemed like a strange place to end up, so I didn't hold
out much hope when I called Christopher Street Pets and asked
for Ballard. Miracle of miracles, he not only worked there but
was present and accounted for. They got him on the line and I
told him who I was and what I wanted to talk with him about.

I also mentioned how I tracked him down, which served as
my bona fides.

"Sure, I'll talk about Susie," he said. "But not now. My manager's giving me the stink eye. And I'm leaving on Sunday to

visit an artist friend of mine. It'll have to be tomorrow before my noon shift."

I asked if we couldn't meet tonight, but he nixed that.

"I'm sorry, I've got to shop for three weeks in Cape Cod. It's tomorrow morning or wait until I get back."

I said I'd meet him tomorrow morning at a café near the pet store and hung up.

"Shit."

"What's wrong?" Holly asked from her spot behind Ms. P's desk, where she'd been listening on the other line. "He says he's willing to talk about Susie Beck."

"Yeah, but tomorrow morning. Which is Saturday morning," I reminded her. "That means canceling our open house. Ms. Pentecost won't be happy about that, but I guess it has to be done."

"I could do it," Holly said, starting to put everything back in the accordion folder in the order it came out.

"I appreciate the offer," I said. "But as much as the people who show up for our open houses might not be able to afford a detective, they do come expecting one. It's already bad enough they're not getting Lillian Pentecost . . ."

Holly was giving me a look.

"I mean I can meet with Louis Ballard," she said in her "yes, child, the stove is hot" tone.

"I don't know. If this guy lied to Klinghorn, he could be dangerous."

"We'd be meeting in a public place."

"Okay, but interviewing people—even friendly ones—can be a touchy thing and you're . . ."

"I'm what?" she asked, coming around and tossing the folder on my desk.

I tried to stand up, but she leaned over me, forcing me back into my chair.

"Will Parker," she said. "I will have you know that I am perfectly capable of moving through the world and talking with people and asking questions when they need to be asked. That includes talking to strangers, especially if I have time to prepare, which I do. Also, if we're assuming that Louis Ballard is a homosexual and that he'll respond better to someone who is sympathetic to that fact, may I remind you where I slept last night."

If that doesn't tell you why Holly rang my bell, I don't know what to say.

"All right," I said.

"All right?"

"Let's get you prepared."

CHAPTER 29

By 9:55 the following morning I was regretting everything.

I was regretting letting Holly tackle Louis Ballard alone. I was regretting holding the open house. I was regretting the two soft-boiled eggs I'd inhaled for breakfast, which were threatening a repeat performance.

I'd never run a Saturday open house by myself. I contributed plenty, but the only time I ever took the wheel was when Ms. P gave me the nod. Which only happened when her multiple sclerosis was getting the better of her, or the issue at hand was one I was better equipped to deal with, and those instances were few and far between.

But here I was, sitting at my desk—I absolutely was not going to use Ms. Pentecost's—watching the first woman of the day file in, and my stomach was doing backflips.

All right. The only way out was through.

"Hello, I'm Will Parker. What brings you by today?"

"Mrs. Norton. Mrs. Priscilla Norton."

"How can I assist you, Mrs. Norton?"

And we were off.

Mrs. Norton was a thirty-two-year-old mother of five who made her home in the Lower East Side. Her husband worked graveyard shift security at Consolidated Meatpacking. She worked part-time sewing buttons on blouses for a little concern in her neighborhood.

Needless to say, her children were on their own most of the time. She was worried the eldest, her fifteen-year-old son, was up to something.

"Jimmy's always been a good boy. Now some mornings I wake up and he's gone," she told me, sitting in her chair, twisting a tear-soaked handkerchief into knots. "He says he's going to school early to practice basketball, but I heard from his English teacher that sometimes he misses her class, he gets to school so late. Now he's away all day some weekends. Like today, he was gone before I woke up and—and . . ."

She started hiccupping here and I had to wait for her to get her breathing under control.

"I know he's running with a rough crowd," she finally said. "These grown men—rough-looking men—say hello to him on the street. And when he's home he smells like a French whorehouse, pardon my language."

"That's all right," I told her. "I don't mind the French."

"I know he's in a gang," Mrs. Norton declared. "Like those boys that are always in front of McDougal's. Fighting, stealing. Girls hanging all over them. My God, he's fifteen! He's too young for that kind of thing."

I wasn't sure about that. At fifteen I was learning to play with knives and making passes at tattooed women. That's not true, I thought. Mostly I was shoveling tiger shit and going to sleep smelling like . . .

A light bulb flickered.

"How's money been, Mrs. Norton?"

That question made her uncomfortable, but eventually she admitted things had been snugger than usual.

"George broke his ankle and couldn't work for a couple of weeks," she said. "That was hard. He's a proud man. Hates that I have to work. But Mr. Babbit, our landlord—bless his soul—didn't want to lose us because we were such good tenants. He lowered our rent by twenty dollars a month. I'm usually not one to take charity, but I'm not foolish, either. Mr. Babbit is a saint, I tell you."

I didn't know about that. I was betting Jimmy was covering that twenty dollars and maybe one or two extra to bribe Babbit to play the saint.

There were a lot of places on the Lower East Side where a fifteen-year-old could pick up work on the sly because he didn't want to anger money-proud Papa. The early mornings and weekends narrowed the list a little. But the French whorehouse was the big tip-off.

Spend an hour slinging tuna at the Fulton Fish Market and the smell could be on you for a week. If you're running back to school or home, you don't have time for a soak, so you pick up the trick that some of the older guys use. You douse yourself in whatever cheap perfume you can get your hands on.

"I think you were right, Mrs. Norton."

"That he's in a ga—" She hiccupped. "A gang."

"No, ma'am. That he's a good boy."

I told her to swing by the fish market on the way home. And while she could take Jimmy by the ear, it might be wiser to have a conversation with his boss and figure out a schedule that didn't interfere with English class.

"Stock up on bars of Ivory," I suggested. "That cheap perfume will give him a rash—believe me."

She thanked me profusely, shaking my hand so hard I thought it would fly off, then practically running out the door, anxious to confirm that her son was hanging around with halibuts instead of hoodlums.

Not bad. I started thinking I could maybe do this after all.

I poked my head out of the office.

"Who's next?"

.   .   .

And next, and next, and next, from eleven in the morning until five at night.

When Ms. Pentecost was there, I'd take an hour and go into the basement to run my regular self-defense class, where I got to stretch my legs showing a group of women how to turn mashers into mashed potatoes.

No stretching this time. My butt was in that chair for six hours, minus two five-minute bathroom breaks and a quick trip to the kitchen to ask Mrs. Campbell to slap some of that ham she was feeding our guests onto a couple slices of bread.

When I did that, I was surprised to find Holly sitting at the kitchen table. She had a mouth full of ham, so she was only able to give me a thumbs-up. But she was back and alive and had not been abducted and murdered by Louis Ballard, which might seem like a foolish worry, but when you're in this business, a murderous pet store clerk is within the realm of possibility.

As for the other cases that came through the door that day, none were as swift and satisfyingly solved as Mrs. Norton's, and my elation at that early success swiftly faded.

I could spend a dozen chapters recounting the assortment of failures and frustrations, but I won't. The only one I'll tell you about are the Zhaos.

The mother, Li-Hua, was supposedly around sixty but looked eighty. Maybe it was the sag in her shoulders or the black lace-cuffed dress that was more like something out of Dickens than a New York department store.

The daughter, May, looked exactly her twenty-five years, and was at least wearing something from the current decade—an orange wrap dress in a white-carnation print. May did most of the talking. When Li-Hua spoke, it was in Chinese, which her daughter translated.

Their husband and father, Junfeng, had been a toy maker specializing in hand-carved pieces with mechanical innards—trains that rolled, soldiers that marched, bears that waved. They used the past tense because he'd been killed the last weekend in September, shot to death at his workshop, which was located in an alley off Mott Street. The victim of an apparent robbery.

"He never kept much money at his workshop," May explained. "All he had was his wallet. To kill him for that? It makes no sense."

I could have told them that most crime doesn't make sense. People get murdered for pocket change, and sometimes for nothing at all.

The mother went on a tear, and I waited patiently for the translation.

"Everyone loved him," May said. "His customers. The other shopkeepers. For every three pieces he made, he gave one away. That was the kind of man he was. But the police, they do nothing. They ask questions about enemies. About gangs. One of them asked about Tongs. As if it were forty years ago."

I asked some questions, got some details. The address of the workshop, the stores Mr. Zhao sold to, names of other shopkeepers, his schedule. Zhao's hand-crafted toys were so highly sought-after and took so long to create that Christmas orders started arriving in March.

Sometimes he worked so late he would sleep on a cot in his workshop, which is what he was doing the night he was killed. All of this was passed on from mother to daughter to me.

After I finished jotting down her answers, Li-Hua spoke again, only a few words this time.

"Where is your toilet?" May asked.

I gave her directions, and she passed them on to her mother. Once Li-Hua was out the door, May turned back to me, the neutral face of the dutiful daughter gone. She looked disdainfully at my notes.

"I told her we shouldn't come here."

"Fair enough," I said. "Mothers and daughters don't always agree."

"My mother is . . . hopeful," she said, smoothing her dress against her knees. "Both of my parents are. Were. My father was a great craftsman. He could have made furniture. Or art. He could have carved friezes for fancy Manhattan hotels, but he made toys because he liked the smiles of the children."

"That's very sweet."

"Yes. Sweet."

She said the word with acid instead of sugar.

"You think differently?" I asked.

She shook her head. "No. He was sweet and kind and hopeful. So is my mother. Though they have no right to be. They saw their friends and family slaughtered in Peking because they were Christians. They escaped here. When they arrived, they were treated like dogs. My mother destroyed her body working in a cannery. Four miscarriages. She still prays for their souls. I was their miracle child. Their reward for so much misery. Except it didn't stop, did it? During the war people spat on us as we passed them on the sidewalk because they thought we were Japanese. Still, my parents believe America is a good place."

"But you don't."

"I was born here," she said, as if that explained everything.

I guess it did.

"The one thing my mother and I agree on is that the police will do nothing. Nearly a month and not a word. They will never find my father's killer because they do not care."

"We've had success where the police haven't."

"Yes, but Lillian Pentecost is not here. She's in prison. How can she help us when she cannot even help herself?"

I tried to fumble out an answer, but May's mother chose that moment to come back into the office. The mother said something and the daughter replied in Chinese.

Li-Hua smiled at me, nodding vigorously.

"I told her you will try but that you promise nothing," May said, standing. "If you must contact us, you can reach me at PS Twenty-three. I am a teacher there. Please do not contact my mother. I do not want to get her hopes up any further."

With that last punch to the gut, they walked out.

CHAPTER **30**

Holly found me spread out in the middle of the office floor, staring at the ceiling, wishing the Egyptian rug were the sort that could lift up and fly me away.

"Was it that awful?" she asked, sitting cross-legged next to me.

"If you could dig the hole, I could probably manage to crawl in myself."

I went on to tell her about the Zhaos. I did not tell her about the Nortons, because who remembers your victories six hours after the fact.

As I talked, Holly moved the pair of us up to the sofa, maneuvered my head into her lap, and began untangling my curls with her nails in a not-unpleasant way.

"The daughter was right," I said. "Any other time, we'd be all over this case. Murdered toy maker getting ignored by the police. Ms. Pentecost would be wandering down Mott Street right now, knocking on doors. Don't get me wrong— I'll start digging. But right now it's third in line and I'm flying solo."

Holly tugged hard on a lock.

"Ow. Not entirely solo. How did it go with Louis Ballard?"

Seeing it upside down, it took a moment to decipher Holly's expression as a smile.

"You found something?"

"I found something."

She told me.

Holly had met Susie Beck's old co-worker at a café off Washington Square Park, a few blocks from where Ballard now worked as a clerk in a pet store.

Holly got everywhere an hour early, so she was already sitting outside the café when Ballard walked up: a man of about thirty, handsome but too thin, with peppery hair that had a dash of salt thrown in and ears you could get a real grip on. He was dressed in a sweater-slacks combo but carried a pair of brown coveralls with the name CHRISTOPHER STREET PETS stitched on the breast.

There was some awkwardness at first when Holly announced herself as my associate rather than the expected article. He had to be at work in twenty minutes, but the pair spent five of those talking about shared acquaintances, books they'd read, clubs they'd been to. Not exactly a secret handshake, but close enough.

Holly's pitch was exactly as we'd rehearsed it the night before.

"Her husband can't move on," she told Louis. "He still gets up, eats breakfast, goes to his job like everyone else. But inside he's stuck, trapped in the moment that he walked in and found his wife dead. Can you imagine that? He needs to understand why she did it. Or he'll never be free."

I'm sure she said it with her usual flutteriness, which can be very disarming. You want to answer her questions just to get her to be still.

"Susie was unhappy," Ballard began. "I could see that right off. That smile of hers was like my grandmother's china. Very pretty, but a spiderweb of cracks. That's probably why we got along. It was like looking in a mirror. Also, she grew up in a small town and I was a curiosity. I try to butch it up at work, but the girls always seem to know.

"When I found out her husband was a cop, I almost shut her out," he continued. "Then she explained he wasn't really a cop—that he took pictures. I saw him a couple of times. He seemed nice. Lowercase *n*, you know? That's why I didn't say anything before. Who wants to hurt a nice man like that? Also, the private detective who came around the first time was a bit of a jerk."

"What didn't you tell the jerk?" Holly asked.

"About Loverboy," he said. "She didn't like it when I called him that, but I was only teasing."

"Who was he?"

Louis shrugged.

"I never met him," he said. "She barely acknowledged his existence. I sort of figured it out on my own. She goes out for lunch one Tuesday and comes back and—well, you know how you can tell sometimes? Glowing and everything slightly askew. I asked her, 'Did you sneak out for some exercise? They say exercise is very important.' She turned absolutely crimson."

"Could it have been her husband?" Holly asked.

"I told you. He was nice with a lowercase *n*. Those sort don't make you glow."

According to Louis Ballard, these lunchtime liaisons commenced sometime around January of 1946 and continued until shortly before Susie Beck died. Throughout that time, he continued to tease and she continued to keep mum. But he noticed that those cracks in her visage were starting to mend.

One morning, while the two of them were alone in the supply room, sorting through old travel brochures to decide which ones could be tossed, Susie Beck asked him apropos of nothing, "Have you ever been with someone who really makes you feel alive?"

When Louis asked if she was referring to Loverboy, she clammed up.

"Another time I said something cheeky about how she better watch out because men can gossip, too. She said something like, 'Not when he has just as much to lose.'"

Then one morning she came in an hour late and the cracks were back and twice the size.

"I asked what happened and she gave some story about breaking a heel and having to go back to change. She could barely say it without bursting into tears."

That was the first week of July. Two weeks later, Susie Beck was dead.

"Did she ever let Loverboy's name slip?" I asked Holly. She shook her head.

"I asked Louis," she said. "Several times. Too many, probably. I think he was getting annoyed with me. He said she was always very careful not to say too much."

However, because the travel agency wasn't a thrill-a-minute gig, Louis had been living vicariously through Susie and had made some observations.

She always walked in the direction of the subway for her long lunches, so their liaisons likely weren't held near the office. She never wore any new jewelry. No new clothes. But at least once a week, she'd come in with a box of cherry cordials, her favorite treat.

"How do you know they weren't from her husband?" Holly asked Louis.

"Three reasons," Louis told Holly. "First, they were from a very upscale shop. Somebody was trying to impress, and husbands generally don't make the effort. Second, she always left the box at work. Never took it home. See? And third—you really only had to see her eat one of those cordials. She was reminiscing, if you get me."

Holly got him. So did I. By now we were off the sofa. I was at my desk, Holly in one of the armchairs usually reserved for clients.

"I think I like Louis," I told her. "If he gets bounced from the pet shop, we should hire him as a stringer. Scratch that. We already have one. Good job, beautiful."

"Thank you," she said. "But don't praise me until you've heard the best part."

She was practically vibrating.

"What is it?" I asked.

She stood up and started pacing for the next bit, but you can't get much distance in our office, so she eventually settled for shifting from one foot to the next.

"You know how I kept asking him if she ever mentioned his name and he said no, no, no, she didn't. The whole point of having a secret lover is to keep him a secret. But as I was leaving, I asked one last time, and he said, and I quote, 'She never said his name, but I'm sure she wrote it down in her diary.'"

It was a solid three seconds before my tongue caught up to my brain.

"Diary?"

"Apparently she wrote in it during slow stretches at work."

"Am I getting forgetful or was there not anything about a diary in that heap that Wally Beck gave us?"

"There was not. But . . ."

"But?"

"When I first started writing, really writing, I didn't want my mother to know. Not because she wouldn't have approved, although I'm not terribly sure she would have if she'd known exactly the sort of things I was writing about. Anyway, I wanted to keep it to myself for a while, so I never worked on my stories at home. Always when I was out or she was at work."

A secret diary for Susie Beck. Because she was scribbling things she didn't want her husband to know. Things she didn't even want to write about when he was in the next room. Like lunchtime rendezvous and cherry cordials.

"So," Holly said, flopping back down in the armchair. "Did I do good?"

I went over and kissed her.

"You did great," I said. "But in the future, how about you lead with the secret diary, okay?"

"I have to go in order, Will. You know that. Besides," she added with a little smile, "the suspense is half the fun."

CHAPTER 31

Holly and I discussed Loverboy: meeting somewhere remote; no names; no gifts that couldn't be gobbled. Men weren't usually so careful for the woman's sake.

Then there was what Susie said about him having just as much to lose. The last case Ms. P and I worked, there was a woman who had a secret lover and it had taken us far too long to clue into the fact that the secret was he was married.

Not this time. Susie Beck was having an affair with a married man and wrote about it in her diary.

Holly and I went through Beck's file. No married men stuck out as good candidates.

"What do we do now?" Holly asked.

"*We* do nothing," I said. "I need to pay a visit to our favorite extortionist."

I told myself I needed to see Beck to grill him about married men in their circle. Really, I was hoping that this progress—an actual, possible suspect in his wife's death—would be enough to appease him. It wasn't an answer, but it was proof we weren't shirking.

I hoped it would be enough to get Ms. P free.

Beck's apartment was on the fifth floor of an unassuming building in Jackson Heights. It was a popular neighborhood for young families—the kind of place that tried to achieve small-town charm with big-city excitement and only half failed at both.

I'd called ahead to make sure Beck was there. He was. He demanded to know what I wanted to talk about. Since infidelity is a touchy subject to introduce over the phone, I demurred.

He was already asking questions when he opened the lobby door. Questions all the way up the stairs.

"What did you find?"

"Was she killed?"

"What does Lillian Pentecost think?"

He asked that last three times between the stoop and his fifth-floor apartment.

"I don't know what she's thinking because she's in prison and Ma Bell doesn't service cell number 302, you selfish piece of shit" was what I wanted to say. But I managed to hold my tongue until we were in the apartment, sitting in a pair of upholstered armchairs.

It was one of the saddest places I've ever seen, and I've seen a lot.

Taken as a snapshot, the apartment was cheery enough. Lots of light, yellow-daffodil wallpaper in the kitchen, embroidered pillows in the living room. Clearly decorated with a woman's touch and unchanged by Beck since his wife's death.

But the door to the bathroom was open, and I could see the edge of the tub. I'd seen it before in celluloid black and white and featuring Susie Beck's slit-open wrist.

Then there were the photos. All over the walls of the living room were photographs of Susie, some of which Beck had included in his file. Almost all were of her caught unawares: moments of repose, reading a book, looking out the window. Never looking at the camera. Wistful, I would have said.

Knowing about her lover, though, I saw them in a different light. A woman with a secret.

Beck was sitting across from me, barely on the edge of his seat, back hunched even more than usual, hands gripping his knees like he was front-row on a coaster at Coney.

I saw him in a different light, too.

Middle of the afternoon on a Sunday, lounging in corduroys and an oversize sweater that looked like a stiff breeze would unravel it. No radio playing. No book open on the arm of the chair.

What had he been doing? Sitting quietly in the same apartment where he found his wife dead, staring at the wall? What kind of man did that?

The same kind who would come up with a plan to frame my boss so she'd take his case, that's what.

I held my tongue and kept it professional.

"Mr. Beck, did you go through your wife's belongings after her death?"

He was expecting a statement, not a question, but he fielded it anyway.

"Yes," he said. "I never . . . I mean, everything is still here. But I went through it."

"Did you find a diary?"

"She didn't keep a diary."

"She was seen by a co-worker writing in a diary," I said.

He shook his head.

"Susie didn't keep a diary. She wasn't . . . I mean, she wasn't the sort."

"What do you mean, she wasn't the sort?"

"To write things down like that.

"Maybe it was an address book," he added helpfully. "She had one of those."

"You said all her things are still here. I'd like to make a search if you wouldn't mind."

"Looking for this diary? I told you, she didn't keep one."

"Maybe she did and you never saw it," I suggested.

I want to draw your attention to the fact that I was trying to be nice and circumspect and what was about to happen was as much Beck's fault as mine.

"Why wouldn't I see it?" Beck asked. "While I might not be Lillian Pentecost, it's still my job to notice things, Miss Parker."

"A woman sometimes . . . she sometimes likes to have some things to herself—you understand?"

Beck obviously didn't.

"What do you imagine she wrote in this diary?"

This guy. All I wanted to do was search his wife's things. I could have broken in when he was at work—should have broken in, because then I wouldn't have to see his placid, nobody face and have him ask stupid questions.

"What would she write? Well, Walter, sometimes wives have thoughts. Things they don't want their husband to know. Because women are people with feelings and desires and occasionally they like to write those things down."

But Walter was a cop, or at least he worked with them. He could put two and two together.

"You think she wrote about something in particular, don't you?" he said. "Her murderer? Do you think she wrote about her murderer? Why would you think that?"

I was really getting tired of his answering-my-question-with-a-question shtick.

"I'm going to ask you a question and I want you to think hard about it," I said. "What married couples were you and your wife friends with?"

"Why do you want to know about married couples?" Beck asked.

"Just answer the question, Walter."

He appeared to give it some thought.

"There's no one," he said eventually. "We didn't really do those things. Dinner parties and all that."

"What about married men?" I asked. "Any of those hanging around? Someone in the building, maybe?"

"Why do you want to know that?"

My face was getting hotter and hotter. He must not have noticed my freckles disappearing in a wash of red, because he kept at it.

"Why are you asking about married men?"

"Because we have reason to believe your wife was having an affair. With a married man."

He started shaking his head before I got to the second sentence.

"No, no, no. That's ridiculous. Susie was not— That's ridiculous. Where did you hear that?"

"From a co-worker. She was seeing someone before she died and wrote about it in a—"

"Which co-worker?" he snapped. "Which one? Was it that man?"

His tone made it clear there were some very strong quotation marks around *man*.

"I met him once. You can't trust that sort. They make things up all the time."

"This is good news, Walter," I said, clenching my jaw to keep from shouting. "This means someone might have had a motive to kill her."

Beck was shaking his head like a dog with a flea in its ear.

"No, no, no. Susie was not having an affair. She wasn't like those other girls. I told you that. You need to go back to that fairy and find out why he lied. Because he is lying. He's making up a story. You should look at him. Maybe he did it. Maybe Susie found out something about him and threatened to tell."

I took a breath. It was meant to be a calming one, but it was like tossing coal into an overheated boiler.

"Listen here, you little shit." And, yeah, this time I really said it. "This is what you wanted. You wanted us digging into your wife. You wanted it so much you framed Lillian Pentecost for murder. Now here I am, giving you an honest-to-God lead.

I'm sorry it destroys the romantic fantasy you've built in your head, but that's the job."

We were on our feet now, facing off like pugilists in a daffodil-wallpapered ring.

"You are going to sit down with me and we're going to figure out who this other man could be," I told him.

"There was no other man!"

I stepped forward and grabbed him by the collar. He didn't move back, didn't grab for my arms. That only made me angrier. That he wasn't taking this, or me, seriously.

"Then you're going to go get that real bullet and march right down to the nearest precinct house, or I swear to God—"

I felt the gun barrel press into my stomach.

"It's a Mauser C96," Beck said. His breathing was short and quick, but the words came calm enough. "I brought it back from the war."

As if its provenance was what I was concerned about. He must have had the thing tucked into his waistband underneath that sweater the whole time.

"Look, Walter—"

"I'm not stupid, Miss Parker," he said. "I knew you could come here and try to force me. I am resolved. You must understand that. I am resolved."

He stepped back so the barrel wasn't poking me anymore. But he kept the gun trained on me while he moved to the door and opened it.

"Please leave."

I walked out into the hall and turned.

"My wife was not unfaithful," he said. "Please keep looking. I don't like . . . I don't like doing any of this."

He shut the door in my face.

CHAPTER **32**

From the journals of Lillian Pentecost

This week is very difficult to write about.

On Saturday Val and I returned from lunch to find our cell smelling like a latrine. Someone had urinated on our mattresses.

We informed a guard and were told it would take a few days to replace them and that we should flip them over and make do. It was implied we had soiled them ourselves.

"You act up like this, you're going to have to sleep in the consequences."

On Sunday I was delivered a basket of food from Eleanor. Cured sausages and apples and a dozen of her famous scones.

"Whatever that is, it smells like heaven," Val said when it arrived.

When I opened it, a rat leapt out. Had I been a half-second slower, its jaws would have clamped on my hand. As it was, it still nipped a finger. Then it ran to the door, squeezing its body through the narrow gap at the bottom and disappearing into the depths of the prison.

The food was scattered on the floor, my finger was bleeding, and I heard quiet chuckling. I looked out the barred window of our cell door to see Andrews there in the hall, grinning like a schoolboy who'd stolen the sweets.

"Nobody likes a rat, do they?" he said, then walked away.

Val and I gathered up the food, but I was reluctant to eat it.

"You think he'd poison you?" Val asked.

"I think poison is unlikely. Though other . . . contaminants are possible."

He smelled one of the scones and took an experimental bite. Then a bigger one.

"You know what? I'm gonna chance it."

On Monday I woke up and knew it was going to be a bad day. It started as many bad days do, with a worsening of the always-present ache, beginning in the smaller joints and progressing throughout the rest of my body as the day went on.

My balance on the way to breakfast was acceptable, but on the way back was starting to suffer. By the afternoon, the dysarthria had begun. It is certainly not the most debilitating symptom of my disease, but it is one of the most frustrating.

The muscles of my entire vocal apparatus become weak. My speech slurs, and it is difficult to modulate breath and volume.

Then came the tremors, which made writing impossible.

It is a cruel thing not being able to communicate when you are in pain.

To paraphrase Will, I was very much hoping that my bad day would not become a bad week. Or longer.

As it happens, it was a bad five days. The symptoms continued through today, Friday, with Wednesday being the worst of it. On Wednesday I stayed in my bed the entire day. Val was kind enough to bring me food from the dining hall, though my appetite was hardly robust.

It was during the evening meal that it happened.

I was alone on my bed, trying desperately to sleep, when I

heard the cell door swing open. I assumed it was Val returning from dinner. Then I felt something poke me hard in the ribs.

I opened my eyes. Andrews was standing over me, nightstick in hand.

"Howdy," he said.

I tried to rise, but he pushed the nightstick into my chest and I fell back.

He cocked his head and smiled.

"You really are as weak as a kitten."

I thought about calling for help, but my voice was all but gone. Besides, who would answer? I tried to remember the various self-defense techniques I'd learned over the years. The things Will has taught me. None seemed possible. Not in the state I was in.

With no possibility of defense or escape, I was determined to at least learn the reason for this torment. I managed to croak out a single word.

"Why?"

His smile vanished.

"Why? Why do you think, you . . ." I saw understanding dawn across his face. "You don't know who I am, do you?"

Understanding was replaced with anger.

"You cost me my life and you don't even remember."

I tried to think. Sort through my memory for a former police officer named Andrews. But it was difficult. My mind wouldn't cooperate. It was too clouded with fear.

"You wrote my lieutenant telling him I was selling evidence out the back door. Ten years on the job and all of it gone because of you. My wife walked out on me. Took our son. Now I'm here. Corralling the animals."

Of course. Derrick Andrews. The evidence room sergeant who I'd discovered had a sideline selling evidence from murder cases. Whose client list included Jessup Quincannon.

It was one of many letters I'd sent this past year in my

efforts to keep Quincannon from pursuing his obsession. Still, I should have remembered.

He sat down at the foot of my bed, and I shrank back.

"Don't you worry," he said. "I'm not going to do anything. Not right now, anyway."

He patted my leg.

"We've got all the time in the world, don't we? Murder trials take a long while to get going. Lot of things can happen."

There were voices from down the hall. Women returning to their cells after dinner. Andrews stood, went to the open door, and looked outside.

"Guess I gotta go," he said, then turned back to me. "Now, you get better, all right. Don't want you dying on me."

He smiled again. It was perhaps the most awful smile I've ever seen on a human face. I squeezed my eyes tight against it. When I opened them, he was gone and the door was shut. I hadn't even heard it close.

I am not too proud to admit that I cried. I was still crying when Val returned. At first, he assumed I was in pain because of my symptoms. I thought about keeping Andrews's visit a secret. But Val is my roommate, and very much in the line of fire. He deserved to know.

It took some time, my voice being what it was.

"Jesus Christ, Lil," he said when I finally finished. "We should tell someone, but . . ."

But who? The casual abuse of prisoners by guards was hardly novel. And it was my word against his.

"You got anyone on the outside who could . . ." Again, Val trailed off.

"Who . . . could what?" I managed to ask.

"Pay him a visit?" he suggested.

I considered the possibility. There were people I knew who would gladly pay a visit to Derrick Andrews. But that would likely only make him angrier, and might escalate his plans for revenge.

The only way to stop him would be to kill him. I cannot ask someone to do that. There are lines I will not cross. Not again.

This means I can tell no one. Not Mr. Whitsun. He would certainly use it to press for my bail, which would likely fail.

Not Will. She would kill Andrews. I'm certain of it. She is loyal and ruthless when she needs to be. Cunning enough to get away with murder. But I've seen how killing someone—even someone who deserves it—weighs on her.

No one can know about Andrews.

I will have to find a way to deal with him on my own.

I asked Val to tell no one, and he reluctantly agreed.

"I don't know what you did to that guy who took your eye," he said, "but you might have to do it again."

Perhaps. But I was a younger woman then, and the circumstances were very different.

I can take other action, though. It will be risky. Foolish, even. But necessary.

My symptoms have now eased to the point where I can hold a pencil. I have asked to make a phone call. I will tell Mr. Whitsun my intentions.

He will not be happy.

Then I will meet with Will and Dr. Hubbard and do my best to behave as if I'm on the mend.

Even though I have written these pages in code, I might still destroy them. Or perhaps not.

I am very tired.

CHAPTER **33**

"She wants to do what?"

I had the receiver pressed between ear and shoulder while I worked on turning my face into Nurse Palmer's, so I assumed I'd misheard.

"She wants the goddamn case expedited," Whitsun repeated. "No delays. No motions. Speedy as it can get."

"Hang on," I said, putting down the compact. "This is Ms. Pentecost? She's asking for this?"

"Pearl and I met with her this morning. She wants to get to trial as quick as possible."

"That doesn't make any sense," I said. "You told her we need more time, right?"

"I explained it six ways from Sunday. She wasn't having it. She was . . . I don't think she was feeling all that good."

A week ago, she'd been fine. Okay, not fine, but hanging in there. What had happened to make her want to leap in front of a jury when there was so much work left to do?

The previous five days had been less than productive, though not for lack of trying.

On Monday I took another run at the caterers. This time they didn't even open the door to me.

On Tuesday I paid a visit to Quincannon's. I'd called ahead and Alathea told me that Silas Culliver was ensconced in Quincannon's office working on preparing the dead man's financials for the audit.

For ten minutes, he didn't even acknowledge my presence, just kept mashing away at his adding machine. Undeterred, I tossed questions at him and tried to read the answers from the gleam off his bald head.

"You went upstairs to talk to Quincannon that night. What did you two discuss?

"What was his mood? Did he seem worried?

"What about his finances? Did anyone at that party owe him money?

"Where did he meet Billy Muffin? Did you find him for Quincannon? Where did you dig him up? Is he there now? Has he been in touch?"

Nothing.

"What about the will?" I asked. "Whitsun was supposed to get a copy of that last week. Judge's orders."

Finally, Culliver looked up.

"I will have a messenger deliver a copy to him," he said. "Anything else will require a subpoena. Now, if you don't mind, Miss Parker, I have work to do."

As Alathea showed me out, she commented, "From your questions, I take it you haven't had much success."

It would have been pointless to lie, so I told her, "Yeah, I'm getting all lemons."

"But you're still convinced Lillian Pentecost didn't kill Mr. Quincannon."

It wasn't quite a question, but I answered it anyway.

"I'm positive," I said. Then I added, "The bullet's a frame-up. Problem is the frame and the killing were done by different people."

I don't know why I told her that. Frustration, I suppose.

"Interesting," she said, as she unlocked the gate. "My offer stands, Miss Parker. If you need assistance, please let me know."

I told her I would, though I couldn't imagine a scenario where I'd take her up on it.

That afternoon, Holly moved back into her apartment. Her help with the Beck case was done, and she had her own work to do—revisions on her novel and an endless stream of stories to write for the pulps.

That night, I changed for bed, but didn't lie down. My mattress still held Holly's shape, my sheets the lingering smell of Chesterfields. Sleep suddenly seemed impossible.

I got dressed and went for a drive. Chinatown. The Zhao murder. I had this fantasy of getting some brilliant Pentecostian bolt from the blue.

I found Junfeng Zhao's workshop—or what used to be his workshop. It was a narrow room with a door that opened onto an alley off Mott Street. The door was chained shut, but I was able to peer through the crack. It looked like somebody had moved in. A seamstress, I guessed, by the rolls of fabric in the corner.

I circled the block, walking into every shop and restaurant that was still open, asking questions.

I found a few people who admitted to knowing Zhao, but that was about the extent of what they'd tell me. One grocery owner who I caught in the middle of locking up for the night told me the police had already covered that ground.

"They ask me about a car," he said.

"What kind of car?"

"Chevy sedan. Dark blue."

Someone, the police didn't say who, had seen it parked around the corner from Zhao's workshop. A dark blue Chevy. About the most common car on the road.

The grocer might have been thinking the same thing.

"They will never find who did it. It was nobody. A thief," he said. Then added, "It's late. You should go home, miss."

That's what I did.

I slept in late on Wednesday and was awoken by a call from Jules—my reformed cat-burglar friend. He'd been out of the country and had just returned. He confirmed that, yes, he'd been the one Alathea had hired to burglar-proof Quincannon's mansion.

"No one is getting into that third floor unless they break into the first floor," Jules declared. "They will find that difficult. The locks, they are very good."

That limited my pool of suspects, and I didn't know if that was good or bad news.

Also on Wednesday, Culliver sent Whitsun a copy of the will. Pearl called me after they'd had a chance to sift through it.

"Not many surprises," she said. "Most of his money goes to various charities."

"Not many surprises suggests more than none."

"There was one. Quincannon willed ten thousand dollars to the Church of the Holy Redeemer. Did the Novarros say anything to you about that?"

They certainly hadn't.

That night I swung by the church as it was letting out. This time I wore the Hi-Power in a holster under my coat. While ten grand might have been pocket change to Quincannon, it was serious dough to the Novarros, and sinners don't hold the patent on temptation.

I made sure I had a good line of sight on both their faces when I asked them if they knew about the money Quincannon had bequeathed them. If they were faking their surprise, they'd taken time to practice.

"Maybe that's why he invited us that evening," Novarro suggested. "To tell us about the will."

"Why do you think he did it?" I asked. "You said he toyed with you, then blew you off."

"I have no idea why," he said. "God works in mysterious ways."

Thursday I finally got around to developing the rest of the photos from my tour of Quincannon's, which took me most of the day; I even took my meals in the darkroom.

My only break was when Max Roberts called in the afternoon.

"I wanted to give you a heads-up," he said. "I'm writing a story for the Sunday paper. A retrospective of Lillian Pentecost's career. It's mostly a rehash of previous stories I've written. But . . . my editor asked for additional context."

"What kind of context?" I asked.

"He had me talk to this doctor—guy at Bellevue—about multiple sclerosis."

I was already dreading the rest.

"He told me it can impact a person's mind over time. He explained how it can impede judgment and make someone more emotional and . . . prone to poor decision-making."

I thought about what Backstrom had said about using Ms. P's disease as a defense. It felt like giving up. Worse than giving up. It would be flushing her career down the toilet.

"Just because he said it doesn't mean you have to print it," I told him.

"My editor knows about the quote, so . . . I kind of do," he said. "But I've got room for a quote from you. Or from her. But I need you to get it to me by—"

I hung up. If I hadn't, I would have started yelling at Max, and he didn't deserve it.

Okay, maybe he did. But he wasn't the one I wanted to yell at.

I'd called Walter Beck at least three times a day for the previous five days. He wasn't answering. I called Lazenby, and he told me Beck was out of work with the flu.

Flu, my ass. He couldn't handle the truth about his wife, and he was making my boss suffer for it.

I woke Friday dreading my visit with Ms. P. I'd have to tell her how badly I'd blown it with Beck. I was putting my face on and practicing how to break the news when Whitsun called and told me about her order to expedite the trial.

"I'm seeing her in half an hour," I told him. "I'll talk some sense into her."

"You'd better," he said. "If we went to trial today, it'd be a gimme for Bigelow. Although maybe his case isn't as strong as he'd like us to think."

"What makes you say that?"

"He called to talk deal. Fifteen years with the possibility of parole," Whitsun said. "You don't start talking deals this early—especially not with a sure thing. We need time to find where the crack in his case is."

"Does Ms. Pentecost know about the deal?" I asked.

Whitsun made a noise that was a bunch of vowels strung together. "I'm taking my time getting it to her. My worry is she'd take it."

"I'll talk to her."

"You'd better."

"You said that already," I told him.

"I know," he told me. "I'm driving the point home."

Twenty minutes later I was standing by the curtain-enclosed bed with Dr. Hubbard planning out everything I needed to tell Ms. P. There was Louis Ballard and Loverboy and my confrontation with Beck; my call with Jules; my one-way conversation with Culliver; and Quincannon's will and the ten grand he left the Novarros.

Then there was Bigelow's deal and Whitsun's belief it meant the case against Ms. P had a crack in it. Was it possible Bigelow had found out about Beck? About the bullet swap?

I was still debating whether to tell her about that last item when the clinic door opened and a guard escorted Ms. P across the room. Except by "escort," I mean she was responsible for keeping my boss upright. Ms. P didn't so much sit on the bed as crumple. The guard left and I closed the curtain.

"On your way up or down?" Hubbard asked her, meaning was she heading into a bad stretch or on her way out of one.

Her index finger pointed skyward.

"How bad has it been? On a scale of one to ten."

She held up five fingers.

"That means it was a seven," I told Hubbard.

Ms. P shook her head.

"Not . . . that bad."

Three words, and she could barely get them out. It wasn't a mystery anymore why she was pushing for a speedy trial. If she was like this after a few weeks, what would she be after the months that it usually took for a defendant to go to trial for murder?

How could I stand here and tell her not to worry? That everything would be fine? How could I say that with a straight face when she was suffering like this?

"Nurse Palmer?"

Hubbard was looking at me like he'd said my name more than once.

"Yes?" I said, my voice cracking almost as bad as Ms. P's.

"I think I'm going to need the full time with my patient today," he said, kind but firm.

That meant no whispered updates. No distractions for my boss while Hubbard worked to determine how bad things were and how worse they might get.

"You can, of course, assist if you wish," he added.

I shook my head.

"I'm going to go. There's . . . um . . . there's nothing we need to talk about."

I put a hand on Ms. P's shoulder and said, "It's going to be okay. Understand?"

She gave a small, shaky nod.

Then I walked out, muttering something to the clinic doctor about there being another patient I needed to see to. He found a guard to escort me back to the front entrance.

Without Hubbard at my side, I was subject to more whistles and hoots from the prisoners, but I wasn't hearing them.

All I could think about was what I was going to do about Walter Beck.

I was still thinking that as I walked through the open door into the cold, crisp air of the last day of October.

October gone already? How did that happen?

I walked through the Village, noticing for the first time the carved pumpkins sitting on doorsteps. I tore the blond wig off, bobby pins yanking out some of my own hair in the process, and stuffed it in my bag. Then I proceeded to the drugstore and used their pay phone.

There were two paths I could take with Beck.

I'd tried directness and that had gotten me the barrel of a Mauser in my stomach. The smart play now would be softness and sincerity. Sit him down and talk to him as honestly as I could.

Ms. Pentecost was ill. She couldn't handle prison. He needed to come forward now, or there wouldn't be anyone left to investigate his wife's death.

I'm not sure I could do that without crying, but it was long past time to take pride out behind the woodshed and shoot it.

Holly would be good to take along. She could do sincerity and honesty like no one's business. She was accidentally insulting sometimes, but at least you knew she wasn't sweet-talking you.

What if he still said no? What then?

By the time I walked into the drugstore, I'd chosen a path.

I dropped a nickel and dialed.

CHAPTER **34**

Halloween night, driving through the streets of Queens, homing in on Beck's apartment.

Clouds had come in during the late afternoon, and now a steady drizzle was falling. There were still trick-or-treaters out, and I'd had to slam on the brakes multiple times to keep the Caddy from turning a goblin into a ghost.

"We should park a few blocks away."

I turned to the woman in the passenger seat.

"Why should we do that?" I asked.

"In case."

I didn't ask in case of what. I was afraid Alathea would tell me.

I'd chosen the other path. The one that involved pulling fingernails, though I hoped threats would be enough.

I'd told Alathea to dress to intimidate, and she'd delivered: narrow black slacks, a tight black sweater, a long white box coat under which she could have hidden a shotgun. With her porcelain complexion and that jet-black hair of hers, she looked like a Tourneur film come to life.

With my gray pinstripes and my fedora resting between us, we were a matching set of Halloween costumes: detective and femme fatale.

In stories like that, the detective really shouldn't trust the dame, but I was doing it anyway. She hadn't been surprised when I explained what Beck had done.

"That makes sense," she said. "When you said the bullet was a frame job, I knew it would have to be a police officer or someone close to them."

"You don't mind putting the screws to someone whose friends wear badges?"

I hadn't been able to see her shrug over the phone, but it was implied.

"He's interfering with discovering who killed my employer," she said.

That was that.

As per Alathea's suggestion, I parked the Caddy three blocks away from Beck's apartment. Then I opened the trunk and pulled out the suitcase holding the recorder—the one that usually lived in a secret compartment behind a bookshelf in our office. When Beck started talking, I wanted it on tape.

I also pulled some goodies out of the hidden compartment in the Caddy's trunk: lock picks, handcuffs, and a Smith & Wesson .38 that I'd taken off a mook who had thought it was a good idea to try robbing my favorite deli while I was waiting for a late-night pastrami and cheese.

I hoped I wouldn't have to use it, but I needed to get that Mauser away from him. If a bullet happened to intersect with his kneecap, I preferred it be one that couldn't be traced back to me.

We walked there in the rain, Alathea carrying the umbrella while I carried the case, our respective boot heels tapping out a two-part melody on the wet concrete.

"We start with the wife," I said as we walked, reiterating the plan I'd outlined over the phone. "She's his soft spot. He can't stand to even think she might have been unfaithful. I say I'll put it out for everyone to see. From prison, Lillian Pentecost proves that a year-old suicide might have been murder."

"Might it?"

"Who cares? As long as the story includes the phrase 'Susie Beck's lover.' If that doesn't work, I threaten to call Lazenby. Beck can deny it, but I think Lazenby can make sure his career is over. And if that doesn't work . . ."

I didn't have to say the rest. Didn't want to say the rest.

That's why I'd called Alathea. When put to the test, I wasn't sure I was capable of torture. If I faltered, I needed somebody there who wouldn't.

I found myself having second thoughts for the tenth time. Like the previous nine, I thought about my boss sitting there, struggling to get words out, willing to play chicken with the justice system because she knew she couldn't go the distance in that joint.

She'd hate this. When she found out, I might not have a job anymore. But if it worked, she'd be free.

Holly wouldn't like it, either. She was at a Halloween party Marlo and Brent were throwing. I'd begged off. I wasn't in the mood for crowds, I said, but she should go alone.

"You're going to miss seeing me in my cat costume," she said on the phone.

"You can put on the ears for me some other time."

"Promise?"

She told me to not stay up too late typing out notes, told me she loved me and would miss me, and we said goodbye. Right after that I left to pick up Alathea.

One burnt bridge at a time.

My lock picks made quick work of Beck's lobby door. We'd just stepped inside when a young couple came out of the stairwell with a two-foot skeleton in tow.

Alathea turned her head to the side, and I followed suit. No use taking chances.

Then we were up the stairs to the fifth floor and Apartment 514.

I held my hand over the peephole and knocked. No answer. I knocked again, louder this time.

I took my hand away.

"Come on, Beck," I called. "Open up."

A door down the hall cracked open and a wizened face poked out, peering at us from behind cat's-eye glasses.

"Hello, ma'am," I said, putting on my winningest smile. "We're spreading the word of the Lord. Do you have a—"

The face darted away and the door shut firmly behind it.

Alathea looked at me. "The word of the Lord?"

"It was the scariest thing I could think of."

I got out my picks again. Either Beck was there and not answering, or he wasn't there, and we could start scouring the place for the bullet. I was about to try the first skeleton key when Alathea tried the knob.

"It's not locked," she said.

She cracked the door open and we both smelled it at the same time: blood.

I drew my .38, Alathea an ugly snub-nosed revolver. I went in first, slipping to the side, making way for Alathea to come in after. She was taller and could fire over my head.

There'd be no shooting. We saw that right away. The apartment looked like a cyclone had hit it. Cushions had been torn open, furniture overturned; in the kitchen all the drawers and cabinets were open and cutlery and canned goods were scattered everywhere.

The reason there would be no shooting was lying on the floor of the living room, right in the eye of the storm—Walter Beck. He looked like he'd been dead for a while.

We searched the rest of the apartment. The storm had visited the bedroom, too. The mattress had been thrown off the bed, the closet emptied, clothes piled high in a corner. Half the baseboards had even been pried away from the walls.

The bathroom was untouched, though. I wondered if that

was because the killer ran out of time or if they had found what they were looking for.

Satisfied there were no murderers waiting to leap, we went back to the body. I knelt in an area clear of blood and debris and got as close as I could without touching.

He was curled on his side, the Mauser clutched in his right hand. There was a bullet hole on the underside of his chin and a corresponding, messier one on the crown of his head.

I looked up. A thick spray of congealed blood marked the ceiling above the body.

I leaned closer and sniffed the barrel of the gun. If there was gunpowder lingering, I couldn't smell it over the blood. I took a handkerchief out of my pocket and used it to check the magazine. I counted rounds.

One bullet fired.

Divorced from everything else, I would have said suicide. But there was a lot of everything else. The apartment cyclone, for one. Also, Beck's shirt was untucked and torn open, with several buttons missing. His knuckles were scraped, and there was a long, thin scratch along his cheek. I checked the Mauser's gunsight and found a fleck of skin still attached to it.

"Will."

I looked up, startled at the use of my first name and the worry in Alathea's voice.

"We should leave," she said.

I shook my head.

"We have to find the bullet. The one Beck replaced."

"A bullet is small enough to hide anywhere," she reminded me. "If it's still here at all."

She was right. Even if the killer hadn't gotten to it, finding the bullet could take hours. During which we'd be sharing a room with the corpse of a police photographer.

I tiptoed my way through the mess, and we left as quickly and quietly as we could. Twenty seconds later we were back in the rain. Two minutes after that, we were in the Caddy moving south on rain-slick streets smeared with streetlights, dodging soldiers and ghouls and fairy godmothers.

All the while I thought about how I was going to have to tell Ms. Pentecost that our best hope of setting her free had turned into a pumpkin, and there was no magic wand in the world that was going to bring him back.

The good news was that I didn't have to wait a whole week for Nurse Palmer to break the news about Beck. Judge Creed called a hearing on Monday to discuss Ms. Pentecost's request for an expedited trial.

Whitsun managed to wrangle a private room where we could conference before the session, and I talked him into giving me five minutes alone with her.

She was still wearing the eye patch, but she was back in her own clothes for the event—a worsted wool suit in chestnut brown. Skirt instead of trousers, though. Something about how if her roommate wasn't allowed to wear pants, she wouldn't either.

I didn't know and I didn't ask.

I'd had the full weekend to think about how to tell her everything that needed to be told. I'd even canceled our open house once again. She wouldn't be happy, but there were bigger disappointments in store.

I gave them to her quick, like pulling off a Band-Aid: Ballard and my blowup with Beck, the radio silence followed by finding his body. I didn't even skirt around why I'd had Alathea riding shotgun.

To that, all she asked was, "What are Alathea's intentions now?"

"She intends to keep her mouth shut," I said. "When I

dropped her off at Quincannon's, she asked that I leave her name out of it if the police come calling. Which they probably will. At least one neighbor saw us."

"Your interpretation of the scene?"

"Beck was killed with his own gun," I said. "Probably while he was still holding it. I'm going to rule out suicide on account of how roughed up he was. I think there was a fight. Beck comes in and finds somebody tossing his place. He pulls his gun; there's a struggle for it; the gun goes off. Beck loses the coin flip."

She motioned for me to continue.

"My guess is Beck's killer and Quincannon's share a set of fingerprints. Somehow he or she figures out Beck was the one who switched the bullet. I mean, the killer must have known somebody did it and figured they had the best luck in the world. But they needed to make sure that bullet stayed switched. So, break into Beck's, et cetera, et cetera, dead Walter. Now, unless Beck kept his own diary, which I doubt, there's no way to prove he swapped that bullet."

Ms. P sat silently for half a minute. I couldn't tell if she was nodding or rocking.

Finally, she said, "We should not discount the possibility that Mr. Beck's murder was related to his wife's death. That your investigation instigated something."

That had occurred to me, and I didn't like it. It would mean that said instigation came courtesy of one of Holly's phone calls. Also, it would mean there were two killers running around, and I was having trouble nailing down one.

"I won't discount it," I promised, "but right now we have to tell Whitsun and Pearl about Beck. We can't have them wasting energy figuring out how Quincannon was shot with your gun. And we need to put the brakes on this speedy-trial deal."

She shook her head.

"I will tell Mr. Whitsun about Beck and his tampering,"

she said. "But I will continue with my request for an expedited trial."

"Boss, you've got to—"

"Will."

She looked at me and I looked at her. Really looked at her. She was thinner, yeah. And paler. There were new hollows under her eyes and beneath those heavy cheekbones of hers. Like her flesh was slowly evaporating.

She hunched a little in her seat, and every time there was a noise in the hallway, her eyes darted to the door.

She seemed . . . fragile.

"All right," I said. "But you're telling Whitsun. I've broken my share of bad news for the day."

We invited Whitsun and Pearl in, and Ms. P spilled everything. While she was the one who'd ordered that Beck's tampering be kept a secret from the lawyers, I was the recipient of their wrath.

"I swear to God, Parker. I knew I should have gotten my own investigator. I knew it!" Whitsun said, seething. "We could have had this guy subpoenaed and under oath. We could have had a dozen investigators going over him with a fine-tooth comb."

I sat there and took it because I deserved it. Ms. Pentecost was the one who spoke up in our collective defense.

"Let's say that Mr. Beck came forward and confessed. What would it have changed?"

"What would it have changed? What would it have changed?"

I thought Whitsun's head was going to pop.

"If he was believed—and please consider that he had reason to want me beholden to him, so that is hardly a given—the district attorney would still have motive, means, and opportunity," Ms. P explained patiently. "I would still be the clearest and most convictable suspect. The only change in the state's case would be that I used a different gun and disposed of it on my way home."

Steam was still escaping from Whitsun's collar, but his boiler no longer seemed in danger of blowing. It was Pearl who found the crack in the argument.

"Every bit of that may be so," she said. "The fact remains that both of you lied to us. You turned down Walter Beck on three separate occasions in the past, and that makes him prejudiced against you. A prejudiced man was one of the first people at the crime scene. We could have made hay with that. Maybe we still can, but right now I don't see how."

Then she added, "Let me remind you that you only have this man's word that he didn't kill Quincannon himself."

I didn't think that last bit was likely, but it wasn't the time to argue. The rest of what she said was true, and Ms. Pentecost and I both knew it.

"Mr. Whitsun, Miss Jennings—I understand if you feel compelled to excuse yourself from this case," Ms. P said. "I won't hold it against either of you."

The pair of lawyers exchanged a look. Pearl nodded at her boss, who turned back to mine.

"You aren't the first client who's lied to me; you won't be the last," Whitsun said.

"This means no more focusing on finding the real killer," Pearl added, turning to me. "You need to look at everyone, whether you think they did it or not. We need every possible suspect trotted out for that jury. If we give them enough, maybe we can turn it into reasonable doubt. You understand what I'm saying?"

I nodded.

"Any chance I can talk you out of this expedited-trial nonsense?" Whitsun asked my boss.

"I'm afraid not," she said. "And I agree with Miss Jennings's direction to look at any and all suspects. Because I believe in our collective ability to solve this case. Not to merely provide reasonable doubt, but to demonstrate who, in fact, murdered Jessup Quincannon."

It was a good speech. I almost applauded.

I almost believed it.

The court hearing was short. That's what happens when the defense asks for something that the prosecution is all too happy to give. Judge Creed was the only hesitant party. He made Ms. Pentecost stand up and say directly that she wanted to go to trial as soon as possible.

"I do, Your Honor," she said.

"May I ask why," the judge queried.

"Because I'm of the opinion that an innocent person should not have to remain in prison any longer than necessary."

Creed reluctantly agreed to the defense's request and scheduled jury selection to begin the first day of December. Then he banged his gavel and made it official.

We had a month. Twenty-eight days, actually.

If there was a bucket underneath my seat, I might have thrown up into it.

After Ms. P had been escorted away, Max Roberts shouldered his way out of the herd of reporters and approached me. His story on Ms. P's career since she'd arrived in New York City had run the day before, and he'd been right: It had been mostly fair. It included all the big numbers: the Collins murder; the Sendak arsons; the Fennel case. Then he ruined it by quoting Dr. Whatshisname from Bellevue, whose description of multiple sclerosis ended the story on a "she's guilty as hell, but she's sick" note.

"Why's she doing this, Parker?"

Parker, not Will. He was mad at me for hanging up on him.

"You heard her," I said. "She's innocent."

"That's a horseshit answer, and you know it."

I grabbed him by the elbow and led him to a vacant corner away from the press and the peanut gallery.

"Maybe she wants to put her foot on the gas because every day she's in jail is another day when her reputation gets dragged through the mud," I growled.

"I warned you about the story," he said. "She had the chance to respond."

"Oh, yeah, you're one of the good ones."

"Compared to some of these guys, you better believe it."

"Here's a quote, Max: Go to hell. Don't call me again."

He stayed put for a moment, probably waiting to see if I was serious. I was. He walked back to the crowd of reporters, who were swarming Whitsun at the door to the courtroom.

I was getting up the gumption to push through the crowd when I felt a tap on my shoulder and I turned around.

It was Bigelow. Santa's favorite helper, in an overcoat and homburg.

"There's a back way out of the building," he said. "If you want to avoid the reporters."

When forced to choose between two devils, I like to pick the one who doesn't slap my face on the front page. He led me out the door that Judge Creed usually entered from, then down a short hallway to another door that opened on a narrow staircase.

"I appreciate the shortcut," I said, as he started down the staircase, with me a few steps behind. "But I'm too old to expect free favors. Especially from civil servants."

He turned back and smiled shyly.

"You caught me," he said. "I wanted to have a word."

"I'm not sure I feel comfortable doing that," I said. "Not without Whitsun present."

He nodded. Or at least I think he did. It was hard to tell from the back while mid-descent.

"I understand," Bigelow said. "Though he's the reason I wanted to talk with you alone. You see, I've made him an offer.

Or I've made his client an offer. But I don't think Mr. Whitsun is providing the best counsel. He made a few—well, a few disparaging remarks when I phoned."

"This is the offer for fifteen years, maybe parole?"

He looked back, surprised.

"He told you."

"He did," I said. "I don't know what disparaging remarks he used, but consider them seconded."

"It's a generous offer," Bigelow said. "Fifteen years. Less with good behavior. As opposed to life with no possibility of parole. I really do wish your employer would consider it."

"I'm not a lawyer," I told the back of his head, "but it seems a little early in the game to talk deals, doesn't it?"

He paused at the third-floor landing and turned to face me.

"Yes, it is," he said. "But I don't like to waste the court's time or resources. The sooner Ms. Pentecost accepts the deal, the sooner she can begin serving her time and the sooner she'll be free. Since Mr. Whitsun doesn't seem amenable, do you mind conveying that to her?"

Whitsun was right. There had to be a hole in their case. Bigelow was afraid that if he went to trial we'd find it and Ms. Pentecost would use it to slip free. But where was it?

"Miss Parker?"

Bigelow was looking back at me expectantly.

"Sorry," I said. "Woolgathering."

"What do you think? About talking with Miss Pentecost?"

I thought it was bull.

"I was thinking that this is bull," I said.

His fluffy white eyebrows shot up. "Excuse me?"

"This offer. Making it seem like you're doing my boss a good turn. Fifteen years, maybe ten. What a gift. Can you throw in a new stove? A genuine Westinghouse? I think your case is weak and you know it's weak. Somewhere there's a crack, and we're going to find it. You're tossing out a deal now so you can chalk up a conviction and not chance us making you look foolish in court. That's what I think."

I expected Bigelow to storm off in a huff. He just stood there, unfazed. He never blinked, never looked away. When I was finished, he glanced down at his hands like he was looking for crib notes.

Then he looked back up. If I had to nail his expression to a single word, it would be "pity."

"I imagine you've done some research on me, or Mr. Whitsun has," he began. "If so, then you know I don't usually handle cases like this. Big headline-grabbing affairs. Now I'm getting fifty calls a day from reporters. I imagine it's no better for you.

"To be honest, I find it all disgusting," he continued. "People are making money on a man's murder, on this trial. It's not only the papers. There's a betting line. Did you know that? I didn't. Someone else from the DA's office told me. As if it were business as usual. A betting line with the odds on a conviction."

I did know. Every morning I'd been calling to find if the line had shifted. As of that morning, the odds were four to one in favor of guilty.

"All that's to say, Miss Parker, that I have no interest in dragging this out," Bigelow said. "I realize the irony of it, considering Jessup Quincannon's hobbies, which I'm sure Forest Whitsun will lay out in detail for the jury. I, in turn, will reveal how he planned to abuse your employer, expose her family's history. I don't know the details, but the broad strokes are ugly enough. The papers will make a meal of it."

Somewhere on a floor above, a door swung open, the sound of it echoing down the stairwell. Bigelow started, as if he'd forgotten where he was.

Son of a bitch, I thought. He's on the level.

"There's no hole in your case, is there?"

He shook his head.

"There isn't," the white-haired elf said. "If we go to trial, I will absolutely prove the state's case and Lillian Pentecost will go to jail for the rest of her natural life."

He added, "To be honest, I don't think Jessup Quincannon is worth that."

"But it's worth fifteen years?" I asked.

"Ten with—"

A woman appeared above us on the stairs—a court stenographer wearing the quietest pumps ever made. Bigelow and I each took a quick step away from the other, like lovers caught necking.

She passed between us without a glance. Once she was out of earshot, he continued.

"Ten years with—"

"With good behavior. I know," I said. "For Ms. Pentecost, ten years is life."

That last was more to myself than the prosecutor, but he understood.

"I can recommend she be sent to a prison with good medical facilities," he told me. "Someplace where she can have her own cell. Someplace comfortable."

Bigelow had too much white hair to be that naïve. A prison was a prison. Some gave you a few more square feet, but Lillian Pentecost wasn't going to survive a decade in any of them.

"We should probably get moving," I said. "Four weeks. You've got to work on your opening statement."

As I started down the steps, he called out, "Will you talk with her? Make sure she understands."

"She understands," I said, without looking back. "Airtight case or not, she's pretty sure we're gonna kick your ass."

CHAPTER **36**

As I walked out a side door of the courthouse, the thrill of telling Bigelow off was already fading, snuffed out by the reality of the situation. Twenty-eight days, and we had even less than we started with.

The list of questions that I needed answers for was as long as my arm and they needed to be answered yesterday.

But when I tried to focus on any individual question, I couldn't manage it. In my head they were this massive tangle, like fishing line left to dry in a tackle box. Each one ended in a hook driven deep into Ms. Pentecost's future.

I found the Cadillac where I'd parked it, slipped my fingers through the handle, and stopped.

The thought of going back to the office and beginning the work of untangling that mess made me physically ill. A hundred things to do. A dozen calls to make. No idea where to start.

I let go of the door handle and kept walking. I headed north, moving quickly through Chinatown and into Little Italy. I walked up Bowery, then cut west, skirting the edge of Washington Square Park, almost, but not quite, close enough to the House of D to put it in my sights. I could still feel it, though.

The place radiated. And like the radium they used to paint watch dials with, it made everyone who touched it sick.

I kept going north. With the House of D in my rear view, the city seemed to open up. The first Monday in November, and the sky was clear and the air was crisp and light, like breathing it in would pull you straight up into that bright blue.

Everyone I was sharing the sidewalk with seemed to feel it. The cluster of secretaries dragging their heels on the way back from lunch; the doorman peeking out from under his awning; the pair of girls roller-skating, taking corners hand in hand. Even a flock of nuns walking past a playground looked like they wouldn't mind playing hooky themselves, monkeying over the wire fence, and taking to the swings.

Everyone with the same idea. Soak it in before it's gone.

North.

No thinking, just walking. No destination, only a direction.

Up University and then through Union Square Park and out onto Broadway.

It was around the Flatiron when I felt the tangle loosening. I didn't pick at it. I was content just to know that it was happening.

I walked past Madison Square Park, took a detour to get a better view of the Empire State Building. I even paused to stare up and gawp like a tourist. I liked to imagine King Kong hanging off that spire, swatting biplanes like mosquitoes.

I laughed out loud, then started moving again because that stretch of sidewalk was known for suicides.

By Thirty-eighth Street, my head had cleared enough that there was space to think, and I figured I could address the tangle without feeling like my heart was going to claw its way out of my throat.

When she's on a cleaning spree, Mrs. Campbell likes to say, "You do the chore in front of you. The rest will still be there when you're done."

I grabbed one of the lines and started pulling. I never stopped walking, though.

The first line I yanked on was Muffin. The best suspect of the bunch and not hide nor hair. How did I dig him out?

I was reminded of how my father lured the gophers out of

his garden, and suddenly the answer was simple. Why hadn't I thought of it before?

Oh, right. Because I'd spent the last three weeks mired in panic and guilt and making desperate decisions instead of smart ones.

I moved on to the next line, then the next. With each, the tangle became smaller and looser, and each subsequent problem easier to solve.

The whole process took another hour of slow strolling, and when I was finished I looked down at my watch to see two p.m., then up at the street signs to see I was at the corner of 106th and Fifth.

Three hours of walking and I'd almost cleared Central Park.

And I had an honest-to-God plan.

The first place I needed to go was only another twenty blocks, but I hailed a cab anyway. Twenty-eight days. Time was short.

I told the cabbie to take me to Harlem.

Sam Lee was still in bed after working the night shift. His landlady eventually agreed to rouse him, but only after I swore that my intentions were purely professional.

I had promised myself not to drag him into this case, but promises—especially those whispered in private—are made to be broken. It was all hands on deck, and I needed to know if Sara Johnson and her son had seen or heard anything while they were slinging canapés at Quincannon's party.

They were the only people there without skin in the game, or at least I hoped so.

"There's always an outside chance they had something to do with it. However you make your approach, make it careful," I warned him. "If you sniff a cop, get out of there. I don't want you losing your job."

"Don't worry, Miss Parker," he said. "I'll get you what you need."

With that done, I hopped on the number 2 train south, clearing in forty minutes what it had taken me three hours to walk. I retrieved the Cadillac and drove back to the office and started making calls.

The first was to Lazenby.

"This is Mrs. Crapper again. Any word on Muffin?"

"A couple sightings of him around Gravesend. Rumor is he has family out there, but no one's claiming it," Lazenby said.

"How bad would you like to catch this guy?" I asked.

"About as bad as you would."

"Let me tell you my plan."

Lazenby didn't like it, but he agreed that it had a chance of working, and that he'd hold up his end if it did.

My next call was to Whitsun's office.

"Whitsun, it's Parker. If you asked Creed for access to all of Quincannon's financial records, would he give them to you?"

"I think so," Whitsun said. "It might take some sweet-talking to prove relevance."

"I have faith in you," I said. "You can be charming when you put your mind to it."

I was about to make my next call when the phone rang. It was Lazenby.

"Don't tell me you're having second thoughts," I said.

"And third and fourth. I just found out that Walter Beck turned up dead."

I counted to two and a half—my personal calculation for the amount of time a sharp human brain can process shocking news—before asking, "Turned up dead where?"

"In his apartment. Don't you want to know how?"

"That would be the next question, right before when and why."

Lazenby made a sound—a kind of huffing sigh—that over the years I'd come to translate as pained resignation.

"His apartment," the big man said. "Gunshot to the head.

His own weapon, probably during a struggle. He'd been there for a while. Early guesses are he was killed as much as a week ago. They're saying the place was turned over good."

"Look, if you want what we have on Susie Beck, I'm happy to give it to you."

"I don't, but Staples might. Beck was part of his regular crew. He's the one running the case."

"Tell Donald I'd be happy to share."

That comment was a little too glib, and Lazenby picked up on it.

"Parker—tell me this doesn't have anything to do with you and your boss."

I constructed my own huffing sigh, which I hoped translated to exasperation at being regularly and wrongly suspected of misconduct.

"I don't know who wanted Beck dead, but I can swear on any book that Dewey ever decimated that neither I nor Ms. Pentecost was responsible."

Which was cousin to the truth, in that Beck's death was almost certainly his own damn fault.

"I know you're not telling me everything, Parker."

"Listen up, Lazenby." I didn't mean to growl his name, but I didn't feel sorry about it, either. "You asked a question, I gave an answer. If you don't like it, tough. Now, you can tell Staples I'll be happy to hand over everything I have on the death of Beck's wife if he happens to give a shit. Personally, I've got bigger things to worry about than Walter Beck. Like drawing out Billy Muffin. If you're really as interested in catching him as I am, stop jawing with me and start laying bait. Now, if you'll excuse me, I've got a long list and twenty-eight days to get through it."

I hung up before he could reply. You might think that wasn't very nice, and you'd be right.

But I was done playing nice. I had work to do.

CHAPTER 37

If you haven't figured it out by now, there are no straight lines in a murder investigation. Certainly not the way Ms. Pentecost goes about it, and that's who I learned from.

Rarely do you pluck a thread and follow it all the way to the end. It's more about the accumulation—sometimes painfully slow—of facts. And all due respect to Mr. Conan Doyle, rarely are those facts the presence of cigarette ash or an errant boot print. Mostly it has to do with behavior and with character. Figure out someone's character, and you can recognize when they've done something contrary to it.

Investigations are also mostly waiting, which I've never been good at. With everyone given their marching orders, waiting was all I had left to do. I used the lull in activity to pick at the Zhao case some more.

I called one of the few cops I could trust not named Lazenby and confirmed the detail about the dark blue Chevy seen lurking that night. I also confirmed that was the only lead they had.

They hadn't bothered dusting for prints. And the bullet was another fragmented mess. Unlike Quincannon's killer, Mr. Zhao's hadn't been kind enough to fire a second shot into a more forgiving target.

Which meant I needed to drum up my own leads.

I went back to Mott Street during business hours and found Junfeng Zhao's old workshop open for business. A half-dozen women were sitting at sewing machines churning out faux-silk kimonos.

The owner, Mrs. Liu, used to have a smaller shop around the corner and had known Zhao for years. I bought a pair of kimonos at twice the asking price and got a conversation thrown in for free.

According to the elderly seamstress, Zhao kept long hours, sometimes arriving before dawn and staying until past midnight, especially as the weather turned cold and it crept closer to the holidays.

He must have been killed very late, she said. Earlier and the businesses on either side of him would have heard the shots.

People were in and out of his shop all the time, picking up toys they had commissioned, requesting new work, or browsing the pieces he'd created that had not yet been sold.

Maybe he kept money on the premises, but she didn't think so, confirming what his family had told me.

"He was a good man. Honest. Trusting. But not a fool," she said simply.

She showed me a few of Zhao's toys, left by the family to sell in case any customers who had not heard of the father's death came calling. I used the last of my cash to buy a palm-sized wooden frog. It was meticulously carved and painted, a red silk tongue stretching out of its mouth, to which you could attach a tiny wooden fly. If you gave the tongue a pull, it would snap back and the frog's mouth would close, gobbling its wooden treat.

When I got back to the office, I put it up in the third-floor archives, right on the floor next to Ms. P's chair. A reminder of how little use I'd been to the Zhaos as a detective.

Come Friday, Nurse Palmer was back on the job, telling Ms. P about the different bits of machinery her assistant had set in motion. She gave her seal of approval.

"Do you see anything I don't?" I asked. "Anything I can do that I'm not doing?"

No words, just a shake of the head. I left not knowing whether I really was doing everything I could, or if Ms. P was too exhausted to know otherwise.

Not a good day.

Saturday was marginally better. While Ms. P forgave my canceling the open house the week before, she didn't want that to become a habit. We had nearly thirty people come through the door. Most I referred to various lawyers or charity organizations. Some I helped, some I didn't. There was nothing as ego-crushing as the Zhao case.

I even managed to take a thirty-minute break to visit the basement and teach a dozen of my usual students that trick Alathea had pulled on me. It was therapeutic. Who needs to take the waters when you can pop a guy's kneecap off?

On Sunday I didn't do a damn thing. I tried my best not to feel guilty.

Tuesday. Twenty days until jury selection. That's when things started to shake up.

First, Whitsun called. Judge Creed had granted a request for every document detailing Quincannon's financials.

"Don't pull the trigger yet," I told him. "This is what you do. Type up a letter in your best legalese. 'Dear Mr. Silas Culliver, this is to inform you that we will be serving blah blah blah. Prior to doing so, we request that you speak with our associate Willowjean Parker to discuss the details of,' and so forth and so on. Make it threatening, but in that polite, snake-in-a-suit way. Get it messengered over to him today."

"What do you expect to find in Quincannon's books?" Whitsun asked.

"Leverage."

On Wednesday, Sam Lee came knocking. He hadn't managed to see Sara Johnson, but he'd had luck with her son, William.

William Johnson wasn't much of a churchgoer, but the girl he was sweet on was. While that girl didn't belong to the same congregation as Sam Lee's landlady, they had mutual acquaintances.

A complex system of levers and pulleys was activated, which resulted in William sitting down with Sam Lee in exchange for the handsome young morgue assistant promising his landlady that he would take a particular choir member to the movies.

"Hey, it could turn out to be a nice time," I suggested.

"I doubt it," he said. "I've met her. She thinks joie de vivre is something you get from French-kissing."

But none of that matters. All that matters is what he learned, which wasn't much. I'd been crossing my fingers that William was the sort who kept his ears open while passing out Champagne.

"He says he blocks it out," Sam Lee told me. "Says people can tell if he's listening. Also, if he gets distracted, he could drop a tray, which happened once and never again."

So much for a case-breaking tidbit.

Also, he was in the kitchen restocking his tray when he heard the shots, so he didn't know who all was in the conservatory or, more important, who wasn't.

It wasn't a total loss. William might have kept his ears shut but his eyes had been working fine. Consequently, he was able to tell Sam Lee two important things.

The first was that Alathea was down in the basement when

the shots were fired. His mother had seen her go down and William saw her run up when people started yelling. There was still the possibility of some secret way out and up to the third floor, but I didn't see how the timing worked.

Considering how much she knew, it was comforting to cross her off the list.

The second thing William saw was less conclusive, but more interesting.

"He was talking about the other two women at the party," Sam Lee said. "He said that the slinky brunette—his words, not mine—purposefully spilled the busty blonde's drink. Again—his words."

"Purposefully? He's sure?"

"That's what he said. Looked right at her and knocked her drink out of her hand with her elbow. It spilled all down the blonde's dress."

Sam Lee spent a needless few minutes apologizing for delivering so little. I assured him he'd done fine and promised I wouldn't hesitate if I needed his help again.

After he left, I sat at my desk for a few minutes, fitting old information to new. A couple of those pieces slotted together nicely, but I needed to confirm the picture that was taking shape.

I picked up the phone and dialed The Carlyle.

The desk clerk told me that Victoria Pelham was still present and accounted for but wouldn't put me through without checking with the woman in question.

"Tell her we had a smoke by Grimké's grave."

A few minutes later, that familiar husky voice came on the line.

"This is the young detective?"

"It is the young detective," I said. "I don't suppose you've reconsidered a more formal conversation."

There was a pause, and for a moment I thought she might bite.

"I think not," she said eventually. "Over the years I've learned never to say anything on the record if I can help it."

"How about this. One question. And I promise no subpoenas."

That was a lie. I couldn't promise anything. But I really wanted that one question answered.

"Ask it and we'll see," she said.

"You thought Quincannon was stepping out with somebody else. Someone new. You said you didn't know, but I think you have a suspicion. I want to know who it is, and why you suspect it."

A longer pause this time. Long enough that I thought I might have to call the front desk to reconnect me.

"All right," she finally said, then answered my question.

I asked a couple follow-ups, but she reminded me I had license for one question and had already caught my limit. I thanked her and hung up.

"Now we're getting somewhere," I said to myself.

CHAPTER 38

PLEASE CALL UPON ME AT YOUR EARLIEST CONVENIENCE TO DISCUSS YOUR RELATIONSHIP WITH JESSUP QUINCANNON, is what the telegram said.

It only took a day for Elaine Novarro to find an excuse to break away from church business long enough to pay me a visit. At noon on Thursday she was sitting in the chair of honor in our office.

For once, I was behind Ms. Pentecost's desk. Not because I thought I deserved to sit there, but because I wanted Mrs. Novarro facing the hidden microphone. There was a good chance she might confess to murder, and I wanted every word on tape.

I expected something along the line of "What is this all about?" But to give her credit, she started with, "Before we begin, I'd like to request that you not tell my husband anything of this meeting."

"He won't hear about it from me."

Not a lie. If he did hear something—whatever that something might be—it would be in court, or maybe from the police.

Since she was cutting to the chase, I decided to do the same.

"Mrs. Novarro, would it surprise you to know that you were seen entering Jessup Quincannon's residence on Saturday, July twelfth?"

She shook her head, but a headshake doesn't show up on tape.

"You're not surprised?"

"I'm not," she said. "I was there."

"This was without your husband?"

"Correct."

"He didn't know you were there?"

She shifted in her seat. I don't know if I'd call it a squirm, but someone might. Last time I'd seen her, she'd been in silky, cheerful number that gave her room to breathe. Now she was buttoned tight into a dark gray utility suit, sleeves to her wrists, collar to her chin, skirt swishing at her ankles.

Armor.

"Timothy didn't know," she said. "He thought I was interviewing a possible new pianist for the church."

"Did you?"

"Did I what?"

"Meet with a pianist."

"Earlier in the evening, yes."

Which meant her husband was the sort to check up on her. Also, that she was the sort to think about alibis.

"When did your relationship begin with Quincannon?" I asked.

"My husband and I first met him last winter," she reminded me.

"I mean when did your personal relationship begin with him?"

She looked confused—an open-mouthed squinting that did her face no favors.

I tried again. "Let me be frank. When did you start sleeping with Jessup Quincannon?"

There was another second of squinting, then her eyes widened in realization and Elaine Novarro started laughing. Full-throated, doubled-over-in-her-chair laughing.

"My God," she wheezed. "I understand now. I thought that

woman was drunk or hysterical. But she thought that he and I
were . . ." The rest of her words were lost to guffaws.

I waited patiently for her to recover. Eventually, she wiped
her eyes and, still smiling, asked, "Was it that woman from the
party who saw me? What was her name? Pelican?"

"Pelham."

"She was looking at me all night and then came up and
whispered something crude. Then she knocked my drink onto
my dress. I thought she . . . I don't know what I thought. Now
I see."

I didn't.

"Are you saying you were not in a sexual relationship with
Quincannon?" I asked.

"My God, no," she said. "I know we shouldn't speak ill of
the dead, but I think we can agree the man was disgusting."

"Then what were you doing meeting with him?"

"I went there to ask him for money, Miss Parker," she said.

"I thought you'd already struck out."

She hammered her smile flat and straightened her skirt.

"A single 'no' is hardly striking out," she said. "I wrote to
Mr. Quincannon again in May asking for a personal meeting.
When I didn't hear back, I wrote a second time. Then he sent a
letter granting me an appointment, so I went."

The same night Victoria Pelham showed up, fresh from
San Francisco, a little drunk, a lot lonely, hoping to rekindle
the romance. Instead she'd seen Quincannon coming down the
walk to let in a busty blonde a decade younger than her.

"You didn't tell your husband?"

"He would have insisted on accompanying me."

She must have seen me coming to the wrong conclusion,
because she added, "He wouldn't have approved of the tack I
took."

"Okay, if it wasn't sex that you were offering, what was it?"
I asked.

"Mr. Quincannon asked the same thing. He asked if I

was offering absolution for his sins," she said. "I told him that money won't buy absolution from the Almighty. But it does offer camouflage."

"Camouflage?"

"It's a tradition as old as religion itself," she explained. "The wealthy cloaking their sins in charity. I told him that Timothy was going places. That he would be a force for God in this country, and how useful it would be for the Quincannon name to be attached to the church. A plaque reading THIS MEETING-HOUSE PAID FOR BY JESSUP QUINCANNON. An announcement before every radio broadcast."

I was reconsidering the woman in front of me. How had Max described her? The seen-and-not-heard type? Men can be real dummies.

"I see why you didn't want your husband there," I said.

"Timothy is a good and kind man," she said. "He thinks the best of everyone, wants the best for everyone. He has principles that he absolutely will not bend."

She smiled when she said his name, a patient, loving smile.

"He will be a force for God, but for that to happen, he needs more people to hear his message, and that requires money."

"Even money from someone who's morally disgusting?" I asked. "Money tainted by sin?"

She snuffed the smile out.

"Money is . . . simply a tool. It's what you do with it that matters."

Not a bad argument. One a lot of people have made to themselves when pocketing a payoff.

"Ten thousand. You must have been pretty persuasive."

"I didn't think so at the time," Elaine said. "Now I wonder if he wasn't making a joke."

"What do you mean?"

"He told me the one thing he'd never be in his life was a hypocrite. Those were his exact words."

So instead of writing a check, Quincannon put them in his

will. A private joke to himself, the punch line to which landed earlier than intended.

"You haven't told your husband about any of this?" I asked.

"My husband thinks it's God's will. The money, I mean. A little miracle."

"And you don't?"

A smile crept back onto her lips, but there was little love in it.

"I think if you take a good look at the things we call little miracles, you won't find God's hand anywhere near most of them," she said. "Just normal, everyday people doing their job. No matter the cost."

CHAPTER **39**

I posed a few other questions to Elaine Novarro. The only one worth mentioning was whether she knew the name "Walter Beck." I wanted to see what her face did.

It did nothing, and she said she'd never heard of the man.

After she left, I checked the tape to make sure everything got picked up, then called Whitsun to give him an update.

"This is good. Real good," he said in a tone usually reserved to describe your grandmother's corn bread.

"What do you mean? I thought I was uncovering a torrid affair, and all we've got is some surreptitious God-mongering."

"Think about it, Parker. We only have her word she didn't know about the will. That's a big, fat motive for her and her husband. Nobody was in the bathroom with her during the murder. Who's to say she wasn't really sneaking upstairs? Not to mention we've got a wife having a secret meeting with our victim, and a husband who may have found out about it."

"She says not."

"Would she know?" he mused. "He might have jumped to the same conclusion you did. Either way, it'll be a show for the jury. Two motives for the price of one."

I spent a minute feeling sorry for Elaine Novarro, but not a second longer. Like I said—no more playing nice.

. . .

That went double for the interview I had that evening.

Silas Culliver arrived at eight—the time I asked him to come—and promptly demanded, "What the hell is this court order?"

Again, I was sitting behind Ms. Pentecost's desk, Culliver in the comfy yellow-upholstered armchair, which I'd thought was plenty wide, but barely fit him and creaked precariously when he touched down.

I didn't need reminding that Culliver was a big man. That's one of the reasons I wanted to be behind the desk. It put half a ton of oak between us and it let me have my Colt loaded and ready in the middle drawer.

I didn't answer his question right away. It was pretty vague and I wanted to make him stew a bit. I spent the time examining him. Culliver had come wearing a three-piece in dark gray English wool, complete with silver watch chain.

His own version of armor.

"I ask again, what is the meaning of this?"

"This is us having a conversation, Silas. Off the record."

I gestured to our bookshelves. The secret compartment that housed our tape recorder was standing open, the machine itself sitting over on my desk, unplugged, the microphone with its extra-long cord curled up beside it.

"If it's a conversation about Mr. Quincannon and the work I performed for him, then you must know that attorney-client privilege extends even beyond the veil of death," Culliver declared in that very British way of imparting information that suggests a personal failing on your part for not already knowing it.

"'Beyond the veil,'" I said, sounding out the words. "It's almost poetry."

"However you phrase it, it means I cannot answer your questions."

I shook my head.

"That's not really true, though," I said. "According to For-

est Whitsun, with Quincannon dead, it's your prerogative—
that's Whitsun's word—how much to say. Before you dig your
heels in, let me inform you that if you stay mum, I have a guy
who can make life very difficult for you."

Culliver straightened in his seat, squeezing out every inch
of height.

"Are you physically threatening me?"

"Shucks, no," I said. "The guy I'm thinking of couldn't
punch his way out of a paper bag. But he does know his way
around paper—financial documents, specifically. He used to
work for the mob. Shuffling money around, paying bribes and
whatnot. I'll bet my silk blouse against your silver watch that if
there's a single sawbuck unaccounted for, he'll be able to sniff
it out."

Culliver laughed. I was getting a little tired of witnesses
laughing at me.

"My God—if I'd known you had someone of such skill I
would have hired him myself weeks ago. It would have saved
me hours of drudgery."

"I'm glad you find this amusing," I said.

"What do you or Mr. Whitsun think you're going to find?
Do you think there are lines in the ledgers reading 'Jack the
Ripper's diary—two hundred dollars'? Or perhaps 'procure-
ment of one painter's box in the possession of Reverend Adam
Pentecost—eight hundred dollars'?"

That last was clearly meant to get under my skin, and it did.
But I'd plucked out worse.

"You got scammed, Silas. I know a dozen guys who could
have stolen that box for three hundred plus train fare."

"How very droll," he said. "I'm afraid you'll find no record
of Mr. Quincannon's purchases for the Black Museum. Everything was paid for in cash from his office safe. All filed very
meticulously under 'household expenses.'"

That made sense. I'd done something similar when I paid
Sam Lee.

"Good for Quincannon," I said. "But Sid—that's my money guy's name—Sid will also be able to ferret out any other mistakes in your math."

"What makes you think there will be any?"

I slowly ticktocked a finger at him in a way that I'd seen Ms. P do.

"No dice, Silas," I said. "You could have told me to get bent over the phone. The fact that you're here means there's something in those records you don't want us to find. According to Sid, preparing for an audit like this—unless the books are a total mess, and Quincannon didn't strike me as someone who'd let that happen—he says a job like this should take two weeks. You're on week five. He says the only way it'd stretch out like this is if you're entirely incompetent, which I don't think you are. However, Sid also brought up the possibility you're using this as an opportunity to skim the till. That's blue-collar for embezzling. Which, I have to admit, sounds a lot more likely."

Silas sniffed and performed a series of costume adjustments—smoothing his jacket, straightening his tie, tracing the loop of his watch chain.

"What about it, Silas?" I asked. "Been picking the pockets of a dead man?"

His eyes fixed on the unplugged, unmoving tape recorder. He seemed to come to a decision, and some of the stiffness left him.

"No, Miss Parker, I am not embezzling."

"You'll have to excuse me if I don't—"

"I'm covering up prior . . . withdrawals."

Sid had brought that up as a third possibility, but I'd wanted Culliver to get there first.

"These are withdrawals by you?"

"Minor, I assure you," he said. "A few thousand every month."

I only had a few thousand to my name at any given time, so I hardly considered that minor.

"For how long?" I asked.

There was some more costume adjustment.

"Since shortly after my employment. Five and a half years, give or take."

I did some quick math. Two thousand a month times sixty-six months was . . . a lot.

"I can see how a dent like that might take some time to spackle over. How's it going, by the way?"

"Swimmingly," he said with more than a hint of American-made sarcasm.

"Out of curiosity, how are you fixing the math?"

"Mr. Quincannon made regular cash withdrawals to replenish his safe. I am simply going through the ledgers and recategorizing my own withdrawals to match his."

"When did Quincannon find out?" I asked. "Did he call his bank to get a tally and find himself a hundred grand short?"

Culliver laughed again, this time with what sounded like authentic joy.

"My God, woman, the man wasn't an idiot. He knew the whole time. He ignored it."

Some of the polish had flaked off his accent. I began to wonder how much of Culliver was show.

"Six figures over six years is a lot to ignore."

Silas shook his head.

"Not to Jessup," he said. "Do you know what he told me shortly after hiring me? That it was his father's money and he was happy to let it burn. As long as I was able to procure him this or that piece for his collection, he didn't care. It was a gratuity for my troubles."

Culliver must have read my skepticism.

"I had carte blanche, Miss Parker," he said. "Carte blanche to maneuver Mr. Quincannon's funds however I saw fit. Why in God's name would I put an end to it by murdering him?"

I didn't have an answer to that. And if Culliver was lying, I didn't have anything left to pry him open. I was at the end of my lever.

"What did you talk with him about? When you went upstairs?"

"I was trying to convince him not to go through with his little show-and-tell," Culliver said. "I told him it would be far better used as a threat against Lillian Pentecost to keep her from interfering with his affairs. At the very least, he should think on it more."

"I take it he wouldn't listen."

"He would not. He was quite determined. He said he was finished with delayed gratification. That this would be far more satisfying."

I felt a surge of anger at the dead man. *Satisfying.*

"Why did he hate her so much?" I asked.

"I really don't know," he said. "But his animosity had certainly gotten more intense over the last months of his life. He'd become quite fixated. In no small part due to your employer's own self-righteous meddling."

He leaned back, frowned, and started to go through his series of straightening and smoothing but stopped halfway through adjusting his Windsor.

"He did say something curious once. He asked me if I'd ever met someone who made me question the very core of myself. And if I despised them for it."

We sat with that for a moment, then I asked him my final questions.

"Where can I find Billy Muffin?" I asked. "You're the one who tracked him down before."

"Everything I know, I've told the police," he said. "I have no love or loyalty to Mr. Muffin. He's a common thug."

A common thug who killed people for money and was still missing after fleeing the scene of a murder, but God forbid we be specific.

"What about Walter Beck?" I asked. "What do you know about what happened to him?"

"I don't know who that is."

I gave it a second to see if anything would leak. Nothing did. "Last question," I said. "Who do you think did it?"

He stood and leaned forward, putting his catcher's mitt hands on the table and using all seventy inches of his frame to loom. I didn't open the drawer with the gun inside, but I had my fingers on the handle.

"Lillian Pentecost," he said. "Now if that will be all, Miss Parker, I will see you in court. Though if I am called to the stand, I will repeat none of what I have said here tonight."

With that he walked out. I would have retrieved his hat and coat for him, but I try not to do bastards any favors.

After I heard the front door slam shut, I counted to ten, went out, and locked it. Then I came back into the office and opened the door to the dining room. I walked over to the audio recorder sitting on the dining room table and turned it off.

A cable ran from the recorder under the door to the office, disappearing beneath the rug before emerging to snake up the back of my desk and connect to the microphone. The one Culliver thought was attached to the disabled machine.

I'd bought the second device the day before. Never hurts to have a spare.

I rewound the tape and listened. If Culliver was telling a lie, it was a good one. Quincannon was worth more to him alive.

Still, it was another motive to hand Whitsun. Embezzlement? And Quincannon knew? That was even better than the Novarro situation.

But I was still secretly hoping for a win, not a draw. My favorite suspect was still out there. I just needed to get my hands on him.

CHAPTER **40**

Friday came too quick.

The only good news I had for Ms. P had been delivered to me by Dolly Klinghorn, who called that morning to say she had witnesses to Valeria Lincoln's assault.

"It was clear self-defense, and Dolly has the signed statements to prove it," I told my boss during our clinic visit.

"Excellent," she said. "Please pass it on to the attorney handling Val's case."

While we talked, Hubbard worked her over. He was pushing up her sleeve to affix a blood pressure cuff when he hissed through his teeth.

"That's a nasty bruise."

I took a look and winced. The bruise was purple and black and spread like a thundercloud across her tricep.

"I was making my way up from the dining hall and tripped on the stairs. My arm hit one of the steps. It looks much worse than it feels," she assured us.

I'm not going to play coy here. I'm the one cobbling together this little narrative, which means I've read Ms. Pentecost's journals. That means I know about Andrews and that her bruise did not come from a fall on the stairs.

She was right, you know. I would have killed him. I'd have gotten away with it, too.

At the time, I thought nothing of it. Even at home my boss

collected bruises like baseball cards. I finished my report, gathered a few suggestions from Ms. P on how to move forward, and left.

Saturday was another open house. If anyone walked in with something significant, I didn't make a note of it.

On Sunday Holly dragged me out to see Tyrone Power in *Nightmare Alley*. It was about a con man working a traveling circus, and she thought I'd like it. Of the movie, I remember nothing, other than the churning feeling in my gut that I should have spent the day doing something useful.

I made up for it on Monday, or at least I tried.

I'd mentioned to Ms. P that while I had the feeling Backstrom had been less than forthcoming, I didn't have a way to twist his arm. Not like I had with Culliver or Elaine Novarro.

She suggested a bluff might be as good as the real thing. That made me think of what Dr. Grayson had said about people dropping troubled relatives off for brain-cracking and them coming back the lesser for it.

What were the chances that more than a few were angry at Backstrom? That they might be willing to hire a hotshot lawyer like Forest Whitsun to put the doctor in the crosshairs of a lawsuit? Sounded believable to me.

That was going to be my play when I walked into Backstrom's office that morning, with the suggestion that I could maybe call Whitsun off if the doctor agreed to come to our office for a more formal interview.

Lady Luck was with me when I saw that Mrs. Pervis wasn't at the receptionist desk. Instead, it was a gawky brunette who looked like she might still be learning how the pencil sharpener worked.

When I asked to see Dr. Ryan Backstrom, I discovered that not only was Lady Luck not with me, she had packed up and left town.

"What do you mean he's in Sweden? For how long?"

"I'm sure I don't know," she said. "Awhile, I think. Visiting family. He's from there, apparently. Dr. Delmonte is taking over his clients while he's gone."

"That son of a bitch."

"Excuse me?"

"I'm sorry. I was thinking of someone else," I said. "When exactly did Dr. Backstrom leave?"

"Let's see. This is the seventeenth. I started right after he left and I've been here a little over three weeks so . . ."

So he'd left town not long after I'd paid my visit.

"I can make an appointment for you to see Dr. Delmonte if you— Excuse me? Miss!"

What the hell was this? Of all my suspects, Backstrom was the last I expected to do a runner. Because that's what this felt like. A runner.

He hadn't even been high on my list of suspects. Mathers had said he'd been talking with Backstrom when the shots were fired. Asking him something about gout.

Maybe the old judge had been lying. Or maybe his memory really was shot.

I made him my next port of call.

I didn't have an invitation, but I didn't think Mathers would send me away. For all his rottenness, he was still a lonely old man who wasn't going to turn down a visit from a young woman, no matter how nasty her tongue.

I knocked on the door of Mathers's Bowery flophouse, ready to bat my eyelashes and play nice, only to have the door opened by Jefferson, who delivered the news that Mathers had also done a runner.

"What do you mean he's dead? Who killed him?"

"God and time, miss," the houseman said. "Doctor told me it was his heart, which I suppose is proof he had one."

I choked off a snort.

"Go ahead and laugh, miss. I lived with the man. He wasn't any better in private, let me tell you."

"I don't suppose he said anything to you about what happened to Jessup Quincannon?" I asked.

Jefferson, who had ditched his faded tuxedo for paint-splattered dungarees, a white undershirt, and rubber gloves, shook his head. "No, miss. Not so much. Although his last days he was talking more. More to himself than me. About how Mr. Quincannon never had a chance. That's what he said. That the boy never had a chance."

"What did he mean by that?"

He looked around at the adjacent stoops, which were litter-strewn but vacant. Then he leaned in and said in a hushed voice, "I didn't understand everything the judge said, but it had to do with the man's father. Mr. Quincannon's? About how he was with his son. When he was little, I mean. I think . . ."

"What?" I asked. "What do you think?"

He shook his head, as if coming out of a trance, then stepped back.

"Never you mind. It's not something to talk about. Especially with all involved dead."

I tried for more on that front, but Jefferson wouldn't budge. I asked about Mathers's last days, but there had been no change in his routine. Wake, eat mush, peep at the neighbors, more mush, bed. Until Saturday morning, when he didn't check that first item off the list.

"Do you have a place to land?" I asked.

He laughed, but there was no humor in it.

"Oh, I'm taken care of. The judge saw to that. He left me this godforsaken shithole. It's in a trust, too. Something Mr. Quincannon set up for him. I can't ever sell it as long as I'm alive. I'm stuck with this place until I die. Stinks like him, too. That's what I'm doing now. Trying to scrub the smell out."

I left Jefferson to his scouring and drove back to the office.

I wasn't the type who believed that weeks continued how they started, but this one wasn't kicking off on a hopeful note.

Zero-for-two on the interview front and not much likelihood to improve.

But I've been known to be wrong.

The phone was already ringing when I walked into the office. I picked it up.

"Parker."

"It's Lazenby. I just got word. It looks like Billy Muffin is taking the bait."

CHAPTER **41**

"I bet five."

"Fold."

"Fold."

"I'll see your five."

"I see the five and raise five."

"Bullshit."

"You think it's bullshit, throw another five in there and find out."

"You think I won't?"

"I hope you will."

"Fine. I call the ten."

"How about you, Red? You in?"

"Hell, no," I said. "You were any more eager, Charlie, you'd be drooling on the cards. I don't think you made your straight but I'm betting that queen gave you a sneaky two pair. I fold."

"Shoot. I gotta work on my poker face, I guess."

Charlie turned over his hole cards, revealing queens and jacks.

"The ladies always come through for me," he crowed, dragging the pile of bills his way.

The other guys at the table laughed.

"You wish," one of them said. "The only thing the ladies ever gave you is a case of the clap."

"Hey, don't talk about your sister that way," Charlie retorted.

Peals of laughter. Someone lit up another cigar, blowing smoke into a room already thick with it. I leaned back and groaned.

Three hours of this. Five cops and me playing with borrowed money in a seventh-floor room of the Grastorf Hotel on a Friday night. A formerly distinguished establishment on the edge of Times Square, it was a favorite for out-of-town businessmen. A favorite because a buck could buy you a blind eye from the management, which was a good quality if you were looking to hire a hooker or hold a middle-stakes poker game.

The first half hour was the worst. That's when the boys were trying to be polite. No swears, excusing themselves when they burped, calling me "Miss," folding to every one of my raises.

Some of them had met me before and knew better. But Lazenby was in the adjoining room with an ear to the door, so they were on their best behavior.

Then I told a joke about a showgirl and a donkey and everyone relaxed. Mostly. How loose could you get when you were waiting to get robbed at gunpoint?

Every ten seconds, one of them would look over at the door, which was pointless, since we'd get warning long before Muffin made it that far. Lazenby would get a call from one of his guys—either the one hogging the pay phone on the corner outside or one of the men dressed as bellhops covering the entrances.

At least we hoped Lazenby would get a call. The plan was to let the sting run a full twelve hours—eight p.m. until eight in the morning. If Billy Muffin didn't show, we'd try it again the next week.

"You're up, Red."

I shuffled and dealt.

Lazenby hadn't wanted me at the table. His argument was that high rollers wouldn't let a woman in the game. I reminded him that these were not high rollers, but medium rollers. High rollers invested in guns and bodyguards. Semi-wealthy business owners, like this game was supposed to be filled with, did not.

I also reminded him that this sting was my idea and it was one of my contacts, Brynn Suilebhan, who'd rung the bell. Billy Muffin had been in his bar looking to see if anyone was in the market for a gunman. Brynn whispered the words he'd been told to: "poker game"; "good money"; "lots of booze."

"I could see his wheels turning," Brynn told Lazenby on the phone. "He asked lots of questions. He looked hungry."

Hungry was good. Hungry people made bad decisions. The game looked like a nice, soft target, but an experienced holdup man might still stay away. It was at a hotel, after all. That meant narrow hallways and lots of stairs and a long run to get free with the cash.

But a hotel was consistent with the story of out-of-town businessmen, and it gave Lazenby and the rest of his men an easy place to hide. It also meant nobody's house would get bullet holes in the wallpaper.

It was a good trap, and Lazenby and I had spent much of the week ironing out the details. Nurse Palmer even called in sick that morning, asking Hubbard to pass on her regrets to Ms. Pentecost along with the message that there might be good news in the offing.

I was dealing the sixth of seven cards when a knock came on the adjoining door—three, then two. Someone had given Lazenby the signal. Billy Muffin was on his way up.

Everybody tensed and looked at the door to the hall. Everyone except for me, since I was given the chair with its back to the door, and you better believe I wasn't happy about that.

"Stay in character," I said. "He comes in and sees five guys staring daggers, he could bolt. Stanley—you've got a pair of sevens showing. If you're gonna convince us there's a third in the hole, you've got to bet."

Stanley tossed in a bill without looking.

"Come on, you've got to at least talk. He's gotta hear a game going. Charlie—tell that joke again. This time everyone laugh."

Charlie told the joke. It was a lengthy number about a farmer's daughter and a Bible salesman. By the time he got to the punch line, he almost sounded natural. Everyone laughed for exactly three seconds before clamming up again.

We should have hired actors.

Suddenly the door to the adjoining room burst open and all six of us jumped out of our seats, guns already clearing hidden holsters. Lazenby filled the doorframe.

"Something's wrong," he said. "He got on the elevator in the lobby, but he didn't get off on this floor."

"He could have jumped off on another floor and be taking the stairs," I suggested.

Lazenby shook his head.

"We chained the stairwell doors to this floor, remember?"

I did. So where was Billy Muffin?

There was a thump from above and the sound of muffled shouts coming through the ceiling. Seven heads tilted up. Stanley was the first to say it.

"You think maybe he got the room number wrong?"

The stairwell doors were out, so we ran to the elevator. I was about to step in when Lazenby held up an arm and barred my way.

"You stay here."

"Come on, Lieutenant."

"We catch him, you'll get your shot."

I stepped back, letting the doors slide shut. Then I ran to the door to the stairs. The padlock was a brand known to open if you even breathed on it, and the second skeleton key on the ring did the trick.

I cautiously stepped into the stairwell and listened. Nothing from above but voices several floors below.

"Who goes there?" I yelled down.

"It's Perriman!" That was the officer that Lazenby had stationed at the bottom of the stairwell. "What's going on?"

"We think he's on eight!"

"He's what?"

"I said we think he's on eight!"

I was halfway through that last sentence when I heard a door open above me, followed by footsteps running up the stairs.

"He's going up!" I yelled before following.

I passed the door to eight, then nine, ten. Every time the stairs jackknifed, I took the corner gun-first, heart hammering in my throat.

Narrow stairs and a man known to carry a sawed-off. Not a good combination. But if Muffin got away, he'd find a hole so deep I'd never ferret him out again.

I wasn't about to lose my best shot at setting Ms. Pentecost free.

There was a loud bang from above and I threw myself against the wall. It was a full two seconds before I realized it had been the door to the roof slamming open. I took the last two flights at speed. The door was still swinging shut by the time I got there.

I put my foot in the way to keep it from closing. Then I paused to calculate the odds that Muffin was standing just out of sight, shotgun aimed at the doorway.

I slipped my jacket off. Then, with the hand not clutching my Browning, I held it up and out through the doorway. The wind nearly whipped it out of my grasp, but I clung on and waited for the blast of buckshot.

Nothing.

I let go and my jacket went flapping away. Then I peeked out. Nothing but empty roof. I stepped out, keeping my back to the stairway bulkhead.

The lights of Manhattan drenched the roof in tungsten-filament twilight. The wind had scoured the sky of clouds. The same wind that was whipping my hair into my eyes and roaring past my ears so I couldn't hear a damn thing.

That side of the rooftop was empty. I skirted around the first corner of the bulkhead, gun first.

Nothing but concrete and shadows, and none big enough to hide a man. He had to be up here. There was no fire escape and no adjacent buildings at the right height to leap to.

I skirted around the next corner. Nothing.

Were we doing ring-around-the-rosy? I looked back over my shoulder. Nothing.

I was about to take the next corner when I heard the sound of metal scraping against concrete. Not in front, not behind.

Above.

I looked up.

A white face peering over the edge of the bulkhead. The dark, double-barrel stare of a shotgun so close I could see the tool marks from where he'd sawed it off.

Time slowed. I was still trying to bring my gun up and around when Muffin pulled the trigger.

CHAPTER 42

When I was with the circus, I liked to say I'd try any-thing twice. If I flubbed a trick on the first try, I was always game for another. How else was I going to get better?

Except with the aerialists. It was with them that I found my line.

It was a simple move. Something the Flying Sabatinis taught their kids when they turned eight.

Leap off the second-highest platform, keep hold of the swing until the end of its arc, then let go. Marco would be there to grab my hands and carry me safely to the other side.

"All you have to do is let go at the right time," Marco told me. "And don't look down."

But I did look down. The strength left my hands and my fingers slipped. I felt this cold emptiness blossom in my gut as I began to fall.

Then I hit the net.

Of course there was a net. I was brave, not suicidal.

I felt that coldness again as Muffin pulled the trigger. My body giving me a preview of the death that was about to come.

Click.

A puff of smoke spat out of the barrels and was whipped away by the wind.

Suddenly Lazenby was in front of me. He grabbed the barrel of the sawed-off and pulled. Billy Muffin's grip on the gun was so firm he came flying off the top of the bulk-head and crashed to the rooftop. Lazenby put one foot on Muffin's chest and tore the shotgun out of his hands like he was yanking up a weed. Then Stanley and Charlie and the rest were there, throwing kicks into the gunman's head and ribs.

They got a few dozen in before Lazenby shouted over the wind, "That's enough, boys! Cuff him and bring him downstairs for a chat!"

The chat was in the room adjacent to where we'd been playing poker. The one where Lazenby had been hiding. My spare recorder was set up on the floor behind a curtain. I turned it on before Lazenby brought the stickup man in.

This was my payment for coming up with the idea for the sting. Ten minutes with Muffin before he was hauled away.

None of the chairs were sturdy enough, so Lazenby handcuffed Muffin to the metal frame at the head of the bed. Then he ordered everyone else out.

Caught in the bright light of the hotel bedroom, my prime suspect was an average specimen. Muffin was pushing forty, a little short, a little heavy, with a shock of bright red hair and the kind of wide, affable face that would fit nicely behind the wheel of a New York City cab.

It was the eyes that gave him away.

"What's happening here?" he asked, pulling himself up to a sitting position on the mattress. "This is all a mistake. A big misunderstanding."

If you're ever wondering what a killer's eyes look like, don't hunt for malice. Look for calm. Muffin was acting nervous, but his dark eyes were as placid as a lake on a summer's day.

"What's happening is, we're going to have a chat before I take you down to the station," Lazenby said, finding a spot in the corner of the room while I pulled up a chair.

"Take me there now. I ain't got nothing to say."

Lazenby nodded slowly, one hand tugging thoughtfully at his beard. "If that's what you'd like," he said. "The problem is, my boys are a little worked up. I hand you off now and they hear you didn't cooperate, I can't guarantee what condition you'll arrive in."

Muffin laughed, then winced.

"Spare me. They already broke a rib. Might as well go for two."

"How about this," I said. "You answer my questions now and I'll have amnesia about exactly what happened on the roof. You'll go in for robbery but not attempted murder."

He shook his head. "Nah, nah. That scattergun's all for show. To scare people."

But I'd seen the surprised look on his face when it hadn't fired. I got up and retrieved it from the desk.

"Doesn't look like a showpiece to me," I said, breaking open the gun. "Cartridges, on the other hand—I'm guessing someone had these sitting in their basement and water got to them. You should get your money back."

Muffin looked at Lazenby.

"This on the up-and-up?" he asked. "I talk, you don't go for attempted murder?"

I hadn't cleared it with the lieutenant ahead of time and I could tell he wasn't happy. I didn't care. I wasn't looking to nail Muffin for attempted anything.

"If Parker doesn't say you pulled the trigger, there's not much the DA can do, is there?" he grumbled. "But we're sure as hell getting you for the stickups."

Muffin shook his head and laughed.

"I swear I heard Room 801. Guess I got lucky, huh? Otherwise your boys might have shot me full of lead. This is all entrapment, by the way. God—the look on that guy's face when I busted in on him and that broad. He's gonna have a story when he gets back to Poughkeepsie."

Usually, I love a little wry humor, but I was still remembering that coldness, that feeling of falling.

"Take it or leave it," I snapped. "But choose now."

Another thing about a certain breed of killer—they're real quick about calculating the odds.

"All right," Muffin said. "What are we chatting about?"

The timer started on my ten minutes. No chance for finesse. Body shots only.

Will Parker: Why'd you run that night at Quincannon's?

    Billy Muffin: Ah, Jesus. I shoulda known that's what this was.

WP: Answer the question.

    BM: You serious? I know gunshots when I hear them. Of course I ran.

WP: Worried you were going to get shot?

    BM: Worried I was gonna get arrested. Guy with my pedigree.

WP: They arrested somebody else.

    BM: I heard.

WP: Why keep hiding?

    BM: Who's hiding? I was staying with my cousin. Looking for work.

WP: Or a good poker game.

    BM: This is a misunderstanding. My lawyer will explain it.

WP: Yeah, yeah. When did you first meet Jessup Quincannon?

    BM: Last spring. I think it was April. Maybe May.

WP: Where did you meet him?

    BM: His place.

WP: How'd you come to be at his place?

    BM: He sent an invitation.

Nathan Lazenby: Don't play games, Billy.

    BM: Okay, fine, fine. I was staying with this girl I knew over in Flushing. One day I get a knock on the door and it's this guy—Quincannon's lawyer. He says his boss wants to meet me.

    This guy don't look like no lawyer I've ever seen. He looks like a leg-breaker. I tell him no way.

But he hands me a hundred bucks and says there's another three if I agree to meet. I wasn't in a position to turn down four hundred dollars.

This lawyer—Culliver—he drives me over to Quincannon's house. Brings me up to his office.

WP: What did you think of the joint?

BM: What do you mean, what did I think?

WP: Ever been in a place that upscale?

BM: I see what you're getting at. Sure, I had ideas when I walked in. Who wouldn't? Then I met the broad. The one with the hair and the legs. Weird name.

WP: Alathea.

BM: Yeah. Her.

WP: What did she say?

BM: At first, nothing. She didn't have to. I know a killer when I see one. On my way out, she said if I ever thought of having something fall into one of my pockets, she'd know and she'd trim my inseam, you know what I'm saying?

Anyway, that was after I talked with Quincannon. By then I wasn't having no more thoughts like that.

WP: Why not?

BM: I didn't want to spoil a good thing. The guy was handing out C-notes like candy, and all I had to do was answer questions.

WP: What kind of questions?

BM: Just questions.

NL: I swear to God, Billy. I've got half a dozen men outside who want a shot at you.

BM: He asked me about . . . certain activities. Things I can't really talk about in front of somebody who works for the city, you know?

WP: How about hypothetically?

BM: How about what?

WP: Like you're not talking about yourself. You're talking about some other guy.

BM: Right, right. I see your game. Sure. He asked me about a guy I know. Used to know. Might have killed some people. You know—a long time ago.

WP: *What did he want to know about this guy?*

BM: What it was like killing those people. How this guy went about it. Figured out their patterns. Followed them. Lay in wait. That kind of thing. About the gun I—that this guy used. How he got away with it.

WP: *You were okay talking about all this to a stranger?*

BM: Not at first. I thought it might be a sting, you know? Then he took me up to his collection. Started pointing at things. This was the Torso Murderer's hacksaw. This was Lizzie Halliday's underwear. Two minutes listening to this guy, you know he's not a cop. I mean, cops can't fake weird that good.

Some of the questions got a little too much, you know? Even with the money, I thought about walking.

WP: *How were they too much?*

BM: He had all these questions about my—about this guy's family. His upbringing. How he . . . how he might have ended up doing what he did.

I told him I didn't know what he was talking about. He kept asking, so I made some shit up. He seemed to like it.

Another thing he was on about was how it changed me. Changed this guy. Pulling the trigger. How it changed him on the inside, you know?

I told him. I don't think this guy felt anything. Not like that. This guy wasn't a freak. He was a Joe with a job, end of story.

Anyway, there was an hour of that and then he gave me the three hundred and the broad threatened to cut my balls off and I was out of there.

WP: *But you came back.*

BM: A couple times over the summer. Same deal. Four hundred for the hour. Except after the first time, I had to take a cab.

WP: *What did you talk about those times?*

BM: Same deal, but more specific. Specific . . . instances. I don't care how hyperflexible we're getting, I ain't saying more than that.

WP: *Then you got an invitation to the salon.*

BM: Yeah. Fancy envelope and everything. He'd told me about his club. Bunch of freaks like him. Thought maybe there'd be some money in it, so I borrowed a tie from my cousin and went.

NL: Two minutes, Parker.

WP: *Was there? Money?*

BM: Hell, no.

I was talking to this one guy. He was asking questions like Quincannon did. Like how often I got angry. I said as often as anybody else. He said he was a doctor. Said he wanted to put me in a study. I said sure—how much does it pay? He said it pays nothing. That'd it be for science.

Nuts to that.

WP: *Is that where you were when Quincannon came downstairs?*

BM: Maybe it was.

Yeah, yeah. I think it was.

WP: *He say anything to you?*

BM: I asked what the hell I was doing there. It wasn't my scene. He said go have a drink. Enjoy myself.

WP: *That's it?*

BM: Nah, he said something else, too. He said I was right.

WP: *Right about what?*

BM: Hell if I know. He just said, "You know, Billy, you were right." At least I think he did. He was turning away to talk to that doctor.

WP: *He talked to Backstrom? What did he say?*

BM: Nothing. He walked off.

WP: *Quincannon?*

BM: No, the doctor. Funniest thing. He turned on his heel and walked across the room like he was getting a drink, but his glass was full. I saw his face, too. Doctor should study himself if he wants to know about anger.

WP: Backstrom was angry at Quincannon?

    BM: Looked it to me.

NL: Time, Parker.

WP: What did you do then?

    BM: I did what he said. I got a drink. If I wasn't getting paid, I
could at least get loaded.

WP: You stayed in the conservatory the whole time?

    BM: Yeah.

WP: You didn't go upstairs?

    BM: What did I just say?

WP: Nice try, Billy. But someone saw you.

    BM: Saw me what?

WP: Saw you going upstairs.

    BM: That someone is lying.

*WP: I mean, here was Quincannon asking you about specifics.
The things he could do with that kind of information. He had you
on a hook.*

    BM: Uh-uh.

*WP: Or maybe it was heat of the moment. This freak you don't
know from Adam asking you about your childhood. Prying into
your head. A man can't stand for that. Not a real man.*

    BM: Screw you, bitch.

WP: You getting angry, Billy? Like you got angry that night.

NL: Parker.

    BM: I didn't do it!

    I didn't go upstairs. I didn't shoot him. I didn't do nothin'.

*WP: I think you did. I think you got angry at this rich son of a bitch
and you decided to take care of business. It's just a job, right?*

    BM: Exactly. A job. And nobody was paying.

    You know who did pay me? Quincannon. Why would I mess
with a good thing?

    Besides, that Pentecost broad killed him. Everyone knows
that.

NL: Will.

WP: I know, I know. Time's up.

Lazenby took Muffin to the precinct to book him while I stayed behind to pack up the recorder and microphone. As promised, the charges against the gunman would not include attempted murder of yours truly. One count of armed robbery and assorted misdemeanors would have to do, with perhaps a few more armed robberies thrown in if Lazenby could get the victims to testify.

As I rolled up the microphone cord, I thought about how I'd played Muffin all wrong. I got him angry, sure. But it was all denial, denial, denial.

I needed another go at him. Maybe after he was arraigned. At the very least I wanted to put Walter Beck's name in front of him and see how he reacted. Not something I was able to do with Lazenby in the room.

Muffin had given up at least one interesting detail: Backstrom was angry with Quincannon. What did that mean? And why had Backstrom run?

Time. I needed more time.

But we were almost out of it.

CHAPTER *43*

From the journals of Lillian Pentecost

It was long past midnight Friday evening when I heard footsteps walking up the corridor toward our cell. A guard's hard-soled shoes, moving slowly but with purpose.

My stomach clenched. The fear settled over me like a shroud. I hated it and I hated myself for feeling it.

Then the footsteps were outside our door.

Three soft taps from a baton.

I forced myself to stand and walk to the door's small barred window.

Through it I saw a petite woman in a guard's cap and uniform.

"Hello, Ms. Pentecost."

That voice.

"Good evening, Dr. Waterhouse."

I would not have recognized her. She looked nothing like the mousey academic we originally met during the Collins murder, and little like the elegant woman Will described being abducted by last spring.

The woman on the other side of the window had limp blond hair and pockmarked cheeks. A forgettable face.

Except the eyes. So dark, the pupil and the iris seemed to bleed together. I will never forget those eyes.

"Have you come to gloat?" I asked.

She appeared honestly insulted.

"Do I really seem the sort?" she asked.

"I suppose not."

"I came to offer my assistance."

"Do you know who killed Jessup Quincannon?"

I asked the question casually, but not lightly. Olivia Water-house had created an elaborate network for gathering infor-mation about the city's—maybe even the country's—high and mighty. She used that information for leverage, extortion, and sometimes the elimination of people she felt the world would be better off without.

It was very possible she knew the identity of the real killer.

She shook her head.

"I'm afraid not," she said. "Quincannon was one of those nuts I couldn't crack. He let very few into his inner circle."

"What about his guests?" I asked. "Do you know anything about them?"

She cocked her head and smiled.

"Lillian, are you interrogating me?"

"Interviewing," I corrected. "A confidential informant."

Waterhouse might have been a criminal of the highest order, but she was also a singular source of information and she had delivered herself to my door.

"As long as it's confidential," she said, twirling the baton expertly in one hand. "Now, let's see. I know little about the surgeon. Quite a bit about the judge, though nothing useful, and now quite moot. He's dead, in case you haven't heard. Nat-ural causes and far kinder than he deserved. He was the sort who, after helping light the match, was happy to sit back and watch the world burn down around him."

"She used different metaphors, but that was Will's impres-sion," I said.

"Miss Parker is nothing if not an astute judge of char-acter. As for the rest, I've met Timothy Novarro, though

I doubt he remembers me. He seemed like a true believer. The most dangerous kind; they're always willing to kill for a cause. There's the lawyer—Culliver. Unless his character has changed significantly, he is almost certainly embezzling from the estate. And Victoria Pelham. Everyone thinks she killed her husband."

"Did she?"

Waterhouse shrugged.

"I've never asked. Though from what I've heard, it was nothing he didn't deserve."

I had heard the same. I did not pursue that line further.

"There's the reporter—Roberts," she continued. "A good writer, all in all. But too beholden to power to make a difference. I do look forward to reading his book, though."

"His book?"

"About this case. As I understand it, a publisher has already given him an advance."

Will hadn't mentioned it. I wondered if she knew.

"Then of course there's the bodyguard," Waterhouse said. "An exceptional woman. I looked to recruit her for a time, but I believe she's almost entirely amoral."

"And you are not?"

Again, she looked disappointed.

"I am deeply concerned with right and wrong. But I don't let the powers that be dictate which is which."

She looked down the hall at the line of cell doors that stretched all the way to the stairwell.

"If I could, I would open up every single door in this forgotten Circle of Hell and fill it with the people who really belong here."

As she spoke, she began turning, tilting her head to the floor, to the ceiling, as if they were made of glass instead of cold concrete and she could see the bodies encased within.

"I would lock up the monsters who built it, who feed it, who toss women down its throat until they are chewed or spat or shit out. I would fill it with those people and then I would burn it to the ground."

She stopped turning, the look in her eyes almost pleading.

"Is that such a terrible dream?"

"It depends," I said.

"On what?" she asked, extending up on her tiptoes, face pressed against the bars.

"What price you would pay to light your bonfire."

"I would pay anything," she whispered. "I *will* pay anything."

"Even when the currency is lives?"

"Oh, Lillian," she said. "It's only us here. The press aren't listening. Will isn't here. You pretend that the people I prey on are worthy of your sympathy, that you wouldn't do the same if . . ."

"If?" I prompted.

"If you let yourself go."

I owed her more than a rote answer, so I gave it some consideration. It took a moment to remember the names, but eventually they came.

"Jane Howard, the daughter of Byron Howard. He plummeted from the Brooklyn Bridge in 1941. Two years later she jumped from the same spot. Then there was the timber baron who vanished into the Great North Woods. His company collapsed after he disappeared. Hundreds lost their jobs, their homes. It's slowly becoming a ghost town."

She shrugged.

"This country is full of communities destroyed by men like him."

"And Jonathan Markel?" I asked, naming my friend. The one who first made the connection between the name Olivia Waterhouse and the string of strange deaths and suicides she'd left in her wake. "You murdered him when he got too close. What about him?"

"Hardly an innocent."

"No," I admitted. "None of us are. Here or anywhere."

"Certainly not," she said, tapping her baton against the badge on her chest. "But there are some men the world is simply better off without."

"He was my friend," I snapped. "For that alone, I will not stop hunting you."

"Hunting? How . . . frisky."

She stepped away from the window.

"Despite that," she said, "I've come to make you an offer."

"Of what?"

"Freedom," she said. "I can't open every cell in this prison, but I can open yours. Right now. I have a car waiting outside."

"To deliver me where?"

"Anywhere you wish."

Anywhere I wished. I admit, I considered her offer. Olivia Waterhouse was not the only one who had the resources to change her identity. There were places I could go, hide, begin a new life.

Though not as Lillian Pentecost or anyone even resembling her. My work would be finished.

And how many years would I have to enjoy this so-called freedom?

"No," I said finally. "It would be very difficult to be both hunter and hunted. Also, breaking out of prison would destroy whatever credibility I have left. No, Olivia. I think I will stay where I am and take my chances in court."

She laughed at that. A harsh, cold laugh.

"The same court that put all these women in here?" she asked. "That keeps them here? Did you know there's a woman a few cells down who was arrested for having nowhere to live? She'd been released from prison just two weeks before. Can you guess the charge she was serving time for?"

"I suppose for having nowhere to live."

"Vagrancy. Imagine that."

"You should go and open her door," I suggested.

Another smile. It never quite reached her eyes. Will once described them as a shark's eyes. But a shark's eyes are lifeless. Hers are not. If you have ever seen Henri Regnault's *Salomé*, which depicts the Jewish princess with platter and sword, awaiting the head of John the Baptist, then you have seen those eyes. Dark and fierce and resigned to her actions, however bloody.

"Goodbye, Lillian," she said. "If you change your mind, ask Will to put an ad in the *Times*. Use the name Adler. She'll like that. I'll see it and come. In the meantime, here."

She reached into the jacket of her guard's uniform and pulled out a familiar item and slipped it through the bars for me to take.

"Sleep in peace," she said, before turning and walking away down the hall, hard-soled shoes echoing on the cold concrete.

Val rolled over in his bunk.

"Friend of yours?" he asked.

"No," I said. "Not as such."

"Sounds like she's got an itch for you. Not sure what kind, though."

"Neither do I."

I sat on my bed and looked at what Waterhouse had passed to me. My notebook. The one stolen from my cell.

I thought about how she'd tapped her baton against her badge.

There are some men the world is simply better off without.

I do not think Andrews will be bothering me again.

I'm ashamed to say I slept well that night.

CHAPTER 44

One week until jury selection. I forgot how to sleep again. All the gibbering panic I had managed to stomp flat during my Manhattan-high hike came surging back like acid in my gut in the middle of the night.

I'd snap my eyes open at three a.m., fresh from a nightmare where they were strapping Ms. Pentecost into the electric chair. I was clawing at her leather bindings, but I kept breaking nails. What the hell was I doing with nails that long?

I'd look down and see I was in my Nurse Palmer drag and the warden would turn to me and say, "Nurse, help hold her down while we throw the switch."

Then he would throw it and I'd wake up panting.

It was my brain rebelling. I was beating it senseless trying to jostle loose a clue I hadn't noticed. As if putting the puzzle pieces back in the box and giving it a shake might rearrange things to my benefit.

My week went like this:

On Monday I took all the photos I'd snapped at Quincannon's and tacked them to the walls and bookshelves on our third floor. Ms. P had told me about a woman up at Harvard who made dollhouse re-creations of crime scenes to help train investigators. This was my way of creating a sort of life-size photographic diorama of the Black Museum.

I put Ms. P's chair in the center and sat and pondered. The

only conclusion I came to was that everyone gets nearsighted when they've been squinting at photos for two hours.

On Tuesday Mrs. Campbell talked me into trying a hot bath. "It clears my mind right out," she said.

I used half a box of bubble powder and some relaxation techniques I'd learned from my sword-swallowing mentor. When you're sliding three feet of steel down your throat, tense is the last thing you want to be.

I was lying there feeling the water cool and my skin shrivel when I heard the whistle of a train in the distance and a thought came to me: They all did it. Everyone at that party colluded to murder Quincannon and so could tell any lie they wanted and no one would call them out.

I jumped out of the bath, wrapped a towel around myself, and was halfway down the steps to the office before all the other thoughts arrived behind that first, the most prominent being that there was a reason those sorts of things only happened in fiction. People don't trust one another like that in real life. Not when the stakes are so high.

I made my way back to the bath, but not before getting another towel and cleaning up my trail of soapy water. No reason to make Mrs. Campbell pay for my desperation.

That wasn't my only brainstorm. Wednesday evening I woke at the usual three a.m., but instead of yelling, "Don't do it!" I blurted out, "The elevator!"

Ten minutes later I was explaining my idea over the phone to Alathea.

"What if Quincannon wasn't murdered when we thought he was murdered?"

"Explain yourself," she demanded, her voice clogged with sleep.

"It's those gunshots," I said. "Everyone heard them and so everyone can say exactly when Quincannon was killed. What if they were faked? What if someone killed Quincannon earlier? Five minutes would do it. They use a silencer, then they set up something that would mimic the sound of gunshots. Ms. Pentecost heard the shots when she was going up in the elevator, and I was thinking—"

"What if the device was in the elevator shaft?"

"And it was rigged to go off when the car was going up."

"Effectively framing whoever was traveling to the third floor," she finished.

"Exactly!" I blurted. "Now what I need to do is get into that elevator shaft and take a look around. I figure I can send a rope down from the third floor, or maybe ride on top of the car. You can stand inside and stop the car every few feet so I can get a good look around. You think we can do that?"

The sigh she gave was so long I thought a nor'easter might have blown past the receiver.

"Yes, Miss Parker. We can do that. But if you don't mind . . ."

"What?"

"Can we do it tomorrow?"

What had seemed like such a sturdy theory at three a.m. was looking pretty rickety in the clear light of Thursday morning. Still, I spent an hour on top of that elevator looking for machinery that didn't belong or scorch marks from fired shells.

Bupkes.

I left apologizing to Alathea and feeling like a fool. On the way out she asked if anyone with a badge had come asking questions about Beck's death.

"Nothing yet. Staples will get to me eventually, though," I said.

"When he does, you won't mention my name?"

"Who are you again?"

When I got back to the office, there was a message waiting for me from Whitsun. He and Pearl had met with Ms. Pentecost that morning and she'd passed on a bit of information.

Max was writing a book? Since when?

And how had Ms. P heard about it when I hadn't?

First thing I did was call up Marlo Chase. Besides being Holly's other better half, she was an editor, publisher, and something of a prodigal-daughter socialite whose family had deep connections.

"I'll ask around and see what I can dig up," she said.

She must not have had to dig deep because she called back less than an hour later.

"He's received a sizeable advance from Viking," she said. "The editor I talked to is expecting big things. The trial of the century told by someone who was there when the murder happened."

I thanked her, grabbed my hat, and drove uptown. This time I didn't call ahead and arrange to meet over burgers. I walked right into the *Times* offices, took the elevator to the fourth floor, and knocked over two copy editors to get to Max's desk.

He looked up as I approached, and whatever he saw on my face had him out of his chair and glancing around for the nearest exit. I got to him before he could bolt.

"A book?" I snarled. "You're writing a goddamn book?"

He grabbed my arm and pulled me away out of the bullpen and into an empty office.

"Keep your voice down," he said, closing the door. "It's not public knowledge."

"No shit. I had to hear it thirdhand."

"The paper doesn't like its writers moonlighting," he said. "They're worried we'll hold the best stuff back."

"Are you?" I asked. "Holding the best stuff back? Ms. Pentecost's father said he was getting calls from reporters. Did you find yourself a town gossip?"

He didn't have to answer. I saw it all over his face. Max never could lie worth a damn.

"Goddamn it, Max."

"Come on, Will. Someone's going to do it. It might as well be a—"

"A what?" I asked. "A friend? Ms. Pentecost is looking at life and you're hoping to make a buck. That sound like something a friend would do?"

He tilted his head down and peered at me over his glasses.

"I'm getting old, Will," he said. "My sources aren't what they used to be. One of these up-and-comers is going to take my seat eventually and I'll be left with a newspaperman's pension and a closet of clippings I can use to stoke the fire on cold nights. This is my cushion."

Say what you will, Max could really string some syllables together. Five years ago, it might have charmed me.

"You write your little book, Max. Your crime-of-the-century tell-all. But when this is over and my boss is free, don't call me again. Not me or Ms. Pentecost. Not for a quote, not for a cup of coffee. And if there's one misplaced comma, you better believe I'm going to sic Whitsun on your ass. He'll rip those thirty pieces of silver right out of your pockets."

I walked out before he could answer.

Blowing up at Max might have been a tonic for the soul, but it was short-lived. By Friday morning I was feeling as low as ever.

At the House of D, my Nurse Palmer costume chafed more than usual. Maybe because of that dream. Or maybe because I had no new hope to hand Ms. P.

She didn't seem to mind. In fact, she was looking better than she had in weeks.

"I don't know what you're doing differently," Hubbard said, "but keep at it."

That evening I picked Adam Pentecost up at Penn Station. On the way back to Brooklyn I filled him in on the sorry state of the case. If he was despairing for his daughter, he didn't look it.

Poker faces must run in the family.

I got him settled into the guest room and told Mrs. Campbell to put out word that Saturday's open house was canceled for the foreseeable future. There was simply no way I could sit there and concentrate on penny-ante problems, no matter how important it was to Ms. P.

The weekend was spent in conference with Whitsun and Pearl, talking through everything we could hand the jury as an alternative to Ms. Pentecost. There was the embezzling lawyer; the money-hungry preacher's wife; the spurned lover; and the gunman on the run.

"I was thinking on it last night, and I believe we should concentrate on Muffin," Pearl said over a Sunday breakfast of bagels and lox. "If we give the jury too many options, they could get confused and take the easy way out. We can show he needed money. He confessed that much on tape. We'll get Lieutenant Lazenby on the stand to speak to Muffin's history of getting away with murder. Put Muffin up there and he'll invoke his Fifth Amendment rights for everything we ask, which will look guilty as hell. That's an alternative the jury can understand."

Whitsun agreed, and we spent the rest of that last day relistening to the Muffin tape and jotting down ways we could trip him up on the stand.

A dozen times I opened my mouth to say, "I think I

believe him when he says there was no profit for him in killing Quincannon."

But I never said it. It wasn't my case anymore. It was Pearl and Whitsun's.

It wasn't about finding the real killer. Just making sure that Ms. P didn't take the fall.

CHAPTER 45

Jury selection began Monday, and if you want to read all the details, you can look up Max's story in the Tuesday, December 2, 1947, edition of the *Times*.

JURY SELECTION BEGINS ON PENTECOST TRIAL—DEFENSE AND D.A. BUTT HEADS OVER WOMEN ON JURY.

There were plenty of other arguments and nuances and objections and all the usual courtroom hubbub, which is about as exciting as getting to a Dodgers game early to watch them scrub the bases.

Ms. Pentecost was there for the proceedings. Whitsun had me deliver one of her old glass eyes. She didn't say what happened to her other one. A photographer for *The World-Telegram* managed to snap a shot through the bathroom door as it swung open, revealing my boss bent over the sink, popping it in. That shot would eventually run with the caption LILLIAN PENTECOST APPLIES LIPSTICK, ROUGE, AND HER EYE BEFORE COURT.

As the *Times* headline promised, the big story was that Whitsun wanted women on the jury and Bigelow didn't. Women had been serving on juries in New York for years, but it wasn't mandatory like it was for men. They had to opt in. Which meant there were fewer women to choose from overall and it was easier for Bigelow to make sure they didn't get a winning ticket.

What the *Times* didn't know, but I'll tell you here, is that it was all for show.

"If this was a domestic thing—a wife killing her husband because he beat her, I'd want a jury box packed with women," Whitsun confided to me during one of the breaks. "With garden-variety murder, a woman will send another woman to jail just as quick as a man will. Maybe quicker."

Whitsun wanted to put up a fight so that all the prospective jurors would see Bigelow as against women, which might edge them the tiniest bit in Ms. P's favor.

At the end of the day—Thursday, December 4, to be exact—we had our jury. All men, with two women among the alternates.

There was a grease monkey, a guy who repaired musical instruments, an electrician, a couple of fellas who were out of work, a retired typist, and other assorted citizens. Not a one I'd consider peer to Lillian Pentecost.

Judge Creed instructed the jury to keep mum, stay sober, and spend the weekend with their families, since they'd be sequestered for the trial, which would start bright and early Monday morning.

That's when we'd all find out what kind of show we had tickets to—and if it was going to be a tragedy.

I spent Friday night at Holly's.

It wasn't that I didn't appreciate Adam Pentecost's company. When he hit the half-hour mark at lunch describing how biblical translations were responsible for many of today's commonplace phrases, it was almost like having my boss there.

Except she wasn't, and every time I looked up from my soup, I thought, Your daughter is in jail and I can't do a damn thing about it.

To make matters worse, I'd skipped that morning's visit with Dr. Hubbard. I figured, why bother now that I was seeing Ms. P regularly at court.

Except now I was regretting it. It felt like shirking. Like I was laying down on the job.

I spilled all this out to Holly while we were sitting at her tiny kitchen table sharing a slice of cheesecake the size of my head.

"It seems to me," she began, "and I know I'm not a professional, at least not in the strictest sense, that you have done exceptional work, especially considering you've done most of it on your own."

"Yeah, but none of it includes who actually killed Quincannon," I said. "Or Walter Beck, for that matter. Can't forget about that son of a bitch. Which reminds me—I need to get Lazenby on the phone and see where Staples is with the investigation. Usually, I'd be territorial. But right now, if Staples finds Beck's killer, chances are he finds Quincannon's killer, and if he does, I'll give him a big ol' kiss."

"You'd better not," she said.

"A metaphorical kiss," I assured her. "Besides, you're the apple of my eye. Which was originally coined by William Tyndale in his sixteenth-century translation of Deuteronomy."

"You're such a flirt."

I laughed and she laughed, and I could have mistaken it for a normal evening.

After we finished the cheesecake, Holly threw the latest Billie Holliday on the record player, and we kicked off our shoes and danced in her living room. That eventually led to the bedroom, where we kicked off everything else and Holly managed to evict my cares for an hour.

One of the joys and sorrows of Holly's bed is that it's so narrow, activities that begin there frequently finish on the floor. Which is why we were sprawled in a pile of dirty laundry when Holly's phone rang from the living room.

She was up in an instant, padding naked out of the room. She didn't get many calls. I was accounted for, and Brent and Marlo were out in the Hamptons with Marlo's parents.

That left her mother's nursing home in Greenpoint. This late at night, it could only be bad news.

"Will, it's for you!"

Shit.

I ran into the living room and snatched the receiver out of Holly's hand.

"Hello?"

"Will, it's Adam Pentecost. I apologize for calling so late."

"What is it? What's wrong?"

"Nothing's wrong," he said. "Or I should say, nothing that isn't accounted for by the fragile mortality of the human race."

I spied my slacks hanging from the back of a chair. I grabbed them and started maneuvering one leg in while keeping the phone in place with my shoulder.

"What mortality? Who's dying?"

"Millicent Bridgers."

I paused mid-hop.

"Who?"

"One of my longtime parishioners," the minister explained. "She's been ill off and on for quite a while. Her son called and told me that she's not likely to last through the weekend. If it were anyone else, I would pass it on to Reverend Pike, but she's an old friend of the family."

"You have to go home," I said, finally catching up.

"I do," he said. "I'll get the earliest train I can tomorrow morning. I'm going to try to see Lily before I go. If the prison staff will oblige."

"If they don't, play the man-of-the-cloth card," I suggested. "Even turnkeys have souls. Allegedly."

"I'll do that. Again, I'm sorry for waking you. Good night."

"Night."

I collapsed into the chair, heart still pounding, one leg in, one leg out of the slacks. I looked up at Holly.

"How the hell am I going to make it through this trial?"

"One day at a time, I suppose," she said, sparking a cigarette. "Also . . ."

"Yes?"

"Those are my pants."

CHAPTER 46

From the journals of Lillian Pentecost

I had not realized how much Andrews's daily harassment had affected me. I breathe easier, walk with more confidence, and no longer flinch at every loud noise. These last weeks I have lived within a fog of fear that I did not realize was there until it had lifted.

Clear thinking has been no comfort in court. Sitting through three days of jury selection was demoralizing in the extreme. The questions that were asked, the casual prejudice that was uncovered.

"Sure, women can be plenty smart. I mean, I wouldn't trust one to do math. That's different. My wife—no head for figures. But without her I wouldn't be able to find my belt in the morning, you know?"

That was said by a mechanic who was accepted by both Mr. Whitsun and Mr. Bigelow. He is one of the men who will decide my fate.

The biggest disappointment occurred in another courtroom entirely. Val's trial had been scheduled for early Thursday morning. When I returned to our cell late that afternoon, I found him gathering his few belongings.

"They're transferring me to Bedford Hills. Get me away from the bad influences, the judge said. Six months. That's not bad. I can do six months. I hear it's not a bad place in summer. Mind you, it's December."

"Dolly Klinghorn's report clearly shows you did not instigate the assault."

"Sure, sure. My lawyer introduced that report and they dropped the assault charge like that," he said, snapping his fingers. "But they still got me for dressing like a man. Nothing to do about that one. My lawyer didn't even try."

"I'm so sorry, Val."

"Hey—don't look so glum, Lil. A bull dyke walks into an Irish bar. We all knew how that joke was gonna end."

The guard rapped her baton against the door.

"Come on, Lincoln, hurry it up. The bus leaves in ten minutes."

Val threw the last of his clothes into a bag, then pulled his stack of magazines out from under his mattress.

He handed them to me.

"They won't let me take these," he said. "See if any of the girls want them, would you?"

"I'd be happy to," I told him.

He hugged me and kissed me on the cheek, saying, "Keep your head down."

———————

I spent the night alone for the first time since I was arrested. Or as alone as one can be in the House of D. My newly recovered clarity of mind did not help me achieve sleep, however. I kept thinking how I should be able to solve this puzzle.

For God's sake, I was there! Mere moments after the shots were fired. I practically watched the last glimmer of light flee Jessup Quincannon's eyes.

If only I could have interrogated that final glimmer of consciousness.

"Who killed you, Jessup?" I whispered in my bed.
No voice whispered back.

On my way to breakfast Saturday morning I was intercepted
by a guard.

"Your father's here to see you," she said.

I was taken down to the visiting room, a large, open space
with a scattering of spare tables and uncomfortable chairs. I
found my father already seated at one of the tables. He stood
and embraced me and we sat.

"I'm afraid I have to go back home," he said. "At least for a
few days."

He explained about Mrs. Bridgers, whom I remember well.

"I'll almost certainly miss the first day or two of the trial,"
he said. "Maybe more. I'm so sorry, Lily."

I assured him it was all right. In truth, I was glad he would
not be there. While the prosecution did not know the finer
details of my mother's death, they knew enough.

They knew she'd had a lover. They knew that lover was
murdered and that my mother had been arrested. They knew
she was found hanging in her cell. They knew Quincannon had
planned to parade all of this in front of his guests and the press.

To establish motive, Mr. Bigelow will have to speak of these
things, likely in the most sensational manner.

I wished to spare my father that.

"Hopefully, I'll be able to return quickly," he said. "Although
I suppose that's wishing for Mrs. Bridgers to pass quickly, isn't
it? She could recover. She has before. I should be able to tell as
soon as I see her. You can always tell, you remember?"

"Yes," I said, reminded of all the times I had accompanied my
father on such visits. All those people, bodies sunken into their
beds, waiting for death to place its hand on them. "Yes, I know."

"I would have passed this one to Reverend Pike," he said, "but she has such a history with our family. Also, and I wouldn't say this to anyone but you, I don't trust Pike to do deathbed visits. He's a very good speaker, but his bedside manner is lacking. It's fine when people are merely sick, but . . . Lily? Dear?"

"Yes?"

"Are you all right?" he asked.

"I am."

"You've thought of something. You have that look."

"I have," I said. "I've been really rather stupid."

"I doubt that. I've known you to be many things, but stupid has never been one of them."

"I'm going to need you to do something for me," I told him.

"Anything."

"When the guards run over, insist they call Dr. Hubbard immediately. Then ask to use a phone. Call Will. Tell her to get into costume. Tell her that I know who did it and there's no time to waste."

I stood up and took a wobbling step backward.

"Certainly," my father said. "I'll do whatever's needed. But what do you mean when the guards run over? Why would—"

I threw myself forward, hitting my head on the edge of the table, and knew no more.

CHAPTER 47

I was on my way back from Holly's when Ms. Pentecost's father called, and the message I received from Mrs. Campbell when I got to the brownstone was, "She fell and hit her head and her father says to throw on your nurse's togs and get over there right away."

A frantic thirty minutes later, I was flinging open the curtain around the bed in the House of D's clinic to find my boss laid out and Dr. Hubbard hunched over her, dabbing iodine on a nasty gash in her forehead. Her father was sitting at the foot of the bed, looking infuriatingly calm.

I remembered at the last second that Nurse Palmer does not scream obscenities.

"What happened?"

"She fell and hit her head," Hubbard said, screwing the top back on the iodine bottle.

"It was intentional," Ms. P said, tilting her face my way.

"Intentional?"

"I don't think it was that intentional, Lily," her father challenged. "You were unconscious."

"Hang on," I said, sitting on the edge of the cot while Hubbard started preparing his needle and thread. "You did this on purpose?"

"I needed to speak with you immediately," Ms. P explained. "Though, I will admit, I might have overdone it."

"No shit. Sorry, Reverend."

"I assure you, I employed much stronger language when it happened," he said.

"Quiet, both of you," Ms. P snapped. "I need to speak, and there's not much time. I know who killed Jessup Quincannon."

We quieted and we quieted quick. Hubbard broke the silence.

"Can you tell us while I put eight or nine stitches in?" he asked.

"Yes," she said. "Go slowly, please. I need the time."

"As you say, Lillian," Hubbard muttered. "I'm only the doctor."

As the doc stitched, she talked, explaining between the occasional hiss of pain exactly who put that bullet in Quincannon's skull. Halfway through, Hubbard made a loud show about the stitches being too far apart and pulled them out and started over. That gave me time to ask the obvious questions. The first being how hard she'd hit her head.

"I'm not delusional and I'm not concussed," she assured me. "This is the solution that makes sense. If I'm mistaken, please tell me how."

I thought it through. Yeah, it made sense. It untangled a few of the more persistent knots. But there were holes in her theory I could have driven the company Caddy through.

While Hubbard finished the last of his tailoring, I enumerated them.

"The who I get," I said when I was finished. "The how is the problem. From where I'm standing, it looks impossible."

Hubbard helped Ms. P to a sitting position and checked his work for leaks.

"I think now that we know what to look for, the how will become apparent," she told me.

"It's Saturday," I reminded her. "The jury takes their seats on Monday."

"The prosecution will need at least three days to make their case."

Five days total. And I thought we were playing chicken before.

"The challenge will be in convincing Mr. Whitsun," she added. "Currently he is prepared to lay the blame on Billy Muffin. His cross-examination will be directed toward that end. If he starts down that path, it might leave the jury confused when we reveal the true culprit."

While Hubbard got her on her feet and walking around the bed to see how her balance was, Ms. P and I talked about next steps. Somewhere in there, Adam Pentecost left to catch his train back home.

"Death waits for no man, I'm afraid," he said.

Ms. P paused her circuit to give him a hug.

"I'll still try to get back soon," he told her. "I'm glad to know that you're on the right track."

Then he was gone. Five minutes later, so was I. Sent home to figure out a way to prove the impossible.

It's funny how these cases work.

For eight weeks I had been wandering a labyrinth, aimlessly turning corners, butting my head against one brick wall after another. Now I saw the maze from above. There was the exit! I simply needed to reach it.

When I left the House of D, there were still two big knots left to unravel. Ironically, they were the same ones we'd had before Walter Beck ever showed up: the bullet and the gun.

If we couldn't explain those, Whitsun would never jump onboard, and rightfully so. Just because your story is the truth doesn't mean a jury will buy it. Especially if it's got holes that big.

The answers came with the help of two phone calls and a cheese sandwich.

I placed that first call as soon as I got back to the office. It was to a detective agency in Amsterdam that Ms. P had done some favors for in the past. After a few dropped calls, I managed to get the owner on the line and explained what we needed done. They said they would do their best. I told them to aim for better.

I had just put the receiver down when the phone practically rang in my hand. It was Dolly Klinghorn.

"I don't mean to be a nudge, Will. And I'm sorry to bother you on the weekend. But I wanted to make sure you got my invoice for that Valeria Lincoln job."

"Son of a bitch."

"Don't worry about it. Whenever you get a chance—"

"I have a chance right now," I said. "I'll get a check messengered over to you today."

"There's really no hurry."

"Sure, there is," I said. "There's no excuse for stiffing your friends."

After she rang off, I opened a drawer and pulled out the company checkbook. I scribbled out "Klinghorn Investigations" and the appropriate figure and was dotting the *i* in "Willowjean" when I froze.

I pulled out Walter Beck's file and flipped through it to confirm what I suspected.

One mystery down, one to go.

The second—the bigger one, really—was more persistent.

It was Sunday night. Scratch that—early Monday morning. A handful of hours before Judge Creed fired his starter's pistol.

Ms. P and I had an early-morning appointment with Whitsun during which we were going to present her theory of the crime. But there was one last turn in the maze, and if we didn't have that figured out, the jury was never going to buy it.

I tried to get some shut-eye. The answer wasn't coming in my waking hours, but maybe I'd dream a solution.

No dice. No dreams because no sleep.

I went downstairs, fixed myself a cheese sandwich and a glass of milk, and went up to the third floor. I sprawled on the Egyptian rug, back propped against the chair, munched and sipped and pretended to think.

Really, what I was doing was waiting for the sound of the phone from downstairs. I would run down and answer and be told that Nurse Palmer was needed at the House of D, and I would get dressed and speed over and my boss would have the answer ready and waiting.

The photographs of Quincannon's Black Museum were still taped up to the walls and the shelves—my 360-degree diorama of the murder scene.

I looked at the photograph of the empty glass case where the painter's box used to be. Then I looked down at the photograph of the body taped to the floor, then up at the space where the book with its single bullet hole had been.

Two shots. Bang, bang.

Zhao's wooden frog was still sitting on the floor beside me, a totem reminder of my failure. I idly pulled out its mechanical tongue and let it zip back.

Two shots. Bang, bang,

Zip.

I craned my neck around, taking in the rest of my makeshift diorama. The maybe-faux Bonnie and Clyde car door; the writing desk; the top of the stairs; the elevator.

Bang, bang.

Zip.

The case, the body, the book.

Bang, bang, zip.

The car door, the desk, the stairs, the elevator.

Bang, bang, zip.

The case, the body, the book, the car door, the desk, the stairs, the elevator.

Bang, b—

Just like that, I turned the last corner. There was the exit, in front of me.

Every drop of tension—that feeling of impending doom that had been sitting on my shoulders for two months straight—ran out of my body like bathwater down a drain. It left me feeling clean and fresh and more awake than I'd been in weeks.

There were calls that needed to be made. People who needed to be roused out of bed. Those were afterthoughts.

From start to finish, I knew how it had been pulled off. And I knew what we had to do next.

CHAPTER 48

"The People versus Lillian Pentecost in the murder of Jessup Quincannon is in session. Again, I will remind those present that I will brook no foolishness, no needless theatricality, no disruptions. I won't have any of that silliness in my courtroom. Now, Mr. Bigelow, are you ready to present your opening?"

"I am, Your Honor."

"Then proceed."

"Gentlemen of the jury—"

We were off.

In the audience were Staples and a collection of cops and scientists ready to talk blood and bullets; there were the Novarros, Victoria Pelham, Mrs. Johnson and her son. Silas Culliver was sitting in one of the back pews, perhaps wondering if he could slip out without anybody noticing. Alathea was across the aisle from him, dressed like some bank president's personal secretary. Roberts was with the rest of the press but had been granted an aisle seat in case he was called to testify. If he glanced my way, I didn't know it because I was avoiding looking at him.

The rest of the audience was made up of the press and general public, who thought they had front-row seats to the downfall of a great detective.

Bigelow began the festivities by telling the jury and

everyone else what they were in for: family secrets, old grudges, murder club party, gunshots, corpse, fleeing woman. Nothing they hadn't read in the papers.

Then Whitsun got his turn.

"Ladies and gentlemen, I won't take up too much of your time. Mr. Bigelow is raring to present his evidence, and I'm more than happy to let him. Because my client has spent enough time locked in a cell. She has spent sixty-four days in prison.

"Sixty-four days watching as her name has been dragged through the mud. All for a crime she did not commit. I promise you that by the time this trial is over, not only will we have proved that, but we will hold up the one, true murderer for all of you to see."

Bold, clear, and not even a minute, where Bigelow had taken twenty. I heard the reporters in the back scribbling down every word.

Whitsun was onboard with the plan. Barely.

Not because he didn't believe us. By the time Ms. P and I sat down with him that morning, I'd made some calls and gotten confirmation of my theories. Pearl, as usual, summed up the problem.

"I buy it," she said. "I don't know if a jury will. It's so . . . I don't know if I have the word for it."

"I agree," Ms. P said. "That's why I believe we must act very deliberately."

She laid out a plan of attack, and it was that plan that made Whitsun so reluctant. Because it required the hotshot, charismatic, scene-stealing defense attorney to do something entirely against his character.

Nothing.

It required him to do nothing. So he gritted his teeth and did just that.

For the next two days, as Bigelow rolled out the evidence against Ms. Pentecost, Whitsun barely spoke.

As Bigelow brought up witness after witness, there were hardly any objections, barely any cross-examination. Even when the chief medical examiner flubbed and called the bullet a slug, the best criminal defense attorney in the city kept mum.

Like my boss, Whitsun fixed his face into a look of sphinx-like patience.

The headlines after that first day were all over the map. Some declared that Bigelow was running roughshod over the defense. Others argued that Whitsun was lying in the weeds, waiting to strike.

The only time Whitsun showed signs of life was when Alathea took the stand on the second day. She was sworn in as, I swear to God, Alathea Doe. That was apparently her legal last name, and I use the word *legal* loosely.

She was there to talk about Ms. Pentecost's arrival at Quincannon's on the night of the murder. Bigelow also asked her about the confrontation in September where Ms. P had asked Quincannon to return the painter's box.

"How did the defendant react when she saw it?" Bigelow asked her.

"Distraught," Alathea said. "She clearly had some kind of emotional attachment to it."

Everyone in the courtroom, the court reporter included, looked at Whitsun to object. Alathea was a psychopath, not a psychologist. Even Judge Creed was waiting.

"Mr. Whitsun, did you want to say something?" he asked.

"No, Your Honor," he said. "The defense has no objection at all and will gladly stipulate that the exhibit has a deep personal meaning for my client."

He said it matter-of-factly. Almost cheerfully.

There was so much scribbling from the reporters I could practically smell their pencils smoldering. Whitsun was known for fighting for every inch of ground in a case, and here he was, giving the state a clear highway.

Alathea was the only witness he spent any time cross-examining, and even then his tack wasn't what anyone expected.

Forest Whitsun: He started giving you Saturday nights off again when?
    Alathea Doe: The first week of July.
FW: But he never told you why.
    AD: He did not.
FW: Was there one of these nights that sticks in your memory?
    AD: One morning I arrived back to find Mr. Quincannon with a bruise under his eye.
FW: A black eye? Somebody hit him?
    AD: He said he ran into a door.
FW: Those pesky doors. Always throwing jabs.
Ken Bigelow: Objection! Your Honor, Mr. Whitsun is leading the witness far afield.
FW: I apologize, Your Honor. Just one more question. When was this?
    AD: The morning of Sunday, September twenty-eighth.
FW: Thank you. No more questions, Your Honor.

We were nearing the end of day two when Bigelow wrapped his case. A full day earlier than expected, thanks to Whitsun playing possum.

"Mr. Whitsun, will you be ready to call your first witness tomorrow morning?" Judge Creed asked.

"I will, Your Honor, though I have two motions to present before then."

"I'm sure those can wait until—"

"They're very quick, Your Honor," Whitsun said. "One is a change to our witness order. The first witness we'd like to call is Lillian Pentecost."

I'm sure you've read the phrase "the room exploded" in some book or other, but it's something else when you experience it in person. No fewer than five people blurted, "Holy shit," including at least one juror.

After gaveling the room quiet, Judge Creed turned to my boss.

"Are you sure, Ms. Pentecost?"

The son of a gun got the "Ms." right.

The woman in question stood and addressed the judge and jury.

"Yes, Your Honor. I'm quite sure," she said. "If I'm allowed to tell the story in my own way."

"Which brings us to our second motion," Whitsun added. "We've spent the last two days hearing witnesses describe this so-called Black Museum and seeing pictures of the place. We've heard about the timing and events and the movements of people throughout the house. But, sir, pictures do not do it justice. Which is why the defense is motioning to convene the court tomorrow morning at Mr. Quincannon's home. We believe that's the only way for the jury to understand—with their own eyes—what really happened that night."

Ka-boom.

This time it took Judge Creed a good half-minute to gavel the room into submission.

"In my chambers," he growled. "Now."

Bigelow and Whitsun followed the judge out of the room. I snuck up a row and leaned forward to whisper in Ms. P's ear.

"Your friend in Amsterdam found him," I said. "Got the call this morning. Everything should be ready for tomorrow. Speaking of which, what do you reckon our chances are?"

She leaned back in her chair to respond.

"You're the oddsmaker, Will. What do you reckon?"

I thought about it.

"Let's see. Whitsun spent two days playing meek and mild, all so we could trade in every chit on this single play. Then he made the request in front of the jury and the press. If Bigelow objects too strongly, everyone will wonder what he's scared of. So fifty-fifty."

Ten minutes later, the three men reappeared. Creed wore a scowl, Bigelow a look of stunned confusion, Whitsun an "ah shucks" smile.

We were in.

CHAPTER 49

On Wednesday, December 10, 1947, thirty-six people gathered inside Quincannon's front gate. There was me, Ms. Pentecost, Whitsun, Pearl, Judge Creed, the court reporter, Bigelow, two assistants from the DA's office, seven uniformed bailiffs, Detective Donald Staples, twelve jurors, six alternates, and Max Roberts.

Judge Creed had balked at Roberts. He didn't want to show favoritism to any single paper. We reminded him that Roberts was doubling as a witness in this case and that we might need him.

But that crowd was nothing compared to the one gathered on the other side of the gate. Every morning edition worth its salt had the trial on the front page, and while some of them were calling today's planned field trip a "stunt," they printed the word in three-inch type.

Which is why the street outside Quincannon's manse was a river of bodies—hundreds of people jawing and pointing and clambering to get a glimpse of whatever Lillian Pentecost had planned. Another three dozen police were spaced around the block, keeping people from trying to leap the fence.

I pointed out that elm branch on our way in and suggested they get an officer to take an ax to it.

Ms. Pentecost had requested to begin her testimony as soon as we passed through the gate, but the noise from the crowd meant we had to move halfway up the walk before she could be heard. We stood in a rough circle, defense and prosecution on one side, judge and jury on the other.

Judge Creed, looking like he was regretting this whole affair, gave a protracted spiel about propriety and decorum and how it was still a trial and if we couldn't remember that, he'd call the whole thing off.

"Mr. Whitsun, please call your witness."

"The defense calls Lillian Pentecost."

My boss stepped into the middle of the circle and was sworn in. She moved easily and with grace, her cane having been returned to her for the duration. She was attired in one of her favorite suits—a rust-colored English number in herring-bone tweed. Her self-imposed moratorium on trousers had been lifted.

Whitsun asked the only question he needed to.

"Ms. Pentecost, could you tell us in your own words what happened the evening of October seventh."

Sensing the show was starting, a hush fell over the crowd outside.

"Shortly after dinner that evening, I received an invitation to a meeting of the Black Museum Club," she began. "It was not the first I'd received, but this one was different. In recent months, I had been instrumental in disrupting Jessup Quincan-non's pastime of collecting memorabilia from the most lurid of murder cases. I had informed on officials, intercepted bribes, and . . . and caused the dismissal of men who had accepted those bribes. This invitation advertised a new exhibit in Mr. Quin-cannon's collection. A painter's box. Mr. Bigelow presented it as part of his case and described, with much-appreciated discre-tion, its significance to me. I will say this—it belonged to my mother, who was accused of murder and died in prison before her trial. I loved her very deeply and am protective of her mem-ory, and of my father, who loved her as well. As you can imag-ine, I did not want this artifact and its history used as part of a campaign of revenge against me. Which is all to say that when I arrived here at eight-fifteen on the evening of October seventh, I was not thinking clearly."

I raised a hand and gave a wave to the figure looking out one of the first-floor windows of the house.

"For that, I apologize," Ms. P added. "If I had, I would have noticed certain details in the moment and spared us all these many weeks of hardship."

The front door opened and Alathea walked out. At Ms. Pentecost's request, she was dressed as she had been that evening: a black velvet evening gown with a slit up the leg high enough so she could get to her thigh holster, which was strapped on but unoccupied.

Ms. P waited to continue until Alathea had reached us, which was smart. The jury was all men, after all.

I glanced at Bigelow, half expecting him to object to this admittedly needless theatricality, but the St. Nick stand-in kept quiet. I think he knew, even then, there was a knockout coming. Being an honorable man, he was prepared to set his jaw and take the punch.

"At eight-fifteen I pressed the buzzer and Miss Doe escorted me inside," Ms. P said.

Alathea turned around and we followed her en masse the rest of the way up the walk. She held the door open for us and we filed inside. Because of the numbers, the group stretched all the way down the hall and through the doorway into the conservatory, though the jurors were given the front-row spots.

"I was the last to arrive," Ms. P told them. "The invitation had been hand-delivered late to ensure this. Jessup did not want to give me time to interfere with his plans."

Now Bigelow raised a hand.

"Objection, Your Honor. The witness cannot know the victim's intentions," he said.

Whitsun took the ball.

"Your Honor, Miss Doe is willing to testify that Mr. Quincannon specifically arranged for Ms. Pentecost's invitation to be delivered late in the day for this very purpose."

Creed looked to Alathea, who nodded.

"We'll let it go for now. But please try to shy away from conjecture."

"Of course, Your Honor," Ms. P said. "Miss Doe has already testified as to what happened next. Before coming outside, she had used the house phone here to call her employer, who was waiting on the third floor. She told him that I had arrived. He instructed her to install me in the elevator and then to retrieve a particular bottle of wine from the basement wine cellar. One that had been misplaced. She did as requested. Consequently, when the elevator deposited me on the third floor, fifteen seconds later, I was alone. Now, if you will follow me."

We couldn't all fit in the elevator, so we took the stairs. Even with her cane, Ms. P somehow managed to take them a little quicker than the rest of us, driven by exhilaration, anticipation, and a gleam in her good eye.

On the night of the murder, Ms. P had arrived on the third floor to find herself alone save for a corpse. That wasn't the case this time. We were greeted by the stalwart figure of Lieutenant Nathan Lazenby, standing next to the open glass case that had once held the painter's box. He was wearing a pair of white cotton gloves and held in his hand a double-barreled derringer, similar to Ms. P's own.

Staples moved forward, probably to start a territorial pissing match, but Judge Creed beat him to it.

"Lieutenant? What's the meaning of this?"

"I'm here serving a warrant on another case, Your Honor," he said. "Don't worry, the gun is empty."

Lazenby looked at Ms. P.

"It was exactly where you said it would be."

A ripple went through the jury. Not so much a murmur as an expectant shifting of feet, of bodies leaning forward.

"She told you where to find this gun?" Creed asked.

"I can't take credit," Ms. P told the judge. "It was Miss Parker who unraveled this particular knot. And in doing so, she solved a months-old murder."

"Do you mean Jessup Quincannon's?"

"No," she said, shaking her head. "That of Junfeng Zhao."

A lot of blank, confused stares.

"Mr. Zhao was a toy maker," she explained. "Known for his hand-carved pieces that housed ingenious mechanical devices. His work delighted children and was in high demand among the city's wealthier families. Mr. Zhao was even written up in the papers once. That's probably how he came to his killer's attention."

Now Creed looked like he was regretting getting up that morning or even taking up the profession of jurisprudence in the first place.

"If you don't mind, Your Honor. I believe I can explain everything to your satisfaction," she added.

"All right," he said. "Please make it swift."

"Certainly. May I have the assistance of the lieutenant as a stand-in for Jessup Quincannon?"

Creed gave Lazenby the nod, and we were off again.

"As I mentioned, when the elevator doors opened into this room on the evening in question, Jessup Quincannon was lying on this spot here, dead, a very fresh bullet wound in his head. The air smelled of gunpowder and blood and something else. Something familiar. But as I said before, I was not thinking clearly. What I did notice was the small notebook lying next to the body."

That caused another ripple, among jury and jurists alike, since no one had mentioned a notebook until this moment.

"I examined it and saw that he had written the details of his presentation and about my mother's death. Details I did not want made public, which they would certainly be if taken into evidence. I took it and fled. When I arrived home, I burned it."

Bigelow looked like he wanted to object, but he couldn't figure out what for. For the accused digging herself deeper?

"It was exceptionally foolish, I know," Ms. P admitted. "That rash decision, along with my own distractedness, precipitated everything that followed."

She hung her head in contrition. But only for a moment. When she raised it again, there was another kind of look in her eye.

"I am not entirely to blame," she told the jury. "My actions were carefully orchestrated. My invitation arrived late so that the stage would already be set. That notebook was there so that I would have a reason to flee the scene. Even the slowness of the elevator was deliberate. He needed time, you see."

Nobody saw, and because Whitsun was being leisurely hitting his cue, I piped up.

"Who needed time?"

Ms. P turned to Lazenby.

"Would you do the honors, Lieutenant?"

"Gladly," he rumbled.

To judge and jury she said, "Now please allow me to demonstrate what happened in this room in the sixty seconds prior to my entrance."

Creed looked at Bigelow, expecting an objection. How could Ms. P testify to events she wasn't there to witness?

No objection came. Maybe the prosecutor was as curious as everyone else. Creed nodded to Ms. P.

"Proceed."

She did.

"At eight-fifteen Jessup Quincannon received a phone call from Miss Doe," she said. "He was informed that I had arrived. He asked Miss Doe to retrieve the bottle of wine. Then he listened for the sound of the elevator. Once he was assured I was on my way up, he took up the prepared derringer."

Lazenby displayed the gun to the jury.

"He fired its two shots," she continued. "The first was not into the medical textbook, but into the car door."

Lazenby raised the pistol, pointed it at the bullet-riddled door, and pulled the trigger.

Click.

"Then he placed the gun carefully against his own temple and shot himself in the head."

There were gasps from some members of the jury as Lazenby pressed the derringer against his own brow and pulled the trigger a second time.

Click.

"Ms. Pentecost," Creed said, "I warned against this kind of abject theatrica—"

That was when Lazenby let go of the gun and it flew out of his hand, yanked through the air by the wire that had gone unseen in the dim lighting of the room, and into the open top of the writing desk. Wire and derringer disappeared into the false bottom inside, the opening to which fell and latched with a third and final click, showing only the green-velvet inner surface with its half-finished letter.

Lazenby knelt down onto the hardwood floor and stretched out. Right where Alathea had been. Right where Jessup Quincannon had been.

"This is how he did it," Ms. Pentecost told the jury, who were all standing, gobsmacked. "This is how Jessup Quincannon killed himself and framed me for his murder."

CHAPTER **50**

If you're thinking, "Hey, all of this could have been explained in the quiet confines of the courtroom," you're right, but you're missing the point. Ms. Pentecost didn't just want to absolve herself. She wanted to blow the goddamn doors off the joint.

"Jessup Quincannon spent his last breath in an attempt to destroy me and my reputation," she explained to me that last Saturday in the clinic. "A simple recitation of facts will not do."

Thus the spectacle. Thus having Roberts present. We'd made a deal with him. You get a seat at the table, but only if you agree to leave out any details about Ms. Pentecost's mother from your book.

The newspaperman reluctantly agreed. Now he was scribbling so fast his shorthand couldn't keep up.

"But why?" Whitsun prompted. "Why would Jessup Quincannon end his life in an attempt to frame and discredit you?"

"Because he was dying," Ms. P declared. "Which I should have realized sooner. That very evening, in fact."

She turned to the jury.

"It was the smell," she explained. "My father is a minister. As a child, I accompanied him on numerous occasions to the sickbeds of the gravely ill, many of whom were dying from cancer. They exude an odor. Perhaps from the illness, perhaps as an effect of the medicine. Eventually it pervades any room they spend a considerable amount of time in. That smell was present that evening, even over the smell of blood and gunpowder. But I was too distracted to take note."

Whitsun turned to Pearl and nodded. She stepped forward and handed Judge Creed a sealed envelope.

"Your Honor," Whitsun said, "the defense would like to submit as evidence a signed statement from Dr. Ryan Backstrom, testifying that Jessup Quincannon approached him in June of this year, suffering from nausea, headaches, and a number of other symptoms. Mr. Quincannon suspected, and Dr. Backstrom confirmed, the presence of a brain tumor."

"Right here, in the frontal lobe," Ms. P said, tapping her brow. "The placement of the bullet was very deliberate."

Murmurs from the jury, and Creed reached for a gavel that wasn't there.

"Quiet, please," he said. "Why isn't Dr. Backstrom here to testify to this in person?"

"He's currently in Sweden," Whitsun explained. "I believe he will fight any attempt at extradition."

"Why would he do that?" Creed asked. "Diagnosing a patient is hardly a crime."

Again, Ms. P raised a hand.

"I believe I can clarify, Your Honor," she said. "When Jessup learned of his illness and was told it would kill him within a year, he began to make plans. To orchestrate the scene we have just re-created. First, he swore Dr. Backstrom to secrecy, and he only allowed the doctor to see him here, at his house. And only on Saturdays, when he required Miss Doe to absent herself from the premises. He'd already ended his relationship with Victoria Pelham. Likely—Dr. Backstrom will have to confirm this—due to the tumor's interference with his ability to perform sexually."

The judge looked over at Pearl and then the two women alternates, but they seemed nonplussed at the casual nod to erections. He did not look my way, which I took as a compliment.

"He also began preparing this room," Ms. P continued. "He had the elevator installed. He had likely first intended it to be for his own benefit. He was able to hide it, but he was growing weaker, you see? However, as his plan solidified, he had the workmen set it to as slow a speed as possible without raising suspicion. He replaced a preexisting exhibit—a dress from one of Jack the Ripper's victims—with the car door. It's meant to be reminiscent of the car of Bonnie Parker and Clyde Barrow, but it's an obvious forgery. Its intent was to provide a place to fire the first bullet. Would you mind, Lieutenant?"

Lazenby raised himself off the floor and walked over to the car door. After a moment of inspection, he pointed to a bullet hole whose edges gleamed a little brighter than the rest.

"Right here," he said.

Ms. P nodded once and moved on.

"From Mr. Zhao, he commissioned the writing desk."

Lazenby walked over to the desk. He pressed three hidden buttons on it simultaneously, causing the false bottom to unlatch and reveal the pistol secreted within.

"However, Mr. Zhao was an honorable man," Ms. P continued. "Jessup would have recognized this. He could not expect Mr. Zhao to remain quiet once he'd realized his work had been used in a ruse to convict an innocent woman. So Jessup made use of another acquaintance. Mr. William Muffin."

Lazenby rumbled a word that caused the court reporter's fingers to stutter.

"No, Nathan," Ms. P said. "He did not hire Mr. Muffin to kill Mr. Zhao. He merely gathered advice on the best way to do it. To murder a man swiftly, with a pistol, and leave no trace. He then committed the deed himself. On Saturday, September twenty-seventh with the gun you're holding in your hand. It allowed him to not only be certain of Mr. Zhao's silence but to test out a technique for modifying the derringer's bullets to fragment upon impact. It was a technique he also learned from Mr. Muffin, and it was of vital importance to the success of his plan. A fragmented bullet not only ensured that it could not be matched to any individual gun, but would also more fully obliterate the tumor in his head."

She peered at the derringer in Lazenby's paw.

"I see that there is some blood speckled on the barrel," she said. "Some of that will of course be Jessup's. But it's quite possible that some will be found to belong to Mr. Zhao. The murder was committed at close range. Close enough that Mr. Zhao was able to strike Jessup in the eye."

Remember what Quincannon said to Muffin at the party? *You were right.*

If I was a betting woman, and I am, that had less to do with the bullet trick and more to do with Muffin's insistence that the business of killing was just business. I think Quincannon finally got his chance, did the deed, and felt nothing.

"Jessup also used the opportunity to ensure Dr. Backstrom's silence," Ms. P explained. "He had the doctor drive him to Mr. Zhao's that night, likely making up some innocuous excuse. When Dr. Backstrom discovered that Jessup had committed murder and that he was an accomplice, it guaranteed his silence even after Jessup's death. While I cannot prove this beyond a shadow of a doubt, it does explain the doctor's flight. Also, you will find that a blue Chevrolet sedan—similar to the one owned by Dr. Backstrom—was seen near Mr. Zhao's workshop the night of the murder."

Judge Creed raised his hand. That's how much Ms. Pentecost had taken control of the case. A judge raising his hand in his own courtroom.

Ms. P gave him the nod.

"What about the bullet in the textbook?" he asked. "The one shown to be from your gun?"

"That was a bit of genius on Jessup's part," she admitted. "He bribed a man—Walter Beck, a member of the New York

City Police Department's crime lab—to procure a bullet discharged from my gun, which was already in police custody. Jessup then shot a bullet into the textbook, pried it out, and replaced it with the one from my gun. I imagine he did it the Saturday before his death, when he had the house to himself. A small bullet hole would have gone unnoticed for a few days."

"Can you prove any of this?"

The judge fired the question at Ms. P, but Lazenby intercepted it.

"I've looked in the evidence room. One of the samples we took from Ms. Pentecost's derringer back in November of '45 is missing."

"Also," Ms. P added, "while I'm afraid Mr. Beck has since died, you'll find in Mr. Quincannon's ledger a deduction of one thousand, two hundred, and fifty dollars taken from the cash deposit in his safe on August ninth and listed under 'household expenses.' That exact amount was deposited by Mr. Beck into his bank account the following Monday."

The note in Quincannon's ledger had been confirmed by Alathea; Beck's deposit by Lazenby. All precipitated by Dolly Klinghorn asking me for a check.

It had made me think about the practicalities of being a working detective, which made me think about how Beck hadn't been able to pay for Klinghorn's report until recently. How had he gotten the money? I'd been too busy hating him to ask.

When Klinghorn's report showed nothing and he was still unsatisfied, Beck hijacked Quincannon's plot. He took credit for the swapped bullet and used it to try to strong-arm us into proving that his wife was murdered.

And if you're wondering how, if Quincannon was behind all this, Beck ended up shot dead in his apartment, don't worry. We'll get there.

Back in the Black Museum, we had already spent our

powder, but Whitsun hated to leave the jury on such a dry note.

"I don't want them walking away pondering a fact," he'd told me before we started. "I want to leave them gripped by a feeling."

He asked Ms. Pentecost one final question.

"It seems that if you've only got a few precious months to live, you'd be careful how you spent them," Whitsun said. "But Jessup Quincannon wasted them seeking revenge against you. Why in God's name would he do that?"

The next bit had been rehearsed, but Ms. P delivered it with feeling.

"Part of it might have been due to the tumor. It was certainly impacting him mentally, as well as physically. But that's a generous interpretation," she said. "Mostly it was because of his deep dislike for me. He was someone who focused on mankind's worst impulses. Who believed that they were inevitable."

"You believe otherwise?" Whitsun prompted.

Ms. Pentecost hesitated before responding, taking a moment to look around the room. The jury followed her eyes. To the glass cases filled with straight razors and spent bullets, scraps of clothes soaked in the blood of men and women whose only crime was to be in the wrong place at the wrong time.

Quincannon's evidence that all humans were monsters waiting to happen.

"I do not know," Ms. P admitted. "But I am willing to proceed with the hope that people—individuals, if not our species as a whole—can make themselves better. I think Jessup couldn't stand that. That I saw all that he saw, and worse, and still acted as I did."

She looked at the jury, meeting the eyes of those twelve men, one by one.

"Jessup Quincannon was right in one respect," she told

them. "We are all capable of terrible things. But we are also capable of wonderful things, of compassion and grace. I am truly sorry that Jessup died before he could discover that for himself."

With that, the defense rested.

CHAPTER 51

The doors of the House of D did not immediately fall off their hinges. Judge Creed called for a twenty-four-hour delay so police could confirm everything that Ms. Pentecost had laid out.

Those twenty-four hours turned into forty-eight, which ran into the weekend.

The gun in the writing desk was tested and blood samples were taken that matched the type for both Zhao and Quincannon. Dr. Backstrom's statement was confirmed, as were the corresponding lines in Quincannon's and Beck's respective financials.

Meanwhile, after Max Roberts's exclusive, the rest of the city's papers played catch-up. There were stories coming at the case from every possible angle. Fresh stories about Quincannon and the Black Museum, about the Zhao murder.

There was even a story about Backstrom that tracked down some unhappy recipients of his lobotomies. Or unhappy family members, as those who'd undergone the procedure were not fit to be interviewed.

By the time Monday morning rolled around, everyone in the city knew not only that Lillian Pentecost was innocent, but also that she had proved it, and thrown in the Zhao murder to boot.

When court reconvened that morning, Whitsun called

for an immediate dismissal of the charges. While Judge Creed wouldn't go so far as that, he did strongly urge Bigelow to throw in the towel.

Almost ashamedly, Bigelow told the judge, "I'm afraid I can't do that, Your Honor."

Creed, who wasn't used to being told no, leaned over his desk like he was ready to pounce.

"You *can't* do it?"

"I have been instructed to request that we let this go to the jury."

Someone in the DA's office—probably the man himself—had decided too much money had been spent, too much hay had been made.

And so, at eleven o'clock on Monday, December 15, following some very brief final arguments, twelve men went into a locked room to decide the fate of Lillian Pentecost. Twelve men who I would trust to fix my radio, restring a violin, and figure out the wobble in my axle, but not much else.

The courtroom hadn't even finished emptying when the bailiff came back.

"They have a decision!" he cried out.

Eleven minutes. It had taken them eleven minutes to decide "not guilty." They didn't even drag it out to get the free lunch.

Not that there was ever any doubt. At least not by Whitsun, who had reserved the top room at Zanotti's for a celebratory meal.

We were late getting there, though. My boss, cane firmly in hand and not a handcuff in sight, stood on the steps of the courthouse and answered every question thrown at her. It was a cold, blustery day, but she stood there, hair and coat whipping in the wind, looking like she welcomed the chill.

A million flashbulbs ignited. If you've seen only one photograph of Lillian Pentecost, five will get you ten it's that one. Looking like goddamn Lady Justice herself. One-eyed instead of blindfolded, and this one absolutely giving a damn.

While she held court, I slipped around the side of the building in time to catch Bigelow coming out the back.

"They really threw you to the dogs, counselor," I said, as the door swung shut behind him.

"If we dropped the case, that's on the DA's office," he said. "If we lose it, that's on me."

"Politics."

"Politics."

He added, "The DA—this was before the verdict came in—wanted me to file an obstruction of justice charge against Ms. Pentecost. For burning Quincannon's notebook."

"Did you?" I asked, suddenly worried that maybe this wasn't over after all.

He shook his head.

"No. I suggested that, if he wanted it done, he should file the paperwork himself. To lend the official weight, you understand?"

I did understand. It was legalese for: If you want to be petty, do it yourself. Now, with the not guilty verdict in, it would be political suicide.

"You getting canned?" I asked.

He smiled. "Oh, they won't fire me. They'll ask for my resignation. With the knives discreetly hidden behind their back."

"You gonna give it to them?"

"I haven't decided," he said. "If I don't, they'll kick up a fuss."

A particularly vicious gust chose that moment to tear the homburg off his head and send it flipping, brim over brim, up Centre Street. He moved to run after it, then stopped and watched it tumble away into the distance.

"You should kick up a fuss," I told him, watching as the hat hit a curb and then shot straight into the sky, propelled by some invisible Manhattan twister. "For a lawyer, you're not too big of an asshole."

That got a smile out of him.

"Miss Parker, from you I take that as the greatest of compliments. I will consider it."

He pulled his coat tightly around him and started north, in the direction of his hat, which by then was no more than a black speck against a white sky.

By the time Whitsun and Pearl and I dragged Ms. Pentecost up into the private room of Zanotti's, everyone was already there, elbow-deep in pasta carbonara and slinging back Chianti. And when I say everyone, I mean it.

There was Mrs. Campbell and Hiram and Sam Lee; Lazenby was dabbing a sauce stain off his shirt; Dolly Klinghorn was there, dressed in a McCall's special and deep in conversation with Dr. Hubbard, who looked like he was enjoying the attention. Alathea had been invited but declined to attend.

Adam Pentecost had arrived on the eleven o'clock train; Mrs. Bridgers's illness had been a false alarm. Death, it seemed, had decided to tarry.

He stood up when we entered and came over and hugged and kissed his daughter. Holly, who had been tasked with meeting the minister at the train station and getting him to the restaurant, stood as well, but didn't come over and hug and kiss me, as we were in mixed company.

After we took our seats, a bottle of Ms. Pentecost's honey wine was produced. Congratulations were given, toasts were made. Whitsun gave a speech. It was both eloquent and too long.

Eventually, questions were asked. The papers had covered everything in exhaustive and lurid detail, but there were still corners that had been left unexamined.

"As usual, it comes down to the victim," Ms. P explained to her disciples. "To their life and character, and to the anomalies within it. At the very outset, I wondered why Jessup would trade all that leverage over me, potential years of torment, for a single evening of humiliation. It seemed so rash for him. I should have noted it sooner.

"Then there was Walter Beck," she added. "Whom his colleagues and acquaintances described as a simple, unimaginative man. That he would concoct the plan to switch out the bullets was out of character for him. But to take advantage of Jessup's scheme once he'd realized what was happening—that was far more possible. Again, the clues were there. It simply took us a while to see them clearly."

I excused myself. There was nothing I could add and Ms. Pentecost was having too much fun.

Once outside, I walked down the block to Flannagan's. Lunchtime was over and the bar was empty save for a sleepy bartender, a bored-looking waiter, a table of suits in the back, and the one man I'd spied walking in earlier, now sitting alone at the bar.

I took the stool next to him. The bartender roused himself long enough to shuffle over.

"What can I get you?"

"A glass of the Chateau Haut-Brion."

He frowned. "I don't think we got that."

I slipped a sawbuck across the bar.

"Why don't you go in back and look for it?" I suggested.

He pocketed the bill and got scarce.

The man at the bar watched all of this with curiosity and apprehension. When the bartender was well out of earshot, he turned to me.

"Come to gloat, Parker?" Detective Donald Staples asked.

I shook my head.

"Nah. I'm not the type," I said. "Actually, yes, I am. But that's not why I'm here. I want to talk to you about Beck."

Staples turned back to his drink.

"I can't talk about that," he said. "Wally's death is still under investigation."

"I wasn't talking about Walter. I wanted to chat about Susie."

Not a blink, not a twitch, not a tremor in that movie-star face. Which told me everything I needed to know if I didn't already know it.

"She was a beautiful woman," I said. "Smart, too. Out of Walter's league. I'll bet everyone laughed at him behind his back. The drip sporting the arm candy at all the NYPD balls. Maybe that's where you first saw her. Or maybe it was at their housewarming. When they moved into their new place in Jackson Heights? Timing lines up. It wasn't long after that she got herself a boyfriend."

As I talked, I examined Staples through Susie Beck's eyes. Young, handsome, charming, ambitious—everything her husband wasn't. Staples was smart, too. The skills that made him a good detective would have allowed him to pick up on Susie's unhappiness. To him, she'd be a damsel in distress, and a pretty one at that.

"You were careful," I said. "Discreet. At first, I figured Loverboy—that's what her co-worker called him—was married. Married and he'd done this before, so he knew the tricks. It wasn't until later that I thought it could be a cop. Though I still don't know if you've done it before."

It wasn't phrased as a question, but he gave his head the smallest of shakes anyway.

"Either way, Susie fell for you hard. This was right around when you started to get the spotlight. People began calling you the NYPD's golden boy. If it came out that you were seeing a married woman, it would have kneecapped your career. So you broke it off. She wouldn't take it, though. She pined for two weeks, then invited you to meet somewhere. Someplace remote that served red wine. Don't know if you showed or not, but I know what she did when she got home."

That's right. Susie Beck committed suicide. The one thing she and Jessup Quincannon had in common. Though she did it out of love, while he did it out of spite.

"Time passes," I continued. "Long enough that you probably don't think about her except maybe once a month. Then Walter Beck calls. He found out she was seeing someone. Had gone tearing up the apartment until he found her diary. I'm guessing it was hidden behind one of the baseboards in the bedroom. Found it and saw your name written in it. One of his favorite detectives putting it to his wife behind his back. And if you're wondering how I figured it was you, it was because her neighbor saw me at his apartment. Also, Lazenby would have told you Walter had me working Susie's death. But you never came knocking. You were the dog that didn't bark, Staples."

Finally, he looked at me.

"I loved her," he croaked.

"Did you tell Walter that when you went over?" I asked. " 'Calm down, Walter. Put that gun down. I loved her. I whispered that into her ear every time we fell into bed.' That what you told him right before you put one in his head?"

Yeah, I was being cruel, but I didn't care. Maybe Quincannon was onto something. Cruelty is in our nature.

"It was self-defense," Staples pleaded. "It was his gun. He pulled it on me. I grabbed him, got his arm bent up, and he pulled the trigger. I didn't . . . I didn't mean to kill him . . . I . . . ."

He trailed off. Probably because he heard the same thing I did. The sound of every sad sack in a police interrogation room singing that old "I didn't mean it, Officer" refrain.

Problem was, it was probably true. That's what the evidence had looked like to me and Alathea. The scuffle; Beck's clothes; the blood. Two people having a wrestling match for the Mauser.

"Yeah," I said. "I know you didn't mean to."

While I'd talked, his shoulders had slumped even more, like he was sinking into the wood of the bar. He still looked like a movie star, but I wouldn't have cast him as the hero anymore. Maybe the old drunk. The sidekick who gets shot in the second act.

"What happens now?" he asked. He looked toward the door, as if he expected Lazenby to step through it, twirling a set of cuffs.

"Now I go back and have my tortoni," I said. "I love that stuff."

"What about me?"

"You? You go back to being the not-so-golden boy."

"You're not . . . you're not going to turn me in?"

I shook my head.

"Ms. Pentecost and I haven't discussed it, on account of being busy proving she didn't kill a man. But I think she'll agree with me that Susie was a tragic indiscretion of the noncriminal variety. And that Walter Beck's death was self-defense. My boss is the honorable sort. She knows that the law and justice are two separate things."

Staples kept his eyes on his drink, the bar, the center of the earth.

"Thank you," he muttered. The words came hard, but he managed both syllables.

"Don't thank me," I snapped. "Because I? I am not the honorable sort. Here's how this is going to work. If we're involved in a case, you're not. If you're already involved, you'll find a reason to pass it to Lazenby. And if I find out you're plotting behind our backs, I will stab a knife into yours."

I leaned in and said what came next right into his ear.

"Nobody, and I mean nobody, puts my boss in cuffs. Got it?"

He nodded.

I went back to the party and had dessert.

CHAPTER **52**

From the journals of Lillian Pentecost

It is New Year's Eve. I have been home for nearly three weeks. It feels like a moment. It feels like a lifetime.

This evening, before the sun had entirely set, I went for another walk through the neighborhood. I've been going for many of them, despite the wretched December cold. Partly to sate Dr. Hubbard's wish that I engage in more physical activity. Partly because I no longer feel quite so comfortable in enclosed rooms.

I walk to the market to pick up fresh spices for Eleanor. To the bookshop and the tobacconist and the haberdasher to purchase Christmas gifts. Even to the nearby park to toss stale bread to the pigeons.

Any excuse to have an open sky above my head.

As I walk, I spy neighbors and shopkeepers, who wave, and I wave back. People I have not spoken to in years, or whom I never knew to begin with, approach and congratulate me.

One couple—from Idaho, I believe—recognized me on the street and asked if I would agree to having my picture taken with their daughter.

The girl, about ten years old, could barely stand still. She had a thousand questions about being a detective. I answered them until her parents grew weary and dragged her away.

The girl was proof, more so than any of the newspaper stories, of my success. With his last breath, Jessup Quincannon tried to steal my reputation.

I have snatched it back.

I have no interest in resting on my laurels. In the next few months, I plan to take on every case that I reasonably can. The bigger, the better. I plan to remind them who I am.

Though I will not neglect the smaller cases. I ignore those at my peril, as the murder of Junfeng Zhao has proved.

I have put the Zhaos in touch with Mr. Whitsun, and I believe Miss Jennings is helping them file a wrongful-death suit against the Quincannon estate. A small dollop of justice, bitter and too late.

My errands also included a visit to a local seamstress to commission a set of baby clothes to be sent to Sarah Miller, now Mrs. Sarah Hickman, the former nursemaid accused of theft whose sister approached me in prison.

I'd had to go into the archives to find her last name. But now that I have it, I don't plan on forgetting it anytime soon.

The sun has set, and I am back at my desk. The curtains are drawn and the door locked. Eleanor is in the kitchen icing a cake. I've lost too much weight, she says, and need fattening.

Will is at Holly's this evening. I imagine that will be happening more often.

Good.

They deserve to pry some small bit of happiness from a world determined to deny it from them.

I have only a few blank pages left in this journal before I shelve it with the rest. Though I may revisit it, if only to remind myself what I learned during my time in the House of D.

Tomorrow it will be 1948.

Did I ever imagine I would live to see it?

Will has agreed to drive me to Bedford Hills next week. I've made arrangements to visit Val. I do not know what our relationship will be outside the House of D, but I am interested in finding out.

My new appreciation of open spaces has me thinking of my mother. How in the painting hanging behind me, she imagined herself someplace vast and open. Somewhere she could be free.

I think about how she died, alone in her cell, guilt-ridden over the murder of her lover.

Or so everyone believes.

I do not believe it. Not anymore.

I don't think I ever really did. Suicide was out of character for her. Murder even more so. Character is everything.

Then there's the fire.

Shortly after Jessup Quincannon began his inquiries into my mother's death and arranged to have the painter's box stolen from my father's shed, there was a fire in the old schoolhouse, which has long been used as storage for town documents. All the old records of court cases and criminal investigations—including the murder of Patrick Ebbers and my mother's death—were destroyed.

Coincidence?

Or did someone want to prevent the dredging up of old memories? To keep anyone, myself especially, from looking at the evidence with fresh eyes.

Does a killer still live? Waiting? Hiding in some forgotten corner of my childhood?

I intend to find out.

In the spring, I think. When the world outside has thawed. I will travel home. To reopen the case that has haunted me my whole life.

Willowjean Parker
Lead Investigator
Pentecost and Parker Investigations
New York City

AUTHOR'S NOTE

As always, the events, people, and many of the places in this book are fictional. The House of D, however, was very real. The New York Women's House of Detention stood at 10 Greenwich Avenue from 1932 to 1974. During the years it was operational the prison housed tens of thousands of women and trans men. Few were like Lillian Pentecost. Many were like Val Lincoln—imprisoned not for what they had done, but for who they were.

The House of D is gone now, torn down and replaced with a gated flower garden. It's beautiful there in the spring, with plenty of benches where you can sit and watch the world bloom around you. If you look up, you might be able to imagine those eleven stories of concrete and the women trapped inside.

But history is like a scratched 78—it just keeps repeating itself.

During the drafting of this novel, a wave of laws were passed across the country criminalizing gender and sexuality, and stripping women of their bodily autonomy. As I'm writing this note, cities are looking for further ways to criminalize poverty and homelessness.

Maybe this isn't so much a matter of history repeating itself as it never stopping in the first place. The House of D lives on in prisons all over the country, as do the conditions that created it.

If you want to learn more about the real House of D and not just my fictionalized version, I recommend Hugh Ryan's *The Women's House of Detention: A Queer History of a Forgotten Prison*. It won't give you comfort, but it will make history, and the present, harder to ignore.

ACKNOWLEDGMENTS

A book might get drafted in isolation, but beyond that it takes a team. Special thanks to:

My agent, Darley Anderson, and the crew at the agency who have championed this series from day one.

My editors, Bill Thomas and Carolyn Williams, who have helped make this the best hardboiled mystery/courtroom drama/pulpy adventure it can be.

To everyone at Doubleday who have worked to get this book into your hands or into your ears. They are legion and they do great work.

As always, my wife, Jessica, my very own Holly Quick, who will always provide an alibi when the cops come calling.

And to all the readers who have taken the time to reach out, digitally or in person, and tell me how much they love these stories and these characters. I'm glad I'm not the only one.

ABOUT THE AUTHOR

Stephen Spotswood is an award-winning playwright, journalist, and educator. As a journalist, he has spent much of the last two decades writing about the aftermath of the wars in Iraq and Afghanistan and the struggles of wounded veterans. His dramatic work has been widely produced across the United States, and he is the winner of the 2021 Nero Award for best American mystery. He makes his home in Washington, D.C., with his wife, young-adult author Jessica Spotswood.